Praise for Mary Hughes's
Biting Oz

"I enjoyed this for the unique humor Ms. Hughes brings to all of her Biting Love books, and of course the hot and steamy passion that erupts from the page every time Junior and Glynn come together... I recommend this for those who love a side of humor with their main course of romance."

~ *Long and Short Reviews*

"Well, this is my favorite of the Biting Series by Mary Hughes...this book was fabulous!"

~ *Guilty Pleasures Book Reviews*

"Pulse-pounding danger meets slapstick sausage and cheese wars in the quirky *Biting Oz*. Author Mary Hughes has a way of blending sensuality, danger, and over-the-top oddness in a way few authors ever could, which is why I simply adore her books."

~ *Joyfully Reviewed*

D1713711

Look for these titles by *Mary Hughes*

Now Available:

Biting Love
Biting Nixie
Bite My Fire
The Bite of Silence
Biting Me Softly
Biting Oz

Biting Oz

Mary Hughes

SAMHAIN
PUBLISHING

Samhain Publishing, Ltd.
11821 Mason Montgomery Road, 4B
Cincinnati, OH 45249
www.samhainpublishing.com

Biting Oz
Print ISBN: 978-1-61921-266-4
Digital ISBN: 978-1-60928-958-4

Editing by Christa Desir
Cover by Kanaxa

First Samhain Publishing, Ltd. electronic publication: August 2012
First Samhain Publishing, Ltd. print publication: July 2013

Dedication

To Jessica Mittendorf, whose friendship and support keeps me going (and whose evil writing challenges keep me on my toes).

To Mrs. Missive, SheSwitches, Glitrbug and all the rest of my cherished readers at Goodreads and Goodreads KindleSmut.

To the wonderful Mary Hamilton for sticking with me and getting the story into real shape. You walked where angels feared to tread.

To the brilliant Christa Desir for her energy, talent and focus, stepping into the breach and making this story shine. Thank you for loving my writing.

To my husband Gregg, for feeding me when I get deep in edits and forget to eat. You are so stuck with me ☺.

To you, Dear Reader, for the enormous honor of inviting my story into your life.

Chapter One

I was late. Dinner-skipping, running with twenty tons (including a tenor sax case the size, weight and maneuverability of a dead body), panting late by the time I found the theater house doors.

Chop me into sausage. My first night with the full group and I needed to make a good impression, but I had three minutes to assemble instruments and wet reeds and find my seat and warm up and—

The tuning note sounded. Chop me into sausage and slap me on a bun. Not only was I late, when I did start playing I'd be out of tune like a fifth grade wire choir. I juggled instrumentalia to free a hand, yanked open the heavy house door and ran through—

Straight into a sea of Munchkins. Which, since I wasn't Moses, refused to part.

Chop me, slap me and serve me with ketchup and a side of kraut fries.

Running, squirming Munchkins blocked the aisles, crawled over stinky-new seats and generally terrorized the otherwise empty auditorium. Not real Munchkins, of course, but local kids who hoped to sing and dance their way to fame and fortune in the new musical, *Oz, Wonderful Oz*. The inaugural production would open our brand-spanking-new Meiers Corners Marlene Dietrich Performing Arts Center. Actors and musicians had been rehearsing separately and tonight was our first time together. I was playing reed two in the pit orchestra.

If I could get to the pit, that was.

The house lights were at fifty percent, high enough to see two harried adults patting makeup on chubby cheeks. A couple teenage babysitters tried to run herd but were hard pressed just to keep the kids from ripping themselves or the house to shreds. Mayhem in the form of youngsters shed hats and bows and bits of costume like auto parts in a San Francisco car chase. I craned my neck for a way through the seething mass.

My future depended on getting into that pit on time. We were going to Broadway—if a certain unnamed big-bucks backer was impressed with the show on closing night. All of us, including the musicians. Including *me*.

If I could just get to that damned pit.

Bull my way through? At five-two, I wasn't much bigger than the rugrats. But with the tenor sax deadweight... I eyed the sea of Munchkins and sighed. It was vital I get to my seat but not at the cost of hurting a kid.

Besides, those poor harried teenagers needed help. I sloughed my cases and music stand and went to render what aid I could.

A Lollipop Guilder, scrambling to escape the auditorium, rammed into me. I snagged him by his suspenders and plopped him into a seat. Just as I straightened, a scuffling pair of boys with missing front teeth (not from the scuffle, I hoped) rolled into me. I broke them up, rescued their hats and sat them next to the Lollipopper—who Lolli-popped out of his seat. I grabbed him, but the gap-toothed boys bubbled up, timing it like a tag team. I managed to corral all three with a bear hug and wrestled them into their seats.

I huffed to catch my breath. No wonder Mom only had the one of me.

Two giggling girls darted past and bumped me into the boys. Or into their empty seats, as they'd climbed out and were now Spidermanning into the next aisle.

"Overture, please." Up front the pit director called the musicians to attention.

I forked fingers into my hair, forgetting my scalp-tight braid, and nearly tore out a chunk. Not only was I officially screwed, I couldn't even corral a few kids. Cocktail weenies on a stick, could it get any worse?

Of course it could. "I'm a filly!"

Speaking of corral. A stampede of girls playing horse galloped into me, knocking me off my feet again. I fell, trampled under their small hooves. Terrific. My obituary would now read, "Gunter Marie 'Junior' Stieg, pit musician and sausage queen, pounded flat by a herd of size-three Mary Janes." I braced myself for death, or at least a bad bruising.

Big, warm hands slid under my arms, drew me to my feet.

"Here now," said a musical baritone. "I'll take care of this, *babi.* You sit here, out of the way."

The hands assisted me to a plush seat. I sank in. Mmm, comfy. The city sure had gone all out remodeling the theater...*babi?*

I blinked. A pair of shoulders wider than a freeway waded out into the sea of kids. The leather-jacketed shoulders belonged to a man, black-haired, tall and strong-looking—but even Gulliver fell to a raging river of Lilliputians. I called out a warning too late. Kids grabbed the man's hands, his jacket, and climbed him like a tree. He was swarmed, overwhelmed, swallowed up by the horde of prepubescent terrors. I covered my eyes.

"Sit now, younglings. All in a row, that's it. Sit quietly until it's your turn to have makeup."

He had a lovely accent. I uncovered my eyes. Somehow he'd freed himself from the swarm of kids and was calmly shepherding them into the first two rows of seats, adjusting a tie here or hat there as they filed neatly by.

Holy Dr. Spock. There was a handy man to have if I ever wanted kids.

I smacked myself discreetly between the eyes. No children, at least not right now. First, make a good impression on the director of this show, turn the show into a smash hit, and go to New York.

Which meant getting into that pit before the overture started. Maybe I still could. I jumped to my feet, snatched up my Manhasset stand and corpse sax, shouldered my instrument bag and trotted down the rapidly clearing aisle.

And nearly slammed into a six-kid pileup.

The adults doing Munchkin makeup had stopped the kids from filing into the third row of seats in order to fix one Munchkin's smears. I screeched to a stop on my toes, off-balance. My bag slipped, dropped off my shoulder, jerked me into stumbling. I nearly dropped the sax, did drop my stand, tangled feet with it and had to wrench myself backward to keep from falling.

Except the sax didn't hear about the change in plans. Momentum carried it in my original direction, popping it from of my grip.

To my horror, the tenor case pitched straight at the kids.

The man turned instantly, as if preternaturally aware of the danger. But he was behind the kids. He'd have to hurdle like Jesse Owens to get between the deadly sax and those small bodies.

Palming the wall, he levered against it to kick up and over Munchkin heads, clearing them with incredible grace and ease, landing on my side.

On the way he snatched my tenor. Midair.

I set down my instrument bag and blew out my tension. "Wow. Thanks. I..."

Straightening to his full height of six-OMG, he faced me, emanating strength and energy. Powerful chest muscles pushed into the jacket's gap right in front of my nose.

I gaped, realized I was starting to drool and looked up.

Sondheim shoot me. His face was all dark, dangerous planes. His eyes were twin sapphire flames that hit me in the gut. My breath punched out and none came to replace it. Bad news for a wind player.

He turned to set the sax down. I started breathing again.

A tapping caught my ear, the conductor ready to start. I needed to get into that pit *now.*

Half a dozen kids and two makeup adults were still in my way.

I'd have crawled over the seats myself but my joints weren't as limber as the kids'...unless I used my black Lara Croft braid as a rope. I was desperate enough to consider it.

The man, turning back, saw my predicament. He lifted my instrument bag and music stand over kids with the same strength and grace as when he'd snatched the tenor. Then he turned to me.

And swept me up into his arms.

An instant of shock, of male heat and rock-hard muscle. A carved face right next to mine, masculine lips beautifully defined—abruptly I was set on my feet beside the pit. The sax landed next to me with a thump.

"There." His accent was jagged, as if he were as rattled as me. "There's your instrument." He bounded to the back of the theater and was gone.

I blinked, not sure what had just happened. A handsome, good with kids, preternaturally aware man had swept me off my feet. Literally.

Checking said tootsies, no ruby slippers or glass pumps had magically appeared. So I hadn't sideslipped into a fairy tale, which left him being real, and, hey—I was real, which made me shiver with possibilities.

No. Oh, no.

I hauled the sax case next to the pit wall, threw it open and put the tenor together by instinct. I grabbed beat-up brass...pale gold, like his smooth skin. I fisted hard plastic mouthpiece...he had rock-hard muscles, and something else I fisted would be rock-hard too. I realized what I was doing and jammed mouthpiece onto cork without the benefit of new grease. It was tough, but I reveled in twisting it down tight.

Because I could not afford to get sidetracked by sex. I had priorities. Family duty was A-*numero-uno*. Plans for my future were a close second. This show was a big step toward satisfying both. Right now, any attraction would be a *dis*traction. A huge, muscled distraction. A broad-shouldered, black-jacketed distraction... The overture started.

Lust was making me solo in stupid. I snatched up everything and ran to the pit, pushing sapphire eyes and lilting accents out of my head. Whoever the *babi* guy was, I'd have to stay far, far away.

Entering the pit, I slid slowly and carefully through the tightly packed musicians. We'd had a couple instrumental-only rehearsals before this (the pit didn't join the cast until the first dress rehearsal), but not in the theater, so this was the first time I'd had to navigate the squeeze. I chafed to find my seat, but a bull in a china shop is nothing compared to a bull with premenstrual bloat wading through a pit of high-priced, handmade horns. Only in my case, it was instru-menstrual bloat, ha.

I finally found my chair and was assembling my clarinet when the oboe played a two-measure figure and paused.

A gap went by. My solo, missed. Stuff me in a tuba and blast me into space. Late and now this. I slammed music onto stand, flipped a page and found my place. We were at Dorothy's entrance. I jammed clarinet into my mouth so fast I nearly broke teeth, and sucked breath to play.

"Stop-stop-stop!" Six feet of coral chinos, cravat and Fuh-Q cologne sashayed onstage, clapping his hands. With a coral-and-chartreuse silk scarf wrapped around his head like a fashion patrol Rambo, the man reminded me of Darren Nichols in *Slings and Arrows*, or a bendy fashion doll. Or a metrosexual Gumby. Obviously the show's director, the guy who called the shots—like whether I got to New York or not.

Act professional, act professional... Distracted, my sucked breath released—into the clarinet. My note squawked into the sudden silence like a skewered pig.

"What, exactly, was that?" The man loomed over the pit. I fussed with my music, pretended not to notice him. *This is not the cantina droid you're looking for.*

He receded, tapping an impatient, silver-capped toe. "Where is the offstage choir? They *must* be in place before you start. And who said you could start?" He pointed into the pit. "Did I say go?"

Our music director, Takashi Ishikawa (no relation to the wrestler), fingered his short white stick. "I—"

"Did you hear me give the go on your headset? Do you have a headset? Who has their headset? Soundboard? Light board?" The director tapped his toe faster. "Come on, people. I know this isn't Broadway, but that's where we're *supposed* to be headed. Everyone must have a headset and use it. Steve! Where is that boy?"

A skeletal young man slunk sullenly from the wings. His head was shaved except for a fringe of bangs, and ripped jeans hung from his bony ass. He looked like a deathmetal Gollum from *The Lord of the Rings.* "The name's not Steve. It's Shi—"

"Steve. Do we have headsets distributed or not? How else am I to make such a large endeavor a brilliant success? Because only Brilliant Successes go to New York." The director whirled, glared at Takashi. "Turn on your headset."

Takashi obediently clicked, then surreptitiously clicked again. His set had already been on.

"Good." The director very deliberately clicked the button on his control set. "Ready? Then—go." He spun offstage.

We started from the top. My sax was only slightly sharp from jamming the mouthpiece to the hilt. No time to fix it now, not with all my fingers engaged in low B-flats and Cs. Five measures in, I switched to flute. This time the "oohs" of the offstage choir joined us, and when my clarinet solo came, I dropped it in perfectly. (If this sounds like the movie or Royal Shakespeare Company version of *The Wizard of Oz,* well, the instrumentation was the same. *Oz, Wonderful Oz* was a completely new production, but you gotta sound like the movie or patrons get weirded out.)

We segued into "Dorothy's Got Trouble", and the house doors opened. A spotlight clicked on, catching traditional ankle socks, gingham and braids.

Our Dorothy. The lynchpin of the show. If she was good, we were headed for New York. If she was bad, we'd be playing dinner theater in What Cheer, Iowa, and then only if we offered free soft-serve.

She glided up the aisle, something furry in her arms, and spoke her first lines. And then suddenly I was *there*, in Kansas, and here was Dorothy worried about her dog and her mean neighbor.

The girl wasn't simply good. She was stunning.

We went through the plot setup, the wicked old witch neighbor threatening Dorothy's only friend, Toto. Nobody on the farm seemed to care, too busy with their own work.

Leaving Dorothy to sit on the stoop of her farmhouse and sing her hopefully-soon-to-be-famous lament, "Dreams Beyond the Rainbow". Hearing her rich voice, filled with longing, I shivered, and I don't shiver easily.

The girl used the wavering, pouting Judy Garland alto but imbued it with something more, something that made it her own. She took traditional Dorothy and layered it with her own interpretation, making it fresh. I wondered how old the girl was, really.

As she sang, a shadow appeared in the wings. A big shadow with shoulders that brushed the curtain on either side. The *babi* guy. His sapphire eyes were intent on Dorothy.

Another shiver hit me, this one down low, and I missed my changeover. No big loss as all ears were on Dorothy—except for Takashi's. He gave me a short, meaningful stare. For a grad student, the guy heard everything. Even without this *Oz*, he'd make Broadway someday.

Me, I wouldn't even make the soft-serve follies unless I got my head out of my panties and focused. I put flute to lip and concentrated on playing the tag, a little triplet fillip. That segued into "Mean Old Nieghbor" (Neighbor to the rest of the world, but Nieghbor on the hand-notated, hand-lettered part. Welcome to the world of pit music). The change to clarinet took my full attention. When I looked up again at the end of a menacing chord, Mr. Babi was gone.

Despite concentrating on the music, I was still shivering. That worried me. I'm a musician but also a businesswoman. Emotions tempered by, as Pop puts it, hard-headed dollars and sense. Ha.

My part had nothing until the tornado, so I had a few scenes to try to figure it out. Did I want to? Hell no. I poked around in my own innards with dread. But the missed cue said it was eating me bad enough to throw me off. I had to poke or potentially screw up this pit gig.

And the gig was bottom-line, underscore-underscore, red ink important.

So. What was throwing me? Being so blasted late? Squirting a clarinet fart in front of the show's director? Dorothy and her soul-shredding voice?

Surely my shivers weren't from the gorgeous hunk of sapphire-eyed male who'd watched her.

Not thinking about him. I latched on to my last thought, Dorothy's voice...yes, that alto certainly was haunting, especially singing about her rainbow dream.

Emotion hit me so hard I gasped. Rainbow dream. That was it.

I'm an only child. Not the doting-parents-smothering-with-money-and-affection kind. The you-have-a-duty kind. I'm rather of proud of that.

Duty to my parents was vital to me. They raised me and gave me food and a roof, not to mention the whole gift-of-life thing. My mother even gave up her career for me (although that's another issue). They're older, maybe a decade from retiring, but they can't because they run their own business and sink every spare *pfennig* into it.

So I help them in the store and I'm glad to do it. I love them; they're my world.

But sometimes I want...more.

Dorothy's rainbow dream resonated deep. Like Kansas, my home is small. Meiers Corners is just west of Chicago in miles, but it's worlds removed in attitude. In some ways, the Corners is even smaller and more black-and-white than Dorothy's Kansas. I feel trapped in my small backyard, knowing there's a big, wide, Technicolor world out there, just waiting for me.

New York is my Emerald City. That's why this pit gig was so important. The director was aiming to do a *Rent*, go viral and get to Broadway. My friend Nixie, who had recruited the pit orchestra musicians, managed to work an agreement out that if the show went, the Meiers Corners's musicians would go along.

That was when I signed up. Not only would I get to New York—I'd get there with a job that'd support me *and* have cash left over for my parents.

If the show did well. If I was a professional and could cut the part.

Takashi raised one finger, our cue that the tornado was coming. I checked my music for the proper instrument (pig squeal ain't nothin' on honking a flute part out on tenor). I used color highlights to reinforce instrument name, and in this case CLAR was highlighted in blue, like eyes as blue as an Irish sea...

Dammit, I had to concentrate on my part, not blue-eyed hunks. Business Truth #2 was "Focus on the job at hand". I couldn't get distracted, not with my dreams so close I could taste them, like tasting beautifully defined lips...crap.

I lifted my clarinet, concentrating on fingering the upcoming tornado, not fingering gorgeous...shizzle. Concentrating on the music, not musical baritones murmuring *babi* sweetly in my...phooey.

This was going to be harder than I thought.

By the time we got our break two hours later, I decided I'd overreacted. The guy couldn't have been as gorgeous as I thought. I'd been swept off my feet, waking romantic fantasies and understimulated hormones (being the dutiful daughter means I don't date much).

I'd test his nongorgeousness by giving him another look-see. Snatching up my water bottle, I stood.

Next to me, the woman playing reed one rose too and stretched out her back, throwing her pregnant belly into relief.

Nixie Emerson is the only person in my world smaller than me. At five feet even, wearing clothes bought in the kids' department at Target before she got pregnant, she could have doubled as a Munchkin—until she opened her mouth. A punk rocker, Nixie could swear like a Marine. When you could understand her. She used a mishmash of cultural metaphors and punkspeak, a kind of a *Star Trek: TNG* "Darmok and Jalad at Tanagra" for the terminally tattooed and pierced.

"Hey, Nixie," I said. "I'm going to find a water fountain. You want anything?"

"Nah, I'm chill," Nixie said. "Want some aitch-two, Julian?"

17

That was to her husband, on her other side, wiping down his cello. Talk about gorgeous—Julian was the original poster boy for Yowsa. He said, "After that first half? Beer, maybe."

"You talking about rehearsal? Or that thing with Dumbass?"

"Dumbass?" I asked.

She turned to me. "Yeah, Director Dumbass. You know, the guy who dinged Takashi about the headset, then screeched all his directions voice-naked?"

"He was rather colorful."

"The rehearsal," Julian said. "Missed light cues, sound cues, lines dropped. Tin Man's plate sliding off his bony body. Kids behaving like rampaging monkeys. I can't believe we open in just four days."

"The stars are exceptional," I said. "That'll help."

"And the pit's fearsome great." Nixie grinned and popped another vertebra.

"Maybe, but the rest was a train wreck." Julian set his cello on its ribs. "All those sugar-rush Munchkins chasing Toto didn't help. The director's screeching and cajoling made it worse."

I shrugged. "It's the first rehearsal with all the players. Not everyone is professional, and there's a lot to coordinate." I reveled in it all, even the flubbed lines. The pulse and thrum of life past the edge was so un-Meiers Corners. "It'll be miraculously wonderful by Thursday night."

"It had better be." Julian's tone was dark.

"True dat," Nixie said. "I'm not planning on NYC but I know a lot are."

"The backer's not coming until closing night. We have time." I double-checked my flute and clarinet on their homemade pegs. "At least long enough for me to find some freeway-broad shoulders...I mean water."

As I set my sax on my chair, flutist Rocky Hrbek leaned up, her wealth of shining chestnut hair falling forward. She pushed it back as if it was an annoyance instead of a hunk-magnet. "Um, Junior..." She shoved at the bridge of her clunky glasses. "Not to be presumptuous or anything. But I could use some water too. Can I go with you?"

I shook my head at her "presumption". Rocky had been overweight and acne-ridden in high school and still saw herself that way. Though she was slim and gorgeous now, nobody in the Corners had bothered to correct her. She was just as shy and unsure of herself as she'd been in the black cesspool known as seventh grade.

Fortunately it didn't matter when it came to her playing. Hell on wheels in band, first-chair flute her freshman year, she'd only gotten better.

"Sure. C'mon."

She grabbed her water bottle, tucked her flute case under her arm and followed me out of the pit. I'd left my flute on its stand, but mine was a thousand-dollar Armstrong and hers was a twenty-thousand-dollar gold Miyazawa. Or maybe she just saw it as one of her few faithful friends.

"Do you know where the water fountain is?" she asked as we hit the aisle.

"Probably near the restrooms. Let's try the outer lobby." The PAC had two lobby areas, outer and inner. The building's main entrance led to the outer lobby, with ticket counters and restrooms. Straight through the outer lobby was a set of doors leading to the inner lobby. The inner lobby had two sets of double doors leading into the audience section of the theater, or the house. As we made our way up the house aisle, a couple of Munchkins zipped past, knocking into me. A harried-looking teenager ran after them. "How've you been?"

"Good." Rocky swayed to avoid the worst of the Munchkin meteors. "How're things at the sausage store?"

I pushed through the house doors and we schussed over the thick red carpet of the inner lobby. "Working our asses off to make ends meet, but that's par for a mom-and-pop shop." I shouldered open the outer lobby doors, revealing two stories of new sage walls, contemporary art and recessed natural light. "Somebody put real money behind this remodeling. You'd never know this used to be a toilet paper factory."

Rocky slid her glasses up on her nose and looked around. "Mayor Meier did some tax credits and a special loan program at the bank. He's pushing to get all the city's empty buildings retenanted. Oh look, there's the drinking fountain."

The hiss of water zeroed my attention on the far wall. Dorothy had just bent her beautiful, graceful head to take a drink.

Standing behind her like a personal shield was Mr. Couldn't-Be-That-Gorgeous. He wasn't.

He was more.

19

A glow of sapphire eyes, a flash of dangerous planes, the impression of broad shoulders. Glimpses through lowered house lights and dark wings hadn't prepared me for seeing him in full light for the first time.

Big became huge, several inches over six feet, deceptive because he was perfectly proportioned, like Tom Cruise in reverse. Broad shoulders were really acres wide, flaring from a narrow, flat waist. He had perfectly chiseled features, his five o'clock shadow emphasizing a honed jaw, his perfect skin taut over sharp bones, his lips masculine yet bold. His black hair gleamed under the lights, thick and lustrous.

Great Braunschweiger, he was beyond gorgeous, as in punch-out-my-heart-and-use-it-to-club-me-senseless stunning.

A sudden, searing need to know his name pushed me toward him.

Rocky's hand on my shoulder stopped me. "Junior, wait. They're busy."

"How do you know?" *And busy doing what?*

"Look at her back. It's bowed. Whatever she's hearing, she's not liking it."

Rocky was right. Shove a trombone up my ass and play "Yankee Doodle". I'd violated Business Truth #6 of my parents' Eightfold Business Path—"Keep your eyes open and on the customer". It told a savvy shopkeeper what the customer was looking for. *And what would Mr. Gorgeous be buying, Junior?* I shook myself.

As if Dorothy had heard our whispers all the way across the lobby, she turned toward us. Without stage lights washing her out, she was as stunning as he was. Her eyes were the bright green of spring leaves, framed by coal-black lashes and filled with intelligence and determination that made them even more striking.

Here was no little girl, but a young woman of consequence.

Her expression eased into a welcoming smile. "Please, come have a drink. Don't mind Glynn and me."

Her soft voice carried across the lobby, great acoustics or a truly brilliant actress. As we approached, she stepped back from the water fountain, leaving her hulking male no choice but to do the same.

"Thanks," I said.

"You're in the pit, aren't you?"

"Yes." I eyed Glynn (such a lovely, musical name, lyrical as his deep baritone...phooey, when did I go poetic over *names*?). If he wanted to be alone with her, he didn't give me any nonverbal hints. Of course, if he wanted to be alone with her, he shouldn't have hogged the water fountain to do it.

The drinking fountain activated with a side lever handle. I turned it halfway to get a moderate stream and sipped.

Rocky said, "I like your Dorothy."

"Thank you." The young woman gave a silvery laugh. "I have to admit, she's a bit of typecasting for a small-town Iowa girl like me."

"Iowa?" I backed off for Rocky. "I thought all the stars were from New York. Where in Iowa are you from?"

"Coralville. I'm not quite New York yet."

"I bought my flute in Coralville," Rocky said between sips. "It's not so small. Just a few miles from the University of Iowa."

The girl gave Rocky a dazzling smile. "Most folks think we're all corn and cattle. I'm Mishela." She held out a hand.

Rocky shook. "I'm Rocky. This is Gunter Marie, but everyone calls her Junior."

"My parents' idea," I said. "Hey, it's better than a female Gunter." Mishela's hand, when I took it, was slim yet strong. I nodded nonchalantly at Mr. Gorgeous. Well, trying to be nonchalant. "And your shadow?"

Mishela gave me a rueful smile. "Glynn Rhys-Jenkins. But I call him Warden."

"Mishela." The warning in his tone was plain.

"Custodian? Keeper?" She smiled at him, a playful beaming that, aimed at anyone else, would have turned him into a pile of mush.

Glynn just glowered. "Seventeen is not too old to spank."

Her smile turned saucy. "Some might say it's the perfect age to spank." She touched a finger to his massive chest. "If you were my type."

Glynn's glower darkened. "Just because Elias lets you get away with your sass—"

Oh great, a lovers' quarrel. I suffered a rush of heat, backed away. "Nice meeting you both. But, um—"

"I'm sorry. Please don't go." Mishela turned from Glynn to touch my arm. "It would be nice to talk to other women. Especially other performers."

Her tone caught at me. She seemed...lonely. Even if she was older than I thought, she was still a young woman away from home. I heard myself say, "Want to do something after rehearsal? Sodas at Nieman's Bar?"

She perked up immediately. "I'd love to. If you don't mind the looming watcher."

Big, muscular Glynn, *watching* us... My belly heated and my panties felt a little too tight. Which annoyed the crap out of me (I had goals), so I said, "He doesn't have to come." And promptly flushed. *Come.* Perfectly innocent, except in connection with this hunk of striding sex...in the same sentence...much less the same room...*uh.* "We're adults, Rocky and I. We'll chaperone you."

"Mishela doesn't go anywhere without me." Glynn crossed arms, pumping his bold chest into the opening of his jacket. Mounds of muscle strained against cotton and leather. My eyes fell out my head and my panties shot directly to broil. Phooey.

"Glynn speaks. End of discussion." Mishela sighed. "My guardian would agree."

Rocky and I exchanged a glance. So who was Glynn, beyond being insanely gorgeous? Her brother? Bodyguard? Lover?

A clap sounded behind us. "Places, ladies." Coral-and-chartreuse buzzed past and through a side door.

"Yes, Mr. Dumas," Mishela called after him.

Ah, Dumas. That explained Nixie's Director Dumbass.

"You heard the man." Glynn took Mishela's elbow and hustled her toward the theater.

She called back to Rocky and me, "Nice meeting you both. See you after rehearsal."

"Well, that was interesting." I saw Rocky juggle flute case, water bottle and fountain handle and automatically stepped in to help, twisting the handle so Rocky could fill her bottle...all the while trying not to panic. Glynn was even better than I remembered. How could I focus on duty and goals now?

Sure, the music would absorb me during rehearsal, but what about after? We were going out for drinks together, for pity's sake. How could I avoid seeing him, wanting to touch, to kiss...no, Rocky would stop me. And Mishela. She'd joked about Glynn the Warden, but how could any woman not want such a prime male? If I got too familiar with Glynn, she'd intervene. "Mishela sure doesn't look seventeen."

"She doesn't. I wonder when she figured out she's gay."

My hand jerked on the handle, spraying water. "What? How do you figure that?"

"Didn't you catch it?" Rocky pushed her nose piece. "The comment about 'if you were my type'?"

"Well, yeah, but...wasn't she flirting with Glynn?"

"More teasing him, like a sister."

"And his sticking to her?"

"Protective hovering." Rocky capped her water, only half-full because of my ham-hand on the handle, and started back. "Maybe he's her bodyguard."

My underwear roller coaster had evidently made me miss some things. I felt strangely lightheaded and lighthearted—missing yet another obvious fact, this one about me.

Then I thought of a downer. If Mishela was gay, only Rocky would stop me if I slid my hands under Glynn's black jacket to pet those broad shoulders...panic flared and I ran to catch up.

Rocky said, "So how do you know Glynn?"

"I don't."

"Oh." The normally neutral syllable was lengthened and pitched high, filling it with her skepticism.

"I don't," I repeated, as if saying it again would convince her. "I just met him tonight."

"So I only imagined he was looking at you 'that way'?" She elbowed open the house doors and trotted down the aisle.

"What way?"

"Like he wanted to eat you up. Which reminds me, did you see Rob brought pit chocolate?"

My voice wouldn't work. Glynn was looking hungrily at *me*?

Panic flared anew. More people. I needed more people between me and Glynn. Rocky, and...and... "Rob brought chocolate?" Speaking of hungry, I'd worked my folks' register right up until time to go and hadn't had dinner. I couldn't think. "Chocolate goes straight to my pads."

"Think that'll stop Nixie?"

"No. But with her tiny body, if she doesn't eat every hour she'll

23

implode."

"Her metabolism," Rocky agreed. "Worse now that she's pregnant. Good thing Julian feeds her regularly."

Hey. Nixie and Julian were more people. I could ask them to come to Nieman's.

And Takashi, who stopped me outside the pit.

But before I could harangue...I mean ask him if he wanted to go out, he said, "Dumas noticed a solo missing. I didn't tell him specifically it was you but..." He fingered his baton. "Try to be on time tomorrow, *hai?*"

I winced. "Of course."

Could have been worse. At least Takashi had covered for me. But Dumas had noticed, a ding against my professional image. I sank into my seat. Then I straightened, determined to play my ass off.

Next to me, Nixie was chowing down on Rob's bag of chocolate bars. Seeing me, she offered the bag.

"That's cruel," I said. "You know I can't have any until we're done. Not unless I want a two-hundred-dollar repad."

She snatched the bag back, chomped down another bar and heaved a contented sigh. "Shoulda brought a toothbrush." She grinned, showed me her foldaway.

"Buy me one for Christmas. Hey, I've got a new joke."

Her husband Julian groaned, but Nixie stopped chomping. "Feckin' awesome. Lay it down."

"A conductor and a viola player are in the middle of the road. Which do you run over first, and why?"

"The conductor," Nixie said. "They're all puffed with their authority. Except for Takashi."

"The violist." Julian set his bow on his stand. "All your jokes are bad viola jokes."

"Nope," I said. "The conductor. Business before pleasure."

Nixie laughed. Julian's head jerked up.

Steve, the Gollum-like assistant, darted from stage right across the proscenium. He had what looked like a pair of pink and green bikini underwear dangling from his hand. A dark jacket arrowed after, Mr. Chiseled 'n Sexy. I frowned. Nixie half-rose.

"Stay here." Julian snapped to his feet, one hand on her shoulder.

"Stay out of trouble." He vaulted onto stage and dashed after Misters Gollum and Gorgeous on very long legs of his own. Nixie sat.

"What was all that about?" I asked.

She shrugged. "They're trying to catch Steve to ask for a headset? It's theater people. Who knows?"

"Julian is theater?"

"No. But if there's any trouble, he's the suit who'll have to deal with it with his Lawyerly Loquaciousness. He's probably just mitigating the risk factors or whatever has more syllables than is healthy."

"I see." I didn't, but had given up figuring out the weirdness that seemed to follow Nixie around. "Speaking of trouble, how much can you cause, weighed down by ten pounds of kid?"

Nixie unwrapped chocolate. "If I put my mind to it, or just on instinct?"

"Sorry, forgot who I'm talking to." I snorted. "By the way, Rocky and I are meeting Dorothy at Nieman's after rehearsal. Want to come?"

She stopped mid-unwrap. "You guys and Mishela? Going out at night...with Mishela...uh-uh. Not a good idea."

"What? Why not?"

"Well, because...um." She hesitated, not at all like herself.

"Why not?" I repeated.

At that moment, Mishela emerged stage left and stalked across the stage, something pink clenched in her fist. As she disappeared into the wings, Takashi gave a short, hissed "Entr'acte" and raised his baton to start the second half. "Why not" would have to wait.

We ran the second half of the show minus Munchkins, sent home at nine. They'd have to stay for the full run tomorrow, if only to get them used to being up past their bedtimes. That, and we still had to choreograph the bows.

Good thing the kids had gone, though. With the secondary characters and even some of the stars flubbing it, Director Dumbass harangued us until midnight. By the time we played the last note and packed up, I was more than ready for that drink, whatever Nixie's "why not".

Which remained unexplained. The instant Takashi laid down his baton, she abandoned her instruments and dashed out of the pit. I leaned over to ask Julian if he wanted to come to Nieman's, but he was turned from me, face pressed to his phone, talking earnestly and inaudibly.

So I disassembled and cleaned my instruments. Even with three, he was still on the phone when I finished, so I gave up.

Rocky and I were trudging up the aisle (thankfully with less equipment than when I came, as my stand and light would stay for the duration of the run) when Julian stopped us.

I blinked. "You're off the phone?"

"A bit of a problem with my household." Julian's voice was a deep, cultured baritone that slipped over a woman's skin like pearls, so it took a moment for his words to filter through my primitive slobber-brain. Not only does he have a voice set on sex, the man is inhumanly gorgeous. Black hair, startling blue eyes, aristocratic features, and a body that, when he chooses to show it off, can turn a woman's chair into a Slip 'N Slide. But he's so totally in love with Nixie that he has the letters VT stamped on his forehead: Very Taken. Not really. Almost, though. His devotion to his wife only makes him more attractive.

Black hair, blue eyes, unnaturally handsome...actually, Julian reminded me of Glynn. Though there were subtle differences. Julian's eyes were laser-sharp, Glynn's were dark jewels. Julian's hair was perfectly trimmed, Glynn's was spiky and a bit too long. Julian's nose and jaw were exquisitely honed, the Renaissance noble; Glynn was the druid prince—watchful, secretive, yet possessing great power and able to fight when necessary.

I flashed a mental image, a tall, broad-shouldered figure swathed in a dark cloak, twirling on a nighttime battlefield, huge silver blade dancing in the moonlight...ooh. That made me hot.

Julian cocked a brow at me.

I flushed. What had he been saying? Oh yeah, trouble with the household. Julian owned a set of townhouses, so I mentally substituted "apartments". He occasionally used odd words, probably because he was old Boston money. At least that's what Nixie said. "We're going to Nieman's," I began.

"Yes. I heard you're going out with Mishela." His tone was unusually cool.

"Her and Glynn. Want to come?"

"Junior, the thing is, Mishela and Glynn aren't like you and Rocky."

He was warning me off, just like Nixie...no, not just like Nixie, *because* of Nixie. The bricky titch had pulled a Sales Maneuver— siccing a well-meaning relation on me. (Cousin Liese had tried to get me to talk her mom out of marrying a reformed bad boy. It backfired because I kind of liked Race.) "Not like us? Are they brain-sucking zombies? Space aliens?" I gasped. "Mimes?"

"No, of course not." He looked away. "Not exactly."

"Then what? Exactly."

"Well, I..." Frustration shaded his features. "I can't say." His eyes returned to mine and they were an eerie shade of violet. "But be very careful."

Though I mostly ignored Nixie and Julian's weirdness, that shook me. Smiling to cover it, I latched on to Rocky's arm and pulled her out the door. He watched me with those strange violet eyes the whole way.

Chapter Two

Even having to swab and dismantle three instruments, the little interlude with Julian, dropping off my stuff at home and walking to the bar, Rocky and I got to Nieman's first. Well, Mishela had to take off stage makeup and get notes from Director Dumbass, a gruesome experience. That pancake's nasty too.

I chatted with Rocky on autopilot, thinking about Glynn, or rather thinking about how to not think about Glynn, which is fairly screwed up if you consider it. But so far my separation tactic had tanked, and the only new one I'd come up with was to find some way to immunize myself against his attractiveness. You know, find something that made him less gorgeous, like maybe he picked his teeth with a knife or something. Yeah, pathetic.

Nieman's barkeep, Buddy, had gotten new tables, those tall postage stamps where you have to jump to get up on the matching skyscraper chair. Or at least I did. We snagged a table in a dark corner and worked through our first sodas, discussing missed entrances and other fuckups. We expanded into other musicals we'd done. A brief diatribe on poorly erased parts segued into a friendly discussion about which were the best erasers (I favor Staedtler Mars plastic, not just because they're made in Germany; Rocky prefers to photocopy her parts and physically cut and paste the cuts), which segued into, "Hey, Rocky. How do you get a pair of piccolos to play in unison?"

"Shoot one," she said. "Why did the chicken cross the road?"

"To get away from the sax recital. What's the difference between a violin and a viola?"

"The viola burns longer. That one never gets old." As she answered, a buzz hit my spine, immobilizing me. She raised her head, her eyeglasses flashing briefly. "They're here."

Teeth picked with knife. Okay, I could do this. I turned.

Mishela stood in the doorway, casual in jeans, baggy flannel and a ball cap to hold her loose hair.

Behind her...damn.

If Glynn had a knife, it wouldn't be for teeth-picking. He hovered protectively over her, the epitome of big, dark and dangerous.

My bra and panties suddenly felt two sizes too small. Those cheekbones alone could have cut diamonds. I stuffed my lolling tongue back in my mouth, wished I could do the same to my drooling sex, stood and waved to Mishela.

She didn't see me. Her hands were shoved deep in her pockets and her head was turtled. Intuition screamed that here was loneliness beyond simply being homesick.

Yeah, I'd had my head up my ass until now. Normally I'm very good at sizing up a stranger, knowing at a glance what kind of sausage he's looking for—better yet, the kind of sausage he'll fall in love with. And no, I'm not making sly sex jokes. I have some dignity. Mostly.

I looked at Mishela, really looked at her for the first time. Lonely. Sure, she had a guardian, and pseudobrother Glynn. But they were hovering men who'd love her, protect her and care for her—but wouldn't understand her. I wondered how many real friends she had.

We all look for like-me's. People we don't have to explain ourselves to, who understand the raw us. It's hard enough for average bell-curve humpers like me.

Artistic Mishela was way off the bell curve in a number of areas. Beautiful, brilliant—an uneasy combination even under normal circumstances. Add in gay and young, and top it off with her hovering males...well. She had to be one of the loneliest people on the planet. She'd be hungering for people like her. There wouldn't be many.

I wasn't one. Oh, I was nice looking, with Pop's good German bones and Mom's striking Italian coloring. And I was talented enough to play reed two in a dark pit. But I didn't have Mishela's grace and off-the-charts ability.

Still, I was close enough that I could understand her. Not a true meeting of minds, but I was like-*enough*, and maybe she'd sense that.

So even though I wasn't all that sure of my immunity to Glynn, Mishela's loneliness and need prodded me into brighter light (at least as bright as Nieman's gets) and I waved again.

She saw me. The relief sagging her body, the way she fairly tripped back, made it clear that tonight, understanding would be good enough.

I'd done the right thing. My Good Deed.

Behind her, Glynn strode like a dark force of nature. It wasn't until I pushed my tongue back in that I realized I'd started drooling again.

Yeah, no Good Deed goes unpunished.

He was tucked up behind her like a Chicago cabbie, eyes cutting left/right, drilling the shadows like he expected trouble. I didn't get that. At seventeen Mishela was almost an adult. She didn't need a 24/7 chaperone, and she certainly didn't need a babysitter.

Unless he really *was* her bodyguard.

Oh, right. She was a good actress, on her way to being great, but she wasn't the Olsen twins or Emma Watson or anything. Why would anyone do a Godfather business maneuver and kidnap her? No profit to it.

Unless she really was someone's heir.

She'd mentioned Mr. Elias. If that was the name of her legal guardian...if he was business mogul gazillionaire Kai Elias...in little Meiers Corners? Naw.

Mishela bopped up. "Hey, guys, thanks for inviting me out. I was going crazy with only gloomy Glynn as company." She slid into the high chair next to Rocky.

"Our pleasure." Rocky poured two more glasses. "Hope you like diet cola."

Glynn made a face as he pulled out the remaining chair. I might not have understood his hovering, but that I *did* get. Business Truth #8 is "Be deliberate in your ordering". Guys don't like diet anything.

Yeah, I know that's a whacking great stereotype. And if a guy wants to buy low-fat sausage, I'll sell it to him. But for ninety-six percent of the male population, it's true and I stock my shelves that way. So scold me for prejudice. We're still in business.

He sat "beside" me. Could've been in the parking lot for as much airspace as he put between us. Considering the tiny table, it was almost insulting. Hey, I bathe regularly. He hadn't looked at me once, which pissed me off because I was all too aware of him. That black hair, those deep blue eyes, that gorgeous skin... I shifted on my stool, trying not to squish as I did. So much for immunization.

I was irritated and set the conversation accordingly. "Mishela, love those silver slippers. Are they yours?"

Shoes. Next to diet cola, a guy's worst nightmare.

"Oh yes. I have a whole closet of character shoes. I believe it builds the foundation of the character. I have high heels and flats and the cutest pair of strappy sandals..."

Glynn fidgeted, caught me looking, relaxed rather deliberately. He stretched out with a calculated-looking yawn. His feet touched mine.

I zapped straight, my feet jerking under me automatically.

"Of course, in the movie, the slippers were ruby. But for this version, the writer went back to the original Baum for some things."

Rocky said, "So what about Broadway? Do you think the show stands a chance?"

"Sure." Mishela sipped soda. "In fact, we would've opened there if it hadn't been for the fire. It ruined the theater, burned up all the costumes and sets."

"How horrible. Is that why you had to come to Meiers Corners?"

She nodded. "The backers wouldn't put up extra money to rebuild and new backers were impossible to find. They took the fire as a sign of bad luck."

I relaxed as she talked. My legs loosened from their tight hold on the stool...my bare legs rubbed denim...warm denim, hard muscles beneath... I jumped and quickly shimmied upright again.

"Your bad luck was our good luck," Rocky said. "We're getting a top-notch production to inaugurate the PAC."

"The musicians' good luck too." I rejoined the conversation, determined to ignore warm denim. "If your stars hadn't lobbied for quality musicians, your producer wouldn't have cut the deal with Nixie to get us to New York."

"Assuming we get to New York," Mishela said. "A big backer is interested, but we have to impress him. More than put on a stellar show, I mean. Our audience will have to be standing room only, beyond SRO. Gene Roddenberry is tough to impress."

I wondered momentarily why, if Mishela's guardian was Kai Elias, he didn't just fund the show. But I only said, "Not *the* Gene Roddenberry. He died decades ago."

She smiled.

"So what was that thing with Steve before the second half? He took something of yours?"

"Yes." She colored. "I don't want to talk about it."

So those *were* bikini panties I'd seen. I wondered if Steve had stolen them on a bet or if there was more to it.

Rocky was paging through a copy of the program booklet. "Hey, Mishela. Your bio lists *Juliet Capulet: The Musical* at Ravinia. Do you know Barron Scarpia?"

Mishela nodded. "Sings like an angel and gropes like a schoolboy. Not as bad a pig as Lechnowsky, of course. He'd be screaming at you one minute and trying to get you in the sack the next."

Rocky rolled her eyes. "Boy, that sounds like Carrion. He did a music clinic when I was in college and made a pass at me, but I think he'd try for anything wearing a bra, including some cars."

Glynn gave a disgusted grunt. "Are all musicians philandering sex maniacs?"

"All of us," I said just to needle him. Well hell, he got under my skin, so turnabout, right? "It's the creative urge. I myself would screw anything in jeans and a jacket—" I bit my tongue.

He looked at me directly for the first time. His sapphire eyes were burning.

Burning at *me*?

Rocky's eyes widened, picking up the hot man-sex vibes too. "Um, so." She cleared her throat a couple times, focused exclusively on Mishela. "You've played New York and Canada and Illinois. What's that like, being a glamorous traveling actor?"

"Glamorous." Mishela laughed. "Complete with my 'glamorous' entourage of whichever nanny or warden Mr. Elias assigns to watch over me."

"So you don't jet?" Rocky asked. "Luxury hotels, oyster bars?"

"More like minivans and pizza."

"I think I'm disappointed."

"At least you get to travel," I said. "See new places and new people. I envy that. I've lived in Meiers Corners my whole life." I looked away. "A small life in an even smaller town."

Glynn gave a disgusted grunt. I looked back, was surprised to find him glaring at me, all hunger gone from his eyes. "Your envy does you no credit. You are fortunate to have a home. Many do not."

His condemnation hit me square in the guilt gland, strange because usually only my mother had such bull's-eye aim. I glowered in return—and was confused by a shadow of pain in his dark blue eyes.

Then he hit me with, "You have no appreciation for what you have."

What? "I've lived here my whole life. Don't tell me I don't have appreciation. Meiers Corners has all the amenities. Nosy neighbors, whipped-potato homogeneity—"

"Do you worry about bills? About being attacked? This is a true home, a place where you can feel secure, can be yourself."

My jaw kicked up. "Be myself? Don't make me laugh. I can be myself—as long as I'm a great shopkeeper with a strong sense of family and no other ambitions."

He leaned in. "So you have a few obligations. Do you think living on this planet is rent-free?"

I leaned in too until we were nose to nose. "I pay rent by working for my parents for nothing. By making a deal so that when I do leave, they can hire a real replacement. This show's taking me to New York, and when it does, I'm out of here so fast it'll leave skid marks on the sidewalk." Not true, but I was hyped.

"You are a willful, unappreciative—"

"I have plenty of appreciation—"

"Whoa." Rocky leaped to her feet like a fire was raging instead of a mere argument. "Um, excuse me, but I have to go to the, um." She blushed and gestured toward the back. "I have to go."

Mishela jumped up too. "I'll go with you."

Rocky edged away from our table, not taking her eyes off Glynn and me until she was out of the blast radius. Then she turned and practically ran toward the restrooms.

Mishela wasn't looking at us. Her gaze was on Rocky. As Mishela followed, there was a wistful tilt to her head, watching Rocky's hips sway. Talk about tailing.

It hit me like an obvious bomb. Mishela was attracted to Rocky.

Well, hell. I'd been Meiers Corners blind, seeing the fading snapshots of persons past rather than the present. Rocky was beautiful, brilliantly talented and an even closer match to Mishela than I was. A possible soul mate.

Still, it was all innocent enough. Mishela was young and protected. Even if something budded, it would only be a crush. And though Rocky was incredibly hot, attracting both men and women, she didn't have a clue. I turned to Glynn to say something of the sort—and fell into ocean-jeweled eyes and drowned.

This close, I could see the sleek feathering of each eyebrow, the black velvet of his dilated pupils ringed by coronas of blue fire. The straight edge of his nose, the elegant flare of nostril, the perfect curl of upper lip, begging for a graze of my fingertip. My tongue throbbed to trace the full swell of his lower lip.

Our argument's passion blew into runaway lust blasting between us.

"Junior. The way you look at me, your golden-brown eyes..." Glynn sat back abruptly. His eyes clenched. "Insane. I must have gone stark raving mad." His eyes opened again, intent on mine, his stare as hot as if I were dressed in nothing but his favorite sausage. "I want to kiss you."

I swallowed hard. I had a duty, and the last thing I needed was to get trapped in a relationship. This man, blistering-hot sexy, said complication the way gravity said down.

But blistering-hot sexy didn't drop into Meiers Corners every day. I licked my lips.

His gaze fell precipitously to my mouth and sharpened. "Insane," he repeated, reaching for me, snagging the base of my braid with strong fingers. "I'm not looking for involvement."

"Perfect," I breathed. "Neither am I."

"All right then." And his mouth found mine.

Even if our dark corner hadn't cloaked us, that kiss would have driven any concern about being seen clear from my head. Hell, it drove out any thought whatsoever except for *oh my.*

Glynn didn't kiss tentatively. Didn't try to entice with tempting brushes or soft licks. His mouth covered mine, hot and demanding, pure power channeled into heat and thrust, passion and drive.

Or maybe he was just meeting me where I already was—midlust. My heart pumped hard, my tongue welcomed his heat. He tasted so right. I went straight from *oh my* to *hell yes,* as if I'd known him for years.

His hand tightened on my hair. His head slanted, mouth opening, tongue thrusting deep, opening me wide. Warm, wet, it explored me, dipping, cresting, diving again. A dark groan filled my mouth, his. "You taste like heaven." Seizing my head with both hands, he took me with deeper thrusts of his tongue.

I clutched his arms to steady myself. My fingers dug past buttery-soft leather into biceps big and hard as boulders.

He growled, plunged his tongue so deep I choked, or maybe that was my throat constricting with need. To my embarrassment I opened wider, clutched harder, whimpered for more.

He hauled me into his arms, standing as he did so. Spinning us, he bent me back against the table and drove himself between my legs. His chest superheated my breasts, his abs burned my crotch, his mouth devoured mine and we were two seconds away from a public offense when I heard a horrified, "*Glynn.*"

My sight cleared to Mishela's pale face just beyond Glynn's leather-covered shoulder. Next to her was Rocky's face, red. Mishela's nostrils were flared like she smelled something shocking. Rocky just looked shocked.

Glynn stiffened. Then, with an apologetic glance at me, he stepped back. I slid onto trembling feet and nearly buckled. His hand shot out, steadying me until I could stand on my own. I swallowed but no words came.

Rocky cleared her throat. "Well. Um, I should be getting home. Being that it's late. Being that it's—" She glanced at her watch. "Wow. It really is late. Nearly one. Okay, well, see you all tomorrow." Flushing and stammering, she turned toward the door.

I didn't see Glynn move, but suddenly he blocked her path. "The night is dangerous. We all go together." Snaring a wallet from his jacket, he dropped a twenty on the table. "Come." He threaded his way out, started north on Fifth.

We followed like baby ducks, each lost in her own embarrassment. But walking brought a sense of normalcy back. Mishela, with the exuberance of youth, shrugged off the awkward moment first. She dropped back to walk with me. "Is Meiers Corners really dangerous? Or is the warden just being himself?"

"We have crime," I said. "If you count lawn flamingos. And those fat-butt garden ornaments have to be at least a felony."

Rocky, coming up alongside us, shot me a look.

"Hey," I said. "They ought to be a crime."

"Junior. For your information, my mother has one of those."

"She has a garden gnome too. That cancels out the fat butt. Garden gnomes are cool."

"No way. Garden gnomes are creepy. They're like weeping angels." Rocky shivered. "Or mimes."

"Or clowns," Glynn said over his shoulder. When he caught my surprised look, he flushed slightly. "I've had to comfort children scared by clowns."

The thought of big, protective Glynn, comforting children... I wasn't looking for entanglement, but here might be a man worth it— no, no, no. That was exactly what had gotten my mother, once an operatic mezzo, limited to the small pond of Meiers Corners.

Mishela danced out in front of us. "So where do you live?" She said it to both of us, but her eyes made it clear it was Rocky she was asking.

Which Rocky totally missed. "Junior's on Fourth and Jefferson, over her folks' sausage shop. Across from Kalten's Roller Rink. Well, it was Kalten's before it burned down in November."

"That's nice." Mishela smiled, waiting for what she really wanted to know.

I took pity on her. "Rocky lives on Eighth and Eisenhower."

"Elena O'Rourke's old apartment," Rocky said. "Before she married Bo Strongwell. Then it was Nixie Schmeling's before she married Julian Emerson, and Liese Schmetterling's before she married Logan Steel...huh. I never realized that before."

"What?"

"That so many women lived there just before they got married."

I had. Nixie called it the Fucking Fangtastic Flat, but she had a strange sense of humor. "It's not so odd, statistically speaking. Midtwenties is when most women get married."

"Maybe you're next, Rocky." Mishela fell into step with her. "Do you have a boyfriend?"

Subtle like a Hummer, but she was only seventeen. I waited to see if Rocky caught it, but where her own attractiveness is concerned, she's dumber than a sack of hammers. She said, "Me? No. Both Junior and I are confirmed singles."

"Right." My eyes flickered to Glynn, skulking in the shadows ahead of us. The man even skulked like sex. "Confirmed."

Mishela nudged Rocky. "Nobody you have the hots for?"

I blushed. I definitely got hot around Glynn.

Strangely, Rocky blushed too. "No boyfriends. Oh, look. Here's

Jefferson. We turn here."

"I can do one block alone," I said. "You don't have to walk me to my door."

Glynn spun, took me by the nape and steered me onto Jefferson.

I fought a shiver from the heat of his strong fingers. "What are you doing?"

"I said we'd walk you home." He didn't add the duh but I heard it anyway. Only in his accent, it would be a caressing *deh*.

"This is out of your way if you're headed for Rocky's. Or if you're headed for where you're staying—hey, where are you staying?"

"We keep together," he replied, ignoring my question.

"And when Glynn speaks, you'd better listen," Mishela said.

"Seriously, Meiers Corners is as safe as a tricycle with training wheels, pink flamingos aside," I said. "It's only one block. If something happens, I'll yell and you can come running."

"Trouble blows up quickly." Glynn's voice was low and rough, almost a growl.

"Glynn's expecting a disaster," Mishela said.

I muttered, "Something tells me Glynn's always expecting a disaster."

"That he is." She chuckled. "Gloomy Glynn, sucking the joy out of everything."

"Enough, Mishela." His gruff tone was leavened by an affectionate note.

"You're better than Mr. Elias. At least I can tease you."

"Mr. Elias only wants you safe—" Glynn stopped abruptly, and since my neck was still in his long fingers, so did I.

Behind us, Mishela made a strange noise. Low, angry, almost a snarl. I tried to look, but my head was immobilized, Glynn's fingers strong as a vise. I slanted my eyes back, which gave me a headache, but it was enough to see her eyes harden, her features sharpen and her stance turn distinctly threatening. Her hair furled in a sudden wind, snapping behind her like a cape.

Sharpened features, hawk-like eyes... I'd seen that look somewhere before. A book.

"Mishela." Glynn's voice was cool, a warning. "We have company."

She blinked a couple times. And just that quickly, the threat ebbed from her.

"Good. Stay here." Glynn finally released me.

Only to disappear around the corner. Around the corner to...*my home.* "Hey wait!" I dashed after.

And yanked up like a dog on a chain when Mishela grabbed my wrist. For a slip of a girl, she was strong. "Glynn said to stay." Her face was as stern as his.

"He's your guard, not mine." I tried to shake loose, but she had fingers like a concert pianist's. And yeah, that's superstrong. I tried a wrist-twist, but apparently she'd had training because she only shifted hands.

I shook my wrist again, gently, a nonverbal phooey. "That's not fair."

Her stern expression melted into a grin. "That's what I always tell Glynn. Know what he says? 'It isn't, is it?'"

"Such sympathy. I'm not surprised you feel stifled."

Vulnerability flashed across her face, just as suddenly hidden. She gave a little laugh. "Oh, it's not so bad." Her acting was perfect, but her tone was a quarter step off. "It's like I have five big brothers. Lots of girls would love—"

A howl cut her off, followed by the roar of a lion. I froze as metal sang like the crossing of swords.

"What the—that's from the store!" I leaped into motion, only to yank up short against her grip. "Let go!"

"Junior, I can't." Mishela's eyes were sad, and far older than her seventeen years.

"I can," Rocky said simply, and dashed around the corner onto Fourth Street.

With an anguished cry, Mishela released me to dart after her. "Rocky, no!"

I kicked after them both and—

Plowed straight into them. Mishela held Rocky, stroking her hair. Rocky didn't seem to be aware of it. She clutched her instrument bag to her stomach and stared at the vacant street.

Totally empty. No lion, no swordplay.

No Glynn.

A light snapped on above us. The *shoop* of a window rising and a clap of shutters presaged a head poking from the second floor of the storefront. The face had my features but was tubby, older and male. A lick of silver hair winged out from under a striped nightcap, a cookie elf complete with the ruddy cheeks.

My dad.

"Junior! *Was ist hier passiert?*"

Just what I needed, family yelling in the street. And poor Rocky hated conflict. "English, please, Pop." Meiers Corners was founded in the 1800s by German immigrants, and Pop, though second generation, was raised speaking it and still dreamed in it. Sometimes I had to remind him not everyone spoke fluent *Deutsch*.

"*Ja*, all right. Junior, what are you doing? Do you know what time it is?"

"After midnight, Pop."

"Then get your heinie up here and get some sleep. The store opens at eight *pünktlich*—whether you are awake or not."

"But Pop—"

"Bed, Junior. Sausage doesn't sell itself." The window banged closed.

Good ol' Business Truth #1 on the Eightfold Business Path. Other kids got "Early to bed and early to rise" or "The early bird gets the worm". I got sausage slogans.

I turned to say goodbye. Strangely, with all Pop's yelling, Rocky was still shivering in Mishela's arms, staring at the empty street. I frowned. "What's wrong with her?"

"Nothing," a deep voice answered.

Glynn glided toward us. His clothes were neat and clean, and not a bruise or scratch marred his hewn, stubbled jaw. If he'd been in a fight, it didn't show.

He stopped so close to me I had to crane my neck. Damn, he was tall. I fell back a step.

His fingertips on my chin halted me. I hoped for a kiss. No, I didn't. Yes, I—

"You saw nothing." His murmur was soft, soothing, yet rang strangely in my head. "Neither of you saw anything."

"But...but I did." Rocky's croak was far from her usual honeyed alto. "F...fighting."

"You didn't see fighting." Glynn's tone darkened, echoing. I shook my head.

"I did," Rocky insisted. "You and someone...or some*thing*..."

Grimacing, Glynn flicked eyes to me. "Junior. You saw nothing."

"Nope. But Rocky did. Hey, what's with the cave voice?"

"Bloody hell." Mr. Grimace intensified, joined by his little brothers Glower and Hands-on-Hips. "Both of you are immune?"

"I had a flu shot," I said. "Working in retail you come into contact with all sorts of double-nasties. What does that have to do with what Rocky saw?"

"Bollocks." Glynn's blue eyes took on a distinctly icy cast.

Mishela laid a slim hand on his sleeve. "Why don't we call Mr. Elias? He can explain everything to Rocky."

Their eyes met and an understanding passed between them.

Clearly they were close. I felt a moment's yearning. My father was the only person I had a link like that with, via sausage. Ha ha.

Then their heads turned in tandem to look at me, and I got a weird shiver. Close? Or unnaturally attuned?

"Junior," Mishela said. "You don't need to stay."

I considered that. Though shows make for a feeling of family, I'd only met Mishela and Glynn tonight. I didn't really know them, especially Mr. BDD—big, dark and dangerous being the very definition of mystery.

Rocky was my friend, she'd seen fighting, and I'd heard strange things. Not cute-funny strange, but the howling and clanging metal kind. From the way Mishela and Glynn were acting, they knew about it.

They probably meant Rocky no harm, but I couldn't count on it. "I'll stay. I want to hear the explanation too."

Mishela opened her mouth to argue, but Glynn said, "Let's get this over with." He flipped out a phone, hit speaker, then a speed dial. The phone rang once before the line clicked open.

"Rhys-Jenkins."

I took a physical step back. The voice was that deep, that powerful. Like hearing the color black speak. Whoever this Elias was, he had some serious testosterone going.

"We had an encounter, sir," Glynn said. "Mishela's fine, but there's a young woman here who needs a bit of an explanation. Her name is Rocky."

"Put her on. Without speaker, if you would."

"As you wish, sir. Thank you." Glynn clicked off the speaker, offered the phone to Rocky.

She took it gingerly, put it to her ear. "H...hello?" She blinked. "Yes. Yes, sir." She blinked several more times and added in a low whisper, "Raquel."

Then there was only Elias's murmur. Rocky's eyes slid shut. The tension drained from her slowly, as if she were a candle melting. A moment later, she blinked like she was wakening, and smiled. "It's all right." She closed the phone and handed it to Glynn. "It was just a stray dog."

"Excuse me?" I said. "Dogs don't roar."

"That was a howl. Mr. Elias explained everything. The dog is a wolf-husky mix, raised by an old man for protection. When its owner died, the poor thing was dumped near here. Glynn used to be a forest ranger, so the park service asked him to catch it."

"A ranger." If anyone could be a woodsman, it was Glynn, but that didn't mean I believed word one. "So the howl was a wolf-dog, and Glynn was deputized to shag it?"

Glynn raised a single black brow.

I blushed. What about the man made everything coming out of my mouth sound dirty? "I mean catch it. Shag, meaning fetch. Um, did you? Catch it, that is?"

The brow made an arrogant arch. "Of course."

"And caged it?" I made a show of looking around. "Huh, no cage. So did you spear it with your trusty sword?"

Both Glynn's sleek black brows winged up.

"I meant..." I winced. "I heard metal. Ka-*shing*," I added, lamely.

"Oh, certainly." The brows came back down. "That was the tranquilizer dart."

"O-kay." That singing metal had not been a mere dart. "And the wolf is now where?"

"Someplace safe. Which is where you should be." Glynn seized my hand and dragged me to my front door, his heat searing me.

I jerked away. "No! My entrance is in back." Yikes. "I mean..." What was it about the man that made me vomit these glorious freaking double entendres? "The front door is for the store. The family entrance

41

is around the side, back between buildings."

"I see." He took my arm, steered me to the walkway. "So this is your...private entrance?"

"Uh, yeah." My cheeks fired. A change of topic was prudent. "Thanks for the escort."

We'd reached the door, small, unmarked and barely visible in the shadows between buildings. Glynn waited silently while I unlocked it (MC was safe, but we had neighbors who didn't exactly appreciate us). He waited while I opened and entered, waited until I shut, even waited while I locked up. I didn't see him, but I could practically feel his dark, hovering shadow.

I leaned against the closed door, caught my breath. Ordinarily after a rehearsal, I'd maybe have a beer with friends, then head home alone. I did not stay out late, I did not hear sword fights and animals howling, and I certainly did not kiss darkly sensual forest men. Ordinarily.

Tonight was seriously out of the ordinary orbit.

Yet according to Glynn, nothing had happened. Mr. Elias had "explained" things to Rocky. From my perspective, it had looked more like hypnosis. But hypnosis over the phone? None of this made sense.

I wanted to think. I pushed away from the door and ran up the stairs past my folks' flat, straight to the small attic space that was my room.

My "room". More of a crawl space really, its ceiling low even for my five-two. Some days it felt cozy, others it felt cramped. Rarely did it seem like the only safe place in a world gone insane.

When I was ten, I wanted to paint the walls dark purple. My parents had insisted on Realtor beige. To give the space color, I'd slapped up a poster of Times Square at night. Flowers blooming in the Mojave Desert came next. Then pictures of Paris, the Eiffel Tower, the Louvre. A map of Boston, and next to it a subway map. Eventually I had pictures, maps and posters from every corner of the world, covering every bit of beige. The latest addition was the colossal Burj Khalifa skyscraper in Dubai.

My room, a cubby in the family homestead, was me being a dutiful daughter. My pictures were me wanting more.

I ran into my room, slowed. Touched a picture at random and dreamed of going to that place, of seeing its color and life. This was part of my going-to-bed ritual, as important as brushing my teeth.

Tonight my fingers caressed a London evening. Lights cascaded off the Thames, blues and violets slashing through rows and rows of gold. I'd take that image to bed with me, dream rainbow dreams...

But I'd come up here to think. Instead of crawling into bed, I went to my window.

My single window faced south. It was a reverse dormer notched into the roof. I opened sash and shutters to the warm May night, heard Rocky and Mishela's voices fading away to my right, heading west on Jefferson. And with them, though I didn't hear him, was Glynn. Big, silent Glynn.

I shimmied outside, into the small box of roof space that encased the window. Small for me even when I was a child, I now fit only with my knees drawn to my chin. But that was the best position for staring at the stars and thinking. I'd meant to mull on the weirdness that had happened, but somehow it didn't seem nearly as important as the fact that Glynn had kissed me.

Glynn had kissed me, and I had responded to every big, dark, dangerous bit, lust igniting my very cells. I'd never known anything like it. Granted, I hadn't experienced a lot because the store kept me sixty-hour busy, but I wondered if anything could have prepared me for the instant union I felt with him.

Glynn had *kissed* me. Was that normal, a guy going straight from "hi how are you" to locking lips? And then seem almost angry that he'd done it?

Glynn had kissed *me*. Why me, why not Rocky, who was a hundred and ten pounds of hot? Or one of the other pit or adult cast members? Hell, why not the flamboyant Director Dumbass, who was cute in a driven, psychotic sort of way?

A pounding came from below. My dad, hitting the ceiling with a broomstick. "Get to sleep! Work tomorrow."

I sighed. What Pop lacked in subtlety, he made up for in volume.

But in this case, he was right. Worrying over Glynn's inexplicable behavior wouldn't make it into sense. The only way to deal was Business Truth #7, courtesy of Queen Elizabeth I. "Never decide today what you can put off until tomorrow." It would either disappear or grow until the solution was obvious.

Tomorrow I'd work hard in the store, forget about *Glynn kissed me*—forget about *all* tonight's crazy—by reminding myself where my duty really was. My parents, the store, my dreams.

Chapter Three

My alarm went off at five. I'd dreamed about Glynn kissing me and woke sweet and heavy and even more determined to lose the events of last night in my work.

Showered and dressed, I staggered downstairs at five twenty into the familial abode—not thinking about Glynn. The Wurstspeicher Haus didn't open until eight, but I had tons to do before then. A big store has accountants and salespeople and a purchasing department and the IT guy. A small store still has to pay taxes and deal with customers and buy product and fix the things that buzz and blink. We had Mom and Pop to do all that—and me.

No lights, so I followed the lifeline scent of freshly brewed coffee and stumbled into the kitchen, then poured by feel alone. It was dark because Mom and Pop left for work before dawn. The kitchen smelled of bacon and eggs and buttered toast.

Mom's opera music was blaring. *L'Orfeo* by Monteverdi, early music to start the day. She'd save Stravinsky for evening.

Not thinking about sweet, hot kisses, I grabbed a bagel, hoisted my coffee and hit the stairs down. I shivered, not lust, just simple chill. May mornings were still on the cool side and the stairwell was unheated. I gulped hot coffee as I trotted downstairs and through the door.

The office area was warmer. Our building was a storefront, literally. The store was the front half. The back was originally my grandparents' flat, converted into offices and storage after Grandma and Grandpa Stieg went to the Happy Sausage Shop in the sky.

The stairwell opened into the dining room, now a general work area. To the right was the kitchen, now storage. Straight ahead were two bedrooms, Mom and Pop's offices. Left was the store.

Time to forget Glynn and kisses, which I had *not* been thinking about anyway. I squared shoulders and headed left to work and duty.

My father looked up from his paperwork as I stumbled by. His face gleamed round and ruddy in the glow of his accountant's lamp. "Junior, *gut*. Help me carry in the *wurst*." *Gut* meant good. *Wurst* was what we called sausage. He heaved to his feet, which made him maybe an inch taller. At five-six, not only his face resembled a cookie elf.

"Where's Mom?" Or actually I said "*Wo ist Mutti?*", as he and I spoke German at home (I knew a bit of Italian too, courtesy of Mom). I took a quick bite of bagel, set it and my coffee on his scarred desk and trailed him to the kitchen.

"Your mother is on the phone with suppliers. They are asking why we need so much *blutwurst*."

"Because people are buying it?" I snorted. "Why Mom? The only German she speaks is the stuff she learned to sing."

"She has decided it's time to get more fluent. She says to me, 'Gunter, I wish to learn, to be better'. Your mother is a strong woman, Junior. You could do worse than to be like her."

"Yes, Pop." We'd had this conversation before. The problem was I *was* like her, too much. To me, learning meant not making the same mistakes she had. Time to change the subject. "It's going to be a warm day. That's going to stress the coolers in the store."

"*Ach*, those coolers are practically brand-new." He jerked the dolly into place and we hoisted boxes of product onto it. "Younger than me."

"Pop, they're fifty years old. The warranty expired before I was born. They clank like Marley's ghost. If we could just get one new cooler with the fund—"

"That cash is for emergencies." His tone said end of conversation.

Well, wonderful. Hold off thoughts of Glynn and kisses with the distraction of work? Silence to fret in was so helpful.

But work in silence we did. Pop threw heavy boxes on the stack like they were Styrofoam. He was strong enough to have loaded alone— for all his diminutive size, he was built like a mule. But I always helped, and not just because of duty. Pop made me, to "build up my strength". He was big into the Protestant work ethic—but secretly I think he still wanted me to be a son.

Nixie Emerson has this thing about names having power. Her parents christened her Dietlinde in a subtle attempt to mold sassy-punker her into a normal German.

My dad naming me Gunter, nickname Junior? Not nearly so subtle.

Mary Hughes

One of the reasons I grew my hair down to my ass. Before I got the breasts, it was the only way people remembered I wasn't a boy.

In silence, we rolled product into the store, like Glynn's lips rolling over mine... Time to talk again. "So, um, Pop. Any problems with the shipment?"

"The usual tampering with the boxes. Mustaches drawn on the Usinger elf. 'This side up' pointing down. These *Käsegecken*. So petty." My father sniffed.

The *Käsegecken* were the Cheese Dudes, our next-door neighbors. Lately they'd taken to stealing or defacing our shipments if we didn't cart them inside right away. Sometimes they'd even go through our personal mail. I knew that because Lady Liberty stamps don't generally sport beards. Messing with US mail is a federal offense, but magic markers aren't exactly uncommon. And the Dudes managed to stick the mail back in our box within a day, so we couldn't prove it wasn't just slow delivery.

Never mind that the MC post office was so punctual they had a "thirty minutes or it's free" policy—and a record better than Ritsa's pizza delivery.

I said, "I still don't get why they hate us. Selling Limburger and Brie right next to our bratwurst and kielbasa. You'd think that'd be a perfect pairing. Cheese and sausage, right?"

"They are jealous. Ours is the better location. The larger store."

"But why the vandalism? There's more, Pop."

"Sure, they accuse us of being old fashioned fuddy-duddies, of scaring away their customers. How silly is that? They, who are the newfangled flash-in-the-pans, are scaring off ours. When you walk into a tourist shop, you expect a cheery little tinkle-bell, *ja*?"

I had to admit their deathmetal recording screaming "Cheese, Marvelous Cheese" certainly changed the ambience of the area. But all I said was, "Their Web site is pretty kickass."

"Watch your mouth."

And that killed the conversation again. Not because I'd said "ass". Because I'd used the W-word, Web site. In my dad's view, anything that wasn't built out of sausage was suspect. So while ass was totally allowable, Web site was *verboten*. Which made me consider Glynn's totally allowable ass...no, no. Thinking of work, not Glynn. Thinking of opening the store, unpacking sausage. Opening a pack of large, fresh sausage, unzipping Glynn's... I sighed.

46

At eight sharp I slipped on my Wurstspeicher Haus apron and took position behind the register, ready for business. Surely dealing with the rush of customers would take my mind off Glynn.

Oh yeah, the rush of maybe fifteen customers. A dozen were regulars who still bought their meat daily, ingrained by a lifetime of routine. (At least I hoped it was routine, not necessity. Meiers Corners was pretty old-fashioned, but I didn't think they had iceboxes instead of refrigerators. Probably.)

A couple of midweek tourists were salted among the dutiful dozen. Not a lot of traffic.

I chafed. Nothing to do behind the counter but dream of Glynn. And I couldn't leave. Despite doing most of our business weekends and holidays, even though I'd started an Internet presence, someone needed to run the daily cash register. The sum total of the work force was Mom, Pop and me.

Why not just hire someone? Well, our net on fifteen customers was maybe fifty dollars. Fifty a day versus $8.25 an hour minimum wage (Illinois's is higher than the national)—not a lot of options. The only people you could pay less than minimum was family or a slave. Sometimes I thought they were the same thing.

Yeah, whiny, I know. I had a roof over my head, three free squares and as much gas money as I needed as long as I walked everywhere. I loved my parents and they needed me.

But I couldn't live at home forever.

The store's bell tinkled, barely heard over the clank of our old coolers and the soaring notes of *La Traviata* (Mom had moved into the nineteenth century). A customer. No matter what I wanted, my motto was "If you have the job, *do* the job". I snapped on my professional smile and my brain snapped on its sausage-selling instinct.

My body snapped on a tingle, imagining a doorway filled with lyrical baritones of the Big Dark and Dangerous kind.

But it was Twyla Tafel.

"Hey, Junior. I've come for my blood sausage." Twyla sauntered in on Kenneth Cole heels, a hundred and forty pounds of curves and detours wrapped in a Donna Morgan suit, blue-green. Only she'd probably call it teal or azure. An art major in school, Twyla was the mayor's executive admin, emphasis on Executive. We have a mayor, but like king and prime minister, he does the handshakes and Twyla, the daughter of an African diplomat, actually governs.

I pulled up her order. "More blood sausage? Didn't you just get some last week?"

"What can I say? Guests seem to like it." She signed for it. "Oh, I need to add a personal blood sausage order. Five pounds."

"We're selling a lot of *blutwurst* lately. I wonder why. I can't imagine cooked blood being widely popular."

"Maybe don't question it too closely. It's all money in the register, right?" She gave me a bright smile as she pulled out her wallet. "Speaking of which, the city's order is covered by our PO, but is credit okay for mine?"

"Sure. The Wurstspeicher Haus has made it into the twenty-first century in some things."

"Thanks to you." She laughed as she flipped out a card. "I think your dad would still be asking 'paper or canvas'."

"Or pigs' bladder. Speaking of which, is a plastic bag okay?" When she nodded, I started filling one. "So what's with the personal order? Party?"

"Julian and Nixie have a few guests."

My head snapped up. Twyla's a resident of the Emerson townhouses, living there with her hot Greek, Nikos. "Guests? Like for the PAC opening?"

"You've heard of it?" She gave a quick, rueful smile. "Of course you have. Nixie told me you're playing in the pit. Sorry. I've just been so worried about it. It's the culmination of some pretty serious budget retooling."

The bell tinkled. I glanced at the door, hoping for Big Dark and Dangerous, but a couple tourists wandered in. I said hello and smiled helpfully at them. They ignored me to check out the coolers.

Out-of-towners. They didn't mean to be rude; they just didn't know any better.

I turned back to Twyla. "Budget retooling?"

Twyla angled closer and lowered her voice. "You know the economy is pretty grim, right? Well, Meiers Corners is mostly self-sufficient, but it's affecting even us. The mayor had a brilliant idea."

I groaned. "An all-polka channel on Hulu?"

"Please. I had some hand in this. Problem is, we're a local economy. That limits us. To expand, we need to go regional. We picked tourism as our vehicle, and are sinking cash into all things quaint and touristy."

"But that's awesome." Little dollar signs floated before my eyes. The sausage store was the epitome of quaint and touristy.

"Sure. Except to finance the expansion, Mayor Meier talked the Sparkasse Bank into making loans. Lots of them, and some pretty serious money, including the renovation of the PAC."

"But the bank makes money on loans, doesn't it?"

"If the touristy places pay the loans back. If they don't...well, we're not just sitting back hoping tourism takes off. We're actively promoting it. *Oz, Wonderful Oz* is our kickoff. We're counting on the pull of a Broadway-caliber show to bring in the out-of-towners. If they like it well enough, they'll come back with a couple thousand of their friends."

"That's no problem. I saw the show last night. It'll be terrific."

"That's not what I heard." She leaned in. "I heard it was awful."

"Julian?" I shrugged. "It was the first dress. The stars are outstanding. It'll be awesome."

"I'm glad you're confident. The bank went out on a bit of a limb. Not as bad as the bottom dropping out of realty, but if the tourist businesses don't turn a healthy profit and can't pay back the loans, the bank will be in trouble. Best scenario?" She lowered her voice once again until I was practically reading her lips. "The bank gets sold. And the buyers might not be so friendly to locals."

"Ouch. If our coolers go, I'm hoping to get a loan myself."

"Then play that show like it's your ticket to Coolerville."

Not only my future was riding on this production. The city's financial health was too.

At five thirty I turned the register over to my rent-a-kid and ran upstairs for the traditional before-rehearsal, five-second shower and degreasing. Cotton really soaks up the odor of garlic and marbled fat.

I had just pulled black jeans and a black T-shirt over a lacy powder-blue thong and demi-bra (they were next in the underwear drawer—really) and was brushing my teeth when a knock came at the attic door.

"That's weird." No one ever knocked. Because of the setup, my parents were the only ones who had access to the attic, and they took unholy delight in bursting in on me unannounced. Especially (to my chagrin) when I was "going through puberty", if you know what I mean. Curious, I spat and rinsed and headed for the far door. It took me across my "hallway".

Picture a capital T. Turn it sideways and set it on our house, the top bar along Jefferson in the south. My room—bedroom and tiny bath—was at the intersection, sitting like a tree fort in the branches of the attic, the rest being bare rafters and blown insulation.

The stairwell door was at the foot of the T. A set of two-by-fours laid over the joists was my hall. I traveled it by instinct, ignoring the fact that one wrong step would put me through my parents' ceiling. If I ever got out of here, I'd be a shoo-in for a high wire act.

I hurried to the door and opened it. Swallowed my tongue.

Filling the doorway and then some was Glynn, hands thrust in his black leather jacket pockets.

His jaw, freshly shaved, was more honed than I remembered, his skin almost dewy. His lips... I groaned. The upper begged for a nibble, the lower demanded a full tongue-swipe. Those edible lips parted, revealing strong white teeth. The tip of his tongue peeked through.

A storm of lust broke in my belly, drenched my thong.

Glynn's nostrils flared, elegant yet animal. His eyes—smack me with a kielbasa, his eyes burned deep, hot purple.

"H...how'd you get in?" I croaked. More thong-dousing— apparently parts of me wanted to know how he'd "get in" too.

"Through the store. Your teenager wasn't very attentive. I found my way into the house."

"You penetrated the family abode?" *Penetrated.* Just club me. "Um, why have you come?" *Come.* "Here, I mean. Why have you come here...to the store? Yes, that's what I meant." *Shut* up, *Junior.*

I heard a soft grunt, a stifled groan. Him or me, I didn't know.

"I've come to pick you up." His mouth barely moved, lips stiff. "We've Emerson's limo." He shifted his hands from his jacket to jam them into his jeans pockets.

"Limo?" My eyes automatically latched on to his hands, which framed a rising zipper. "You're offering me a fast ride...?" Oh, thank you, Dr. Freud. I cleared my throat and pretended I wasn't an ass. "You do know the PAC is only a block from here?"

"It's on our way. I didn't like the thought of you toting those heavy instruments when I could do something about it."

"That was nice." Trapped in a limo with Big Dark and Dangerous, porn flick fantasy number five. Maybe I should have refused, but lugging the headless-corpse sax *was* a pain. Besides, how much trouble could we get into in just one block? "Give me a sec to pack up." I started to close the attic door. Manners took over. "Why don't you come back? Be careful to stay on the walkway." I started for my room.

No footsteps clunked behind me. I took a couple more steps but still heard nothing, so I twisted around to see if he was there.

I managed to twist myself off-balance. I tried to catch myself, but my foot hit the edge of the narrow walkway, skidded off. No nearby walls or even studs to grab, so I fell.

With incredible speed and grace, Glynn snared me just before I put a Junior-size hole through my parents' ceiling. I was ridiculously grateful—until I realized he'd caught me around the breasts.

And that one big, hot hand was gently squeezing.

I sucked in a breath. Jagged darts of lust fired from that rhythmically squeezing hand and arrowed down my belly to detonate in my groin.

"Ah, Junior. You're so soft." Glynn's breath heated my hair. "So lovely." He rolled me around until I was facing him. His arms wrapped me, bands of hard muscle. "I didn't sleep at all last night, thinking about you. Your scent, your feel. Your taste."

I stared up at him, wondering if I had really fallen through the ceiling gypsum and was lying unconscious on my folks' kitchen floor. This gorgeous stranger had been thinking about me all night? My brain tried to make sense of it... He dropped his head and kissed me.

His mouth took me slowly. Not leisurely slow but purposefully slow, thoroughly, his lips circling gently. Like we lay entwined on a summer beach, cool sand below, warm sun above, with nothing to do but each other. And he was going to do me oh, so right.

My eyelids drifted shut, my palms slid onto his chest. His hard, thick pecs were warm slabs of brick.

He dipped in, tongue licking lightly at my mouth. My lips parted, my breath mingled with his and I tasted masculine fire. I opened more eagerly for him—but he backed off, tonguing the corners of my mouth, tracing the outline of my lips. Rubbing lightly yet thoroughly. Sweetly, as if we had lifetimes to explore each other.

Like a kiss of commitment.

I pulled back. "No involvement" was more than an aim, it was a mantra. Duty to my parents, followed by my dreams. Commitment didn't figure in except as a stumbling block to avoid.

"Don't be afraid," he murmured. "I won't hurt you."

I *was* afraid, not that he'd hurt me physically, but that he'd take over my future.

He didn't know that and only held me more firmly. Securely. Despite my doubts, I felt safe in his warm, strong arms.

Until he bent and kissed the stuffing out of me, tongue swirling masterfully, pure, hot sensation. I squeaked but he distracted me by rubbing his muscled chest into my palms. My fingers tightened compulsively. The man's pecs were sauna rocks set to steaming. My fear melted away, leaving only need.

I stretched up, kissed him back.

He gripped me tighter, practically fusing me with his burning body, and rocked his pelvis into me. His hips were the blacksmith's hammer and mine the anvil, sparking red-hot lust between. And oh, what a fine, large sword was developing.

I clutched his jacket, pulled him toward my room. We'd fall into a tangled heap on my bed. I'd be eager and open and suck him in for some mind-blowing sex.

As if he read my mind, Glynn purred, "Ah, Junior. This is what filled my dreams last night. You, all warm and wet and ready for me. It seems I have been waiting a lifetime to make love to you."

Okay, that finally broke through the red haze of my mind.

Sex, sure, in small doses. But making *love*? Lovemaking led to neglect of duty, which led to regret. To rainbow dreams shattered. I had been a dutiful daughter for five years, and I was just on the verge of having it all, setting my parents up while fulfilling my dreams. I was *not* getting distracted now.

I jerked away. And stumbled, again nearly sailing through the joists.

Again Glynn caught me, but this time he set me away from him, his eyes violet-blue slits between black lashes. "What's wrong, *babi?*"

His voice sounded like maybe he was insulted and I wondered if that startling color of his eyes signaled strong emotion.

Time for "distract with any truth that was not The Truth"—a Wurstspeicher Haus Sales Maneuver, for those of you keeping score at home. "I don't want to be late again. For rehearsal."

"Oh?"

"See, if I do good, when the company goes to Broadway, I go with. So I have to do good."

His eyes stayed narrow a moment longer, almost glittering. Then he nodded and held his hand toward my room, indicating I should go first.

I stared for a moment at that long-fingered hand, as sexy as his honed jaw and talented mouth. "But you knew that, right? If Mishela goes, you're going too."

"I have other obligations." He flexed his fingers, a reminder that he was waiting for me to lead the way.

His long, strong fingers flexing, flexing between my thighs... I swallowed hard and went, but I kept my gaze glued to my feet the whole way. Not to avoid tripping. To avoid sexy *hands*. "Aren't you going to New York?"

"I'm not."

"Why not?" My instruments were where I left them after practicing at lunch. Normally I put them away, but there had been an emergency in the shop. A sausage emergency, now there's an oxymoron. "Mishela needs a bodyguard for little Meiers Corners but she doesn't need one in New York?"

"It would take too long to explain."

"I have to pack up. You have time." I disassembled instruments, mindful of Glynn with each joint. Stupid hands.

"New York is a different...territory, for want of a better word. Elias will hire a bodyguard who is native to the area, to avoid conflict. What's all this?" He came into my room to point at my African collage—Pyramids, the Sahara and Mt. Kilimanjaro.

"Places I want to visit." I knew he was trying to distract me, but I'd barely managed to stop thinking about sexy, strong hands, and now in this tight space I couldn't avoid the heat of his big body, overwhelming the cool spring evening. Or his scent, masculine and leather-clad, mingling intriguingly with the light smell of new-mown grass. It made

53

me think of laying him down in a field, climbing on top, snagging my thong out of the way and...stuff me into sheep guts and boil me, I was such a sausage-brain. I slammed the sax case shut and picked it up.

Or tried to. Somehow Glynn was there, shouldering me aside and snaring the handle in his own big strong hand. "You can carry the little ones, *babi*."

I tried to think of something to say to take my mind off his fucking hands. Ooh, fucking hands rubbing between my... I cleared my throat. "*Babi*. What language is that?"

"Welsh."

Which explained the lovely lilt to his words.

We managed to make it downstairs without me jumping his big, hot...*damn* or his lovely, strong...*fuck*. A limo awaited us at the curb. I'd never ridden in one before and wanted to savor the experience, but Glynn hustled me in next to Mishela, barely pausing to toss my sax in before sliding across from us and slamming the door.

I frowned. "What's that smell?"

Mishela quirked a smile. "Hello to you too, Junior."

"Hi. Don't you smell that? Something's burning."

"Is it?" She blinked big green eyes, and her eyebrows lifted like she was the most truthful being in the world. I knew it as a Sales Maneuver. Maybe actors had Truths and Maneuvers too. I wondered if they used different numbers.

The limo turned in to the underground parking structure and dropped us off on B1 (I didn't see who was driving but I did catch *Hybrid* on the back of the limo...yeah, environmentally conscious extreme consumption). From there, we trotted upstairs. With Glynn carrying the sax, we made good time, despite my still-wet thong hitching every other stride. He wasn't just decorative but useful. If a guy like that were mine...dammit, Queen Bess was wrong. The problem hadn't gone away, it had gotten worse—and I still had no idea what to do about it.

The nice thing about being dedicated to your work is that you can put awkward questions on hold to do the job. Mishela peeled off to go to the dressing rooms. Since Glynn had my sax, he continued alone with me, but I was confident that my professionalism would not let me trip him and grind his naked hips into the plush new carpet.

Mostly confident.

He held the house door open for me. I said a professional thanks and slid by him with a professional foot of airspace. I shivered at his body heat, but dammit, it was a professional shiver.

The moment Julian Emerson saw Glynn, he set down his cello and jumped to his feet. Tucking my sax next to the pit, Glynn took off with Julian. Huh. Blue-blood lawyer and Welsh bodyguard, BFFs? That might explain why Glynn had Julian's limo, but I wondered why Julian had warned me to be careful around Glynn if they were friends.

But hey, maybe here was the secret to dialing down my attraction to Glynn. Maybe Nixie and Julian had the goods on him, some personal wart since the whole knifey, teeth-picking thing hadn't worked out. Grilling was in order. After assembling my sax, I grabbed my gig bag and slid into the chair next to Nixie, who was already warming up. "So we went out with Glynn and Mishela last night and didn't explode or catch any communicable disease."

"Sad for you," Nixie said around her clarinet mouthpiece. Blowing a couple more notes that squeaked like fingernails on chalkboard, she grimaced and yanked off the reed, slid it into its case and pulled out a new one.

"Julian warned me off Glynn too. What is it with you guys, anyway? Mishela's perfectly nice. And Glynn..." Well, Glynn was Glynn.

"So nothing happened? " She stuck the new reed in her mouth. "Nothing at all?" The reed wobbled like a sucker as she spoke.

Besides wolf-dogs and Rocky's strange reaction? "What counts as nothing?"

Nixie sucked on her reed a long time, seriously thinking, which worried me. I'd wanted a wart, but Nixie doing serious meant a plague.

Finally she drew a breath. "Knowing how dedicated you are to your folks, I shouldn't worry. But if there's even a chance of you and Glynn coupling up, you need the 4-1-1. He's not what you think, Junior. He's a—"

Clapping hands cut her off. "Places, people."

Hot pink, lime green and saffron yellow sashayed onto the stage, making my eyes water. Director Dumas. He called, "Places for warm-up. Last night was a disaster, so we're going to do mirrors. Everyone up-up-up." He glared into the pit. "Including musicians."

Takashi waved his baton as if it could parry Dumas. "We need to run the overture and entr'acte."

"Later. Get your asses onstage for the warm-up. Stage crew." Dumas whirled, waved to the hesitating, black-clad figures. "Everyone means ev-ry-one."

Mishela glided into view in the wings, Dorothy braids swaying. Glynn was a dark, faithful shadow behind her. Near her, Scarecrow, Lion and Tin Man also poked their heads around the side curtains.

"Everyone! Actors, crew, musicians. Now-now-now, what are you waiting for? Yes, even you stars." Dumas pointed at Dorothy and her companions.

Scarecrow shrugged his bony shoulders. "Let's do this."

"Parents and sitters too. You, skulking there." Dumas jerked two fingers at Glynn. "Let's go!"

Glynn edged back into the wings, ready to bolt. Smart boy. Acting exercises held as much appeal as flossing with barbed wire.

Dumas simply strode into the curtain legs, latched on to Glynn and pulled. The director was surprisingly forceful, but Glynn was a Welsh mountain, obstinately not going anywhere.

Until Mishela gave him a pleading look. Glowering, Glynn came.

Whoa. She wasn't the boss of him. Which meant not only did he not pick his teeth with a knife, he was the rare male who set aside his own desires just to be nice.

A primitive need flared in me, an elemental *me want.*

Glynn's big, dangerous body hit a pool of light. Dumas's glare shattered into an agog stare. I sympathized. No matter how many times I saw that man candy, I went into hyperglycemic shock too.

But here was an opportunity marked obvious. I'd never want to throw anyone to the sharks, but if Glynn had diverted Dumbass, I was taking advantage of it. I hunkered down, disaster narrowly averted. Julian and Nixie exchanged a relieved glance.

Until— "Musishuns up here. *Nowsh.*" Dumbass's diction was a little off, but drool will do that.

With a sigh, Takashi clicked baton onto stand. "We'll get done sooner if we cooperate." He gave us all a look of apology. "Please?"

Grumbling, we moved out like nonflossers lining up for Jill "The Drill" Schmerz (MC dental hygienist and WWII reenactment enthusiast), nobody wanting to be first. Takashi grabbed my elbow and marched me to the stage. He certainly would be successful, doing what needed to be done. Ass hat.

"Everyone pair up. Quickly now." Dumas tried to tug Glynn onto center stage, but Glynn was doing his Welsh mountain thing again. He didn't move an inch, which wasn't surprising considering he probably had a good fifty pounds of pure muscle on Dumas. Dumas glared, found himself glaring at strong throat, shifted up.

I saw the exact instant Dumas intercepted Glynn's sapphire Scowl of Dismemberment. Dumas fell back a step. "You then." He pointed indiscriminately, his eyes still locked on Glynn. "You, come here."

Unfortunately, he pointed straight at me.

I pretended I hadn't seen his Judas finger, but Takashi oh-so-helpfully shoved me forward. Somebody was *so* getting a gumwad under his stand at break.

But Business Truth #3 is "If you can't run, gut it out". I went.

Dumas snatched my wrist, twirled me and shoved me ass-end into Glynn. I stumbled, would have fallen had not Glynn caught me—again. I blushed at how clumsy I was around this hard, sexy male, both tongue and feet. At least this time he grabbed waist, which was less intimate than breasts.

Or so I thought until my butt landed against his hips and his big, warm hand splayed over my stomach, covering my *whole* stomach. A bright bolt of need shot through me.

With a clap of hands, Dumas spun away. "Pair up, pair up." He pranced center stage, heading for Mishela.

"Mine!" Gollum-like Steve darted in and grabbed for her wrist.

Glynn growled, low and not quite human, eerily like the animal last night. Pressed to him, I felt him tense to leap. Big, muscular Glynn, stick-thin Steve. This would be bad.

But before Glynn could jump, Julian Emerson seized Mishela's wrist out from under Steve's bony fingers. Julian drew her to the slim guy in patched jeans and a straw hat who was the Scarecrow, Jon Wise. Jon smiled adoringly at her.

Steve pouted.

Behind me, Glynn tensed more. He didn't seem to like the idea of Mishela with Jon either. I tried to diffuse the situation. "Jon's a star. Besides, how much trouble can he cause in the middle of a crowd?"

Glynn only growled, real animal this time. It jacked me straight, which rubbed my bottom against him. His growl cut off as he jacked straight too. And something else jacked stiff.

I'm not totally inexperienced, so I recognized the blooming in his jeans. What I didn't recognize was the size. What, did he have a pneumatic XL sock? An inflatable, deluxe rubber raft? I deliberately tried to come up with the least arousing comparisons I could because, sweet lord, Glynn's XL—make that XXL—nestled warm and snug into my bottom like coming home.

Speaking of coming home...he rubbed his cheek against my hair and murmured, "You're right, *babi*. Sometimes I become too distrustful. Thank you." He curled close.

I leaned automatically into his warmth. If I had the comfort of this strong male to come home to every night, it might almost be worth giving up dreams...ring me up as produce. Warts, picking teeth, professional distance, none of it seemed to work with him. I had to get away—

"Face your partner. Mirrors, everyone." Dumas zoomed in and twisted me in Glynn's arms, making escape impossible. Damn him. I wasn't sure if I meant Dumas or Glynn.

The director flitted from pair to pair, a shrimp-pink butterfly with lime peel wings. "One person moves. The other matches it. Try to anticipate your partner. Come on, people, I want to see some synergy here."

I put space between me and Glynn, trying to lower my blood pressure, but my eyes landed automatically on his fly and I coughed, waved a hand at his portable power tool. "I don't think I can mirror that."

He blew air. "Just do the exercise. Let's not make this difficult. I'll follow you."

His eyes didn't follow me. His gaze was over my head, on Mishela.

That cooled me off like nothing else could have. I was trying not to be interested, but I was a moderately good-looking female. Couldn't he at least give me a courtesy ogle?

"I don't need to look at you." He growled it, a man-growl this time.

"What?"

"You pouted because I'm looking at Mishela instead of you, but that's my job. Besides, I don't need to look at you to want you. You're burned into my memory."

"I never pout. It's not professional."

"You do. And it's adorable."

"I don't—huh?" Adorable? He was sweet as well as sexy? Here was a man who might be worth giving up duty and rainbows...spank me with a sackbut.

Other pairs were doing a sort of mime-in-box thing. I held up one hand, flat like I was pressing it to a mirror, and circled it. Time to get some mental space too. "Hey, how many viola players does it take to make a batch of chocolate chip cookies?"

Glynn matched his palm to mine and followed me effortlessly. Without looking. "How many?"

"Ten. One to make the dough and nine to peel the M&Ms. It's funny because they're violists."

"Ha." His eyes were still on Mishela.

"Why does she need a bodyguard, anyway? She's no Hollywood star." I did a quick double hand wave.

He followed, again effortlessly, again without looking. "She's important to Mr. Elias, and Elias is important to us."

"Us." I snapped my fingers and so did Glynn. Damn, he was good. "Who's us?"

"A neighborhood watch."

"I see." Glynn the Dangerous. A homey neighborhood watch guy? I circled double figure eights. "This important Mr. Elias... You don't mean Kai Elias, do you? President of Steel Security's board?"

"Among others." Glynn followed, hands level with mine. "Mishela's his ward. If something were to happen to her, it would...distract him from more important matters."

"What, like counting his money?"

"Like government consulting."

"So you're telling me that business mogul Kai Elias not only lives in Iowa but is part of your neighborhood watch?" I'd just realized Glynn's palms traced his figure eights over my breasts. Blushing hot, I changed to patting my head and stomach. "What government consulting does he do? Coralville's city council?"

"A bit bigger. The Pentagon and White House."

That sounded more like bazillionaire Elias. So what was he doing playing around with a neighborhood watch? "Does Elias—"

"He's a very private person. That's all I know."

It cut off that topic, at least for now. I switched motions and subjects. "So you bodyguard in Iowa for a living?"

"I do a variety of things, of which guard is one. And I'm only based in Iowa. I work all over the world." He mirrored my new gesture, a taffy-pulling motion. It made his pecs dance under the wedge of T-shirt revealed by his jacket.

My tongue lolled. Oh, for the jacket totally off, so I could see the whole chest ballet.

His tongue poked out. Oops, apparently my tongue-rolling wasn't purely mental. I sucked my lust—and tongue—back in.

But it reminded me. "Why the jacket all the time? You don't strike me as the cold type." In fact, the times we'd touched, he'd struck me as very, very hot...yeah.

"I'm more comfortable with it on. Are you done with the interrogation?"

"Interro—" I stuck fists on hips. "And what does that mean?"

His fists hit his hips at exactly the same instant. "Interrogation. To ask questions, or a formal examination. What would you call it?"

"Having a conversation." I frowned.

He frowned in exactly the same way. But something, maybe the quirk of a black brow, made me realize he was teasing me, confirmed when he added, "Such a cute pout."

"I do *not* pout." Sweet, strong and funny. I was closer than I'd ever been to throwing aside duty and dreams to clamp on to his ass or chest and never let go. If I had to endure much more of this enforced closeness...but it had to end, hopefully soon, and then I'd run away. Permanently. I'd never again be close enough to feel...to smell...to kiss...

"Stop, people, stop-stop-stop!" Dumas clapped. "That was terrible. Clearly we need to go back to the basics. Report tomorrow at six for a half hour of drill. *Everybody.*"

I jerked back. There was a general groan, but I groaned loudest.

I was such a schmuck.

If you've got the job, do the job. I wanted to grab Glynn and never let go. I wanted to run away and never come back. But I trooped down into the pit, took up instruments and played my very best. Tomorrow I'd come back. I'd try like heck to get out of acting drills, but I'd return.

Sometimes the personal code of honor thing sucks.

Rehearsal went better with the local fill-in actors not so spooked at trumpets and drums coming from the pit. Even the dog playing Toto, a little terrier belonging to my uncle (everybody is related in Meiers Corners, even the livestock), stopped trying to hide behind the scenery.

Dumas staged the final bows, and when the house lights came up, he clapped his hands. "Good job, people. Sit down for notes."

Mishela slid to the edge of the stage, her ankles dangling over into the pit. Her expression was a poignant combination of eager and hesitant. "Hey, Junior. Where's Rocky?"

"She's at another rehearsal tonight."

Her face fell. "Oh. Well. Meet you at Nieman's?"

And chance her shadow? Not. "I would," I began, and her face fell further. Still I plowed on. "But money's a bit tight—"

"Glynn could pay." She smiled at the dark essence back in the wings. "Right, Glynn?"

He couldn't have possibly heard her, but he nodded. Or rather the top of the shadow folded once like a nod.

"So, Nieman's?"

Her face lit so hopefully. I remembered she was lonely and sighed. If Glynn could suck it up and do what was needed rather than what he wanted, so could I. "Sure. Nieman's."

"Mishela." Dumas trotted up to the pit wall, a frown on his thin face. "As the star, you need to be in top form."

"Glynn will make sure I don't stay out too late, Mr. Dumas." She nodded toward the big shadow.

"Ah, Glynn." Dumas repeated the name like my dad would say "profit margin". "Well, all right. But just to make sure—I'll come along." After dropping that bombshell, he raised his voice. "Let's go, people. I want to get these notes done before I expire."

Chapter Four

At Nieman's, Glynn sat between me and Mishela. Then Dumas wedged a stool between me and Glynn. My head knew that was a good thing, but my body wanted to shoot him. Then Dumas monologued on Method acting until I wanted to shoot myself.

One drink of that was about all I could take. "I'd better get home. The store opens early."

Glynn rose too. Maybe he was as bored with the lecture as I was.

But I was trying to keep my distance from him, so I waved him down. "I'll walk myself home. It's not like Meiers Corners is dangerous."

His stance, muscular arms over jutting chest, said quite firmly we were leaving together or not at all.

Mishela rose. "Might as well give in. Glynn's made up his mind." As we headed out she added. "And sausage doesn't sell itself."

"You sound like my dad." I'd probably be okay with Mishela chaperoning.

"No, this sounds like your dad." Adopting a booming, jolly voice, Mishela said "Sausage doesn't sell itself, *ja*?"

"Whoa. That's uncanny."

"Wait," Dumas's tenor whined from behind us. "I haven't finished telling you about Strasberg's students. James Dean, Marilyn Monroe—"

"Anybody in this century?" I tried to derail him. "Allison Scagliotti? Seth Green?"

Dumas sniffed. "Method acting is continuing to evolve." He strutted east on Main.

Which wasn't my way home, but I was curious, so I followed. "Meaning they're not?"

"Meaning it doesn't matter. All of today's stars are Method's philosophical descendants."

We passed Bob's Formalwear and Ritsa's Pizzas. (The owner's name was actually Rita, but the sign maker messed up and gave it to her for free. She liked it better and kept it.) Dumas was talking at a clip that would make any fine-print announcer proud.

I had to trot to keep up. Behind me, Glynn kept pace merely by stretching his long, muscled legs. I wished he'd lead the way so I could watch his glorious glutes, but he insisted on covering our rears—just sear me to seal the juices. What about the man made me think body parts? Rubbing, heating, damp body parts... I refocused on Dumas, expounding on how Method acting revolutionized American theater.

Mishela was trotting alongside me, her face confused. "Where are we going?"

"Otto's B&BS, my hotel," Dumas said. "Now the Method was actually created by Konstantin Stanislavski, who—"

"BS?" Mishela grinned. "I've heard of a B&B, but what's a B&BS?"

I said, "Bed and breakfast smorgasbord. Uncle Otto runs it."

She turned to me. "Isn't smorgasbord Swedish?"

"Uncle Otto isn't restricted by geopolitical boundaries. Surely you've heard of such traditional German favorites as dumpling pizza, sauerkraut egg rolls, sausage-fried chicken—"

Dumas gave a pointed little *ahem*. "Interesting tangent—if you like complete irrelevancy. As I was saying..."

He started in on sensory-memory exercises. That led into the tale of the anorexic actress, who recalled what she ate so clearly that she revomited it. Yeah, good times.

Dumas was describing the regurgitated orange juice in loving detail as we passed the stone edifice of the Sparkasse Bank, when Glynn snarled and grabbed him by the collar.

I thought maybe he'd finally had enough of Dumas's babbling. But Glynn tossed Dumas behind us, then barred Mishela and me, his powerful arms thrust out like a special forces crossing guard. Skidding to a stop, I peeked under his jacketed arm.

Three men were running across the bridge toward us.

Nylons smashed their faces, but their eyes glowed like red coals. Two waved knives. The third brandished a black cloth bag.

They zoomed in, over the river and on us before I could even gasp.

And I thought, *well hell*. Meiers Corners was dangerous after all.

I considered what to do. I'm a black belt so it might seem

obvious—just kick and punch my little heart out. But while Joe Shmoe could kick and punch and even scratch, my training required my response to be reasonable and appropriate. It's counterintuitive, but the martial arts don't train you to fight—they train you so you don't have to fight.

If these guys were only thieves wanting my wallet, they were welcome to my buck ninety-five. I pulled my cash and tossed it onto the sidewalk, the pennies clunking like plastic.

They didn't even look. So, not after money. Then what? Or who? Their red eyes made them look like Star Wars Jawas.

Or zombies.

Ooh. I could go all Jackie Chan on their asses if they were zombies. Zombies couldn't sue. I bent into ready stance just as Glynn reached into his jacket and pulled something out with a menacing ka-*click*.

A dagger sprang into his hand, scary-long and gleaming silvery-white. He held it steady, its sharp point angled slightly up. Serious. Deadly.

I nearly peed my pants. But at least now I knew why he wore that leather jacket, even indoors.

It hid his long, elegant weapon.

Dammit, looming danger. No time for naughty thoughts.

Glynn surged forward, met the first goon. His left fist knocked the man back even as his long leg came up, snapping a kick through the goon's head. Muscled lightning snapped back for a second hit, *bam-bam*. With a crack of bone the goon's jaw sagged, white shards poking through skin and stocking. His eyes rolled back, his knees folded and he collapsed in a dead heap.

As he fell, Glynn rammed his knife straight into the second goon's breastbone.

I froze in shock.

It was them or us, but the casual violence stunned me. Bone is the human equivalent of concrete, but the knife embedded to the hilt, goon blood blossoming. The thug fell to the pavement with a thud, a second dead heap. Glynn's dagger stuck up from his chest like a flag planted for king and country.

The third man flashed by, a bag ready, headed straight for Dumas and Mishela. Mishela jerked Dumas away at the last instant and the bag swished air. The thug pivoted, spun in for another try.

That unfroze me. Reasonable and appropriate went poof. I snapped a roundhouse kick into the third attacker's ribs.

And hopped back, shrieking. I'd just kicked Frankenstein. Or a flak vest, but I'd cracked my fricking toes, at least two of them. I'd broken them before, knew they'd be numb in seconds, but it *hurt*.

A roar split the night, louder than ten lions. I was seized by huge hands and pushed gently back. Glynn. He grabbed the goon by the neck, his long fingernails digging into goon throat, squeezing hard...the goon's neck snapped, head flopping like a rag doll.

I sucked air.

Glynn released the attacker. The body fell to the sidewalk with a sick *whump.*

"Oh my God." Dumas backed away, face sickly yellow.

I whirled toward grass. The horror...and my soda...came up in acid rivers. Glynn caught my shoulders, steadied my head until the waves of nausea passed. When I was done, he gently wiped my mouth with a soft cloth, another surprise from his jacket.

I looked up. Mishela was inspecting the bodies, going through pockets with a cool professionalism that struck me as profoundly at odds with her seventeen-year-old innocence.

"Chicago," she said. "But we expected that."

"Wh...what did they want?" I found myself clinging to Glynn, had to consciously release him.

"Dunno. But they tried to bag Mr. Dumas."

And now they were dead. My eyes found the first man, his horribly mutilated jaw... The holes were still there, but I couldn't see the shards. I tried to get a closer look. "Something's wrong. Look at that guy's—"

"Time to go." Glynn grabbed my arm, hauled west.

"Come on, Mr. Dumas." Mishela reached for the director.

A black-gloved hand got him first.

The hand was attached to a figure that materialized from a dark cleft between the bank and a yarn shop. Average height, slim, wearing a trench coat, a full mask obscured his...her—*its* features. It threw Dumas over its shoulder and disappeared between buildings before I was even fully aware of him/her/it.

Mishela sprang after, her face like a raptor's.

"*No.*" Glynn's voice rang with stark command. More—with mastery.

She yanked up like a puppet. Her raptor face disappeared but I'd remembered why it was familiar. It was Diana, Greek goddess of the hunt.

Demons, monsters—gods? Had Nixie soaked my reeds in vodka again? Just what was going on here?

"Mishela." Glynn's voice eased back to musical. "Before we pursue, we must see Junior safely home."

"No time," I said. "Every second counts in an abduction. We need to call the police, get them on Dumas's trail."

"We don't need the police." A smile crooked the corner of Mishela's mouth. "Not when Glynn's the best tracker there is."

"Okay." I believed her. After all, he had that whole nature's king/druid vibe going. "But the police have equipment and manpower. And a ton of paperwork to start, so we need to let them know."

But Mishela wasn't listening, and Glynn was absorbed by the dark cleft between buildings where Dumas had been taken, touching the brick, sniffing it. When he moved off, Mishela followed.

If I didn't want to be left behind with three bodies, I needed to leave too.

Normally I wouldn't have worried about staying by myself. But we'd been attacked on Main Street—safe-as-cottonballs Main. Attacked by three thugs whom Glynn had not just fought but annihilated. Dumas had been abducted. It was a nightmare.

Hmm, we *were* standing one block north of Elm Street.

None of it made sense, and I needed it to. What you don't know *can* hurt you—and worse, can seriously reduce your profit margin.

So when Glynn and Mishela disappeared between buildings, I ran after.

Or rather, limped. Broken bones are screamingly painful. Numb cracked toes are just awkward.

I found them behind the bank, in an employee picnic area bordering the alley. Glynn was examining the landscaping hedges, Mishela watching closely. While they were absorbed, I pulled out my phone to call the cop shop.

Glynn took off again, west down the alley. I clutched the phone and followed. Hitting sidewalk on Second, he dropped to his hands and knees and put nose to concrete.

Like a hunting dog...or wolf.

He got to his feet, brushing off his hands. "This way." Nostrils dilated, he loped off, going north on Second.

Very cool, slightly scary and another note stacked onto the weirdness chord.

As I shuffled behind, I punched in the phone number for information and got myself routed to the cop shop. As it rang I wondered what I would say. The police needed to know, but what Glynn had done...what could I tell them?

Alice Schmidt, nightshift dispatcher since the Kennedy administration, and recipient of so many bowling 300 rings she wore them on her toes, answered immediately. I still hadn't decided what to say so I just asked for Elena.

Maybe I'd say that it was self-defense. It had been. Mostly. Yes, Glynn had killed three goons, but they'd been trying to hurt us. I listened to the phone ring, trying not to remember Glynn's deadly precision, his destructiveness well beyond reasonable response. With the last thug, Glynn had been almost brutal. Just after I'd cracked my toes, when I shrieked...

Hey. Glynn hadn't thought I was in danger or hurt, had he?

"Strongwell."

Elena Strongwell was Meiers Corners's top detective. I took a deep breath and reported. I tried to downplay the worst, but had to tell the truth.

She seemed strangely unconcerned by the dead goons. "Junior, the important thing is that you're safe. But I doubt Glynn actually killed those guys."

"You didn't see it. The embedded knife, the blood..." I lowered my voice. "Elena, they were *dead*."

Glynn paused to scent the air, paying no attention to me. Beside him, Mishela closed her eyes and sniffed it too.

Elena said, "Well, I'm on-site now. You said three? Only two here, so at least one's alive."

"That was fast."

"Hubby and I were in the area doing our neighborhood watch thing. Bad news, Junior."

"What?" My fearful gaze shot to Glynn's broad back. It had been self-defense, but did killing those men mean jail for him? Or worse? "They're...they're..."

"Going to be fine."

"What?" I couldn't help it, I squealed. Glynn gave me a brief glance. I grinned with a thumbs up. Turning, I lowered my voice. "Elena, one was knifed in the heart and the other's neck was snapped..." I petered out as I realized just how bad that sounded.

"Choked unconscious, maybe. The guy's neck is fine."

"But I saw his head flop!"

"People do a rag doll when going unconscious. And really, it's a lot harder to poke through bone than it looks on TV."

"I *know* that." Was I going insane? I'd seen three men struck with killing blows. Could I have imagined it?

"Junior, you're a businesswoman. Practical, right? Bottom line is, these guys are going to be fine. Facing stiff charges for assault, but fine."

Nothing had happened, just like the "wolves" last night. Good news, except now I was possibly going nuts. I clipped the phone shut and stowed it. I couldn't go insane. If I checked in as a permanent guest of the MC hospital's Arkham psych wing, who'd run the register?

Wait. Dumas had been kidnapped. He'd validate me.

Glynn headed east. We were nearing Settler's Square when he said, "There he is," and broke into a run. Mishela was right behind. I limped along, finally catching sight of the saffron, lime and pink heap on the park bench.

Dumas wasn't moving. His face stood out white as a sheet. I said, "Is he...?"

"No, he's breathing." Glynn touched a hand to Dumas's neck. "And his heart's beating."

At Glynn's touch the director groaned. His eyes fluttered open, focused slowly on Glynn. Dumas smiled. "Ah, heaven."

Glynn snorted. "Not quite. Let's get you sitting. You'll be fine in a moment."

"What happened?" I asked.

Dumas opened his mouth.

"You don't remember," Glynn said.

Dumas frowned. "I...I don't remember. But—"

Glynn's tone darkened. "You're completely unharmed."

"Completely unharmed," Dumas echoed, eyes blanking.

"All's well that ends well," Mishela added brightly.

Good old Business Truth #4. And people think only fairy tales have morals. But I wasn't going to dismiss it that easily. "Mr. Dumas, what *do* you remember? The fight, the kidnapper?"

Dumas's eyes snapped to me. "The fight. I was sick." The frown returned. "I remember crazy bright eyes, like pinwheels, and then...nothing. The next thing I remember is—" He smiled fatuously at Glynn. "My hero."

Crazy pinwheels. Sounded like Dumas had been hypnotized, but why? And why kidnap him just to let him go?

And why Dumas and not Mishela, who was an heiress?

I'd thought Dumas would help me understand what was going on, but instead I only had more questions.

Just then the new dancing figurine cuckoo clock in Settler's Square (sponsored by the Volka Polka radio station, "All Polkas, All the Time") bonked, clanged and tweeted its quaint and touristy way through twelve strokes. Midnight. It was late, and I'd had a long and tiring day. "I need to get home."

"Me too," Dumas said from the park bench. "But I'm too weak to walk. Carry me?" He held his hands up to Glynn.

With a sigh, Glynn picked up Dumas and strode off. From the way Dumas's arms clasped Glynn's neck, fingers massaging those broad, jacketed shoulders, I thought maybe Dumas was faking the too-weak-to-walk a little.

Wish I'd thought of it first.

We slogged the six blocks to the sausage shop in silence. Glynn set Dumas on his feet at the front door. "Wait here."

"But," Dumas started.

Glynn didn't even bother with his death-o-matic glare. Mishela clamped the director's wrist while Glynn escorted me to the side entrance, where I turned to say goodbye.

A round mechanical eye stared me in the face.

I exploded. "Those penis heads."

Glynn followed my glare and saw it too. Mounted on a plastic bracket on the brick wall across from us was a webcam.

Bad enough when the Cheese Dudes were peppering us with petty harassment. This stunk, and I don't mean Limburger.

The webcam was aimed straight at our private door, so I was sure it wasn't for customers. No, the Dudes had graduated from petty vandalism to voyeurism. Maybe to catch me and Glynn in action and hit us with charges of public indecency. And in case you're thinking "big deal", in the Corners we take public indecency as seriously as murder—unless it's stripping in Nieman's Bar, which is recreational nudity.

Glynn's hand flashed under his jacket. He whipped something at the camera too fast to see. *Clunk-crash.*

The camera, plastic bracket neatly severed, hit walkway.

"Handy," I said as he picked up his knife. "Titanium blade?"

He just shrugged and turned to me. His face was drawn with concern. "You're all right after what happened?"

I blew a frustrated breath. "Elena made it clear that *nothing* happened. She didn't say all the death blows were my imagination but..." But she'd pretty much implied it.

Glynn took my face in his hands. "*Babi,* if I could remove this horrible memory from you, I would. But since I can't...there's nothing wrong with your perceptions."

"It wasn't my imagination?" I searched his warm sapphire eyes. Looking for affirmation of my sanity? For connection, comfort, closeness...all a single dictionary letter away from duty and dream, but in reality, an uncrossable chasm.

"If this were my territory..." He heaved a breath. "Junior, I'm not saying anything—except you're the bravest woman I know. Wrap those toes."

I blinked. I hadn't made an issue out of it, but he'd noticed. *He noticed,* and hard on its heels, *he cares.* "I was trying to kick with the ball of my foot."

"You did. The bastard moved last minute." He gathered me into his arms. I let him, just for a moment, hungry for the warmth, for the simple contact. Just a moment. A moment wasn't a lifetime.

And when he kissed me, I let him do that too.

His mouth was gentle, persuasive. His tongue was tender slipping along the seam of my lips.

A hug and a kiss. A simple connection, a bit of warmth and

tenderness before I went back to duty and dreams.

My eyelids closed, drugged by soft sensation. I sighed.

At the cue, he cupped my head and his tongue stroked with more purpose, urging my mouth open. My lips parted and his tongue swept in.

He tasted fresh, exciting. Like the sweet grass of a spring field, ripe with adventure. Kissing him was like opening my mouth on a shout and swallowing fresh mountain air. Curling fingers over his shoulders, I raised myself for more.

He wrapped arms around me. His head angled sharply, mouth opening, tongue driving. His breath turned scorching.

I arched against him. His arms tightened, fusing us, his powerful pecs digging into the hollows of my shoulders, his belly rubbing mine. My breath quickened to panting, scrubbing my stomach against his abs. Excitement thrilled me to flashpoint. I tunneled my fingers into the softest, thickest hair in the world.

He raised his head and stared down at me. His pupils were black, passionate pools ringed by violet fire, riveted to my face as if gauging the smallest nuance.

I moistened my lips, an invitation.

He thrust his knee between my legs.

I clutched his thigh with a moan. He flexed his quadriceps, swelling denim, as hot and muscular as a stallion. I bit back a groan.

His head dropped and he kissed me again, hard and deep, rhythmically flexing his thigh. The thick muscle bunched and released like a living vibrator.

I started rocking against him. Caught myself. This was going way beyond a hug and kiss. I had to stop.

He grabbed my nipple and plucked.

I bowed back, groaning. His big mouth took my groan, muffled it into a whimper. His tongue thrust like fire. His fingers pinched like clamps.

He pressed my back to the door and drove his thigh against my vulva. I screamed into his mouth. He began to rock hard, fast, beating like a bass drum. I cinched his thigh between mine and rocked in answer, doubling the friction, the fire. My arms melted, hands dropping to his massive shoulders.

His kisses turned sharp. Sucking bites and nips pulled my tongue and lips. My hands slid to his biceps, my fingers clutching weakly.

A deep thrum filled my ears. His body vibrated with it; mine trembled in response.

His mouth traveled down my jaw. "Ah, Junior." His breath caressed my throat. "Your heat inflames me, your sweet scent conquers me. Your pulse is the music that drives my soul." He licked my skin. I shuddered at the hot swipe. "Your taste—sweet *Duw*, your taste drives me mad."

I swallowed past a throat swollen with need. "Mutual, Dylan Thomas."

"Ah, to taste you fully." He nuzzled my neck. "For now I must settle for pleasuring you." He lowered his leg. Air cooled my now Glynn-less crotch, making me very aware of how aroused I'd gotten.

It woke me up. "Wha...?"

He thrust a hand down the front of my black jeans, finger hitting the sweet spot. I yelped. He smiled, half-lidded and lazy.

And stroked.

It was like thumbing a lighter. I sparked instantly. A stab of pure lust cinched my hips back, rolling them—

Taking his hand with me. His finger slid into my body while the rest of his huge hand splayed over my pussy, hot, electric.

My eyes flared wide. He wiggled his finger and I gasped.

He thrust his thigh between my legs, nailing his hand to my crotch, and slammed into a kiss. And then he started thrusting that thick finger. I clutched his brawn as anything resembling sanity blew out of my skull. I rode his finger and sucked at his tongue and felt the sweet need I'd fought since meeting him come to a head.

He thumbed my clit and I cinched tighter, winding closer to the summit of sensation. His fingers rubbed faster, plunged deeper. I moaned into the hot cave of his mouth. My body stiffened, trembled. My skin flushed hot.

"My sweet *babi*." Glynn lifted his head, his eyes so bright they practically glowed. "Come for me. Come hard."

Devouring me in an open-mouthed kiss, he grabbed one breast and fondled it possessively as he plunged into me with his finger, stroked me with his thumb.

My pleasure crested. Broke over me, an ocean wave of satisfaction. I gasped through the release. Sighed into the afterglow.

His hand gently wound me down.

Awareness returned and I remembered just where this sort of abandon led. It felt like heaven, but the consequences were hell. I had duty. I had dreams.

I scrabbled off his leg. At first he held on to me, but when it turned into an actual fight, he removed his hand from my pants and set me firmly on my feet, his fingers circling my upper arms until I found my balance. When he did let go, he backpedaled like I'd erupted in full-body pustules.

Which hurt, but I'd started it. Or ended it. Whatever. "That was unacceptable."

"You seemed fine with it at the time." The music in his voice was as tight as his expression.

"Seduction does that to a gal." I tried to put a sneer in my own music, fell short. "Don't do that again." I jerked out keys, tried to stick one in the lock and was mortified when the keys jangled from my shaking.

He slid them from my hands, thrust one and opened the door. Sighed. "Junior, wait. I—"

"Don't. Just—don't." I retrieved the keys and slipped into the dark hall. Closed the door by pressing my back to it. Or maybe the door was holding me up. I took a deep breath to calm my thundering heart.

A click.

The light blared on. "Do you know what time it is, young lady?"

My mother was waiting up for me.

The bright, bald glare of light burned my eyeballs. The voice glared too, pitched to scrape old guilt raw.

Great Galloping Galbraith. Must have pissed off the demons of the bottom line. I hoped like hell she hadn't heard me orgasming against the door.

She stood before me, hair as black as mine, body as slender. My height too, but the way she stood, hands on hips, spine ominously straight, made her seem ten feet taller. The Egyptian-style headwrap straight out of *Aida* didn't help.

I was the mirror image of her physically. I'd run from Glynn because I was afraid I was like her on the inside too.

No. I took a deep breath. I'd escaped the worst of the lustful urges that had been her downfall.

"Where have you been?" And when she got a look at my well-kissed mouth— "And what have you been doing?"

"Nothing." The fallback of every child from two to sixty-two.

"Don't take that tone with me, Gunter Marie Stieg." She wagged one scolding finger as she spoke. Chunky gold bracelets jingled, underlining her scold. Maybe a stereotype, but my Italian mother very definitely talked with her hands, and by thunder, I'd better listen to both gesture and voice.

"It's not what you're thinking, Mother." I quickly ran through the eightfold path. Used Business Truth #5, "Tell the customer, not what you want to jabber about, but what they need to hear". "I was investigating a new sales avenue."

Hey, I wasn't lying, I was marketing. Besides, this was an emergency.

"New sales. After midnight?" Her flying hands shouted her disbelief.

"A business opportunity." I added a Sales Maneuver, "Distract with any truth that's not The Truth". "You know how the mayor pulled in Broadway stars for the PAC opening?"

"Actors." She sniffed, like she hadn't been one herself. "They have no money."

"Well, one of them does. Or rather, her guardian does. Maybe you've heard of him." I paused for effect. "Kai Elias?"

My mother's stare was an awl. She glared like I was lying so bad I wouldn't sit down for a week. Although if Glynn was doing the spanking... She scowled. "Elias, of Steel Security. Of half a dozen more Fortune 500 companies. Billionaire recluse Kai Elias sponsors an *actor*." Again she sneered the word, but it was the flicking finger that made me wince. "Next you will be telling me he lives in Nowheresville, Iowa."

"Mom, really. His ward Mishela is Dorothy, here with one of his employees. I spent the evening with them." No need to spell out how.

"Let's say I believe you. What opportunity is this? Is the king of information getting into sausage now?"

Put that way, it did sound unlikely. I backpedaled. "I'm just laying the groundwork. Social connections, but who knows where it might lead?" I skimmed by her, headed upstairs to the family kitchen. A rehearsal takes a lot of calories, and all that running around after...not to mention the physical stimulation...well, I was hungry.

"A social connection." She followed. "You're trying to defect from the family business?"

Yeah. About that.

I have duty to family and I have dreams. My plan to go to New York with *Oz, Wonderful Oz* would take care of both.

My parents didn't quite see it that way. Nobody was as loyal and hardworking as family. As the fruit of their loins, I was the epitome of family, and therefore nobody could replace me. Hiring Donald Trump wouldn't be good enough.

Or maybe they wanted to keep me home forever.

Still, I tried. "Mom, I'm not going to leave without seeing you and Pop set up. This was just an exploratory meeting." In the kitchen I started rummaging through cupboards. "I'm just feeling him out. Feeling *them* out." I buried my sudden blush in the pantry closet. "I mean, I'm getting to know them. Mishela and her, um, companion." I found a box of popcorn, extracted one of the bags.

"You'd better not be thinking this 'feeling out' will involve leaving. It would upset your father. You know he relies on you."

The plastic-wrapped bag smashed in my clenched fist. Without turning I said, "You make sure I can't forget."

"You should never forget. He slaved for you. I slaved for you. I gave up my career for you," she countered in a disagreement we'd had so often it was better rehearsed than any theater. "The least you can do is commit a few hours a week to the business your father gave his life to, the business we Stiegs have spent generations building."

You're not a Stieg. At least you weren't until you married Pop.

"I do, Mom." I stared at the popcorn, trying to work back to reasonable, to make this have a different ending. "Nine, ten hours a day, six days a week. It's most of my waking life. I've earned the right to dream a little too."

"Have you? What would you be doing with those hours if not honest work? Be grateful you are not on the streets, not starving or doing drugs or playing in a punky rock band like that Schmeling girl."

"It's Nixie Emerson now," I said tiredly. Diverting this scene was like trying to turn a runaway soloist. "She married a Boston lawyer. Even by your definition of success, she's made it."

"I gave up my career for you," she repeated. "A star mezzo with the

Italian opera. I gave that up for our family's business, for your heritage."

What she meant was she and Pop had done the nasty and I came along, putting the kibosh on singing professionally.

"You must always remember, Junior. *Business comes first.*"

And there it was, of course. The stinger. I tried one more time. "Mom, I'm not going to run off just because I got horny and pregnant—"

She slapped me. Which I guess I deserved.

"Do not speak that way to me. Your father didn't have to marry me. But he did the right thing by me and I have done right by him. I have loved him and honored him and the least you can do is the same. Family duty is more important than any dreams. Home is more important, because it is *real.*" She seared me with "The Look", spun from me and stomped off. Each stomp rammed my conscience.

I thrust the popcorn back into the box, hunger gone, and headed upstairs. The same conversation, the same stomping, the same guilt. It only made me more determined to change the ending, at least for my own life. Mom had been trapped in the small pond of Meiers Corners by marriage. Not me.

Family duty was top priority; we agreed on that. But we had a different idea of how that duty needed to be discharged. I'd see my parents taken care of, no question. But one way or another, I was getting out. Getting my own life.

Fulfilling my own rainbow dreams.

Entr'acte

Glynn Rhys-Jenkins glided through the night shadows, silently, like the dangerous beast he was. His hands were relaxed, ready. Though three of the vampires had been shipped back to Chicago by Elena Strongwell and her vampire husband, one had escaped. That one, the one who'd captured Dumas, was arguably the most dangerous.

Glynn hunted the bastard now.

Good thing Mishela was safe at Emerson's, because the hunt wasn't easy. The rogue had disguised his scent by wearing pungent human clothes. He'd strewn the trail with distractions and red herrings. He'd even waded across the Meiers River at its highest point.

Glynn sloshed through the river now, gritting his teeth. Running water, a body-sized gag buzzer for vampires. As jags sang through his system, he blocked them by dint of long training. The buzz, annoying as it was, would only get worse with age. By the time he was ancient, he'd be so sensitive he'd have to train half the day to cope with his raw animal self. He wondered how Elias managed.

In Glynn's pocket, his cell phone vibrated. He splashed onto the far bank, blew into mist and let the water fall through. Relaxing his concentration, his body snapped together, clothes now dry. For some reason it reminded him of the first time he'd misted, when he'd snapped back naked with his clothes in an embarrassing heap at his feet.

The phone was still buzzing. He dug it from his pocket and thumbed it live. Speak of the devil. "Limited progress, sir. The trail's...obscured."

"I know. That's why I'm calling." Elias's cave-deep voice was disturbingly potent, even over the phone's tiny speaker. "Your quarry is aware that you're a tracker."

Which explained the human clothes and water trick. Glynn snarled. "How? Is there a traitor?"

"Not exactly. Mishela has been boasting of your prowess."

Glynn rumbled his disapproval.

Elias made a clicking sound, an aural shrug. "She is young. She will learn. It does tell us the vampire is closely involved with the show."

Which narrowed it down—to several dozen people. Including one who smelled like heaven and made his fangs ache to taste her. That mind-blowing kiss... He shook himself, annoyed. He avoided humans in general and snippy little immune humans in particular. "Perhaps the vampire has a human minion in the show, sir. One of the cast or crew...or pit orchestra."

"You have someone specific in mind, Rhys-Jenkins?"

"I don't. Well, maybe." He cleared his throat. "Junior Stieg was with us both times we were attacked."

"Unrelated. You told me she's immune to mind-control. Ergo, not a minion." A beat. "It does make her a potential mate."

"Not for me." Glynn throttled back a growl. "She has no appreciation for home. I find her attitude irritating."

"I see."

Only Elias could imbue two simple words with such heavy sarcasm. Glynn blew air in frustration. "Sir, if I could get back to the point. Two attacks by rogues. Intel from the Watch indicates they're related to the show, but not how. Did tonight's trio talk before Strongwell shipped them back to their masters?"

"They talked. Strongwell can be quite...motivational. But they didn't know anything."

"Cock." Glynn fought not to grind his teeth. "They may be after anything from kidnapping Mishela to simply disrupting the show."

"Perhaps the escaped rogue will know more."

The call ended.

As Glynn clapped the phone shut, the tips of his fangs extruded, pricking his lower lip. The rogue who attacked tonight could have taken Dumas by mistake, could have really been after Mishela...or even Junior.

The last thought pushed him to prowl the riverbank, seeking the rogue's scent. Elias was right—Junior's immunity made her a potential mate, attractive to many of his kind. Not him, of course. He could never live with someone so unappreciative of home and family. True, she was immune. True again, as both businesswoman and artist, she had depths to fascinate a male for many centuries.

But she was not for him. No matter how...*heavenly, sublime, incredible*...good she smelled. No matter that he ached to taste her. He would never drink from her. Though the thought of anyone drinking from her other than him...

He spun away from the bank, stalked toward the nearest bridge. The trail had gone cold.

Bollocks. What did he do now? He couldn't think. His two problems—who was stalking the show and for what purpose, versus what to do about his attraction...*need, lust*...for Junior—were jamming his brain.

He knew he had to set the attraction aside and focus on the job. It was hard. No attraction had ever been this bad. He glided along at the deceptively fast pace of his kind and reminded himself that protecting Mishela was his first priority. He should concentrate on that.

Right. Decision made.

If only Junior weren't so wrong for him. He'd grown up without a real home, had spent the rest of his eight hundred years trying to recreate one. And here she was, just a score and handful of years on this earth with the very things he craved. Home. Family. Love...

Enough. Job at hand. Mishela. The attacks.

It was just that Junior smelled so incredible. The softness of her lips, her sweet skin, her plush labia becoming slick with arousal...

His brain wasn't worth a sheep's fart. Fine. He wasn't going to resolve anything tonight, not about the attacks and especially not about Junior. He headed for Emersons.

With the uncomfortable feeling that not deciding about Junior might be a decision in its own right.

Chapter Five

Wednesday was busy with sales at the Wurstspeicher Haus. It put Mom in such a good mood she played *Die Fledermaus* and *The Merry Widow*, her version of opera pops.

Visitors were hitting town for Thursday's opening and they wanted hostess gifts. They'd be back before Sunday to buy take-home presents.

I'd taped my cracked toes and ignored them. But I couldn't ignore the door. Every time the bell tinkled, my body tensed, hoping for Big Dark and Dangerous and sorely disappointed by every tourist.

Not disappointed. Relieved.

Our dozen regulars came in too, including Hermy and her little one. Blonde, blue-eyed and vacantly pretty, Hermy could have been any of a hundred young mothers toting her infant in a front snug sack.

She floated to the counter. "Hello, Junior. May I have my usual? What, Tiny?" She bent her head to the snug sack. "Oh, yes. Tiny would like some more of your homemade baby food. Did I tell you he got his first tooth? I'm thinking of weaning him off the formula."

"Ah. Probably a good idea." I pulled down a couple jars of creamed Thüringer. Inside the snug sack, Tiny meowed his pleasure.

Yes, meowed.

Hermy's baby was a cat. She talked to it like it was her baby, fed it like it was her baby. To her, it was her baby.

Or at least made up for the one she lost.

In the big city, carting a cat in a snug sack would have been a sign of mental instability. At best, Hermy'd be in an institution. At worse, she'd be a homeless bag lady.

But in Meiers Corners...Mrs. Blau came in and glanced at Hermy's snug sack. "I do believe Tiny's gained weight, dear. What are you feeding him? I'd like to try it with my youngest."

Yup, in Meiers Corners people talked to the snug sack too.

"Try the lovely organic baby food Mrs. Stieg makes." Hermy

handed Mrs. Blau a jar.

Also only in MC. Mentally delicate but the Wurstspeicher Haus's number-one promoter, at least for creamed Thüringer baby food.

Mrs. Blau tucked the jar in her bag. "I'll take three more, Junior." As I got the jars she added, "By the way, who was that handsome young man Brunhilde Butt saw you with at Nieman's?"

Another of Meiers Corners's interesting attributes. Secrets were shared with your closest friends—all seven thousand of them. For me, annoying and at times downright invasive. But for Hermy, a blessing. Everybody knew she'd lost that baby, so we treated her with a sympathy verging on town-wide empathy.

When Hermy was ready, she'd rejoin us on the rational side of Main Street.

Glynn came again that night...I mean picked me up...for the final dress rehearsal. Mindful of Mom's history (sexual entrapment was probably too strong a term, but in connection with Glynn, it conjured up all sorts of exciting—I mean *disturbing*—images), I didn't invite him back inside. I didn't need the temptation.

Then I fumbled for ten minutes packing up, *not* thinking about what Glynn could do with an actual bed, and we were late anyway.

On the plus side, we missed the acting warm-ups.

Tonight was final dress. The actors were forbidden to break proscenium—that is, corralled to dressing rooms and backstage. No calling for lines for the actors, no stopping for any of us, not even for a train wreck.

So when Toto flopped down on stage and started licking himself, we kept playing. When he lost interest in his doggie danglies to start watering the potted plants, we kept playing.

When Glinda stumbled asking Dorothy what kind of witch she was, saying instead "Are you a good bitch or bad bitch?" we kept playing. (Our dear Good Witch of the North was actually Lana the part-time Good Hooker of North Avenue. She'd gotten the part because her pimp was one of the show's patrons. Only in Meiers Corners.) When she peeped her song like a toddler on helium, we practically doubled over playing into stands (to soften the volume as well as muffle our laughter), but we kept playing.

At intermission, because the actors had to stay backstage, Rocky and I had the water fountain to ourselves. She pushed her wealth of hair from her face before holding the handle for me. "So I got a new part-time job."

"Another one?" I stuck my bottle into the stream. "What does that make, three?"

"Four. Teaching lessons, the homeless shelter, the community symphony, and now rating for CIC Mutual."

"Insurance?" I stopped filling. "Don't tell Nixie. She thinks buying insurance will lead to the heat death of the universe."

Rocky let go of the handle. "But she's married to a lawyer."

"Julian also plays cello. That cancels out any lawyer cooties." I grabbed the handle and cranked the water back on, resumed filling. "So do you like it?"

"I've only been there a couple half days, but it's pretty interesting. Did you know CIC insures a certain PAC?"

I stopped filling again. "*Our* PAC?"

"Well, I can't talk about specific policies. Confidentiality, you know."

"Huh." I turned on the stream again. "Speaking of confidentiality, a certain Wurstspeicher Haus insures through CIC."

"A lot of Meiers Corners businesses do. Theoretically, that is. The PAC, your store, the Sparkasse Bank, dozens more."

"You know all this how?" I capped my water. "Theoretically, that is."

She blushed. "I didn't look up specific policies or anything. I just had to find some examples to use as templates."

"Right."

"I was surprised at so many. Usually Corners folk buy local." Rocky unscrewed her water bottle.

"We don't have any local insurance companies. Besides, Twyla says local-only isn't good for us anymore, thanks to the latest recession. Did you know there's more riding on this show than getting to Broadway?"

"Really?"

"We're the draw for tourists to flock to our Quainte Local Shoppes to buy quainte shite. No pressure. Hey, how many cellists does it take to screw in a light bulb?"

"None," she shot back. "They're not small enough to fit. Why shouldn't you drive off a cliff with three viola players in a Mini?"

"Because you could fit at least one more in. How many principal flutists does it take to change a light bulb?"

"Only one, but that light bulb really has to want to change?"

I snorted. "That's psychiatrists. One is correct, though. The prima donna holds the light bulb in her hand and the world turns around her."

"Ha-ha. Why do violists get worried when they see the *Kama Sutra*?"

"All those positions!" we said together, bumped fists and went back to rehearsal.

The second half went better, mainly because someone had Palin'ed Glinda and written her lines on her hand. The bows came off perfectly, despite squirrelly kids up past their bedtimes, and when we played the runoff music, I nailed the last low B-flat. I was feeling pretty good as I hauled my instruments backstage to pack up (instrument cases in the audience also forbidden at final dress).

So I was clipping along as I cornered into the back corridor, and nearly ran into the shady form in trench coat and mask.

Instantly I backpedaled, but a tenor sax creates a fair amount of momentum. I almost face-planted into the trench coat's shoulder—which was slung with a black sack.

The kidnapper.

I pulled up at the last second. Beyond the stalker about twenty feet, Dumas gave notes to Mishela.

Shock burned the picture on my retinas. Skulking kidnapper foreground, Mishela background, Dorothy braids swaying as she nodded. Behind her, thick arms crossed over big chest, eyes like lasers on his charge, was Glynn.

Slo-mo, his head swung up to stare right at me. Fear and fury leaped into his sapphire gaze. Fury at the stalker.

Fear for me.

It went fast from there. Glynn shouted "Mishela, drop!" at the same instant the stalker squeaked, jumped like a cat turning midair and ran. Mishela ducked, Glynn leaped. I realized belatedly that here was my chance to catch the stalker.

Just as the stalker plowed straight into me.

I fell on my keister, barely hanging on to my three instruments. The pain flaring in my coccyx hadn't even hit when the stalker grabbed my wrist and yanked me to my feet. Flute and clarinet jarred from my hands, and I heard the clatter of several hundred dollars hitting floor. Dammit, that would leave dents. I tried to punch him (or her or it)—for justice, but also to leave a dent in return.

With a muttered "Fuck," the stalker *shooped* the bag over my head and my punch swept air.

I shrieked. My cry gagged to an *ack* when the drawstring yanked tight.

"Stay back," the stalker hissed. "Or this one gets hurt."

And then I was flying, hefted onto a shoulder so bony it practically cut me in two. Air huffed from my chest at the impact, exacerbated as the guy/gal/thing kicked into a run and bounced me into near-asphyxiation.

A bellow of rage sounded, Glynn, diminishing, like the skinny kidnapper was getting away fast. I scrabbled for a hold on bony shoulders, hoping like hell Glynn could track me—and wondered idiotically if I should be dropping breadcrumbs. I didn't have breadcrumbs, but the way the stalker was rattling me maybe I could drop teeth. Or, like Toto, pee.

Another bellow sounded. Closer. Glynn, athletic tracker Glynn, was gaining. The stalker's breath rasped loud in my ears. Tired gasps, and no wonder. Not only was he/she/it lugging a hundred-some pounds of me, but my sax, tethered to my neck, was a-flopping against its back, whacking with loud, bony thuds. Never was I so glad for weighty and awkward.

Glynn roared again, much nearer and supremely pissed. The trench coat under me squealed—and tossed me to the ground.

Silly me, my only thought was *my sax*. I flipped midair and landed flat on my back.

I hit the concrete so hard my diaphragm froze.

"Getting the wind knocked out of you" sounds like simple inconvenience. But it's a horror of *can't breathe.* You suck air but nothing happens. *Nothing.* You think you may never breathe again. It's all over but for the *My Life* video replay, hopefully with RiffTrax.

I tried to inhale, really I did, but all I got was *gak-gak-gak.* I clawed hood. The sax weighted my ribs like a sandbag. I honestly thought I was dead. End of Junior, small fish in a small pond, never to grow to her full potential. Maybe a comedy instead of a tragedy, but now we'd never know.

Big hands righted me. Warm, ripply muscles pressed to my spine. An intense male heat permeated my chest cavity, eased the straitjacket on my lungs. I sucked in air. Shuddered. Breathed again. Oxygen never felt so good.

"*Babi.*" Glynn's voice was threaded with worry. I felt a plucking at my neck. "Are you all right?"

Not really, but I was better so I just nodded. He shifted me to get to the tie from the front. I cradled the sax in one arm and lifted my chin to give him better access. The tie came loose, his fingers a lot more nimble under stress than mine. When the hood came off, the first thing I saw was his face, gorgeous blue eyes tight with concern for me.

Second was the yellow glow of a street lamp. We were outside.

"Mishela," I croaked.

"Bloody hell." He scooped me up and whizzed back inside, whipping so fast it blurred the walls like hitting light speed. I hugged my tenor like a teddy bear.

In the women's dressing room, Mishela, dressed in a robe, was calmly removing her makeup. Her costume was draped over a nearby chair.

"I can take care of myself, Glynn." She smeared cream on her cheeks. "I keep telling you and Mr. Elias that, but you never listen."

Glynn set me down. I unhooked my sax and cleared off a section of the makeup counter to put it on. Not best practice but I was trembling from adrenaline and not up to carrying its weight.

Around us, trees and Emerald Cityites and other adult females stopped what they were doing to stare at this powerful invading male.

Glinda started doing a little striptease.

To his credit, Glynn ignored them all, even Little Miss Part-time Hooker. "Is anyone missing?"

Mishela stopped smearing, showing she wasn't as unconcerned as she wanted to seem. "I'm sorry?"

"Anyone from the cast or crew not here? Slim build, a bit taller than you, missing right after the bows?"

She paled as the implications struck. "No. But things were pretty chaotic as the curtain closed. Jazzed."

"Who did you see for certain? Lion's too hefty, but what about Tin

Man?"

She nodded. "Both were here."

"The Gatekeeper? Captain of the Winkies?"

"I...I'm not sure."

He pressed. "Steve? Our friend the *Scarecrow*?"

She went white. "Not Jon. You can't suspect Jon, Glynn. He's a Broadway star."

"Everyone is a suspect. And Jon hasn't had a hit in years."

She flinched.

Glynn was scaring her, for no other reason than he was angry. With himself probably, but Mishela looked young and frightened, and I felt for her. Spine snapping straight, I stepped between them. "Oh for heaven's sake. Why stop at actors? Half the pit is the right size and build. Why pick on insiders when it's most likely a stranger? This is just scaring Mishela—who is fine."

He whirled on me. "But *you* weren't. You were in the clutches of that maniac, and I had no idea what he wanted with you or if I would get to you in time!"

I gaped at him. "We barely know each other. Why should you care?"

His eyes widened, then narrowed. "Why indeed?" He shoved out of the dressing room and disappeared.

"I think you hurt his feelings," Mishela said.

She'd turned back to the mirror, toweling off cream and makeup. Trying to seem unaffected, but her hand trembled.

So I reined back my own feelings and tried to edge things toward normal by being domestic and hanging up Mishela's costume. "I don't think it's possible to hurt him. Not Mr. Big, Grim and Invulnerable."

"He's self-contained, not invulnerable."

"Says you." As I picked up the Dorothy dress it revealed Mishela's street clothes, jeans neatly folded beneath her underwear. On top of the pile was a pair of pink panties with a green blob which reminded me of the incident with Steve running across the stage at our first rehearsal. I looked closer. The green was a tentacled monster—with a cute pink hair bow. Under the picture was written "Hello Cthulhu".

Had Steve stolen these the panties? How twee. Mishela's first fanboy was a weenie of a stalker. No wonder she hadn't wanted to talk about the incident.

Then a thought struck me. "Damn, my instruments. They fell in the hallway. I'd better go get them before they get tromped into scrap metal."

My flute and clarinet were propped right outside the door.

Had Glynn found them? Angry as he was, had he really stopped to think about me, take care of my instruments?

Keeper.

No, not thinking about that. I picked up the flute. The G-sharp lever was bent but that was all. I tweeted a few notes, then tried out the clarinet. Everything worked, a huge relief. Hugging instruments, I grabbed a chair, scraped it up next to Mishela, sat and watched her.

Her scrubbing was brisk, expert—not a beauty routine, but as if her face were a palette to be cleaned.

I caught her eye in the mirror. "What I don't get is, why kidnap you? If they're trying to disrupt the show, wouldn't it make more sense just to disable you with an accident or something?"

"You're assuming they're after me." She tossed down the towel, eyes stabbing mine in the mirror. "I'm not convinced. After all, they took Dumas. Now they've taken you. If it's about me, wouldn't they take *me*?"

"I don't know. Why'd Glynn suggest Scarecrow? Doesn't he like him?"

"Glynn thinks Jon has an unnatural interest in me. I keep telling him it's paternal interest. Or maybe a crush, but it's entirely innocent. The man's old enough to be my father." She looked away. "Mr. Elias says it's someone connected with the show."

"Maybe he's wrong."

"Mr. Elias? He's never wrong." She blew a disgusted breath, turned back to the mirror and finished cleaning in silent concentration. It seemed to calm her.

I wasn't calm. I'd been abducted. Despite my martial arts training, despite a building full of people, I'd been taken. Who had done that to me? Slim and connected with the show could be any one of several dozen people. Most were from Meiers Corners.

One of *us*.

If only we knew why the person was attacking. Was he/she after a specific person, or just trying to generally disrupt the show?

I was lost in possibilities and about to panic when I realized I had tools to unravel this. I was a businesswoman, used to solving problems from delivery logistics to the intricacies of stacking pounds of misshapen stock.

I could slice through the whole tangle with one sharp Sales Maneuver: "Follow the money". Long run, who or why didn't matter. Kidnapping Mishela or Dumas or even me would cripple the production at this late date. "Mishela. Who stands to gain if the show is trashed? I don't, you don't. Meiers Corners loses, especially businesses relying on tourists. Who'd gain by disrupting show?"

Tidying her work area, she paused. "A rival show, maybe?"

"Competition. A good, strong motive. Was someone passed over for a starring role? Revenge is also good."

Her eyes widened. "You don't suppose this is connected to the fire that destroyed our New York production?"

"Maybe." Which widened the field of suspects from Meiers Corners to the whole United States. Though I'd asked the right question, it had the wrong answer.

"There are too many suspects," I said finally.

"You're giving up?"

"Not in this lifetime. I have a cunning plan. A plan so cunning it has a British Museum wing named after it."

"Really?"

"No. Look, whoever grabbed Dumas and then me will try again. All we have to do is trap him. Her. It."

"Okay." Doubt shaded her tone. "How?"

"If the kidnapper holds to form, tomorrow after the show he-she-it will try again." I smashed the pronouns together, pronouncing it "heesheeit".

"Bless you."

"Thanks. You're probably the target, but just in case, all three of us will head to Nieman's. You, me and Dumas. We'll make a big deal of it, make sure everyone knows just the three of us are going."

"What about Glynn?"

"See, that's the cunning part. Instead of doing his hulking protector thing, he'll be shadowing. Hidden enough that it looks like we're totally alone. When the kidnapper attacks—"

"Glynn nails him. Her. It." Smiling, Mishela clapped her hands. "I like it. When we get the kidnapper, we sweat him-her-it for answers."

"Gesundheit."

"Thanks." Her smile faded. "The hard part will be convincing Glynn to stand back. Especially after what happened tonight."

She was right. If he'd hovered before, the scare would make him a second skin. Nothing would shake him loose.

Except *maybe* a few well-placed kisses. "Convincing Glynn. Yes." I took a deep breath. For the show. "Leave that to me."

While my brain churned on well-placed kisses, *nibbling carved cheeks, defined lips, flat waist, muscular thighs, thick, long...*my pocket started vibrating. I half-stood and pulled out my cell phone, saw the number and swore. But I answered, ever the dutiful daughter. Yay, me. "What's up, Mom?"

"It's Papa," a booming male voice said. "There is work to be done. I need you to forgo partying with your little friends. Sausage doesn't—"

"—sell itself, I know." Explaining after-rehearsal burn to Pop was useful only if I had five lungs and an hour. Though it'd make a good wind exercise. "What do you need?"

"Uncle Otto has run out of breakfast sausage. How can he make his famous Southern German *Guten Tag Y'all* sausage gravy if he has no sausage?"

"He needs it tonight?"

"It is almost tomorrow. And Otto's wife must be frying by five for the smorgasbord to be ready by six."

Some inns kept business hours, some country hours. My uncle Otto kept military hours. Frying by five meant shower at four which meant up at oh-dark-thirty. "All right, Pop. Be right there."

I lugged instruments home, wishing for a nice limo ride and a nicer kiss... Instead of after-rehearsal rush, I got presausage letdown.

Got the job, do the job. Besides, Uncle Otto was one of our best customers. Stiegs never let nepotism get in the way of profit.

At home, I picked up the box my dad had packed for me, mapping a mental route to haul my tired ass to Uncle Otto's. I'd been the brothers' courier since the age of six, when I'd been a brat pedaling brats on my little bike. I'd ridden or walked every single combination of those eight blocks over the years, knew every flamingo and garden gnome, every decorative pebble. Not much changed in our small town.

I left by the side door, saw a new Cheese Dudes webcam staring at me. Okay, some things changed, and not always for the better. But I was too tired to give them even a courtesy finger.

I emerged onto Fourth. Across the street, lights glowed inside the bombed shell of Kalten's skate rink. For the past month, contractor trucks had parked in front, so I knew they were renovating it. I wondered what business was going in, whether it was compatible with sausage. The builders were working awfully late. Maybe they were close to finishing and putting on a push.

I know I should've been planning a way to "convince" Glynn to help us trap the kidnapper. But it was late and I was so tired. My brain hopped from idea to idea without any of them sticking, that cross-pollination state between Teflon Zen and a kangaroo on crack.

I headed east. Yellow streetlights and early summer mosquitoes were my only company. Here I was, alone, just me and my basket of sausage goodies. Little Red Riding Junior. And we hadn't caught Mr./Ms./Meh Wolf-in-Trench-Coat-Clothing.

In fact, it was almost like our trapping scenario, with me as bait instead of Mishela. Oh, and without Glynn to spring the trap.

I picked up my pace.

If only I knew who the attacker was really after. Why grab me? A deterrent to Glynn, maybe, but why would Glynn care? Just because we'd shared a couple kisses, and a little more...okay, a lot more, but Glynn walked away, acted invulnerable—

"You're alone," a baritone snarled *right behind me.*

Shock spun me into a groin shot, knee rising sharply. With my whole body powering it, testicles would have achieved low earth orbit.

A hard palm blocked my thigh, judo-style, tossing me completely around and pitching me toward concrete.

Sausage leaped from my grasp. The box made a beautiful arc before hitting pavement. The smack-crunch of cardboard was loud but I knew the sausage was fine. One good thing about Pop's *it-vill-be-perfekt* packaging.

I wouldn't be so lucky.

At the last second, hands netted my arms, yanked me flush to a hot torso. A big, familiar torso, the monster sock puppet nestling into my butt like home, cinching it.

"*Glynn?* What the fu...?"

"I might ask you the same thing. Out at night. *Alone.*" He spun me, hands clenching as if he'd like to shake me. "After being attacked

90

by three monsters only last night. I thought you were with Mishela. What are you doing?"

"I'm—"

"What were you thinking?" His voice crescendoed like "Bolero". "Abducted by a maniac just tonight. Yet here you are, *alone*. Are you *trying* to drive me mad?" By the end he was practically yelling.

My mouth fell open. Why was he so angry? Could he possibly be worried about me?

Ridiculous. "What do you care? It's not like you've been smothering me all my life or are here to take the job over from my parents."

Which sounded like I wanted him to. Oh, my foot did not taste good, but I bulled on. "In less than two weeks you're going back to Iowa. I've walked these streets for years. I'll be walking them after you're back in the land of corn and...and corn."

"There's more to Iowa than corn." He growled it, but a glint of sapphire humor warmed his eyes.

"Yeah? Like what?"

"Like trucks. And cows."

"The universities and international businesses?"

"Those don't count." The corner of his mouth quirked. Stunningly handsome lips became downright edible. But I'd be a fool to tell him that.

"Did you know your lips are really yummy?" I slammed a hand over my idiotic mouth.

"That's the nicest thing anyone's said to me."

"I doubt that. I've seen how women look at you."

"Perhaps it's not the words, but the one saying them." He pulled me tight, stroked my head. *"Babi.* I can't live through seeing you in such danger again. As long as I am here, you will not go unescorted at night."

"I'm not helpless." I pushed him away. "I fended off a burglar last year. Side-kicked him on his ass." A Meiers Corners-style burglar, a teenage kid with midnight munchies and no sausage in the fridge, but Glynn didn't need to know that. "And I nearly kneed your balls to the moon. I'm not helpless."

"You're not." He considered me with proper seriousness. "But you're facing a different kind of foe, far stronger and faster than you're used to. Inhumanly so."

"Oh, right. Like monsters? Space aliens?" I snatched up my dropped sausage.

"No. Chicago vam...hoods. Big city thugs."

"Big city automatically makes them worse somehow?" I started across the river. "Meiers Corners folk are narrow-minded because they're stuck in the echo chamber of small-town tradition and don't know any better. What's your excuse?"

He caught up easily with his long legs. "You think big cities are somehow better? I'm to be open-minded simply because I'm more urban?"

"Urban, urbane. They're related for a reason."

"A small town can teach people many things, Junior. Things found only in the smaller group, a tight-knit family, a home—"

"Sure, if you want to learn about being an intolerant, tight-knit idiot."

He made a *tch* of dissent. "Being an idiot isn't a function of community. There are idiots in small towns and big cities. But there is love in both, too. Acceptance, nurturing."

"Sure, but a fish grows to the size of its pond. Simple physical fact. Small pond, small fish. Wanna grow, you gotta get into the ocean."

"That may be true of fish, but not of people. There are big people in small towns, and small people in big ones."

"I'm not talking good-hearted, I'm talking broad-minded. Name one Meiers Corners resident who thinks outside the box. Just one."

"Julian Emerson—"

"Was a hotshot Boston attorney before he settled here last year. Boston's kinda fair-sized."

He blew a frustrated breath. "Nixie Emerson."

"Thinks everyone is out to repress anything fun or spontaneous in her—because they are. She doesn't count, Glynn. She's our oppressed minority."

"Oh? What about your parents? They strike me as worldly. They'd have to be, to run a store with imported sausage."

"Are you joking?" I shook my head. "*Mutti und Vati* are the worst of the lot. So insular they could be used as parka stuffing."

"'Insular' means 'island'."

"Fine. Little islands, never seeing beyond the borders of town. Half the town is related and the other half is married to it."

"Such connection. Such belonging." Glynn stuffed hands into his pants pockets. "It is a rare gift. You should appreciate it more."

"Such inward focus. Such limiting ties. Why defend it so hard?"

"No reason."

"Right." I stopped to punch him with a good glare. "This is the second time you've made an issue of it. We don't have to talk about it, but don't lie to me."

"Fine." He swept by me, snagging my elbow on the way and tugging me into motion. "I have no mother, no father. Be glad you do."

"Say *what?*" I grabbed his wrist, tried to yank him to a stop. Like halting a truck. I tried digging in my heels, but he kept going and I pitched off my feet.

With a growl he stopped to catch me, his big strong hands splayed on my... But he'd stopped, so mission accomplished. I dropped sausage (to another crunch) and took his face between my hands. His skin felt like warm satin. I searched his eyes. "You lost your family? When?"

He didn't say anything. But his eyes twitched away, an answer in itself.

"You *never* knew your parents?"

He turned out of my hands, jammed his deep in his pockets again.

"Oh, Glynn, I'm so sorry." I caught his biceps, stopping him. Facing him, I wound arms around his waist and hugged him tight.

At first, his body was stiff under mine. I rubbed gentle circles on his spine, let my heat sink in. He softened. His arms came around me in return...and then he was hugging me back, so tightly I thought ribs would crack.

The pain was worth it if it helped him even a little.

We stood in silence, drawing comfort from each other. We might have stood that way for the rest of the night.

"Is that my sausage on the ground, *liebchen?* I do not think the health inspector would look on that favorably."

Chapter Six

I spun. Behind us, leaning heavily on his broom, was Uncle Otto. Blushing, I stepped out of Glynn's warm embrace.

Otto's shaped like a kid's top, round in the middle with two pointy ends. He's usually whirling around sweeping. When he's not, he's leaning on something, mostly the broom, but sometimes his wife, Aunt Ottowina, who's built like a tank. I think that, like a top, if Otto wasn't whirling or leaning, he'd tip over.

I should mention there are three Stieg children—my dad Gunter, Uncle Otto and Aunt Hattie. Only Hattie and Pop produced Stieg grandchildren, one each. It makes family reunions both easy and hard. While other families have to rent a park, we can gather in my parents' flat. But while other families play volleyball, we're reduced to lawn darts—far more dangerous because they're nothing but big spikes with wings, and Aunt Hattie's aim isn't so good.

Which, come to think, may have been why Uncle Otto never had kids. Lawn darts and testicles, not a good combo.

"Uncle, what are you doing here?" We'd barely crossed the river. Otto's B&BS was two blocks south.

"Your father called to say you were coming. Then he called ten minutes later to say why have you not arrived? So I came to check. I do not like you alone on the streets, *liebchen*. It is dangerous."

"I told her she needs an escort," Glynn said.

"Because of our dangerous streets. Right." I rolled my eyes. Main had hookers (part-time) and Grant had abandoned factories (now getting renovated). MC was so squeaky clean, city workers ran around checking home porches for the correct pitch. Not that a saggy old porch wasn't dangerous. It's just, where did the whole city get that kind of energy?

"Now, *liebchen*. You should listen to your young man." Otto tapped me on the forehead to get my attention. "He shows good sense."

I puffed in consternation. "And I don't? I'm shocked I've made it this long, traipsing around *alone* since I was *six.*"

"That was before the trouble in November," Glynn said. "Now you need an escort."

Otto nodded. "Listen to your young man."

Second time, I couldn't let that pass. Habits in the Corners were deadly. If you didn't immediately dig them out, they'd take root, like a tree finding a nice juicy sewer line. "Uncle. Glynn is *not* my young ma—"

"It's about time you were settling down."

See? "We're *not* settling dow—"

Glynn's expression stopped me, a gut-jarring combination of sad and wistful.

Well, hell. After hearing he was an orphan, I couldn't quash that hope, even in fantasy.

But maybe I could derail things a little. "Glynn's leaving after the show's over. He lives in Iowa."

"He does not sound like an Iowa boy." Otto, instead of calling me directly on it, started sweeping, a sort of nonverbal accusation. The fact that he was sweeping sidewalk apparently didn't bother him. "He sounds Welsh."

Glynn said, "You have a good ear, Mr. Stieg. I spent my childhood in Wales. I still make my home there several months out of the year."

I blinked. "But I thought—"

"Mr. Elias is my employer. I'm based there but don't live with him."

"I didn't know."

"You didn't ask."

I winced. A very basic, simple question I hadn't asked because I didn't wanted to get any closer to this gorgeous, blue-eyed Welshman. Because I had a duty and dreams that needed protecting.

But protecting dreams didn't mean being an ass. "I'm sorry."

"It's all right."

"*Gut, gut,* you are reconciled. Now for the making-up sex, *ja?*"

My jaw cracked pavement.

"I'll get Junior home safely," Glynn said.

"*Wunderbar,* wonderful." Uncle Otto whirled merrily. "I'll be off with my sausage, *liebchen,* and you'll be off with your young man. *Auf*

Wiedersehen!"

"Uncle Otto! Glynn's *not* my young—"

Glynn put his hand on my shoulder. His big, warm hand. Damn, the man's blood was hot. I wondered what all that blood would feel like inflating his big hot—yeah.

Otto's round form whizzed down the street on its pointy feet like a top. Or maybe a tornado, cuz I sure felt like I wasn't in Kansas anymore. "You shouldn't have said that."

"Why? It's only the truth. I will get you home safely."

"Not that. The young man thing. Otto's twirling home to call Pop, who'll tell Mom, who'll brag to Dolly Barton, and then everyone in town will think you're my boyfriend." When he stared at me blankly, I added, "Significant other. Suitor. Steady Eddy. Relationship partner. You know. Boyfriend."

"Would that be such a bad thing?" The wistful look was back.

"You don't understand things here." I started west. "Once we're hooked up, it's forever, get it? All over but the shotgun and wedding cake."

Glynn fell in beside me with a comfortable glide. "You don't want wedding cake?"

"It's not...look. I don't want the wedding."

He stared at me like I'd announced I was doing a remake of *The Room.*

"I can't start a new family. I already have a family and family obligations."

He gave me a strange look. "I thought you hated family. That you felt home was a cage."

"No. I love my parents and I'm happy to do my daughterly duty. But I also have dreams. I'm trying to make them both work. It's not easy." Crossing the river, I stopped. "Adding another family would make it impossible."

Glynn stood there, watching me with that strange look on his face.

I leaned on the bridge, facing the cop shop. "Speaking of smothering family, why are you here instead of doing your hovering routine on Mishela?"

"She's safe at our rooms."

"Oh. Good." I cleared my throat. Time to sell our idea. "We talked after you left about the attacks. We're wondering who the real target is, since both Dumas and I were attacked." Which reminded me. Elena knew about last night, but she didn't know about tonight. I started south, toward the police station. "Mishela and I came up with a plan."

"Where are you going?" Glynn's stride quickly caught him up.

"Huh?" Plan thoughts derailed. "Oh. To report my attack to Elena."

"No need. Julian would have told her."

"Why? Hunka-hunka hotlove didn't experience it firsthand, did he?"

"Hunka—what did you call Emerson?" Glynn's tone turned very dark and kinda prickly around the edges.

I snuck a look at him. Thunderstorms danced in his eyes, a definite shade of foreboding. "Nixie got real lucky in the mating lottery. Maybe I'm just a mite jealous. You don't want to hear what I call Bo Strongwell."

"You don't want a mate, but you're jealous of Nixie's?"

"I still have hormones, right? Now about Mishela's and my plan—"

"No."

"But you haven't even heard it yet."

"I won't like it. It will involve risk to you or Mishela. Putting you in danger hurts me. Putting Mishela in danger means Mr. Elias will lecture me. Either involves great pain."

"Hey, what do you call a bunch of topless women accordion players? Ladies in pain."

Glynn closed his eyes briefly.

"Get it? Ladies in pain? Like *Lady of Spain*, which is a big accordion piece—"

"Perhaps we can just walk silently for a while."

"But I haven't told you my plan."

"No."

We argued all the way to the police station. The cop shop main entrance is on First and Adams. Most have a locked inner door, but this was MC so we went right up to the detective pen on two. Elena wasn't in. Her partner, Detective Dirk Ruffles, was.

Elena called him Columbo without the cute, always "one more

thing" (he talked nonstop). Skinny and potbellied, Ruffles looked like a strategically shaved chimp stuffed in a Robot Chicken suit. A yellow fedora added to the gangster chicken—er, chic. But he was a damned fine sax player, and we could have used him in the pit if he hadn't worked nights.

Ruffles gave us a big wave when he saw us. "Hello, Junior. I was just cleaning my gun. Well, since my uncle has my gun locked in his safe, I was actually cleaning a picture of it. But I make sure to get it really clean by dismantling it, although one of the prongs on the picture frame broke and I had to use a paperclip to keep the glass from falling out, and did you know Oprah has a Web site?"

Dirk had a voice that rasped like a fart under a wool blanket. I suddenly wanted to poke a pencil in my ear canal. "No, I—"

"Well, she does, and you can watch videos of her. I was watching her on her Web site and cleaning my gun, and wondering if Oprah would have used a paperclip or something else, although maybe she would have bought a new frame, or better yet made one from scratch because she's a goddess—"

"Hey Dirk, I have a crime to report." Interrupting was rude, but I couldn't wait for Dirk to stop talking because, like his favorite TV, he was on 24/7. "Where's Elena?"

"Oh, she's out with Mr. Strongwell on their 'neighborhood watch' wink-wink."

"Their what?"

"Neighborhood watch," he said, his wispy mustache puffing with each syllable. "Wink. Wink."

While I was blink-blinking over that, Glynn latched on to my elbow and wheeled. "Thank you for your time, Detective."

"I'm not done." I dug in my heels but got swept along with Mr. Whitewater Rapids anyway. So when we reached the door, I grabbed the frame. That worked, but probably only because he didn't want to rip my limbs off.

Glynn said in my ear, "It's clear we won't get help here." His breath tickled the small hairs, making me shiver.

"Yeah, but..." But something was strange. Dirk wasn't the fastest cash register in the universe, but he *was* steady. And very, very literal. The only way he'd do a wink-wink was by parroting someone else. I turned back. "You know about last night's attack? Three guys—"

"Three men wearing pantyhose masks attacked Michael Dumas, Mishela Elias, Glynn Rhys-Jenkins, Junior Stieg. One man in trench coat and full mask attacked and carried off Dumas."

Oh yeah, Dirk had a great memory too. Well, he'd have to, to recite Oprah word for word.

"The trench coat attacked again tonight," I said. "He was watching Mishela, so she was probably the intended kidnap victim, but I surprised him and he carried me off instead." I filled in the details.

Dirk nodded seriously, but when I finished he said, "Maybe he just wanted Miss Mishela's phone number for a date."

"Great idea, except for the mask-wearing bit. And Mishela's underage."

"Oh, well, with vampires, age is always hard to tell," he said brightly.

My brain did a pole vault and puke. "With what?"

"It's hard to tell the real age of a vam—"

"He means the neighborhood watch," Glynn interjected smoothly. "Vampire is a sort of code word for monsters."

"And that relates to Mishela how?"

"She's Iowa Watch. We have a loose confederation. I'm a member as well." His face was all bland honesty, but something in his voice said Mr. Truth was screaming a bit on the rack...which made me think of being stretched out under Glynn, him making me scream—

"That would explain those guys attacking," Dirk said. "They're rivals to the Watch."

"Rival *watches*?" I could practically hear the capital letter he put on watch but didn't understand it, and shot an incredulous glance between the two of them. "Neighborhood watch gangs, and you've got watchland warfare?"

Dirk nodded. "The Watch protects us against a gang of vampires—
"

"There's a gang." Glynn cut Dirk off—24/7 Dirkus Uninterruptus—simply by raising his voice. Wow. Glynn could have done some serious damage onstage. "They're monstrous people, code word vampire, who oppose the efforts of the neighborhood watch. They make random attacks to disorganize us."

"Disorganize the loosely organized neighborhood watches? Uh huh."

"It sounds innocent but it isn't." Glynn took my arms. "The gang may have connected you with us, which is why I'm worried about you being alone after sunset. You need to go home and stay there."

"No, I need to tell Elena what happened."

He looked over my head at Dirk. "You'll see that Elena gets Junior's report?"

"I don't know about seeing, Mr. Glynn. But I'll tell her. As soon as I tell her about my gun. Oh, and the yummy sandwich I had for dinner, Colby and ham on rye, lightly toasted and then fried in an inch of butter…"

My stomach growled. Which reminded me I'd burned tons of calories, not only running courier but blowing my little gutsies out at the show. And getting snatched.

"…which melted the cheese until it ran into the butter and fried crisp and golden—"

"Good, thanks!" I held up fingers in the universal *Please God, stop.* "Okay, let's go." I could only hope that when Elena returned, Dirk managed to wedge my info in somewhere, because I had to eat now or implode.

And somehow get Glynn to explain about vampires. "Now about your neighborhood watch—"

"You're hungry." Glynn nudged me out the door with a hand splayed on my back like a blanket. Nice, warm, protective blanket. Hand. Whatever. "Shall we get something at the Caffeine Café?"

"What?" Warm hand warred with *vampire* in my head, but both were eclipsed by FOOD. Unfortunately, I didn't have much of a budget for eating out. "I have food at home."

"I'll pay."

Glynn was offering to take me out—like a *date*?

"Besides, I'd enjoy your company." His voice held an overtone of wistful.

That wistful note decided me. Besides, free food. Added bonus, it'd give me time to work around to the v-subject. Maybe even get him to listen to my plan.

The Caffeine Café was on the same block as the Wurstspeicher Haus, around a couple corners on the Fifth side. We passed my home on the way.

Mistake.

"Junior, there you are." A jolly elf head thrust from the upper window. No shutters banging first, so he'd been lying in wait. "Your Uncle Otto called." He gave Glynn the evil eye. "Who is your young man?"

I suppressed a sigh. "This is Glynn, Pop. But he's not 'my' young—"

"Hello, Mr. Stieg," Glynn said. "I'm taking Junior to the Caffeine Café for a bit of a meal, if you don't mind. My treat."

"You're paying?" My dad's lips pursed as his gears worked. Rehearsals made me hungry, and if my fuel went on someone else's dime, *alles* was *gut*. "I suppose that's okay. But you'll have her back within the hour, *verstehst du?*"

"I understand, Mr. Stieg."

As my dad banged shutter, I said to Glynn, "You speak German?"

"Enough to get along."

"English, German, Welsh...anything else?"

"I learned some Spanish traveling Mexico. A bit of Portuguese in South America last year. Oh, and some French when I was in Quebec."

If only I could travel half that much. "Aren't you full of surprises? There's such a call for linguistics in Iowa?"

"Mr. Elias sends me around. I've picked up a few things in my lifetime."

"Except a home."

Glynn shrugged. "Perhaps that's why he sends me to so many places. To see if I find any of them to my liking."

"That's perceptive." And it was the heart of Business Truth #5, "Tell the customer, not what you want to jabber about, but what they need to hear". It's not about what *you* need, it's about what the customer needs. Or in this case, the employee.

"I never told Elias about my past, but he knows anyway."

And Business Truth #6, "Keep your eyes open and on the customer". I could see why Elias was a big guy in the business world. Although he lived in little Coralville. I frowned. Big guy in little Coralville? How did that square?

Well, Coralville *was* a suburb of Iowa City, home of the University of Iowa. Sure. That made it more urban than its population size would imply.

And Meiers Corners was just outside Chicago, one of the US big three.

That shook me.

We reached the café. I trotted straight to the bar and rattled off half the menu to the night barista, Tammy, tacking on hot peppermint tea to drink.

She shot my order back to the kitchen, drew a pot of hot water, threw in the tea and set it in front of me without looking up. "I'll bring your food when it's ready. Next."

Her eyes lifted. Her pupils dilated, and she brightened like a nova. "Hel-*lo*, handsome." Her expression slipped into something sheer and silky. She leaned against the bar, plumping her cleavage outrageously. "What can I get for you?"

"A Red Special." Glynn was surveying the room. If he saw her smile or cleavage, he wasn't reacting to it.

"Sure thing, hot stuff." Tammy's stare was below Glynn's belt. Maybe she'd heard he could give amazing orgasms against doors and was checking out his door-hanging tools. "Say, haven't I seen you at Julian's? I'm a tenant. Did you move in recently?"

"Visiting. We'll wait for our order over there." Glynn took me by the elbow to a table farthest from the bar.

"You're living at Nixie's?" I said.

"Mishela and I are Emerson's guests."

Almost immediately, Tammy sashayed over with Glynn's drink, a thick, reddish liquid that looked like tomato juice. "Anything else I can get you?" She cranked her smile from nova to super, directed at Glynn but not at his face.

He stared hard at her. My ears heated, and I was about to excuse myself despite being starving when he said, pointedly, "Anything else that I need, Junior can provide."

Whoa. I've heard of double entendres, but that was entendre stripped buck naked.

Tammy's wattage didn't change. "Sure. Let me know if I can help. In the meantime, I'll go see what's delaying her order." She winked and sashayed away.

Help? I tore three packs of sugar into my tea. Fortunately the sweet, hot liquid calmed me enough to remember why I wanted to trap...I mean socialize with Glynn. Vampire and plan. Time for Business Truth #2, "Focus on the job at hand". I picked the direct approach, hoping a hard hit would score me information. "I don't buy 'vampire' as a code word for monstrous people. Dirk's too literal."

"Oh?" Glynn raised an eyebrow, a sort of facial shrug. "Well, you know Detective Dirk."

A soft block, the best counter to the hard hit. Sometimes Glynn's mysterious druid thing got annoying.

"And here comes Tammy with your food."

Misdirection, the perfect follow-up. I wondered if he'd gone to business school too. Of course, Kai Elias as a boss was a top-level education in itself.

Tammy settled my soup and salad on the table. "The tuna melt will be out in a minute." She eyed Glynn. "It's really *hot*." Her sashaying away would have done a cat in heat (or a salesperson with a quota) proud.

But Glynn was watching me, not the waving ass-flag. I tucked in.

"How can you eat all that this late?"

"I burn a lot of energy playing pit," I said between bites.

"Oh? How do other players cope?"

"Pit chocolate. But wind players can't cuz it gums up the pads and valves."

"And Nixie?"

I grimaced. "Has a toothbrush. The cheat. Why do you care?"

He grimaced. "I don't know. I just do."

"Well, stop it. You're heading west next week. And hopefully I'm heading east soon after that. So unless you're into one-night stands..." Which reminded me of last night's stand against the door. "Just stop it. Now, about the vampire remark—"

"I can't stop it. Believe me, I would if I could." He cast one elbow over the top rail of his chair, a relaxed sort of posture except for the tension in his big body. "I'm not into one-night stands. You don't want commitment. What's left?"

My mind was still churning on one-door...I mean one-night stands. "Orgasms," I said and blushed. Bulled on. "I owe you one."

"You don't owe me anything." He stared out the window.

Well, this was going nowhere fast. Good thing we weren't contemplating a relationship. It'd be short-lived, frustrating and painful, like a cheap underwire bra.

Damn. Underwear.

Tammy brought my tuna melt with a brilliant smile for Glynn. "Anything else? We have a full range of coffee drinks. Steamy hot and wet."

Annie on a trampoline, didn't she ever let up? Even if Glynn wasn't interested in her, he was still a guy. She lived where he was staying. All she had to do was offer him turn-down service, and he'd be slipping his peppermint between her sheets.

At the thought, I bit into my sandwich with a snap of teeth.

"Junior and I are fine," Glynn said. "That will be all."

"Later, then." She gave him a wink and sashayed away.

I chomped more sandwich. Fine. She and Mr. Brooding Welsh Sexmonkey could do the nasty. I didn't care. I masticated furiously.

Glynn's eyes stuck on my mouth. As I chewed, the blue got darker and darker.

Finally he clamped his lids shut.

I took another bite. "What?"

"I'm seeing you doing that to my cock."

My mouth fell open. I remembered I'd been chewing, swallowed, then let it fall open again. "Wouldn't that, um, hurt? Chewing, biting teeth…really really sensitive, er, flesh?"

"I wouldn't care." He shifted in his chair. "Anything's better than this bone-deep pain."

I set down my sandwich. Whoa. He wanted it as bad as me. But what could we do? I was phobic of commitment and neither of us were into slam-'n-lam.

I took another bite of sandwich, more frustration than hunger in my chomp now. Glynn finished his Red Special, throwing it back with what looked like equal frustration. I tossed my half-finished sandwich down.

"You're done?" He didn't bitch about me not cleaning my plate, just extracted his wallet and cast a couple fifties on the table. Even with my mondo-order, that would leave quite a tip for Tammy nova-smile. Maybe he was hoping her door would be open, since mine wasn't. He'd lit my fire pretty damned fast. He'd light hers even faster since her pilot was already burning.

Picturing that, I slammed out of the café.

Mr. Long Legs caught up easily.

We walked the block in silence. Our hands were jammed deep in our pockets. Not to keep from touching each other. I wouldn't have touched that hard chest, those ripply abs...yeah.

At my door, I turned and kicked up my jaw to say something snarky. Definitely not for a kiss, much less tongues tangling *bodies melding hips pounding,* but he was already stalking away. *Good.*

Except I hadn't gotten an answer about vampires or the kidnapper-luring plan. Damn the man's mysterious, provoking, tantalizing, arousing... I clamped my thighs tight to shut off my insane desire. That only managed to kick-start desire into *me want now.*

I jammed my key in the lock, threw open the door and stomped inside, more than ready for a fight with the folks. So naturally the hallway was dark and empty. Snoring from the parental flat confirmed I'd go to bed with my full load of vitriolic heat. I stomped up to my room. It didn't wake my parents, but the two-by-fours spat a satisfying amount of dust. Dammit, Glynn itched for me and I burned for him, but we disagreed where it mattered most. Couldn't go two minutes without arguing. I'd probably pushed him toward Tammy.

In my room, I tore off T-shirt and jeans. So what if Glynn got his buzz from Ms. Caffeine? I was glad. It meant no entanglements, nothing between me and my dreams. Which would be wet dreams...my breasts swelled too big for my bra, and a definite raw tingle invaded my lacy panties.

Damn the man. He could have Tammy with the tug of one big finger, but I was alone. Only my right hand, small and cool in comparison to his... Double-damn him. Just one night, one door, one orgasm, and already he'd raised my standards impossibly high.

I needed to get away. I brushed my wall, touching an eighteenth-century map of the British Isles, petting the Irish Sea, which lapped the coast of Wales...

Argh. I didn't need Glynn; I didn't need anybody. Not for companionship, not to fulfill rainbow dreams and especially not for this. I flopped onto my bed, spread my legs and slid fingers under damp lace.

A growl at the window snapped me erect, my hand entangled in lace and my heart thudding. A shape loomed against the glass like something crouched there. Something big. And muscular.

Like Glynn.

Couldn't be. How'd he get up here? The fire escape was a rollaway, currently rolled. Unless he could leap three full stories, it had to be a cloud shadow. It couldn't possibly be him out there. Watching me.

Watching me satisfy myself.

Not Glynn, but it sure made me hot thinking about it. My anger slipped as I imagined his sapphire eyes on me, growing darker as I got wetter. His growl, pure male beast. I took a stroke and another. I imagined him kissing me as I stroked. A moan bubbled up from my belly.

The growl revved rougher. The form at the window blurred, like mist. The shadow solidified inside my room into a very real Glynn, stalking across the floor.

Chapter Seven

Glynn stalked to the bed where I lay, thighs spread, vulnerable in my thin lace and nothing else. He stopped at the foot of the bed, belly rapidly undulating with harsh breaths, like he'd been running. My belly rose and fell in rhythm.

Glowing eyes speared mine. He shucked his jacket and let it fall to the floor. My breath sucked in and held.

He snagged the hem of his tee and raised it, slowly, revealing hard abs ripple by ripple. He peeled the shirt past ribs framed by flared lats, over a cliff of a chest with taut ruby nipples. The buff mounds danced as he stripped the tee over his head and tossed it.

I swallowed.

He mounted the bed, stalking even here, rolling in on hands and knees like a panther. Raw male strength drove me back until my spine pressed against headboard. I panted in anticipation.

He thrust his fingers into my confined hair, holding my head, but I was already tethered by his stunning gaze, the violet fire of his lust.

A moment beat between us, pregnant with excitement soaring so high it was near terror.

Nerves pushed me to lick my lips. His eyes fell to my mouth and he growled, low and soft and feral. Desire skittered through me, an electricity both thrilling and deadly. He was so close I could see the perfection of his skin, the fan of black lashes. His nostrils were flared, his lips slightly parted.

Glinting between their chiseled male perfection were two sharp canines.

I sucked in a breath. "Gly—"

He cut me off by kissing me hard, crushing my mouth with his. He invaded me with his tongue, hot thrusts of bold power. Flame to my fuse, heat stoking heat, he wasn't coaxing my response but demanding it.

I loved it. Desire rushed hot in my veins. I was so hungry for him that I wrapped my legs around his hips. It pressed my panties to my sex.

They weren't just moist, they were sodden.

That shocked me enough to drop my legs and slap my palms onto his chest, to push him away.

His pecs were boulders sheathed in satin. I had never felt muscle like his—lean, rock-solid, covered in warm cream.

Instead of pushing, my palms slid over his chest as he plundered my mouth. My muscles melted and my body trembled, and I felt my control going. Yielding.

Surrendering to lust, like my mother. There'd go duty and rainbow dreams both.

It strengthened my resolve and my muscles. I pushed. "No."

He stopped kissing me, but didn't move an inch despite a damned hard shove. "Did you say no?" His breath played warm on my throbbing lips.

"Yes. I mean no." I gritted my teeth. "I mean stop."

He raised his head. Yellow streetlight glittered in his gaze. He stared deep into my eyes. Despite my mouth saying no, my eyes were probably screaming yes-yes-yes.

Thankfully...unfortunately...he listened to my mouth. After a small eternity, he blew a sharp breath. "Very well."

He sprang from the bed and flew out the window. Leaving me hotter and hungrier than I'd ever been in my life.

"*Damn* it." Despite making him stop, I leaped after him. My body and mind were waging serious war. At the windowsill, I grabbed frame, dragging in hard breaths. I'd wanted him to stop, but not to leave.

My blood was boiling, my skin itchy, my whole body swollen. And my heart...I didn't know what was in my heart except that I didn't want it to end badly like this.

Dammit, I didn't want the complications, but I wanted *him.*

No. I had to slay the sins of my mother. I had duty and dreams. I was *stronger* than this, stronger than *her.*

Yet a need so deep it made me shake, a desire so strong it burned, pushed me after him. I leaned out the window.

This was insane. He was gone, and it was better that way. *No. I had to go after him.* It nearly tore me in two.

Glynn's footfalls sounded on the sidewalk, heading away.

My hold on the sill broke. Need won out over duty, pushed me onto the roof. I scrambled out, skittered to the edge. "Glynn, come back!" Cautiously, I poked my head over the edge of the roof. Then my body. Then not so cautiously, I leaned out as far as I could.

I lost my balance. Scrabbled. Felt myself fall.

Terror sheared through me. Three stories splat onto a Meiers Corners-solid concrete walk. I'd be a Junior-size trash bag of shattered bones.

A hand cinched me back, spun me. Glynn filled my vision, his eyes violet fire.

He also filled my roof crenel, his bare shoulders smashed to shingle on both sides. "What the bloody hell do you think you're doing, woman?"

"Where did you go?" I flung back, gasping. "You were practically crawling into my mouth and then you were just gone!"

"What happened to 'stop'?"

A pounding shuddered from inside, beneath us. Glynn snarled, pure predator.

"It's Pop," I said. "Hitting his ceiling with the broomstick." I had a momentary flash to Otto and his ever-present broom. Wondered if it was a family thing, like maybe all the little Stieg kids got one for Christmas and played shopkeeper instead of war.

Going insane hurt. "My parents are awake. We need to be quiet."

Glynn gave a single sharp shake of the head. "I need to be gone."

"No." I took a deep breath. "No, I need you too much." I grabbed his hands, looked deep into his eyes and committed. "I want you inside." I burned crimson. That sure sounded like more than an invitation into my room. Stupid Freud.

His eyes glowed a violet so bright it was painful. "You don't mean that. You know what will happen. You can't mean to invite me in."

I pulled another deep breath, shuddered with the force of it. "Yeah. I do."

His hands tightened on my arms and he skewered me with that intense stare. "Then let's be clear, shall we? I'm going to screw you, Junior. Screw you in absolute silence. Are you sure that's what you want?"

Was I sure? Hell no. And hell yes. And since I was damned either way... "I want *you*."

He bundled me into one arm and leaped into my bedroom, shut the window one-handed. No more words. He flung me onto the bed, climbed on after and caged me with his huge body.

Biting my lip, I forced myself to relax. Whatever happened now had been my decision. I'd have to live with that.

Yesterday Glynn had been a gentle lover. Sweet, thoughtful, taking it slow, at least to start.

Not now. The wild beast had been restrained too long and ripped free. He spread my thighs and crushed my lace-covered sex with an open-mouthed kiss.

I arched into the mattress. Throttled a shriek. Incredible heat flooded me, his breath and mouth and roving tongue. He licked lace, rolling his tongue, slapping and pushing until I was spread flat. Until each heated breath, each stroke of tongue caught all of me, tender inner flesh to sensitive clit. He licked and kissed until I whimpered. Until I dug my fingers into his thick hair and pulled.

Until I clutched his head with my thighs.

With a soft growl of triumph he pulled away. I mewed at the loss, but he'd only freed himself to tear my panties from my hips.

He thrust both hands under my butt, lifted me and really got to work.

He swiped my sex relentlessly, stroking and grinding with his muscular tongue, scouring me with hot licks until I tossed my head with the need to scream.

Aside from brief, soft growls, he made utterly no noise.

It was frightening; it was incredible. Ravished to within an inch of my life in absolute silence. Tiny rasps of breath and slaps of tongue were the only indication of the passion raging on the bed. I swallowed shouts of pleasure, viciously repressed keens of desperation. They echoed inside my head, caroming off my skull and gaining strength until I thought my head would crack with them.

Denied an outlet, the insane response he wrung from me overwhelmed me. In utter silence he drove me up a peak of lunacy— and swept me over.

I came silently, clutching his head. Screaming in my mind, *yes Glynn yes*—but not breathing a word.

Slowly I calmed. A tenderness rolled over me. An amazement. *I want you so much, Glynn. My heart yearns for you.*

But in the silence, none of the words were unleashed.

So there was no need to explain when I opened my eyes and found his, warm and blue as a tropical sea. I hadn't shouted his name at the peak of passion, hadn't murmured tender words after.

I hadn't said anything that revealed my temporarily unguarded heart.

I had no need to explain at all.

He cuddled me after, long enough that when he kissed my forehead, got to his knees, and unzipped his jeans, I had my guard back up. Mostly. Muscles played in his chest and arms as he shucked pants, and—sweet mystery of economics, his erection was a gold card with heavily compounded interest. Kneeling over me, he fit that monster between my thighs.

"Wait! You're not wearing a condom." I kept my voice to a whisper, though I wanted to shout it.

"*Babi.* I carry no diseases." He pressed the glans into my wet opening like a soft kiss. "And you can't get pregnant."

"You've had a vasectomy?"

"No." His straining muscles shouted how torturous he found it not to thrust home. "But Junior, I'm telling you. You cannot get pregnant by me."

"I'm just supposed to take your word for that?"

His eyes clenched shut. When he opened them, they'd gone pale blue, the pupils constricted. "Another no?" He leaped from the bed, swearing viciously in a whisper that made it even more raw. He paced the small room, hissing expletives. Came to a sudden halt, spine arched, fingers digging into the small of his back. "Bollocks. Are you saying stop?"

I didn't want him in pain, but potential pregnancy was a deal breaker. "I'm saying no penetration without protection."

Before I finished the last word, he was on the bed and covering me, so fast he seemed to blur. "There are other things we can do." He buried his mouth in my neck and nuzzled. "Other ways to find satisfaction."

My eyes closed at the feel of his lips, his teeth sharp on my sensitive throat. "I do owe you an orgasm. Two, now."

"Then lie back." He eased his weight onto me, kissing and

nuzzling and sucking the sensitive skin until I arched helplessly into him. His erection pulsed thick between us, hot silk running the length of my belly. I thought about the "other" ways he could find satisfaction. In my mouth, with licks and sucks...or between my breasts, sliding in the slick perspiration of my own arousal, or...

He thrust against my pubic bone. The hard, driving shock banged pleasure through me. Yeah, that worked too.

He drove against me over and over, until his cock snarled in my pubic hair, until each thrust tugged flesh, wrenching against my swelling clitoris. "Glynn, wait. I want..." I clutched his biceps, trying to slow him. I wanted to give him pleasure. To drive him insane while I remained cool and in control.

To maybe open his heart as he'd opened mine.

But he rode my mons with increasing fervor and my protest went unfinished. Control went out the window and my hips beat up against him, seeking more.

His nuzzling became frantic with nips and licks. "I can smell your arousal, *babi*. Hear your pulse quicken." He groaned, soft, deep. "I must taste you."

"You already tasted me." The hot, broad swipes of his tongue, the heat of his breath was driving me up that spiral of insanity again.

"Fully...your essence... I must taste all of you." His arm circled my shoulders, protecting me from the headboard as he slammed harder, each thrust juddering through my entire body. His breath boiled across the skin of my neck as he nuzzled my throat. "Please, *babi*. Let me taste you."

He sounded so desperate, so unusually needy and vulnerable. Like his heart might be unguarded, just for an instant... I raised my chin, tacit assent.

"Ah, Junior. Thank you." He touched tongue to my throbbing pulse, butterfly-light. I stretched into it, enjoying the sweet flutters—

Pain stabbed my throat. Sharp, hot, so intense it was pleasure. I throttled a scream. Jerked out a hoarse rasp as I exploded in a cataclysmic orgasm.

Glynn thrust one last time and joined me. Hot liquid poured onto my belly in muscular spurts. His mouth moved over the pain/pleasure in my throat, almost feasting in sensual abandon. A dark rumble underscored his kisses, pausing when he swallowed and resuming when he opened his mouth to lick my throat.

A dark rumble like a big cat. Like Glynn was purring.

Connections fired in my brain. Unnaturally handsome men and sated friends and Dirk saying vam—

Glynn's head jerked up. His eyes went far away, iced.

He swore, softly. With a final lick to my neck, he sprang from the bed, started jamming himself into his jeans while I was still processing the fact that he was gone, again. I nearly leaped after him, but with that same instantaneous sort of shimmer he was back, wiping my belly with his T-shirt. "Your parents. On their way up."

"Both of them?" I squeaked it.

But now I'd heard it too, the telltale squawk of the two-by-four I'd deliberately weakened to warn me. A second squawk, lighter. Jeez, it *was* both of them. I only got both for the serious stuff. (I was twenty-five, but they delighted in reminding me they'd always be my parents and I'd always be their little girl. Never mind that I half ran the business. I'd never be too old to spank.)

"Shee-it. Glynn, you have to hide!"

"I know. Pretend to be sleeping." Tossing me under the covers, he paused long enough to kiss my forehead and give the room one last scan before snapping off the light.

My door opened just as he disappeared under the bed.

I curled on my side, clamped my eyes shut and thought blank thoughts, putting myself half-under in two seconds. When you deal with parents like mine, you learn to power-nap.

The door cracked. "Junior?" called a soft mezzo. Well, soft as operatic sopranos went. They probably only heard her a block away.

Mom leading meant they were worried instead of angry. Pop first meant a lecture.

I breathed deeply, regularly. Emanated narcoleptic vibes. *Junior's asleep, fast asleep. Nothing's wrong, go back to bed.*

Silence, but I knew better than to relax.

"I don't like this, Gunter. I know I heard the bed squeak."

Oh please. Don't let my mom say what she's thinking.

She didn't. My dad did, at ninety decibels. "She is having *sex?*"

I clamped my eyes harder, honk-shued louder. *Junior's asleep. Go away.*

Then, because the whole neighborhood hadn't heard it, my

113

mother said at a airport levels, "If she's having sex, where is her young man?"

To my utter horror, I heard Pop drop heavily to his knees and felt the bed skirt lift.

My eyes sprang open. Glynn was rolling across the floor. I choked on a gasp. He scrunched into a corner of the room, put a finger to his lips.

I clamped eyes again. My head hurt.

"Nothing under here, Rosalinda." The scrape of my father getting to his feet and the slap of him removing nonexistent dust evened my breathing. Then, thankfully, I heard the shuffle of his feet toward the door.

"I still don't like this, Gunter."

Dammit.

"What would you have me do, Rosalinda?"

"You check the bathroom. I'll search the room."

Which, postage-stamp size that it was, would give her all of two seconds to find Glynn in his corner. Then there'd be worse than hell to pay. Worse than a lecture. There'd be I-told-you-so.

My mother's brisk stride around the room told me she'd started her search. Fearful, I cracked an eye.

Glynn's corner was empty.

I checked out the second corner. Where the hell was he? Hiding my desperation with a big stretch, I rolled onto my other side. Checked out the other two corners.

No Glynn.

"No man in the bathroom, Rosalinda."

"And none in the room, Gunter."

WTF? If Glynn wasn't in the corners, or under the bed, or in the bathroom, he must be in...

"I will check the closet, Gunter."

I jerked up to stop her—just as she snapped open the door.

Their backs were to me. Two heads peered in, one silver, one black as mine. "I do not see anything, Rosalinda."

I lay back down, pronto. If Glynn wasn't in the bathroom or the room or the closet... My gaze landed on the ceiling.

Where he braced like Spiderman.

I blinked. Fecking freak-my-nomics, he was wedged between the ceiling fan and the wall, obvious as a prom day zit. If my folks had been any taller, they'd have hit heads on his belt buckle as they went by.

I beat my lids frantically in SOS. *Get out of here now.*

He took the cue better than the folks had. While they were head-deep in the closet, he jumped down. He landed silently, all strength and agility, and filtered out the door.

I curled up around my frantically beating heart, hoping my parents didn't hear it. Talk about Poe's tell-tale. That was too damned close.

On the bright side, at least they hadn't caught us bumping happy nuggets. That would've been as bad or worse than the kidnapper catching me...

I barely avoided swearing out loud. I'd had Glynn in the perfect position to "convince" him about our plan to trap the kidnapper, and all I'd done was orgasm. Now how would I make that sale?

Entr'acte

Glynn glided through the night shadows, like the dangerous beast that he was—mostly. His shirt was drying and starting to stiffen, an uncomfortable reminder that he was three kinds of fool.

She'd said no. After giving him a taste of her luscious skin, her sweet sex, she'd said stop.

He'd honored that the only way he could, by getting the hell out of there.

He should have stayed away, but then she'd have fallen from the roof window and perhaps died. Although the explosion of desire had nearly killed them both. It had certainly burned him to cinders.

Sex had never been so good, so...sweet. So fresh and new.

He didn't understand why. Normally sex was no big deal. He had it when he needed it, with vampires because humans were fragile and the few he'd slept with in the early days had the annoying tendency to become enthralled.

Junior not only had not become enthralled, she'd stopped him. It confused him. Intrigued him. Made him wonder about things he'd heard but had dismissed as impossible.

It was still impossible. He was leaving when the show closed. Even if he weren't, he was centuries old to her twenty-five years. He might live millennia more. If she took care of herself, Junior might live a single century.

There was absolutely no future for him and her.

Why was he thinking about Junior, anyway? His job was to protect Mishela. Not from rabid fans, as most thought, but to prevent her from being used as a bargaining chip between the two most powerful groups of vampires in the Midwest, the Iowa Alliance and the Chicago Coterie.

His cell rang. He barely suppressed a jump. When had he changed it from vibrate? He was damned lucky the caller hadn't phoned earlier when Junior's parents were in the room and he was on the ceiling.

He dug the phone from his pocket and checked the number. Elias. Not luck, then. The ancient vampire's timing bordered on eerie. "Sir."

"I have new intel, Rhys-Jenkins. The opposition will make an attempt on Meiers Corners within the week."

Glynn snorted. "Nosferatu's already tried to annex the city, undermine the Alliance protector here and invade the city's blood center. We've beaten him back every time. Hasn't he learned anything from his failures?"

"Strictly speaking, it was his lieutenant who failed. Now that my lieutenant has destroyed his, making him look weak, it's forced him to take a more direct hand."

Glynn thought that over. "Should I be worried about Mishela, sir?" Or Junior.

"No more than before. Although things might turn uncomfortable for you."

"How do you mean, sir?"

"There are only indications...ah, but perhaps I'm being overly pessimistic. I will say this. When the right one comes along, all others fade away."

At the Ancient One's words, Junior's taste rang on Glynn's nose and tongue, clear as a bell, individual as a fingerprint. He could even sense her from here, as if she was a part of him.

He shook himself. All vampires could locate a donor by the unique blood-taste/blood-scent. Though the distance varied by vampire age, Elias and his infernal training had made Glynn one of the best. Of course he could sense Junior. He'd tasted her. It was nothing special. And Elias's words meant nothing special.

Glynn gritted his teeth. Sometimes Elias played his Wise Ancient persona to annoying perfection. "I'm sorry, sir. I don't understand."

"Never mind. I really called to let you know I'll be offline for a few days."

"Still working to keep vampire households from going bankrupt, sir?"

"The economy's hitting us all hard. I'm infusing what liquid cash I can, but we're hemorrhaging money." He made a deep sound of disgust. "I'd rather be funding Mishela's musical, but I suppose vampire civilization takes precedence."

"Yes, sir. Good luck, sir."

"Luck. We all need it, but especially... Well, good luck to you as well, Rhys-Jenkins."

Glynn hoped he was imagining the pity he heard in Elias's voice.

Chapter Eight

The sheer terror of nearly getting caught with a man in my room (even at my age—my parents guilted me early and often, and like an inoculation it's become part of me) gave me a brain-popping burst of adrenaline. As my parents clumped out of the room, everything—Dirk's vampires, the howling, the attacks, Julian and Glynn's unnatural handsomeness, and especially Glynn's teeth at my throat—everything came together with a bang.

Vampires were real. And Glynn, who'd sunk fangs into my throat, was one.

I should have been afraid. A vampire had bitten me. I should worry that it would turn me into a minion.

But hadn't it triggered a kickass climax?

No, no. I needed to be frightened. Glynn was an evil, blood-drinking creature of legends. He'd *bitten* me.

Yet when I put fingers to neck, my skin was smooth and whole. No blood, no holes. And he'd wiped his climax off my belly with his own T-shirt.

Kinda tidy for an evil creature.

I gave myself a mental slap. Vampire. Monster. Not Mr. Clean with an overbite. I needed to be scared, to report him to the authorities. Glynn, and all the vampires, like Julian...

Although what about Julian? If he was a vampire, shouldn't Nixie be paler? More zombielike, less sassy? Infinitely less pregnant? Fear started to fade.

I gave myself another slap. Glynn was a predator. Vampire. When he drank ginger ale, he used real Ginger.

But I wasn't named Ginger, wasn't even a redheaded Brit. And compared to abusive boyfriends, axe-murdering husbands, SOs who picked their noses in public... So my boyfriend was a vampire, so what?

I brain-slapped myself so hard I nearly gave myself a concussion.

My *boyfriend?*

Vampires were not suitable for boyfriends. The whole biting thing, though extremely sexy, was dangerous, especially neck bites. The brain's blood highway ran close to the surface. One wrong poke and I'd be headed to the great Sausage Store in the Sky.

So, okay. I needed to stay out of Glynn's bed.

But both he and I were stuck in Meiers Corners for the moment, me in the pit until Mr. Big Broadway Backer hit us with his money wand and sent us to New York, and Glynn guarding Mishela. Business Truth #3 was "If you can't run, gut it out." I'd just have to suck it up and deal.

Although Business Truth #6 said "Keep your eyes open and on the customer." Being stuck here didn't mean I couldn't keep alert. My eyes were definitely staying on Glynn. On his square jaw and miles-broad shoulders and tight butt...

Maybe I should have stuck Business Truth #2 in there. Focus, Junior.

Business Truth #4 was "All's well that ends well". Glynn might be a bloodsucking creature of the night, but so far all he'd done was protect me, comfort me and give me the best orgasms of my life. Things could have been worse (with a nervous finger-wave to Murphy). Glynn stopped when I said no. He was considerate of my parents. If that didn't prove his self-control, nothing did.

So maybe the bed thing could work after all?

No, no. This was what was most dangerous about vampires. I wanted Glynn so badly I was talking myself into believing he was harmless. Which he definitely was not. Even if his bite didn't bleed me out, a couple more might make me a minion or worse.

So no going to bed with Glynn anymore, despite Mishela's and my plan.

Our *plan.* Crap-ay diem, crap the day. Without a bed, how was I going to convince Glynn to go along with our plan? He'd never leave Mishela open for snatching. Not the guy who was Mr. Protector Universe.

But how else were we going to flush such an unusually strong, fast kidnapper from hiding?

Unnaturally strong and fast, almost faster than Glynn...wait. If Glynn was a vampire, didn't that argue the kidnapper was too?

120

Well, phooey. With all these vampires in Meiers Corners, how would we plain humans defend ourselves?

My mind started wandering, the way it does before falling asleep. Glynn could rescue me, but I'd rather rescue myself. Superstrong, superfast vampires were not the usual enemy, but maybe there were special techniques.

Hmm. Maybe ask Mr. Miyagi. Tae kwon do, hapkido and vampido.

Somewhere between wondering if it would feature kicks, punches or stakes, I fell asleep.

Thursday was the VIP opening, but I didn't remember that when I got my carcass up at the usual half-past ohcrap. My brain was freewheeling on vampires and orgasms, and the gray, drizzly day didn't help. I taped my numb toes, drank a full mug of coffee on autopilot and stumbled downstairs, hazier than a fog machine set on stupid.

No sooner had I turned the sign to *geöffnet* than Rocky Hrbek ran in, sans flute, shockingly enough. But she said, "Junior, quick. I need a pound of blood sausage to go."

"But...but you're a vegetarian."

"It's not for me." She wiped hands on her neat slacks, streaking them a little. "It's for my supervisor at CIC. She goes nuts for the stuff. You know I wouldn't ask just for me, and I certainly wouldn't disturb you before your second cup of coffee."

"How did you know...?"

"Your eyes are cracked open a third. They raise a third for each cup."

Either she was more observant than I knew or I seriously had to consider twelve-stepping caffeine. "I think I have some *blutwurst* left." I did, but not much. I dug it out, weighed off a pound and wrapped it. Made automatic customer service small talk. "So how's the new job?"

"Tough. Interesting. Disturbing."

I stopped wrapping. Disturbing, like vampires disturbing?

"They've raised the rates."

"Oh?" I finished wrapping sausage, hospital-corner neat, no mean feat with unboxed product. "On the insurance policies?"

"Yes. But only on Meiers Corners business policies."

"Can they do that?" I snicked off tape, sealed the package.

"Yes and no. It's supposed to be about risk. A car stored in Windowsmash City will cost more than the same car in SafetyRUsburg."

"Meiers Corners is high risk?"

"Well, maybe because it's near Chicago. But that's not all. I overheard a couple billing clerks talking."

I made *tell me more* noises as I rang up her sausage.

"They were ordered to change the premium payment method for all Meiers Corners businesses. Especially the Sparkasse Bank."

"Payment method? Like from check to credit card?" While she dug for money, I snapped out a bag, slid the sausage into it and held it out to her.

"No. Like from monthly to yearly. Due *immediately.*"

I nearly dropped the bag. My folks' insurance was a thousand bucks a month. If we had to fork over a year's worth *right now*, we'd have to do without little extras, like food.

"I'm sure it's just a mistake." Rocky grabbed the bag. "That's what this is for. I'm hoping to sweeten a few dispositions." She paid and ran off.

Mulling over Rocky's info, I wandered back to storage to get more *blutwurst.* Opening a refrigerator, I stared at empty shelves, my stock sadly depleted. Sure was a lot of blood sausage getting sold, to Twyla and Rocky and Julian...

Blood sausage. *Vampires.* It should have scared me, or at least disgusted me. Idiot that I was, I only thought ooh, a new potential market.

I had my second and third cups of coffee, which helped but not enough. The day was so dreary. Even when the rain finally stopped, it was gray, a fog cloud settled on the street. I wandered to the front windows, thought about being depressed but couldn't summon up the will to care.

I wondered if the weather would help us attendance-wise or hurt. Maybe help. If people couldn't garden or have cookouts, why not go to a show?

Store traffic was down, but the few times the bell did tinkle my body tensed, still hoping for Big Dark and Dangerous, I guess. Although he probably wouldn't show up during the day, since vampires supposedly roasted in the sun. On the other hand, it was cloudy. Probably just a legend anyway.

Then I remembered the burning scent in the limo last night and nearly spat coffee. Not a legend. That woke me, finally.

I by-damn didn't want Glynn hurt, so at six fifteen I tugged on my pink satin jacket (puke pink, and my mother bought it for me when I was in eighth grade, which tells you about the style, but it's my only spring outerwear that's waterproofed) and parked self and instruments on the sidewalk. The instant the limo materialized out of the fog, I tossed my sax inside, catching Glynn square in the breadbasket, which stopped him from getting out and frying.

I didn't have the proper privacy to promote the kidnapper-trapping plan, and I really didn't want to discuss last night. So I slid in with a lot of nontalk, empty pleasantries to fill up the space as I sluiced my braid and shucked the damp jacket. Glynn sliced me a look so narrow I nearly bled and Mishela frowned, but I kept it bright and vapid and kept my hands busy pinning the braid in a giant black cinnamon roll on the back of my head until we pulled into the underground lot at six thirty.

Tonight's performance was for patrons, complete with posh reception. Since their VIP-y review of the show determined whether seats were filled for the general opening Friday, which in turn determined word-of-mouth to pack seats through closing, which finally determined if the Broadway backer was impressed enough to infuse our show with mega amounts of lovely cash, I'd have thought they'd be pouring champagne and caviar into the patrons before curtain. But the reception was after, and they were going with beer and cheese balls, the Meiers Corners equivalent, I guess.

The parking lot was already half-full, which was great. Hopefully that'd mean sell-outs for the weekend. Friday and Saturday were especially good for funny shows because precurtain dining and drinking helped make happy crowds.

Helped, but you never knew. No matter how logically you thought it out, how well you planned, success in the arts always contained an element of luck. That's why theater people are so superstitious.

How superstitious? Just think of the "Scottish Play", which to anyone else in the world is *Macbeth*. Think of "break a leg" instead of a simple "good luck".

I know, I know. In this day and age, how can anyone be that

irrational? But there's a perfectly logical explanation.

Now bear with me, please. I need to get this out of my system. Smile and nod and make an uh-huh now and then, and we'll both be happy.

Like weather, performance is a chaotic system. Night after night you put in the same ingredients, but you're never quite sure what'll come out. Exactly the same gestures in exactly the same voice, and one night the audience will laugh and the next it won't.

Oh, we make up reasons. The audience has been drinking and will laugh at running water. Or it's had a fight with its boss/spouse/stupid fuck on the road and is ready to hate everything.

We blame it on the FUBARs of fellow performers. The actor who jumps lines like a drunk Chihuahua. The followspot operator who screws your solo spot by lighting your left ear. The telephone that, after you pick it up, keeps ringing because the sound gal's texting midshow. The singer who drops measures or misses the starting pitch and does the whole solo in the wrong key—don't get me started.

But those are rationalizations. Simply put, audience reaction is out of our control.

Magic seems the only way to control it.

Theater folk are superstitious because Murphy reigns. Not the imp-of-irony Murphy either, but the mean mutha bent on ruin. And yeah, not to sound the wah-wah-wah brass of doom, but this is unfortunately going somewhere.

Why doesn't life have a soundtrack so we know what's coming?

I kept up the blank chatter as I hauled instruments through the underground parking. I chattered nonstop to the room backstage that the orchestra shared with props. There I waved buh-bye, dropped my revolting pink jacket, turned my back and assembled instruments. Glynn hovered and I thought maybe I'd have to parry a couple pointed questions, but Mishela reminded him she had to get ready and they left.

We were plenty early, but I hid in the prop room until I made myself late and had to haul ass to the pit. I threw my butt in my chair barely in time for the initial tuning.

At seven, the doors opened. Seats filled rapidly and I was hit by the familiar opening-night buzz.

A little preshow cramming usually took the edge off. I'd marked my difficult passages with a star in the margins and now rehearsed them to remind myself how they went. No playing once the house opened, so I just fingered them, which was good enough. When I'd run through them all, it was only seven fifteen.

I leaned over. "Hey, Nixie."

"Not more viola jokes."

"But—"

"No. Tell something else. Tell piano jokes or banjo jokes or something."

"Okay. Why was the piano invented?"

She stared at me. "I didn't think you'd actually *know* any."

"Come on. Why were pianos invented?"

Rocky leaned up. "So the pianist would have a place to put his beer."

We fist-bumped. Rocky said, "What's the least-used sentence in the English language?"

"Is that the banjo player's new Ferrari?" we said together and fist-bumped again.

"Enough!" Nixie glared. "These *baka* jokes can't be good for the baby. I'm supposed to play Brahms and shit, not bludgeon it with stupid."

I smirked. My work here was done.

But it was only seven twenty. "Hey Rocky, how did the sausage bribe go?"

She frowned and was about to answer when Takashi said, "What?"

I looked front. He was talking into his headset, low, intense whispers.

Next to Nixie, Julian arched a black brow. Nixie leaned toward him. "What?"

"Dumas," Julian murmured.

"Something's wrong with Dumbass?"

"Dumas is talking. Telling them something's wrong. Shh."

Vampire ears must be damned good. I could barely hear the electronic chirp from Takashi's headset and was itching to know what was going on.

Fortunately, so was Nixie. She wasn't silent more than five

seconds before poking her husband. "What?"

He sighed. "Something about Lana."

Our Glinda, the part-time hooker with the tiny voice. Not Mishela and not one of the Broadway leads, so probably nothing too awful. Maybe Dumas had found Lana on the job, so to speak. I went back to fingering.

Takashi cued the final tuning and we started. I stopped thinking about anything but the music.

Playing a show is like driving. Your mind can wander, but if there's a hiccup, you'd better be ready to compensate. I try to keep my head in the music. Sure, it's not often some asshole swerves into your lane and jams on the brakes, but it does happen and it's worse with amateurs. Aside from the leads, these were unpredictable newbies. And half were kids.

So when Glinda's swing came out empty during a tremolo, I was surprised enough to stop waggling fingers, but only for a second.

Takashi didn't miss a beat; another sign he'd make it. The show must go on may be a truism, but it's also an imperative. The show is your product and you can't sell excuses. Good news is audiences will forgive a lot if you give them a great product eventually. As long as Lana made it onstage soon (even pulling up her little stardust panties from a good rubbing on someone's wand), the audience wouldn't care. They might not even know. I snuck back into my tremolo.

But onstage nothing was happening, which was a bad thing. We hit a vamp, the musical equivalent of fat pants, and Takashi signaled repeat with a whirl of one finger. Still nothing. I kept flicking eyes between Takashi and the stage. The Munchkins couldn't come out without Glinda to call them, so poor Dorothy and Toto were alone in front of a full audience.

Mishela was desperately improvising when suddenly, a whole number ahead of time, the Wicked Witch shot onstage.

Even Takashi hiccupped a beat.

Wicked was thin and bony and wore the usual fluttery black skirt, granny boots and tall, pointy sorting hat.

And a new green Halloween mask. We *all* lost a bar when we saw that. Well, except Lob, the drummer in Nixie's bar band, who could play though drunken bar fights and Granny Butt stripping. He covered us with a totally bonkers improv.

Takashi hissed, "Number ten." We hit the Wicked Witch theme for two bars and trilled ominously before cutting off. Eighteen faces turned up from the pit to see what would happen next.

Wicked stalked toward Dorothy, claw-like hands menacing. Little Munchkins cowered behind scenery. Toto went apeshit, barking and running in circles.

Mishela's nostrils flared and she took a step back, Dorothy pigtails bobbing.

"I'll get you now," Wicked snarled and followed.

The snarl was male. Fuck, this must be the kidnapper. A *he*, almost certainly a vampire, and definitely after Mishela. I flicked eyes for Glynn, but no dark mountains hovered in the wings.

Julian, though, had set his cello on its ribs to leap to the rescue.

Which would *ruin* the show. Julian's one sexy dude and a fine string player, but not primarily a performer. First rule is if the actors on stage can get themselves out of trouble, you let them. Best case, the audience thinks it's part of the show.

Granted, this bit of trouble was more than your usual dropped line or missed cue. But Mishela was a pro. She'd think of something. Both Nixie and I grabbed Julian before he could bollix things up.

He growled low and feral and not human at all.

Fortunately, Toto's barking covered it up. The dog ran at Wicked and lifted his doggy hind leg, no doubt to tell the impostor exactly what he thought.

Wicked jabbed a broom in Toto's belly. The dog gave a pained yip and skittered back.

Mishela scooped up poor Toto. She stepped forward, hit her light and challenged Wicked with, "Are you a good witch or a bad witch?"

Yay, an actual line from the scene. Damn, she was good.

Wicked grabbed for her again, nearly connected. Mishela swayed back, not quite superspeed. Wicked's claws swished air.

A sucked inhale from the audience said they were caught up in the drama, not knowing it was real.

But Wicked took a menacing step forward, and another, and Mishela backed away, which was bad because the proscenium was only so wide. Once she hit the wing, the audience would know it wasn't an act and the show would be ruined.

Of course that was when Julian shook my hand loose. I tried to grab him and his arm blurred avoiding me. He peeled off Nixie more gently, but his tensed muscles screamed his readiness to leap onto stage the instant he was free. I snatched at him. His arm shimmered again and I missed.

Nixie just jumped into his lap. He couldn't shift her quickly without hurting her. He growled again, more human and disgruntled, and slid her gently aside. She clutched and hissed Latin curses the whole way.

Once again, he tensed for the leap.

Steam boiled from the wings, shot between Mishela and Wicked.

Snapped into a very big, very pissed Glynn, glaring at Wicked. I stopped grabbing for Julian. The scene was lost.

There was a collective gasp, from audience, pit and Munchkins. A tiny gap in the action as even pro Dorothy tried to think up a plausible save. Finally she stuttered, "Who are you? And...and are you a good witch or a bad witch?"

Glynn grinned down at Wicked, his teeth very white, his canines just a little long. "I'm Glynn," he said in his musical baritone. "And I'm very, very good." The canines lengthened a little more.

Wicked turned tail and ran.

The audience cheered.

Without a pause, Glynn turned to Mishela. Pulling a wand out of his jacket, he delivered Glinda's lines word for word. Well, except for calling himself Glynn-deh instead, but I don't think the audience picked up on it.

A quick double-blink and Mishela responded, in character, naturally.

They say the Welsh are a musical people. To our utter shock, Glynn completed the scene as Glinda (Glynn-deh), including singing the come out song to the Munchkins. Down an octave, since he was a baritone, but it was note-for-note perfect. And for once, we could play full volume. That boy had *lungs*.

Although the leather jacket clashed a bit with the wand.

But the audience applauded Glynn-deh, and the scene, miraculously, was saved.

At intermission Julian disappeared, literally. One minute he was setting down his cello, the next he was a river of smoke, running onto stage and into the wings.

Nobody noticed. They were all busy scoring their intermission chocolate from Rob, greeting friends or hitting the bathroom.

Nixie caught me watching Julian's mist. She stopped midswab. "I can explain that."

"No need. I figured it out." I loosened my clarinet ligature and slid the reed out. "The fangs are a dead giveaway."

She smiled slowly. "I thought Glynn was looking a little slugged-stupid around you. Congratulations."

"Thanks. It's not like he made it easy. Say, am I going to minionize or...?" I made fangs out of my index and middle fingers, wiggled them from my upper lip.

"Nope. I'll tell you why later."

"A secret?" Sticking my reed in my mouth, I threaded my swab's weight through the bell.

"Big-time. It'd cost their lives. But the need to bite—" Nixie clacked her jaw "—gives them away every time. When the right mate comes along."

"*Mate?*" I sucked in a breath. Along with my reed, which gouged my soft palate. I spat reed into my stand, coughed and gagged. Nixie pounded my back until I'd replaced the spit in my lungs with enough air to choke out, "What do you mean, mate?"

"Oh, not any sort of destiny mate or shit like that. Just, if you're immune to their Illuminati mind-control, you're a potential. Then the smell/taste thing draws them to couple up."

"I'm not...I mean Glynn isn't...I mean..." Actually, I didn't know what I meant beyond *duh-huh?*

"I was going to give you the 4-1-1, but figured with you so duty *über alles*, it'd never go anywhere. Should have known nature'd win over nurture. Hey, since you're linked in, want to come to the party tonight?"

"You mean the reception?"

"I said party, not puke-fest. LLAMA's doing the reception, you know. They don't throw parties, unless vomiting and mass hysteria count as good times."

The VIP reception was being catered by LLAMA? Not good. The Lutheran Ladies Auxiliary Mothers Association was famous for their liver sausage and cheese balls, second only in popularity—well, maybe notoriety was a better word—to their pistachio fluff with stuff floating in it.

I saw a fluff recipe once. It called for gelatin, whipped topping and cottage cheese, but I think LLAMA substituted cellulite from botched liposuctions.

The fluff was why nobody ever said no to a LLAMA reception. Not twice at any rate. Rumor said they found bits of themselves floating in it. LLAMA pistachio fluff broke down people into desserts, a church-lady Soylent Green. Which I didn't believe until I was sixteen and came eyeball to eyeball *with* an eyeball, staring at me out of my dessert. It turned out to be a pickled egg, but the scarring was permanent.

A rustle caught both our attentions. Rob was opening a new bag of chocolate bars, super dark, the kind that are 70% cacao and 30% orgasm.

Nixie's eyes tracked the bag on its way to Katie Reverend, playing reed three. "Julian and I are doing a do at our place. Glynn'll be there. Get him to tell you about his tchotchkes."

"His what?" I reached for the bag. Nixie snagged it midair. I was practically sucked into the vacuum left behind.

"His knickknacks." Nixie dumped the entire bag onto her lap. Carefully put two back. "He won't tell us anything about them and it's driving me crazy."

"Glynn has knickknacks?" I reached again for the bag.

"Nuh-uh. Pads, girlfriend." She started to pass the sadly deflated bag back a row, stopped. Extracted one of the two bars, and finally passed the bag to the harpist, who simply stared at the lone chocolate.

"Knickknacks." My stomach growled. "Glynn travels. They're probably just souvenirs."

"I don't think so." Nixie popped a bar into her mouth, swallowed without chewing. "He arrived with the clothes on his back and exactly one piece of luggage the size of my clarinet case. And first thing he does is ask for a small table. Well, of course I had to look. He'd covered the table and set up these pieces like some weird shrine." She popped another bar. "You're gonna needle him and find out what they mean."

"I am? Why should I do that?"

"I told you. It's driving me cray-Z." She made short work of two more chocolate bars. I think she unwrapped them first, but I wouldn't bet on it.

My stomach growled again. "Yeah, except these knickknacks are apparently special to him. I'm not going to intrude."

"Aren't you curious?"

"Yes, but..." Glynn was the ultimate mystery man. Vampire. Whatever. He'd lectured me about home, and when he made camp, first thing he did was set out some knickknacks? Huge Freudian thing and much more serious than me slipping up about underwear when he was around.

Slipping, underwear. Argh. "It's private. I'm not going to pry."

"Well, I don't usually bribe. But if you grill him, I'll let you use my toothbrush." Cocking a smile, she offered me a couple bars.

"No, I can't. I mustn't." Without my permission, my hand reached for chocolate. At the last minute, I pulled back. "Glynn has a right to his privacy."

She closed her hand.

I swallowed. "But if he happens to spill, I'll tell you."

She opened her hand and I swiped chocolate from her palm.

Entr'acte

After final bows, Glynn escorted Mishela to her dressing room, sticking like glue until the door clicked firmly in his face. Exiled, he paced the hallway, fury eating up the twenty yards as if it were two.

The rogue vampire had cornered her onstage. Corralled her in front of hundreds of witnesses, trapped her between wicked claws and her damned show-must-go-on duty.

His pacing kicked up a notch. Good thing Elias had sent *him* to watch over her. Who else would've known she would go ballistic at a normal rescue? Only inserting himself into the action of the musical, though it'd taken him almost too long to find a wand, let him protect her in a way she'd accept.

Which was damned stupid, but he knew how performing artists were, the torrents of energy and self they poured into their art. He'd expended similar amounts distracting people as a child, but not for the sake of art. And not because he'd wanted to, but when you were four years old, you didn't get a choice. Which was why he made sure he always had one now.

Except when he was boxed in trying to please others, like Mishela.

And Junior.

His pacing stopped abruptly. He sought her out through her blood-taste/scent, as he'd done only half a hundred times since tasting her. She was safe at the VIP reception.

He let her essence wash over him. It calmed him.

He kicked into pacing again, slower now. Almost eight hundred years he'd been a vampire, and in all that time he'd never met anyone like Junior. He wondered what she would say if he told her, "I'm an eight hundred year old monster."

In his most pleasant dreams, she accepted him, even loved him.

But dreams weren't reality. Reality was she had dreams of her own, and he'd respect that. Would back off, even though it killed him. Well, killed him again.

Damn it, which job was harder? Thwarting rogue vampires and making the world safer for humans, or trying to respect Junior's need to remain unentangled?

He'd have to do both. It wouldn't be easy, but damned Elias had trained him for that too.

He consoled himself that it could be worse. Junior could be the one woman he could love. Not likely, though. He hadn't found anyone in eight hundred years. A good thing too. If Emerson was anything to judge by, he'd fall in love so deeply, he'd not be worth a sheep's fart. Which wouldn't help anybody, not Mishela or Emersons or Elias and especially not Junior.

So. Thwart rogue vampires. Respect Junior's need for distance. Protect Mishela from a wily kidnapper. And try not to fall in love.

Closing night couldn't come soon enough.

Chapter Nine

"Well, that was an interesting show, wasn't it, Gunter Marie? I especially liked the cute little doggie who played with all the Munchkins. And the charming jig he did, raising his little hind leg..."

Mrs. Ruffles, Detective Dirk's mom and this year's Lutheran Ladies president, had cornered me midreception for a "quick" chat. Quick in Ruffles-land was as long as they were breathing, so I'd been there a while.

I would have escaped, but she held a cheese ball in her hand. Mrs. Ruffles is accident-prone like a deer in traffic. (In case you haven't had that pleasure, deer don't have the smarts God gave a peanut. When you swerve to avoid them, they swerve *the same way* to hit *you*.) So I stayed real still and hoped she didn't accidentally bomb me.

Although if she'd had the fluff instead of a mere snot-ball, I would've damned the torpedoes and run.

Mrs. Ruffles kept talking. I kept nodding. Oh for a shield, but I'd left instruments and jacket in the prop room. Smile and nod, smile and nod. If I replaced myself with a Junior-sized bobblehead, would she notice?

Suddenly, Mrs. Ruffles broke off. Wow. I'm pretty sure that's one sign of the apocalypse, after gas prices coming down.

All around me, people turned. Women smiled. Men looked jealous. I turned.

Glynn had glided into the room.

I waved desperately, but he ignored me. The fucker. He was so dead when I cornered him, if being a vampire didn't mean that already.

"Oh look, Gunter Marie. There is the nice young man who played the pretty witch. Well, not pretty since he is a boy, but handsome. He has such a nice voice, doesn't he?" She stared at him and waved too.

I did not get to be MC Sausage Executive of the Year by being slow to capitalize on an opportunity. While Mrs. Ruffles's attention was snared by Glynn, I escaped.

"Such a nice voice, right, Gunter Marie? Gunter Marie?" Without even looking she grabbed me. By the arm.

With the cheese ball hand.

LLAMA balls are a little runny. Nixie says they're made of pus and mayonnaise. Warmed from Mrs. Ruffles's hand, it certainly felt like bodily fluids running viscously (and viciously) down my bare arm. My stomach lurched, trying to escape out my mouth. My brain would have followed if it could have fit.

I whimpered.

Glynn was instantly at my side, his face dark with anger and worry. I'd have been gratified if I weren't so nauseated.

Mrs. Ruffles blinked and actually stopped talking again.

Cheese ball remains dripped steadily down my arm. My expression was probably set on creamed upchuck because Glynn took one look at me and focused his piercing stare on her. He said, "You have work to do."

Her mouth opened. She echoed, "I have work to do."

And then, because she was a Ruffles, she added brightly, "Setting out more cheese balls."

"Cleaning up cheese balls."

"Cleaning up cheese balls." She paused. "And then setting up more?"

Glynn clamped eyes momentarily, as if he was gathering strength. Maybe he was. Controlling a Ruffles brain was probably like lassoing wild stampeding horses. Or herding cats.

His eyes opened and he hit her with a stare so hypnotic *I* almost went under. "You will clean up cheese balls. You will set out sausage from the Wurstspeicher Haus. You will quietly excuse yourself to stand in a corner and contemplate higher things. You will—"

"Glynn! There you are." Emerald, ruby and amethyst paisley beelined in our direction, sans headset. "I've been looking all over for you."

"Correction." Glynn spoke quickly. "You will latch onto Director Dumas and tell him everything you've ever wanted to talk about." Glynn grabbed my arm and beat a hasty retreat.

Ooh, talk about capitalizing on opportunity. Glynn made me look like a noob.

Mrs. Ruffles turned a bright face toward Dumas. He zigged to catch Glynn. Mrs. Ruffles zigged in his direction. Glynn zagged to avoid him, dragging me.

Dumas zagged. Mrs. Ruffles zagged and broke into a trot. Dumas sped up, but he was only a world-class Broadway director. Mrs. Ruffles was a Lutheran Lady.

She stopped, pointed at two Ladies manning the drinks and desserts tables. Two-fingered, she made you/follow/attack motions like a LLAMarine.

The Ladies picked up cheese balls and moved out. Dumas, his attention on Mrs. Ruffles, never saw them coming.

I turned my head away from the carnage at the last minute. But remembering Method acting, I mentally cheered the Ladies on.

"That was close." Glynn drew me over to the buffet, where he snared a silk napkin, dipped it into a glass of beer, and gently wiped my arm.

I stared at his long fingers, cleaning me of cheese snot. "That's an expensive baby wipe."

"Cloth washes." He eyed the napkin in his hand. Streaks of eye-scorching orange, possibly radioactive, smeared its perfection. Bits of fiber bristled as if the cheese stuff was eating through the threads. "Actually, this may need to be destroyed." He smiled slightly.

He had the most edible smile. The most kissable lips. The most tongue-able—I cleared my throat and looked away. "Nice save, by the way. You can really sing."

"The pit helped. I don't think the audience knew the Wicked Witch and I weren't original actors." He dipped more beer, wiped again.

"Sometimes the roles are played by men, so it wasn't so far-fetched." I relaxed as his slow, gentle strokes cleaned me. Warmed me. "You got the lines perfect."

"I'd heard it often enough. The show must go on, right?"

When my gaze flew up in surprise, he smiled again, well-shaped lips and strong white teeth combining into an expression so gorgeous my eyes drooled.

I blinked it away. "Are you secretly a theater person?"

"I'm secretly a lot of things."

I waited for him to expand on that, but he only kept rubbing my arm in that same sensual way, smiling that same smokin' smile. I wondered what that smile would look like rising from between my...the warmth developed an uncomfortable edge. "Um, well, at least now we know the baddie isn't Scarecrow. Not enough time to strip off the Witch costume and make his entrance."

One black brow slashed up. "No, Jon Wise isn't the idiot who took Lana's costume, but he might be the brains and the Witch a confederate." He stopped rubbing. "That actually makes more sense than that cock-up of a witch running things. He didn't even know the lines." Glynn's tone turned distinctly offended, and I realized that, among other things, he was a true performer.

Bodyguard, singer, tracker, performer. What else? *Lover,* my breasts supplied. *Expert lover,* added my pussy with a purr.

Hellooo. My brain waved for attention. *Off-topic here. Mystery-man to discover.*

I'd like to discover his mysteries, my mouth said.

Oh yeah, my sex chimed in. *Muscular, dark mysteries, thrusting mysteries, deep hard myst—*

"Would you guys shut up?"

"I'm sorry?" Glynn said.

"Not you."

"Hey, there you are. You guys ready to dip out?" Nixie breezed up, Julian in tow. Five-nuthin' towing six-plus—like a toddler hauling a Great Dane. It was even more stunning because you knew the Dane was letting the child walk all over him out of love.

A far door swung open. LLAMA VP Mrs. Gruen traipsed from the kitchen with a long silver pan. Cheese balls came on plates so... *Noooo.* "Beyond ready. Just let me collect my instruments."

"Already done. Twyla took your stuff back with mine to the household."

"Our townhouses," Julian clarified pointedly. "They took the instruments to the townhouses."

Nixie bumped him playfully with her hip. "Nah, Junior caught the 4-1-1 herself."

Glynn's brows rose. "Does she ever speak English?"

Julian kissed the top of Nixie's curly head. "Not any that you or I would recognize. One of the many things that keeps our marriage fresh."

Mrs. Gruen catered in another pan. To my horror, she started shoveling up fluffy, bilious green goop. "Yeah, um, could we get going?"

My voice squeaked.

"There's danger?" Glynn scanned the room, only his slightly widened stance and big hands at the ready telling his immediate response to the perceived threat. Damn, he was good. He followed my gaze. "Pistachio fluff, a menace?"

"Did you say fluff?" Nixie shuddered, and Julian too, but they were MC natives. Well, in Julian's case, naturalized. "You don't want to be here if LLAMA starts serving the goo. It's haunted alien slime, slurping everything in its path." She latched on to Glynn's leather sleeve and tried to make for the door.

Glynn stood like a rock. "Come now. Fluff is a staple at every church potluck west of Greenwich. How can it be dangerous?"

"This is LLAMA we're talking about." I grabbed his other sleeve. "Remember the cheese ball you wiped off my arm?"

Glynn's wrinkled nose said he did.

"That's just an appetizer for the fluff. You want to be here when it goes looking for the main course?" I pulled leather, urging him into motion.

This time, he came.

I mean *went along*. Came, as in he accompanied us.

Julian and Nixie owned a pair of four-family townhouses on Eighth and Walnut. The buildings faced each other, two letter Is typed on the dotted line of Walnut. A driveway used to separate them, but it had been seeded over and was now a shared front yard. The mouth of the driveway was still there, leading to underground parking. Julian had apparently remodeled extensively underground, which made a whole lot more sense now that I knew he was Sun-shy the Vampy Guy.

The rain had mostly cleared, so we walked. No masked men attacked us, probably because Julian and Glynn were in extra-growly mode. Though neither were openly fanged up. I think Glynn wasn't because he didn't know I knew about v-guys. Julian wasn't because his neighbors were all nose.

The party was in full outdoor swing, a couple dozen people sharing the small grassy space with a quarterbarrel, a table of munchies and a game of rubber horseshoes. Everyone was having a great time, drinking and laughing.

Except for Julian's "assistants", hot Greek Nikos and Rebecca of Sunnybrook Farm. Nikos was Twyla Tafel's squeeze. I didn't know Rebecca except by sight. She was the kind of woman who wrestled bulls for fun. She wore bib overalls with no shirt and I kept expecting to see hay in her hair. Rebecca was actually her name, but probably not the Sunnybrook Farm part.

They stood like grim-faced bookends to the party, which made sense if they were really Julian's guards, alert for vampire rogues.

Twyla was waiting for me with my pink satin jacket. Lips compressed, she handed it over. "*Where* did you get this?"

"Don't dis the jacket," Mishela said before I could reply. "I'd love it for my costume closet. It'd go great with my poodle skirt."

"Your skirt's the color of cherry vomit?" Twyla's moue of distaste underscored her words. "The style makes Frankenstein's bolts look chic."

"Mom gave it to me." I shrugged the satin on. "Mothers prefer comfort to style."

Twyla raised a fine brow. "Not all mothers are fashion-blind."

"The Lutheran Ladies are."

"I thought your mother was Italian."

"She's a born-again German."

"Huh. Well, if you ever want to give it a facelift, I'll bring the gasoline. Your instruments are inside." She pointed at a townhouse, then exchanged a brief, inexplicable thumbs-up with Nixie, hooked arms with Mishela and wandered off.

Glynn, standing beside me, watched them go.

I frowned at him. "Why aren't you doing the Mishela-hovercraft thing?"

"I'm off duty."

"Go party then." Plastic glasses of beer sat in neat rows on a nearby table. I snagged one. He was still there. "You don't have to hang around for me. I know these people. I'll be fine. Go on."

He nodded. "That would be best."

"Okay. See you later." I sipped beer, pretended to ignore him.

He didn't move. "Do you think tonight's incident will affect attendance?"

I took another sip, but it didn't make Glynn's behavior any clearer to me. "It's theater. Murphy's the lord of chaos. I'm not making bets either way." I took another sip. I was a bit warm—maybe the jacket, maybe the May evening turning muggy. Certainly not Glynn's blue gaze running over my skin like his big, hot hands... I cleared my throat. "Well."

"Well." An awkward silence. Glynn crossed arms. "You'll be all right then?"

"I said I would." My neck prickled with perspiration. Damn hot tonight, not anything to do with Glynn's intense body. I drank more beer.

"I'll just be going then." He turned reluctantly.

I released a pent-up breath.

Behind me a horseshoe whipped through the air, headed straight at me. I swore. At the sound Glynn spun back, eyes red, canines flashing.

I barely registered the shock of seeing Glynn in half-vampire mode before the horseshoe hit...the cup in my hand. Beer kicked up and out, a flying arc of night-silvered amber—and splashed full force on his chest.

His black tee absorbed the liquid with barely a change in color, but I could tell it soaked him from the annoyed *tchah* he made and the way he plucked the shirt from his skin. His fangs abruptly retracted, his eyes cooled to an irritated blue.

"Sorry, guys." Nixie stood across from the horseshoe stake, a second U in her hand. "Guess I threw it a little hard."

Her smile looked more smug than sorry.

Glynn blew a disgusted breath, shucked his leather jacket. "It's all right."

And then in front of me and everyone, he stripped the wet tee over his head and tossed it at the nearest townhouse door.

All partying screeched to a halt. My jaw hit grass and bounced. Sure, I'd seen him shirtless, but hunched over in a cramped bedroom.

Straight on in the bright night...yowsa. Glynn's shoulders were crowned with bowling-ball deltoids, notched with tongueable grooves. His pectorals, swelling big and round from iron-bar collarbones, screamed "pet me". His torso, exposed for the world to drool over, was r-r-ripped.

And big. His chest was wide as a freeway, his pecs twin semis, his abs fast, sexy coupes jockeying for position. His waist was a two-lane country road I'd just love to travel by tongue. The dent of navel and feathering of black hair were two definite tourist stops on my licky way.

Did I say it was a muggy night? I meant steaming. I meant flaming...suddenly way too hot, I grabbed blindly for another beer. Drank too quickly and started choking.

All that chest was instantly in my face, undulating centimeters from my mouth, nipples ruby bull's-eyes...as Glynn slapped my back. Only being helpful. I tried to regain control by sucking in air, got a lungful of hot male and started choking on slobber instead.

He pulled me close. Rubbed my spine as I hacked up lung. "Breathe, *babi*." The heat of his breath on my ear was searing. The heat of his naked skin was incinerating.

"Drink," I rasped.

He gently extracted the beer I was clutching and offered it to me. I managed a sip. That cleared things so I could breathe. He held the cup as I sipped until I nodded that I could hold it on my own.

He handed me my cup and stepped away.

It was like Google maps. Nipples zoomed out to chest, abs, jeans fitting an impressive package... Power and grace sculpted in muscle and bone, the entirety of his male perfection filled my sight.

Desire slugged me, stole my breath like a cold Lake Michigan wave walloping shoreline. My breasts tightened, my nipples peaked.

My fingers ached to grab all that muscle. I clenched my plastic cup as a substitute and knocked back beer. Corners people drink beer in moderation with meals, but sometimes we drink just to get drunk. I opened my throat and poured the whole thing down, trying to douse the fire of lust in my belly.

Yeah, alcohol to douse flames. As a business major, chemistry wasn't my strong suit.

The beer hit my stomach. A fantasy hit my brain. A muscular torso over me, rippling with strength as it drove long strokes of male hips. My legs pulled high over bowling-ball shoulders, ripped power framed by my thighs. Lust slammed me full in the groin. Exploded, a rush of fire through my veins, searing me until I could barely breathe. Until I could barely move.

Until I was scared shitless.

Was I my mother's daughter after all? Had this bonfire of lust been smoldering all along? Was I a late bloomer and now getting wet in my bloomers?

Damn, underwear again.

I tossed my empty onto the table. "I need to go."

"So soon?" Glynn's tone was almost wistful—until the breeze shifted and his nostrils flared. His fingers clenched and his eyes turned a distinct violet. "Right. I'll go change to take you home. Wait here."

"My instruments are inside. I'll come along." I grabbed his forearm. Mistake, because the heat of his skin, the feel of lean and powerful tendons under my fingers... I released him and cleared my throat. "I mean I'll follow."

He nodded and took off for the farthest door. I started after him, got an eyeful of tight ass and clamped my lids shut. Couldn't see to walk so I slit them, but I kept my gaze firmly on my toes.

Which meant when he stopped inside the townhouse, I plowed into his back. My hands slapped onto flared lats, steel cables winding under his skin. My fingers snaked along their tempting length before he stepped away. I hissed an embarrassed breath.

He was kind enough to pretend not to notice I'd been feeling him up like a melon. "They're not here."

"What's not...oh." Once I got my head out of my vagina, I noticed a front hallway of terra cotta tile. My instruments were nowhere to be seen. "We'll have to ask Twyla. After you put on a shirt." I waved in the general direction of his naked, ripped, luscious...everything. I didn't look directly, his chest entirely too much like a solar eclipse in both its temptations and its dangers. I still wanted to run my palms over those hard planes and blind myself licking.

His mouth quirked. "I have a better idea. Come with me."

"What?" I was startled enough to look him in his twinkling sapphire eyes. "Come with you to your room? Are you nuts?" Come, nuts...*oh* fuck *get your mind out of his pants, Junior.*

"A bit insane, perhaps. But I think I know where your instruments are." He glided off, leaving me to race after him through a cozy den. "Based on the snickering from Nixie and Twyla."

"Snickering...oh no. They didn't." My two good friends had not just ambushed me with misplaced attempts at matchmaking.

"I suspect they did." He snared my hand and started downstairs.

Down, to his *bedroom.* Images of him and me, in his room, on his *bed*, rolling and surging and crashing... I grabbed the railing, dug in my heels. "Wait. I can't get...can't do...I *can't.*"

I tried to tell him all the things I couldn't do. I couldn't smell him and not want to bury my nose between his pecs. I couldn't see his powerful muscles without wanting to touch, to pet, to caress. I couldn't be near his naked skin without wanting to lick, to suck, to sink to my knees and...all that came out was an *uhhh* and another, "I can't." Apparently between the beer and raging lust, I was lucky to be using language at all.

"*Babi.*" Glynn took my face between his hands. "I know how you feel about sex. About commitment. I know you have duty and dreams and I understand why you wish to remain unattached. You're safe with me."

"How do you...then what...last night...?" Yup, there went the language.

"Last night was desperation. I am desperate for you tonight as well, but we'll only be downstairs for a few minutes. Junior. You're funny and caring and brave to keep duty first while you attempt your dreams. I respect that. You're safe with me," he repeated. "Hold my hand now. The stairs are steep."

Of all that, the word that stood out was *desperate.* Glynn was desperate for me? The thought of a male wanting me badly, any male but especially one so incredibly talented and attractive as Glynn...there were no words for it. Wouldn't have been even if my brain hadn't unevolved to one step above amoeba.

Midway along the dimly lit basement hallway, Glynn opened a door, paused before flicking on the lights. The gesture made me think he didn't use them, had only turned them on for me. Maybe vampires could see in the dark or had some form of sonar.

There sure was a lot I didn't know about v-guys. I'd have to find out if I was going to spend more time with Glynn...which I *wasn't.*

I took a step back, meaning to wait in the hall, but my gaze smacked on His Bed with a capital Hhhhggg. King-size, five pillows across, with a royal purple comforter the exact shade of his eyes heated with arousal.

Not a bed but a cruise ship for sex.

I remembered his intense lovemaking on my small twin mattress, thought of how much more active he could get on this battleship of a bed...and nearly snapped my neck looking away.

A small, candlelit table sat in the opposite corner.

Even without Nixie's curiosity to prime me, I'd have known that here was something important. Precious, and not referring to Gollum-like Steve. Glynn's mysterious little altar banked my lust. What knickknacks would be on this special table? Sex trophies? Or keepsakes of a lost love?

I floated closer, coming fully into the room. A heavy cloth covered the table, woven brocade. Red, but an old red, like it had been dyed before the colonies were discovered. Not faded from years of sun but whitened with the simple passage of time.

Three tchotchkes sat on the cloth, arranged in an equal-sided triangle. Each was illuminated by a tealight set in front like an offering. One extra tealight was near the center.

A small dragon roared left bottom. Red-painted pewter, it stood fighting-ready, front paw raised. I seemed to remember the dragon was a symbol of Wales.

A white clay pipe was bottom right. Unglazed, long-stemmed, a smell of cavendish indicated it was sometimes used.

And what was the tchotchke at the top of the triangle, clearly the most important by its placement?

A simple clay round with a wooden handle.

I leaned closer, practically put my face down by it, but I finally had to pick it up to tell what it was. Glynn's sharp intake of breath didn't stop me from turning it over to see—a cookie stamp.

What would a warrior-prince vampire be doing with a homey cookie stamp? I cast him an inquiring glance.

Arms crossed, he braced against the wall farthest from the table. Even without the sucked breath, I knew he wasn't happy, not in that defensive stance.

Still, I needed to know. "What is this?"

"Nothing." His tone was flat, not with indifference but from a wealth of suppressed feeling. He pushed away from the wall, strode over and took the stamp from me. With a dark, slashing look, he placed it carefully at the exact top of the undrawn triangle.

Then he turned his back to stride the two steps to the dresser. The conversation was emphatically over.

I'd have thought it a nonverbal slap if I hadn't seen the pain in his eyes.

He pulled a drawer open and rooted for clothes. Muscles rippled across his broad back, rekindling my lust instantly.

Enigmatic little knickknacks, cryptic words, spines going up like a porcupine—and I still wanted to pole vault into his body. Dammit.

I forced my eyes away and caught sight of my sax case, tucked next to the bed. Yup, Nixie and Twyla were indeed channeling Yente the Matchmaker-Matchmaker. Now that I knew where to look, I saw my flute in another corner, my clarinet in a third. Just in case I, you know, needed an excuse to stay a little longer. Matchmaking friends are bad. Clever matchmaking friends are worse. Like STDs, lots of fun but a pain in the end.

As I started gathering instruments, Glynn stretched a T-shirt over his head. I waved a mental bye-bye to his lovely torso, but it was for the best. Just because I loved the taste of sausage didn't mean it was good for me. The same applied to sex. And Glynn's sausage was certainly large and meaty... I bonked the flute case against my forehead.

"*Babi*, are you all right?"

He looked at me over his shoulder. It twisted all sorts of muscles into relief.

I only nodded. And whimpered.

He eyed me suspiciously but went back to changing.

I was going for my sax when I heard heavy cloth drop. Like brocade tablecloth slipping, sending knickknacks crashing. My head snapped around.

Not tablecloth but damp jeans lay on the floor. Beyond were the tight, dusky globes of naked, muscular buttocks.

Glynn was changing pants. His bare behind was actually more gorgeous than his naked torso. So gorgeous I *needed* a lick. And a nibble, a bite... I dropped my instrument cases, a small desperate sound rising from my throat.

He spun with a growl that turned distinctly husky when he saw my face.

My attention was riveted on his hips. A huge shaft jutted boldly, so proudly erect. The effect was like a magnet, pulling me to stand before him.

We stared at each other. Honor warred with desire in his eyes, gridlocked him long enough for me to sink to my knees and take his smooth cock into my mouth.

I took a deep, deep draw.

He hissed. His belly jerked as if he were having a hard time breathing. His fingers combed into my bound hair, pulsed like he wanted to push me away.

He groaned and tugged me closer, slotting me more fully onto him.

I drew my tongue along his length, tickled the knot under the eye with the tip of my tongue.

He made a throttled sound and thrust into my mouth. He jerked back, then thrust again, as if he couldn't help himself, as if he found me so arousing he was helpless to stop.

I gripped the muscles of his thighs and urged him faster, deeper. A rumble started, a dark purr like thunder. It rolled from his chest as he started riding my mouth with quick, sharp thrusts.

The texture of smooth shaft and hot glans was so delightful I swirled my tongue along him as he thrust. He groaned louder, his cock swelling almost out of my mouth. His strokes went so deep the head nudged my throat. I opened it and took him for as long as I could before choking.

At my first *ack*, he withdrew abruptly, drawing me to my feet with fingers still woven in my bound hair. "Junior, *babi*, I'm so sorry..."

I put a finger up to his lips. "Don't." I'd loved the feel of him, the taste of him, and it must have shown on my face because he bent and demolished me with a kiss.

He was a big male, his mouth twice the size of mine, and when he kissed me it felt like he was devouring me. Yet his hands cupped my head, thumbs feathering lightly over my cheeks, a loving, astonishing counterpoint to the rampaging male tongue in my mouth.

I lifted onto my toes and kissed him back. My head swirled with moonlit meadows. With rolling, sweaty bodies, making love on a hillside dancing with fireflies and stars. Need pounded through my veins for more of him, all of him.

He released me to peel off my jacket. As it dropped to the floor, he slid his hands under the hem of my tee and rolled it up my ribs, over my bra. His fingers speared under the bra to tweak my already stiff nipples.

I gasped into his mouth, arching for more. He cupped and

kneaded, tweaked and pinched until I was whimpering. Until I was burning.

Until, as I writhed under his skillful fingers, my duty and dreams seemed pitiful things, burned to ashes by lust.

Writhing in Glynn's arms, I knew I'd underestimated lust. It wasn't a simple temptation pulling in one direction, and I just had to resist. It pushed *and* pulled.

Lust pushed me up the slope of quickening tension, of growing need. Urged me to crown the sweet crest, to finish, heart pounding, sweaty, collapsing in sated bliss.

Lust also pulled with the need to connect. To be part of something bigger, to be loved.

My duties and dreams urged me to leave now. But maybe a better word for lust was passion, because the push-pull to stay was equally as powerful.

And there I was, caught in a moment of crystalline indecision.

Glynn raised his head. He stared down at me, eyes clouded with passion, fang tips glinting between his lips, erection pulsing against my abdomen like the dark throb of a coming thunderstorm.

But he sensed...something. Searched my eyes.

Slowly, he released me.

I couldn't have moved for the world. He did it. He let me go, or I would have been on that bed with my legs open, the push-pull still warring at my soul as I met him thrust for thrust.

It was my only opportunity and I took it. I yanked down shirt and bra, not even having the capacity to apologize. I snagged instruments, ran out the door and thundered up the basement stairs.

Gratefully, I escaped. Gratefully, keening over my loss.

Chapter Ten

Stumbling up the stairs, I tried to catch my breath. But I wasn't going to get any calmer, not with the implications of that internal war flooding me, burning me. I ran to the front hallway and threw open the door to see...nothing.

No people, no beer. Horseshoes lay abandoned on the glistening grass. The party had moved inside the other townhouse because it was pouring rain.

That thunder hadn't simply been my heart or Glynn's purr. It had been real.

Lucking fovely. Walking home in the rain, the overflowing flush to an already-toileted day. I took a deep breath, pushed it out to control my heart rate. Sooner started sooner finished. Thank goodness I had my waterproof—

That's when I remembered my pink jacket.

I spat a ripe curse. The jacket that Glynn had peeled off and dropped to the floor just before his fingers tweaked my already stiff nipples. I swore again. Stupid, leaving my jacket in Glynn's room.

But stupider, what I'd almost let happen. What I still *wanted* to happen. Fuck me, I was a size two dress and a size eight ass hat. The blistering *need* hammered at my preconceptions, chipped at the edges of my very self.

This wasn't just sex.

I *so* did not want to process. Dealing with my physical response to a man—vampire—I barely knew, facing the fact that I'd nearly succumbed to passion despite my mother's history, admitting that I'd almost killed my dreams by tying myself down emotionally and physically...no. It was too big.

Thank goodness for Business Truth #2, "Focus" etc. I'd have to deal with this eventually just to keep sane, but that time was not now. Now I had to get my jacket and escape.

Probably brighter to just escape. But with the pouring rain, I needed a shield or I'd catch a bug, bad because playing a wind instrument with only half a lung sucks green weenies.

So I left my cases and bulled back downstairs.

Several yards away, I saw Glynn's door was open. No noise came from the room. Maybe he was gone. Maybe he'd gone off somewhere to sulk, or had joined the party in the other townhouse. Maybe I was safe.

I peeked in—and froze.

He stood in the middle of the room, braced, muscles pumped huge, fangs fully extended. But that wasn't what shocked me. He was totally naked, but it wasn't that either. He fisted his erection, talons woven like a wreath of thorns around his immense cock, but it wasn't even that.

No, what shocked me was that his nose was buried in my pink jacket and sheer joy shone on his face.

He threw back his head and climaxed with a roar, red light flaring from his slit eyes, fully vampire and nothing less than fully scary.

I wasn't scared—I was stunned. He was jacking off, and apparently having a whopping great time of it, to my scent.

He turned his head, saw me and gave an involuntary groan. Actually started coming again.

The sight of Glynn, powerful, gorgeous vampire, so clearly turned on by *me*, knifed through my gut and groin and heart. *Glynn was aroused by me.* My whole body sang at the thought.

Maybe, just maybe, my mother had made the right decision. Maybe world-shaking, once-in-a-lifetime pleasure was enough to offset a whole lifetime of payment.

Glynn and I stared at each other, each trapped by our own impossible situations, our own unthinkable thoughts. I only realized I hadn't a clue to his when we spoke together.

I croaked, "Do you have a condom?" Just as he stuttered, "Junior. I can explain about the teeth."

Talk about cross-purposes.

"Condom?" He inhaled as if to say something else but he only added, "About my teeth—"

"I know you're a vampire, Glynn."

His response was a stare. "You can't know that."

"Julian and Nikos are vampires too."

149

"Then you don't understand. You'd be more frightened."

"Would be, but Nixie and Twyla are deliriously happy. Ergo vampires aren't the evil creatures that legend says they are."

"We bite." He shook his dark head. "I'll bite you. Doesn't that scare you?"

"It didn't kill me before. Would it kill me now?"

"Now, I won't just bite your neck." He tossed the pink jacket. "If I don't have to hide what I'm doing, I'll bite you *everywhere*." The implications flared in his eyes. His fangs lengthened, straining for me, wickedly sharp-looking. His cock filled and strained for me too, desire unbridled.

"Um...everywhere, everywhere?" Sensitive breast flesh? Soft inner arms...or inner thighs...or places even more orgasmic than last night's bite?

Sweet Carnegie on a pogo stick, the sex would be *even better*. I nearly went to my knees with the thought.

Now I had a choice.

The best sex of my life. A union so potent it would blow my mind.

And with it, the threat of life-changing complications, like the shackles of love.

Glynn made no move, no indication beyond his long, elegant fangs and straining erection. Oh, heavens, just looking at them made me hurt.

I had a choice, but what a Murphy's fuckup of a choice. Duty versus need in perfect balance, like Buridan's ass.

Dammit, I wasn't an ass; I was human. And more importantly, a businesswoman. The decision was important—but just as important was *making* it. And what I did after...but that could wait.

I threw away my reservations and ran to him.

He caught me, swept me up and spun with me. My stomach swooped and I laughed.

He leaped onto the bed and laid me on the mattress, his eyes violet fire.

My laughter died, replaced with breathless anticipation.

He straddled me and raised my shirt to expose my bra. His eyes shaded toward red as he scooped my breasts out like ice cream.

He stared, not saying a word.

I squirmed, heat rising on my cheeks. Didn't he like what he saw?

"Ah, *babi.* Such beauty." Approval rumbled deep in his throat, underscoring his words. With a sharp tug, he tore my shirt and bra completely off, tossed them. He fell to his hands over me, his gaze riveted on my breasts.

My nipples tightened to puckered cherries. I licked my lips in anticipation as he opened his mouth wide. His bared fangs were sharp, long and elegant. He leaned down ever so slowly—and sank the tips into my breast.

Pure, sweet fire sang through me. I arched with a silent scream. Lightning streaked from breast to toe, hitting my clit in between, drenching my vulva in liquid heat.

He licked the hot beads of blood. A deep purr rumbled again my ribs.

My fingers found his hair and I blindly petted, urging him to do the same, again, more.

His dark rumble paused as he swallowed. Kissing and licking up the curve, circling round and round to the peak, his purr roughened to almost a growl. He sucked my nipple into his mouth, drawing hard on it.

I squirmed against the intense suction. My writhing pressed his fangs into my skin, nicking the soft flesh. A shudder rippled through me, and I writhed harder.

He slid down beside me and lay a heavy leg over mine, anchoring me in place while he suckled. I twisted but couldn't dislodge him. So when he licked my breast until it bobbed and sucked my nipple until it stood tight, I could only enjoy.

He licked across to the other breast, eyes closed in pleasure. His mouth left a hot, wet trail on my skin.

I trembled under the weight of his leg, impatient. He only smiled, his fangs flashing...before he sank them in again.

I shrieked. Sensation tore from breast to gut and exploded in my groin, a small but potent orgasm. My blood roared in my ears. The snap and zip of my pants as he opened them was muffled by *whoosh-whoosh.*

But the heat of his hand on my mons was very clear. My clit felt swollen and straining and I was sure I'd die before he touched it.

His fingers slid down. Slowly he split my labia, gently rasping along the hood of my clit. He began thrusting along the pink nose, stroking, burnishing until my lust burned, until I knew dying was the least of my concerns.

And still his heavy leg restrained me. I bumped my hips, trying to open, trying to give him full access. I shoved and flexed, twisted and strained, but nothing budged him.

Finally, I grabbed his ears, dug my nails in and shoved.

He chuckled, a dark amusement underscored by purr. Giving my breast a final lick, he rose to his knees over me. His eyes were blood red, his fangs sharp and white. His cock lined the gap of his muscular thighs, longer than I had ever seen it. It should have scared me. *He* should have scared me.

He lifted a packet from the bedside table.

It was a condom.

"*Babi.* I can't get you pregnant. But since you're worried..."

In that moment I loved him.

"I only have the one..."

I wiggled out of pants and panties. His lips kept moving but no words came.

I parted eagerly, wanting him inside.

He tossed my clothes and thrust himself between my naked thighs. Not his hips, but his chest, in perfect position to sink his fangs into my belly.

He pierced my skin lightly, igniting a firestorm of pleasure deep in my pelvis. I moaned. He palmed my mound, fingers splaying through curls, and used the heel of his hand violently on me until another, bigger climax loomed. He opened wide to bite me again.

His fangs pressed into my mons.

I howled. Grabbed him with my thighs, an involuntary cinching at my sudden orgasm. My legs tightened, nearly crushed him when he began lapping frantically and the climax extended. On and on I convulsed, his purr filling my ears.

His hand was still threaded in my pubic hair and now he tugged on it, pulling me open, exposing my innermost flesh to his flaming tongue. Hot licks accosted my clit directly, pleasure so intense it was near pain. If he didn't back off soon—

He bit me again, piercing my swollen labia. Another climax, driven into my softest flesh, exploded through hips and chest and lungs and emerged as a scream.

As I lay, hoarse and shuddering from that whole-body *pow,* he raised himself over me. A foil rip and a latex roll and he was ready. He tossed my leg over his shoulder, slotted his sheathed cock between my slick lips and drove himself deep with a single thrust.

All screamed out, I merely whimpered.

He set up a steady rhythm. The friction drove my body into another tight spiral, but I was too overwhelmed to care.

Until, still thrusting, he bent over and bit my throat.

I constricted into a black hole, impossibly tight. And then, arching back in a sweep of devoured stars, I came, diamond hard. Harder than I'd ever come in my life: hard enough to bang the mattress, hard enough to hurt myself.

He licked my throat closed as the shudders coursed through me, then took my mouth sweetly.

My orgasm rounded, swelled into something bigger than simple pleasure. Something more than physical release, bigger than my skin could hold, bigger than even my heart.

I shattered, coming apart in the sunrise tide of sensations, the brand-new dawn of me.

When my heart slowed and I opened my eyes, I found myself cuddled in Glynn's arms, his big body curled protectively around me. His rumbling purr had softened, no longer pervasive but ruffled a bit like...like he was sleeping.

He'd fallen asleep. Dammit, he'd fucked like a sex-crazed love monkey and then gone totally unconscious. I wriggled, felt crisp sheet under me.

Huh. At least he'd rolled me out of the wet spot first.

I eased from his heavy arms. He stirred with a murmured question, but I patted one bowling-ball shoulder and he relaxed back.

My clothes weren't immediately apparent. Some hunting produced my pants and panties at the foot of the bed, and my bra in one corner of the room. I couldn't find my shirt.

My search took me past the tchotchke table. I paused.

The dragon almost certainly stood for Wales. The pipe struck me as quintessentially male, the cookie stamp female. Were they remembrances of his parents? I pictured a beslippered father smoking a pipe while an aproned mother baked cookies.

Then I pictured warrior-priest Glynn in the family photo and it went poof. No way he had such normal, homey parents. Besides, he'd never known his parents.

Maybe the knickknacks signified his dream family. They were clearly important and I wondered if he'd tell me, but doubted it. I wondered if he'd ever explained them to anyone but doubted that too.

I donned my pants, zipped them over my belly. Flat, and he'd used a condom, but the fifteen percent failure rate meant maybe my belly wouldn't be flat much longer. We might have started a new family. I might have destroyed my future the way my mother had destroyed hers.

Somehow it didn't feel as devastating as I thought it would.

Probably because it wasn't real. Fifteen percent failure rate meant eighty-five percent success, even higher with proper usage. I put a hand over my belly. Pictured it growing round with Glynn's child.

Nope, still nothing.

I saw my shirt and slipped it on, found shoes and socks and put those on too. I glanced back at Glynn, a mountain on the bed, albeit a sated, snoring mountain. I'd had bloody sex with a vampire. Might get pregnant. I didn't regret any of it.

And it still didn't feel weird.

My pink jacket lay in the middle of the floor. I snared it, flashed back to Glynn clutching himself while he totally orgasmed on my scent.

Okay, that had been weird. Strangely reassured, I shrugged on the jacket and slipped out the door.

The limo was waiting to take me home. Apparently Glynn had ordered it up, whether before or after the events on his bed I didn't know. But it filled me with a warm sense of being cared for, protected.

Although, when I really came right down to it, nothing had changed. I had my duty and dreams. Just because I also had need, and he had need, and we came together in quite mutual satisfaction of that need, it didn't mean answers.

Good thing he'd fallen asleep after. What if he'd wanted to talk? I didn't really know why I'd slept with him. How could I deal with finding out why he'd slept with me?

What if he wanted to talk the next time I saw him?

Time for more avoidance. Hey, remember Queen Bess. The issue would eventually go away. Maybe.

So Friday afternoon, I buzzed Nixie. "Can you get a message to Glynn? Let him know not to pick me up?"

"Why not?"

"Um...I'm meeting Rocky?" I made a mental promise to call Rocky and ask her so it wouldn't be an out and out lie.

"Plenty of room in the limo for two. Glynn could pick you both up."

Friends are damned tricky. "We're walking. For the exercise."

She changed tactics. "Tell you what. I'll pass it along if you spill what you found on the knickknacks."

More sensitive than the sex issue. "Nothing, really." I tried to derail her. "How does Julian get to the PAC if Glynn and Mishela use the limo?"

"He goes earlier and reconnoiters, if you really cared, which you don't. Now dump on the knickknacks, else I'll forget to pass your message on to Glynn."

"Bitch." I gave in to the inevitable. "I saw them, but I don't have a clue what they mean."

"How can you not? *Rowr*, girl, after what Julian smelled passing Glynn's room, he should have been singing the fucking 'Star-Spangled Banner' if you wanted it—"

I managed to finesse my way out of that one by hanging up on her. She called back and I turned off the phone. I waited half an hour before cautiously turning it back on to call Rocky. She agreed to meet me at the Wurstspeicher Haus at six.

The moment my rent-a-kid arrived, I ran upstairs, leaving the store a full hour early, sacrificing another eight and a quarter, and showered so fast my skin steamed. The sun was still high enough to spotlight my picture of Stonehenge when I ran downstairs. It hadn't stopped Glynn before, but I was counting on the element of surprise.

I raced out the side door, screeched to a stop. Oh joy. The Cheese Dudes had something new to annoy us.

A three-story snake flailed from ground to sky like a demented sock puppet.

They're called air dancers or tube men or advertising inflatables.

155

They're big to pull in customers from way far away, so normally they're placed in parking lots or fields, to have room to billow around.

This one was right in front of the Cheese Dudes' building—which put its flopping and flailing right in front of our walkway.

Even more annoying, it had the face of Cheese Dude Two.

The Dudes were two guys who took the geek stereotype and supersized it. Dude One was tall and skinny with greasy, badly cut hair. He wore Hubble-lensed glasses wrapped with the inevitable duct tape. Dude Two was tall, chubby and scruffy, a double for Frank Rossitano on *30 Rock,* complete with ball cap. The Dudes even had the gamer personas, never showing their faces before supper and staying up well past the hour most Meiers Corners stores locked the door and turned the sign to *Geschlossen.*

The snake was horribly unquaint, way over the top—and a great marketing idea. My folks would never have one, which automatically made it cool.

And the little ball cap was really cute.

I reminded myself that the snake was in my way. That it was annoying, like the webcam and petty vandalism. That it was even dangerous with its jerky flopping. Up and flop. Up and chop. A Cheese Dude axe, swinging at the mouth of the walkway.

Thank goodness I'd skipped double-dutch as a kid. Mr. Miyagi's classes had only honed my timing. I zigged out between the roiling curls into the street.

Behind me an electronic deathmetal "Cheese, Marvelous Cheese" presaged a live voice shouting, "Damn you, Stieg. Give us back our Gorgon's Ola!"

I turned. Shaking his fist from the snake-shadowed store was Dude Two himself.

"I don't even know what Gorgon's Ola is," I yelled back.

"The most popular new cheese ever? 'Piquantly Pungent, Like a Striking Snake.'" He shook a threatening paw. "We know you stole our shipment, Stieg. We want it back!"

"I don't have your stinking cheese, Dude."

With a snarl he came after me. I braced for two hundred pounds of Dude. But his timing was off. A coil bonked him in his Cheesehead. He reeled back, tried again. Got punched in his Cheesebelly.

"Damn you, Stieg. Give us back our Gorgon's Ola, or else."

Clutching his head and belly, he made one last dash.

The worm flashed down and under. Blew suddenly up.

Bonked the Dude in his unprotected Cheesedoodles.

He bent over the little Dudes with a howl. Hobbled back inside.

"Wow. Those guys are really mad at you." Rocky trotted up, flute bag clutched to her chest. The outer pocket was unzipped, the top of a paper bag screaming CHEESE just sticking out.

I pointed at the bag. "Consorting with the enemy?"

"I like cheese." She started toward the PAC. "Anyway, they claim you guys started it. Hey, the Kalten remodeling's done."

"We didn't start...it doesn't matter who started it." I hitched instruments. Following, I caught my reflection in Kalten's gleaming exterior. Rocky was right—the remodelers had finished. The place looked better than new. Triangular black marble planters formed an edgy counterpoint to the glossy marble and mirrored glass facade. "I wonder what kind of business moved in?"

"Hope for wine," she said. "Goes with both cheese and sausage. I'm surprised you and the Dudes don't get along better."

"It's not our fault. This latest cheese accusation is pure crock. Um, no pun intended. Why would we steal their product?"

"That's what I thought, especially the Gorgon's Ola," Rocky said. "No sane person'd want to steal that stuff."

"Why not? What is it, exactly? Besides 'piquantly pungent'?"

"Believe it or not, it started as a mistake. See, sometimes cheese bacteria makes gas early. Then the cheese is 'blown', which ruins it."

I eyed her. "And you know this how?"

"Ralphie gave me the Cliffs Notes while I was picking out my cheddar."

"Ralphie?"

"One of the Dudes. Anyway, most cheese gas is CO2, but some bacteria produce hydrogen—think Hindenburg. A company accidentally produced Hindenburg cheese, but instead of throwing it away, some CEO decided it was an 'opportunity'. They marketed the hell out of it, and it became trendy with a certain crowd desperate to be different."

"Good grief. Eating bad cheese just to be trendy?"

"Hey, people eat raw fish. And blood sausage."

"Which reminds me. Did your bribe work?"

"I think so." She held up crossed fingers.

"At least now I know why the Dudes have been so angry lately, if their most popular product disappeared."

"I wonder what happened to the shipment."

"Delivered to the wrong address, probably."

She gave me a look. "With our post office?"

"Stranger things have happened lately." Like vampires. Which reminded me, I didn't want to deal with any sexy vampires, or even snarky spouses of sexy vampires. So I nudged her toward the PAC's side entrance.

For all the trouble I went to avoiding sexy vampires (and snarky friends), it turned out I needn't have bothered. I never saw Glynn and saw too much of Nixie.

Oh, Glynn came. Er, arrived. Whatever. I knew he was there because at seven ten Mishela flitted by with a flirty wave and an embarrassing thumbs-up. She wouldn't be here without her shadow, so he was somewhere in the building.

Just nowhere near me.

I was not dejected, but by the time I made my way to the pit, everyone was already in place and had eaten all the good chocolates. Not really, but it felt that way. Then Nixie latched on to me the moment I sat down—literally, grabbing my elbow in a grip of death. "So, spew. All the gory details."

So much for avoiding confrontation.

I tried to distract her. "Hey Nixie, what's the best thing you can play on a guitar? Solitaire."

"Seriously, girlfriend. Was he any good?"

I almost wished she was asking about the knickknacks. I cut a significant glance at Julian, he of the supervamp hearing.

Nixie grinned. "Nothin' he doesn't know. Or isn't willing to learn. Spill."

"Um, isn't it time to start?" I glanced out into the audience. Less than half full. Earlier than I thought. "Hey, what's the only thing a violin is good for?"

"Lighting a viola. Even I know that one, but it won't work. Details. Juicy. Now."

Thankfully, that was when the doors closed and Takashi cued tuning. So, later than I thought. I picked up my clarinet to match pitch. Nixie snatched up her alto sax and Julian touched bow to strings.

His hand froze. His nostrils flared. The tips of his fangs popped out between his lips.

All hell broke loose in the lobby. Screams and shrieks, the shrill yip of a dog, barely muffled by the closed doors.

Julian was gone in a puff of smoke. A swirl of mist. Whatever. Nixie barely caught his dropped cello.

While she fumbled with his oversized guitar, I tossed my clarinet on its peg and sprinted out of the pit and up the aisle. I expected Glynn to come shooting from the stage, but as I ran, my brain kicked in and I realized where he was and why, and why the hullabaloo was in the lobby.

That was where Mishela was.

Dorothy made her first entrance through the house, coming from the inner lobby. Glynn would be with her.

From the ruckus, so was the bad guy.

I burst out the house doors. Glynn and a knobby masked dude were tussling midlobby. A handful of latecomers, standing just inside the outer lobby doors, stared.

Julian weaved from side to side over the wrestling pair, judging his moment. Suddenly he darted in and jabbed the masked head.

Glynn followed Julian's punch with an elbow smash that would have taken off the head of an elephant. It only stunned the masked guy, confirmation if I'd needed it that this was a vampire.

Nixie edged out behind me. She had a pole and jammed it through the theater house doors as an impromptu bar. Hopefully Mishela had done the same with the other house door. We didn't need more of an audience for this. Nixie said, "Did they get him?"

"I think so."

Glynn pulled the masked vampire to his feet.

"Good. Now we'll find out who he is...damn."

Glynn tore off the mask, revealing Gollum-like Steve.

"Shiv," Nixie said.

I didn't know that could be a name, but maybe vampires took knife names like metal bands added umlauts. "Who's Shiv?"

"A foot soldier, one of the Lestats. I'll give you the 4-1-1 later. This explains why the kidnapping attempts were so lame. Shiv's a fuckup. All Ruthven's homies are."

"Ruthven?"

"A v-guy rogue-lord and businessman who... It's complicated."

"Later?"

"Later."

Shiv was blustering. "Lemme go! You can't pin anything on me. It was dark and I had a mask on so you couldn't know it was me...shit."

Nixie just rolled her eyes.

"You're caught, Shiv." Glynn shook him. "It's over. We know you're trying to kidnap Mishela and why."

Mishela stepped up, fists on hips. "Is that why you took my 'Hello Cthulhu' panties? To get my scent in order to *track* me?"

"No, Mishela, never." Steve—or Shiv—blinked at her. His eyes got big and glossy, and his lower lip stuck out and trembled. "I just wanted a token. Something to remind me of your sweet self."

"Aw," Nixie said. "Puppy love. Cute but messy. Better push his nose in it before it gets any worse."

"Let Shiv go, darlings," a new voice said. "He was working for me."

The voice was a rich alto. The knot of showgoers near the outer doors parted, and a stunning woman step through. Her long black gown was backless—with a neckline down to her navel, almost frontless too. Black eye shadow and blood-red lipstick was a look most women couldn't carry off, but it painted her exotically beautiful. She looked like a perfect fictional vampire.

I blinked. This was probably the real thing.

As she glided past the paying customers, she handed them all colorful slips of paper. They looked at the papers, then each other.

Then the showgoers, *our audience*, trooped out the lobby door. I stared after them in disbelief.

The woman sauntered toward the other vampires. "Hello, Julian. How's the little wifey?" Her voice was a deep purr, Catwoman but for the snide, mocking way she said wifey. I liked Halle Berry but not this woman.

Julian's glare said he felt the same. "Camille."

She sauntered past him to stand before Glynn. "Hello, darling."

He stared down his high druid nose at her. "Is this Nosferatu's minion?" His Welsh accent rolled like thunder.

"Is this the Ancient One's little fetch boy?" A wicked smile on her full lips, she poked a single red nail into his chest. "It's lieutenant, darling. Get it right."

The nail dug, quick and sharp, into his shirt. Through it, a red flower appeared. He growled low.

She laughed. "Second lieutenant, actually, now that Ruthven's gone."

"Congratulations," Julian said. The word was iced with sarcasm.

"Thank you." Eyes never leaving Glynn's, she licked her bloody fingernail. "It opens up the position of third lieutenant. Interested, darling?"

I expected him to smash her face or slash her with his knife. But he only stared at her, breathing through whitened, distended nostrils.

She smiled. Slowly extended all her nails, reaching for his face—to kiss him or claw him, I didn't know and didn't care.

I flew out of the house doorway. "Leave him alone." Glynn could take care of himself, but strangely that didn't matter in my need to defend what was...mine. Aw, hell.

Julian stopped me with an arm. But not before Camille's head swiveled.

"And who is this?" She sniffed the air delicately. Her ruby lips quirked to a nasty little grin. "How droll. What is it with you Alliance boys and your human whores?"

Glynn slapped her. Her head snapped back, the surprise on her face unfeigned and instantly gone. Her nails lengthened to claws and she slashed them across his face.

I jumped, but Julian stopped me. "Let him handle it."

A condescending smile crossed Glynn's face, his striped skin already healing. He raised the hapless Shiv until he dangled. "This yours?"

"Of course, darling." She cocked her head, black hair rippling past her shoulder. "Is that a trick question?"

"Here's the trick." Glynn reached into his jacket and pulled out his long knife. He grinned at Shiv. "This won't stop you, but it will slow you down." With a single muscular slash, Glynn beheaded the rogue. Blood spurted from the stub. The bony head fell with a muted thud.

161

I looked away.

"Camille," Glynn purred. "Don't make the mistake of going after my girls ever again. Any of them." His gaze flicked to me, a stern look that seemed to say, "This is the monster you're getting involved with."

Yet I saw a yearning to be understood beneath the austerity.

Then he looked away. I was left wishing I could comfort him somehow.

"Good thing the carpet's red," Nixie muttered. She touched me on the shoulder, sass softened with compassion. "Don't worry, it's temporary. The only way to permanently stop a v-guy is cremate him or burn him in the sun. They'll slap Shiv's head back on, stick him in the ground for a few days and he'll be good as new."

I still didn't look at the body.

"Don't touch *any* of our humans." Julian's voice was frigid as death. "Go back to Chicago, Camille. Run home where you belong."

"Oh, but I am home."

Camille's sly, loaded tone jolted my gaze toward her, to see what type of snake could talk without hissing.

She wore a ripe gloat, the kind that holds a hand of queens when every last dime has been bet. "Is this any way to treat a fellow Meiers Corners businesswoman?"

"I've no time for games," Glynn said. "Get out."

"Of course. After I give you this." She offered one of her colorful slips of paper.

He just glared.

She held it out to Julian. "You?"

When he glared too, Nixie said, "Oh, for shit's sake," and started for her.

"Nixie, no." Julian snapped up the paper so fast his hand blurred.

Camille's smile broadened. "I have more for tomorrow night. And the night after. In case you find time for games." She gave Glynn one last leer.

Then, with a dramatic swirl, she collapsed into a river of smoke, flowing along the lobby carpet and out the door.

Julian glared like he wanted to snap out his lighter and make her a fuse.

"What the hell?" Glynn snatched the paper from Julian's hand.

Scowling, his eyes darkened to royal blue—royally pissed. "This is why the house is so sparse."

Avoiding the headless body, I sidled over and angled my head to see.

It was a flyer for a brand-new goth nightclub called Fangs To You. The club's address was the Kalten building.

It featured a coupon for free drinks—for tonight.

Chapter Eleven

"Damn." Julian tossed back a shot of whiskey, then plunked it down in a row of empties that stretched the width of the table. Apparently, the older the vampire the more it took to get drunk, because Julian was still red-eyed, long-fanged and apparently clear-headed. "This was their plan all along."

We ringed a table right in the middle of Nieman's Bar, but Julian's fanged state wasn't a problem. Not just the PAC had been emptied by Camille's free drinks.

"I can't believe we fell for it." Mishela, back in her tomboy flannel and cap, toyed with her soda. "The kidnapping attempts were a diversion, to keep us from seeing them finishing the club."

"Not just a diversion," Nixie said. She was systematically destroying every bowl of bar peanuts within reach. "If you'd gone MIA, Scary Ancient Dude would have been flinging-apeshit mad. You know Nosy's MO. Anything to fuck up the Alliance."

Anyone else, I would have asked what the hell they meant. I was sort of used to not understanding Nixie.

Fortunately, Julian had gotten to be a competent translator. "Mishela's kidnapping would have upset the Ancient One, distracted him and disrupted the Alliance. You're right. That could have been Nosferatu's primary plan, with Camille as a backup."

"A one-two punch." Nixie mimed a jab-cross. "Knock us off balance with Shiv, then KO with this shit."

"Perhaps it's not that bad?" Glynn nursed a Red Special, which smelled uncomfortably like brandy and blood. "Perhaps the townspeople will check out the club, find it not to their liking, and life will return to normal."

I jumped on that. "Of course. The novelty attracted them. It'll wear off." Then I shook my head. "But in the meantime, it's free drinks. No self-respecting Meiers Corners—" I tried to think what our noun-forming suffix might be. Corners-ite? Corners-zian? Corners-erella?

Gave up. "No MCer turns down *free*."

"What chaps my ass," Nixie said, "is that those good Corners folk could have come back after downing their drinks. They didn't."

Glynn frowned. "So?"

"So the shiny-new'll wear off, sure. But maybe too late for us."

I tried to steal a peanut, nearly got my hand chomped. Small, fast and pregnant is a dangerous combination. I shook out my fingers. "I hope not. If we lose our audience, that's bad. But all the quaint local shoppes the Sparkasse Bank invested in will be in trouble too."

"And if the shoppes default, well." Julian downed another shot. "The bank will be ripe for takeover or worse."

"Fuck me," Nixie said. "Aren't we as much fun as a barrel of dicks?"

Julian eyed her. "I think you mean 'barrel of monkeys'."

"Dude, the only possible way being mashed in a barrel with a bunch of hairy little things would be fun is if it's dicks."

"Ah." Julian set the shot glass down. "My mistake."

"Remind me," Mishela said. "Why is the Coterie going after Meiers Corners?"

"First tell me what the Coterie is," I said. "And Nosy and the Alliance."

Julian said, "The Iowa Alliance is a group of philosophically like-minded vampires who live in harmony with humanity."

"The good guys," Nixie translated.

"Thanks," I said. "And 'Iowa' Alliance because...?"

"The Alliance is based there," Glynn said. "It's where the leader lives."

"Ah." I nodded wisely. "Scary Ancient Dude."

Nixie snorted. "Better than Ancient 'One', which is totally *baka* fakerific cuz there's more than one."

"But not many," Glynn said. "In our world, age means strength, and the head of the Alliance is a vampire who's walked the earth so long, no one knows how old he is."

"Couple that with his steel will, preternatural intelligence and personal fortune..." Julian knocked back his last shot, grimaced. "He's the most dangerous being on the planet. Thus Ancient 'One' is most appropriate."

I finished off my beer, set it on our tray. "Okay. And the Coterie?"

"The vampires running the Chicago territory," Julian said. "They stand philosophically against the Alliance. Their leader Nosferatu hates the Ancient One. I'll let you explain." With a nod to Glynn, Julian swept the rest of the empties onto the tray, stood and doddered off toward the bar. Apparently not as sober as I'd thought.

Glynn watched him go. "Chicago's the third-largest city in the United States. It's also the third-largest population center of vampires."

I raised eyebrows. "Vampires fill out censuses? Is that one of the race options and I just didn't see it?"

"We have our ways." Glynn shrugged. "The Coterie is a bit of a mafia-like group that uses a gang of rogues, the Lestats, as their muscle. Nosferatu is the head of it all."

Mishela took off her cap and played with it absently. "Nosferatu's after power, territory and blood."

"Especially ours." Nixie scrubbed salt out of the only bowl Julian had left her. "Nosy and his homeboys love to grab up small-town blood centers."

"Don't they have blood centers in Chicago?"

"They're protected," Glynn said. "Grandfathered in on an arrangement the Ancient One made with the federal government. Vampires are powerful, but even a pack couldn't stand against a platoon of Marines or Army field artillery."

"The Coterie'd be jackass stupid to invade Chi-town blood banks." Nixie threw the bowl on the table. "So they score on the streets and in their clubs. But that blood's full of drugs and crap—and they have to hunt it, so it's iffy besides. Funeral homes and hospitals are surer, but most of that blood's old and sick."

"Yuck," I said when I deciphered that.

Glynn said, "Nosferatu is trying every way he can to take over territory west."

"Yum, yum, farm-fresh blood," Nixie said.

Which upped the yuck-factor. "So the government protects big blood centers and the Alliance protects the small-town centers?"

"And small-town people," Glynn said. "It's forced Nosferatu to bargain for blood or, worse yet, buy it."

"I know Nosferatu hates the Ancient One." Mishela popped her cap back on her loose hair. "But why is the Coterie going so hard after

Meiers Corners?"

"Revenge?" Nixie said as Julian returned and passed around refills. She yoinked all the peanuts, gobbled up two cheekfuls and munched like a tiny blonde chipmunk. "Nosy wanted our close and hackable blood center. He's tried like three times to get it or the city under his thumb. But we *pwned* him every time. That's gotta sting."

I took a sip of my beer, smacked my lips at the bright taste of imported pilsner. Julian'd sprung for the good stuff.

"That's possible," Glynn said. "Nosferatu was successful taking over a few small eastern blood centers. Meiers Corners standing firm might taunt him."

"So why bother with it?" Mishela asked. "Why not stick with easy blood?"

"Because he can't go much further east," Julian said. "Not without running afoul of the New York Cadre."

"Sounds like ball teams," I said. "So if he wants to go west, why doesn't he just go west?"

"Because of Project Shield."

I frowned. "What's—?"

"What you'd think," Glynn said. "A line of Alliance households on the Coterie's border."

"Both a defense and an early alert system." Julian lined up an arc of shot glasses. "Like the old DEW line between North America and the USSR during the cold war."

Nixie said, "It's all 'Red rover, red rover let Nosy come over'."

"You mean he's trying to break though?" I frowned. "And he just picked Meiers Corners at random to attack?"

"If only," she said. "We're the Anne Robinson."

"I beg your pardon?" Julian said.

"Suit guy." Nixie winked. "Renaissance dances are his bubblegum pop."

I suddenly got it. "We're the weakest link."

"Yup," Nixie said. "Goodbye."

I got cold.

"The Ancient One won't let that happen," Mishela said. "He'll stop it before it goes too far."

"You weren't around the last time he personally stepped in."

Glynn shuddered, tossed off the last of his drink and shuddered again. "It wasn't pretty."

Julian turned distinctly green around the edges.

Nixie frowned at her husband. "Okay, so top priority is keeping Scary Dude from having to unleash his Ancient mojo."

"But how?" Julian said. "If Camille is in Meiers Corners legally, it's her prerogative to offer whatever sales incentives she considers efficacious."

"Julian, sweetheart, love of my life. Want to tool that down to words invented in the last millennium?"

I said, "If she's not doing anything illegal, we can't force her out."

"That sucks." Nixie upended the last bowl of peanuts into her mouth. She held it out to Julian and batted her eyelids.

With a sigh, he gathered bowls onto the tray and returned to the bar.

Nixie lowered her voice and leaned in. "So, what if we eighty-six legal? Could we run over there, tear off her head, dig out her heart? Blow up her club?"

"It would make life easier," Glynn said. "But the Ancient One tends to frown on that sort of thing."

"Us being the good guys." Mishela grinned.

"So we sit on our thumbs and twirl while the bitch takes our audience?" Nixie frowned at the door. "We should at least check out the club."

I opened my mouth to agree.

Glynn cut in with a snarled, "Too dangerous. Julian would forbid it—and I also."

Though he said it to Nixie, he was glaring at me. I blinked.

"Shoulda sent you to get peanuts too." Nixie said it to Glynn, then gave me an apologetic shrug. "They tend to be a mite overprotective of their mates."

Second time, I couldn't let that pass. My "young man" was bad enough. "Glynn's not my—"

"We could turn Camille's ploy against her," Mishela said.

"I'm interested," Nixie said. "Details."

I tried again. "Glynn's not—"

"Of course, he isn't." Mishela grinned. "Focus here. Camille's snatching tourists, right? So her customers have to be sleeping somewhere, eating during the day when she's closed. We just tell those businesses to talk up other good-guy businesses. We grab the tourists back—and the show."

"We could also offer incentives," I said, my mind starting to work now that the scary mate idea was off the table. "An MC *Quainte Shoppe Coupone Booke* or something. That'll take more time to put together, but it'll work for both tourists and locals."

Julian returned with a trayful of peanuts—and a glass of milk. "Drink." He plopped the glass in front of Nixie. "We'll leave right after. You need your rest."

"We need to prevent Ancient One Armageddon more." She grimaced but drank.

"Hey." I frowned. "If this Ancient guy is so powerful, why doesn't he rule Chicago already? Or New York or London or any of the big cities?"

"He does, in a way." Glynn fingered his empty glass. "He has business interests all over the world, a much more effective leash on things up until now."

"Don't get me started on that," Mishela said. "He's really pissed at the economy. Blames Nosferatu and works insane hours to keep it from tanking completely."

I pictured a sort of shadow mogul, a vampire Howard Hughes skulking in hotel penthouses. "This Ancient of yours is a business tycoon? Then why have I never heard of him?"

Glynn said, "You've heard of him, all right. He's Mishela's guardian. Kai Elias."

Entr'acte

Glynn insisted that everyone walk Junior home that night. He implied it was for safety against rogues, but actually it was so he wasn't alone with her, couldn't touch her and smell her and love her. Emerson eyed him, but wisely said nothing. If the other male had made the twitting comment Glynn could just see on his lips, he'd have turned him into bloody mincemeat.

Or tried. Emerson was a thousand years plus. He'd probably put up a bit of a fight.

Glynn's fangs started to throb at the thought of Emerson putting up a fight. As tense as Glynn was, he might have enjoyed it.

But Emerson said nothing. And when they rounded the corner onto Fourth and met the annoying flying tube with the grinning mad head and Glynn slashed it to pieces with his bare claws, Emerson said nothing again. Good thing, because the flying tube had only whetted Glynn's vampire urge to destroy.

He half expected Junior to shriek in protest when he shredded the tube, but she only choked back a laugh. It made him smile. He found himself doing that far too often around her. She smiled at him in return.

Their smiles died, and they stared for an awkward moment at each other. Her scent became pungent with arousal and he hardened in response. He did that far too often around her, too.

He had to remember they had no future. She wanted it that way. And he had his own dreams.

So he motioned Emerson to walk her to her door while he stood at the mouth of the narrow, dim walkway, scowling when she fumbled her key into the lock. Before he left Meiers Corners, he was damned well putting in a better light.

Mishela glided up next to him. "You want to tell Mr. Elias about tonight or should I?"

Glynn turned his scowl on her. "I don't *want* to tell him. But better me than you. You get overly dramatic." Then he realized Mishela was supposed to be guarding Emerson's wee tornado of a wife. "Where's Nixie?" He kept his voice low.

Mishela's was equally low. "She wanted to scope out Camille's club."

"Cock. That's incredibly dangerous." Glynn glanced at Junior. She'd finally gotten the key to work. Emerson waited stoically at her side, but the lawyer's jaw clamped with a male's imperative to be with his lover and a vampire's need to protect his vulnerable human.

Still, he'd stay with Junior until she was safe inside. Glynn strode across the street, Mishela trailing. He muttered, "If anything happens to Emerson's wife—"

"Relax, Glynn. Nixie's the logical choice. If anyone can do goth, it's her. And Camille's not going to risk starting all-out war in her own club."

"The Coterie risked war trying to kidnap you."

"Using a masked man, so we couldn't prove it. This is different. They won't want any fingers pointing."

"I hope you're right."

At Fangs To You's mirrored doors, two males in identical tough-guy black blocked Glynn's way. The Tweedledum and Tweedledee of bouncers. One smelled human, the other vampire, but it mattered little. Glynn bared his fangs with a snarl and the men fell back. It gave Glynn the instant he needed to slip them a hypnotic suggestion. His simmering irritation made it a bit harsh—one male cupped his crotch and the other bent over puking as Glynn strode through the doors.

Inside was dim, crowded and loud. People mobbed a long lacquered bar to the left. More ringed a corner bar, hazed in smoke. Not cigarette. Glynn tested the air, scented smoke cloyingly sweet. Illegal, but Camille always enjoyed pushing the boundaries. She'd have a battalion of lawyers standing by to get her out of any real trouble.

Red light played over a full dance floor where youngsters, human and vampire, thronged, hopping like a bunch of demented chickens. Glynn wondered if it was modern dance or they were having some sort of fit. Probably dance, though he'd stopped learning popular steps before the waltz. Nixie wobbled in their midst.

She saw him and immediately started over. Good thing or he'd have waded in to drag her out. Emerson would be livid. The small tornado should have known that, having been married to her vampire for several months now. Yet she'd chosen to enter this den anyway. Glynn hoped it was worth it.

Sure enough, Emerson stormed in, eyes blood-red and fangs barely restrained. "If anything the fuck has happened to my wife—"

"Yell later," Nixie shouted over the music as she bustled up.

Emerson turned his snarl on her. "I leave you alone for one moment and—"

"Yell later, Julian," she repeated, motioning them out. "This is bigger. Camille's smarter than the average Lestat. We may be in real trouble."

"What?" As they hit fresh air, Emerson's eyes cooled to a blue Glynn recognized as pissed but in control. "What did you find?"

"Buddy kicked us out of Nieman's at two," she said. "Bar time. Fangs To You should have closed too."

"There's no law requiring it," Emerson said. "Only to cease serving alcoholic drinks—" He stopped mid-stride. "Correction. Only to cease *selling* alcohol."

Nixie nodded as she kept going, looking as grim as Glynn had ever seen her. "Which is why Camille was giving the drinks away free. Open bar for everyone who came early and stayed late. In other words, for everyone who missed our show." She held out her hand. The stamp of a stylized black vampire was on the back. "If I'd come before eight, this would be red. And I'd be drinking my weight for free."

Mishela made a disgusted noise. "That's why our audience didn't come back."

Emerson's long strides caught him up. He picked up his wee wife and they all set off at a more comfortable pace. "The Ancient One isn't going to like this. Who's going to tell him?"

All three looked at Glynn with a mixture of pity and relief.

Glynn sighed. "I suppose. After which I will escape immediately to Wales."

"If it helps any, Mr. Elias probably already knows," Mishela said.

Nixie nodded. "He's an eerie ancient fucker that way."

"He doesn't *know*," Glynn said. "But the way his mind works, I'm sure he's thought of the possibility."

They traversed the nine blocks in just over a minute and headed in through Emersons' driveway entrance. A door led from the underground parking directly into the basement hallway. Inside,

Emerson set his wife on her feet.

Glynn said, "I don't suppose you'd care to wait with me while I make the call? In case Elias really can shoot lightning through the phone?"

"Um, love to. But, um..." Nixie gestured at the first door. "I've got a thing." She disappeared inside.

"Me too." Mishela edged toward the second door. "Got a thing, that is." She slid into her room and slammed the door shut. The lock clicked home.

"I would, but I've got to ride herd on my wife. Good luck, old sap." Emerson cuffed him on the arm. "I mean, old chap."

With a grin, he dropped into mist and ran under the first door.

Glynn sighed and pulled out his phone.

Chapter Twelve

Saturday was the usual mix of regulars and tourists at the Wurstspeicher Haus. But the day itself was anything but usual, and I don't just mean the mayor showing up in full Swiss Family lederhosen and laced boots—although that happening right out of the gate probably should have warned me.

The doorbell tinkled at eight and my body tingled hopefully. But instead of Big Dark and Dangerous with a growled *babi,* I heard, "*Und so* here we are the premiere *wurst* shop ge-having."

Mayor Meier marched in, jolly in the aforementioned lederhosen and boots and slathering his "charming" DeutscheGlish on with a backhoe. Behind him marched half a dozen clog-stomping, embroidered-suspender-wearing, beschnitzeled refugees· from Folk Fair.

I put aside my immediate reaction, which was to hide under a really big slice of bologna, and pasted on my best sausage smile. "Hello, Mayor! How can I help you today?" *And who are these evacuees from Freddy's Oktoberfest,* I wanted to add but didn't. There's a reason "Tell the customer, not what you want to jabber about, but what they need to hear," made it to the Top Eight.

"Hello, Gunter Marie," the mayor said. "These are mayors in my German League of Bürgermeister Towns. The GLBT are here *gekommen* for the PAC opening *und* I showing them the sights was."

It took me a moment to parse that, even knowing *gekommen* meant come and *und* meant and. I was never quite sure what language the mayor spoke. Not English, but not German either. Not even what you'd expect from a native German speaker trying English. It was like the squeezings from a sponge that had absorbed both languages, *Local Color for Dummkopfs* and way too much beer. Eng-Glitch, maybe.

Twyla said he played it up on purpose, part of the jolly German act. I think, like the little boy warned not to cross his eyes, he'd done it once too often and had gotten stuck.

"We have several lovely gift items," I said when I figured out these were visitors. "Sausage boxes, sausage-making spices and supplies, and mugs and scarves." Yeah, sausage scarves. What can I say? They sell well so I stock them. Remember, not broke.

One of the mayors nodded. "Oh, just what we looking for are."

"Ri-ight." I smiled. Apparently the Eng-Glitch bug was not only catching, it could escalate to fevers, hacking and mucus on the brain. "Far wall, feel free to browse."

They wandered into the gift corner just as Mrs. Gelb came in for her Saturday hot ham and rolls.

Hot ham and rolls was our Sunday special, but Sunday was sauerbraten night in the Gelb household. Mrs. Gelb's great-grandma had sauerbraten on Sunday and her grandma and ma had sauerbraten on Sunday and *bei Gott* (by God) she had it on Sunday too. Corners folk elevated tradition to Sistine perfection.

As I rang Mrs. Gelb up, she raved about some new bar. I didn't pay much attention until she chirped, "It's called Fangs To You. Isn't that clever?"

My fingers froze on the cash register. "Clever."

"Alba Gruen and I are going back tonight. Free drinks, you know. Not just with that flyer. If you arrive before eight and stay past two, the whole bar is open. Free snacks too. Isn't that clever?"

"Very clever." Winter swept through the store, lights going blue and my whole body constricting with cold.

Somehow I finished that transaction. I took her money with numb fingers and fumbled it into the drawer. Stood like an ice sculpture as she took her bag and left. Clever, very clever, beyond clever.

This was how Camille was pulling our audience and keeping them. By taking ruthless advantage of Meiers Corners's weakness—free stuff.

I put on a sweater and restocked blood sausage. The repetitive task calmed me—and reminded me we were selling a lot of blood sausage, reminding me of vampires, reminding me of visiting vampires, Big Dark and Dangerous—after which I peeled off my sweater, shivering again but for another reason. When the door tinkled, my shiver changed into a shudder of anticipation.

But instead of one special vampire, a trio of humans entered. Three people, one door...a scuffle broke out. "Hey! Get out of my way." The door slapped wider. Some jostling, some shoving. Oh well, tourists

175

were rude—they didn't know better.

"Move yer frickin' butt." A tourist barreled through, a scowl marring her face... Not a tourist.

My jaw hit countertop. It was Mrs. Roet, wife of Police Lieutenant Roet and mother to eight young kids, including rambunctious triplets just starting to toddle, but that didn't account for this level of belligerence.

Since when were Corners people anything but disturbingly polite? Whap-you-upside-the-head courteous?

Mayor Meier bustled over and attempted to soothe them. While he was doing that, the bell tinkled again. Before I could get up a good Big Dark Dangerous tingle, Rocky Hrbek slid in. She came directly to the counter. "Junior. I need more blood sausage bribes."

We were running low, but this was Rocky. "How much?"

"Another pound. For my supervisor. She's acting weird."

"Oh?" I got the sausage.

"I rated a couple policies yesterday. I did it right, I know I did. But she made me change them."

"Rated?"

"You know, assigned risk factors to determine the cost. I had two taverns, both Meiers Corners, similar in risk, so I rated them the same. But my supervisor changed them—jacked up one to ten times the cost, lowered the other practically nothing. It's Nieman's, Junior. CIC is charging so much that the bar will be driven out of business."

"That's terrible." In many ways, Nieman's was the heart of our community. What would Meiers Corners do without a heart?

Then an even worse suspicion hit me. "What's the other business?"

"Some new club called Fangs To You."

Shocking. But then came the biggest shock of all.

Rocky went to look at sausage spices. The mayors were discussing the various merits of ginger versus mace. The locals had bought their regular meats and were gone.

I was wiping down counters when the doorbell tinkled. I tingled like all the other times, even though I knew Big Dark and Dangerous was only my imagination.

But this time big was bigger. Dark was darker. And dangerous was deadly, real and standing in the doorway.

Glynn had come.

Er, arrived.

He looked a little frayed around the edges, like he'd been zapped with lightning. But he came...er, glided right to me. His sapphire gaze ran over me like he was starving for me, dropped to my mouth and flared that bright violet.

Almost as if he couldn't help himself, he bent and kissed me.

Whoa. The amount of tongue on impact? I think he was as focused on "coming" as me.

And then Glynn added hands and I wasn't thinking at all.

"Was ist hier passiert?"

My eyes flew open. Mom and Pop were emerging from the office catacombs. ("In the Hall of the Mountain King" bopped through my head. You don't have to know the tune, just picture trolls lumbering from a cave's depths.)

Bad news. Pop was in the lead.

It was horrible timing. Maybe all parents have a sex alert, something that goes *ding* when their offspring is up to hanky-panky. Or maybe they just remember their own youth.

Ick. That hurt to think about.

Glynn and I sprang apart. Customers milled around the wares— studiously looking anywhere but at us. Except for Rocky, who was staring like she'd just realized *The Story of O* wasn't a kid's alphabet primer.

My mother went immediately to soothe her, leaving me to deal with my dad.

"Gunter Marie Stieg. *Ich habe gesagt, was—?*"

"English, please, Pop." And a little less than jet-engine decibels.

"What are you doing? Messing around with your young man *while on the job?*"

I blinked. Pop wasn't upset that I was kissing, just that I was taking precious work time to do it. "Glynn's not my young—"

"We didn't get formally introduced the other evening, Mr. Stieg." Glynn stepped forward, hand extended. "I'm Glynn Rhys-Jenkins."

My dad took Glynn's hand.

Time stopped.

A stick will appear jagged or even split into two when poked into a lake. But it's a single stick. These two men, so different—Glynn the druid prince, Gunter the jolly merchant—*felt* the same to me. I stared at them, side by side, my father and my...well, I wasn't sure what Glynn was, but the way my heart was reacting, he was just as important as the man who'd given me life.

That scared me.

"*Guten Morgen*, Glynn. Where do you come from and what do you do for a living?"

Time snapped back into motion. "Subtle, Pop."

Glynn's mouth curved. "I'm a citizen of Wales and the United States, Mr. Stieg, but as a consultant, I travel all over the world."

My father did not look suitably impressed.

Until Glynn added, "I consult for Kai Elias."

"The great businessman?" My dad slapped Glynn on the back, resulting in meaty thuds and not moving Glynn one millimeter. Pop looked even more impressed at the muscle. "What do you think of our sausage, young man?"

"I sampled the *blutwurst* at Julian Emerson's. Very nice. Just the right touch of marjoram."

My father beamed. "*Ach*, we are very selective of our importers for just that. And you know Emerson? He helped save our town, I heard."

Loud as he was, the whole country heard. It meant he was happy. My dad got louder as he got happier, as if jolly were a volume knob on his voice box. (On Christmas Eve at church, he got so happy he outsang the organ. Little kids turned to stare at him during the hymns. Embarrassing growing up, as an adult I took a perverse pleasure in it. In at least this, he was the biggest thing in our little town.)

My dad clapped Glynn on the back again. "I am glad to have met you, Glynn. Take good care of my daughter. Now I must get back to work, *ja*?" And he left.

I nearly choked. Leaving us alone, together, *behind the register*? Holy Schnitzelbank, he had us married already.

My mother had finished settling Rocky and the other customers down. Though my dad was the jolly merchant everyone loved, Mom was the one who fixed all the problems.

She caught my eye, flicked a glance at Glynn and made little finger-nudges at me, a nonverbal "get him while he's hot". Then she followed my dad out.

Gott im Himmel. Married and bedded, with a dozen grand*kinder* on the way.

Glynn said, "Your father's nice."

I shook my head like it'd rattle sense into it. Like it'd settle CIC's disparate ratings or Glynn's desperate kiss or even my parents' nonparental behavior. But some things are murky and incredibly dangerous and shouldn't be attempted except by professionals on a closed track. "Loud, maybe. Twyla calls him boisterous, but she's the daughter of a diplomat."

"He has a certain *joie de vivre.* He's bigger than life."

"So's a clown. Why are you here, anyway? Awake. Shouldn't you be in a"—*a coffin or grave*—"dark place somewhere?" Which reminded me that, no matter how close I felt to Glynn, I really knew nothing about this man. Male. Sweet exploding sausages, I didn't even know what to label him.

"I couldn't sleep," he admitted. "Thinking about you."

Just words, but his blue eyes warmed with meaning. Would it be so bad, giving in to this driving need for him, for his touch, his smile? Giving in, not just to the lust, but what I sensed was behind it?

A real relationship.

Glynn was protective and gentle and strong. Loyal, with how he felt about home. With a mystery or two to unravel to keep things fresh, a relationship might just work.

Hey, my BD&D tingle had finally materialized. Why couldn't other fantasies come true?

Argh. Because it was *a fantasy.* Real relationship, with a vampire? I had rocks for brains.

And yet despite knowing better, hope bloomed at his warm, loving look, for a "would you go out with me tonight?" or "would you mind if I gave you this exquisite piece of jewelry?" or—

"Would you consider leaving town with Mishela for a few days?"

Definitely not on the list. "You mean after the show closes?"

Glynn's gaze swept over the milling customers, then came back to me. "Is there somewhere private we can speak?"

I didn't want to leave the customers unattended. They wouldn't steal anything, but they might leave without buying, which was a crime in my dad's book. Still, if it was as important as Glynn's expression indicated, I should at least try. Maybe he wanted to finish that hot kiss.

"It'll have to be quick." I locked the cash register, let the mayor know I'd be back in a moment and led Glynn through the office to the side stairwell.

A feeble square of sun filtered through the door's window. Glynn flashed up a few stairs, motioned me to join him.

"Mr. Elias is...disturbed by last night. Camille has demonstrated cunning. He's concerned that if customers continue to be pulled away from the show and local businesses, your Sparkasse Bank will be in serious financial difficulties. That it will fold, leaving the city itself vulnerable."

Any hope that our tête-à-tête might be to steal a few sweet kisses died. "Camille's smart and we're in trouble. That's not news. And Mr. Elias isn't the only one concerned."

"Understood. But he is preparing to step in."

I brightened. "With cash?"

Glynn shook his head, once, that sharp, almost angry denial. "He's rich, but Meiers Corners isn't the only place in need, or even the neediest. With the state of the economy, even all his wealth is only a splint and a bandage."

"Then what is he planning?"

"He's put Project Shield on alert."

"Which means what?"

"Meiers Corners could become a vampire battleground."

That didn't sound good. "How many vampires are we talking about?"

"Maybe fifty Alliance, but the best of the best. Perhaps five hundred Lestat."

I rested my head against the stairwell wall, closed my eyes. "Isn't war a bit premature?"

"The alert is only a first step, in response to Camille's tricks. Elias is never rash. But if the show doesn't make a profit by closing night, that'll be a second warning and he'll go to high alert. If, at the end of the month, the Meiers Corners businesses can't meet their expenses and start going bankrupt—"

"It's war. I get it. And the humans? What about us Meiers Corners...sizians?"

"That's why I want you out." Glynn's tone was flat with

suppressed anger. "We'd take every precaution, but even if we win decisively, Lestats may escape. If the Coterie pulls in muscle from other cities, winning isn't even guaranteed."

I processed that. Blood and gore featured heavily. "If we're only at elevated threat level, why do you want me to leave? The fight won't happen for weeks."

"I've worked with Elias long enough to know how he'll probably do things. But in case he doesn't wait until the end of the month...I don't want to stake your life on it. Or Mishela's."

"Glynn, I can't go."

He got all Mr. Grim Vampire. "You must—"

"Don't worry. I'll be careful. But can't you see this is my fight too?" I put fingers on his cheek. "I need to stay and not just for the show. I need to do everything I can to keep us from hitting red alert. We need to win tourists back from Camille. I need to help. Do you understand?"

Reluctantly, he said, "Yes." Even more reluctantly, he added, "I'm very proud of you, Junior Stieg. Honored to know you."

It wasn't a hot kiss or jewelry. But in some ways it was even better.

We returned to find the store packed with customers. I automatically slapped on my sausage smile, unlocked the cash register and rang through pounds of summer sausage, bologna and brats. The work helped me forget about the approaching horrors.

Until I tuned in to nearby conversations.

"That club is just incredible. I drove from Orland Park to visit."

"I stayed the whole night. Tonight I'm getting in line before the doors open."

"That goth club is so exciting. And I love the free little cheese novelties. What are they called?"

"Ooh, the ones that fizz in your mouth? GObubbles. Love those. I could eat those forever!"

While yay, new tourists, boo that they were all being snared by the opposition. Still, they were in my store now and their credit was as good. My smile stayed bright, if brittle.

The door kept tinkling. Rocky and the mayors left, but new people packed in until the checkout line stretched the length of the store. I punched numbers and bagged so fast my fingers bled—but the line only got longer and the store fuller.

Mom and Pop couldn't help. The way product was flying off the shelves, Pop was running his legs off restocking and Mom was in the Wurstmobile couriering in emergency supplies. I was desperate enough to phone my rent-a-kid, who was busy with soccer practice and couldn't help.

I was officially screwed when the line backed out the front door. The May heat poured in. Our aged coolers started clanking like they'd burst. I waved people frantically inside, but they only packed the open doorway, staring like I was demented.

Glynn saw my dilemma. Brilliant guy that he was, he glided to the door and did his vampire compulsion thing. "Inside, please. Form the line here."

He shepherded them all in and shut the door, then nudged the line to wind through the aisles. Oh, wonderful man. Vampire. Whatever. I didn't think I could love him any more.

Until he got behind the counter and started bagging.

Yep, confirmed. Keeper.

Time leaped forward in a flurry of cashiering and bagging. It wasn't until my stomach growled that I looked up. Two minutes to noon. "Wow, that went fast."

My dad insisted on a break every four hours, even in the midst of chaos. I hung up my Wurstspeicher smock and Pop took my place behind the register.

"Lunch?" Glynn followed me upstairs.

"No, I have to practice. There are a couple gnarly parts I need to keep under my fingers." With the outcome of the show so important, I didn't want to do anything less than shine.

"Surely you have to eat."

My stomach growled again, answering him. "I'll power down a bagel when I'm done."

In the attic, he followed me so tight I started getting doggy ideas. So of course upon entering my room, the first thing I saw was my bed. I blushed, suffered my stomach rumbling again, snapped, "Outside. I really do have to practice."

Glynn backpedaled, sat himself on the bare boards just outside my door. "I'll wait here."

"Thanks." I scooted my chair out, sat, assembled clarinet and flute and started woodshedding the tornado scene, lots of fast chromatics.

When I stopped to adjust my reed, Glynn called in, "Why do you practice those nasty parts so hard when they're covered up by brass?"

No real answer for that, so I just snarled at him.

He laughed. "Emerson warned me about that."

"About what?" I twirled the screw of my ligature as I waited for him to expand on *that*, tightened it one crank too tight. "*What?*"

"Just that you might get like this."

I tossed clarinet onto stand and glared out the door.

He sat with his back to the wall that framed my door, eyes closed. I glared harder, trying to poke through his nonchalance. No go, so I snatched an old reed from my clarinet case and threw it at him. He caught it one-handed without even opening his eyes. I snarled louder. "Do vampires practice being cryptic? Or is it like immortality and you're just built that way?"

"We're not immortal. And I wasn't being cryptic." Glynn slipped the reed inside his jacket. "Emerson simply said you're small, so you might get crabby if you're not fed often enough. His wee wife does."

"That sure as hell was crypt...hey. I'm not crabby. Focused on my work, maybe. If you guys aren't immortal, how do you explain Mr. Elias and his older-than-the-mists-of-time shtick?"

"We can be killed. That makes us mortal." Glynn's eyes opened, directly on mine.

I almost fell into those blue jewels. Hell, I nearly dove in like the Hawaiian cliff diver pictured on my west wall. But fortunately I was too crabby...hungry...focused on work. I spun back to my instruments. "You don't age. Immortal."

"Oh, we age."

"You do?" I picked up my flute.

"We just heal it."

"You 'heal' aging. My head hurts. Look, I'm going to finish practicing and get back to the store. Do you need to sleep? I can draw the curtains for you." Although thinking of Glynn, on my *bed*...well, it didn't conjure images of sleeping.

"What about your bagel? You promised to eat."

"Sure, I'll grab it on the way down." I started playing.

"Junior." He blurred to his feet and filled the doorway, eyes blazing—so handsome he'd have gotten my attention even if he hadn't suddenly loomed bigger than life. "You need to sit to eat, take time to digest."

I paused with my flute at my mouth. "Love to, but I need to spell Pop more. With a crowd like that, Mom can only restock solo for so long. If she's even in the Haus." Not to mention all the other behind-the-scenes work they did.

Yeah, I admit it. They couldn't run the store without me, but I couldn't run it without them, either.

"I'll spell your father."

I blinked. "You what?"

"I'll run the cash register while you eat. I've done many things in my time, including a bit of retail. Your register doesn't look too hard."

Glynn was offering to do my job so that I could eat. Not just eat, but sit down with my food. Chew it. Digest it. Maybe even relax a little.

No one had done that for me in a long time. Nobody had sat with me while I practiced, either, not since Nixie and Rocky in high school.

Sitting with me, talking with me, sharing my work... Things a friend did. A good friend.

"Yeah, but—" Words collided inside me, a traffic jam of feeling. I settled for, "I can't pay you."

He wrapped fingers around either side of the doorjamb and leaned into the room to press a quick kiss to my lips. While I was gaping, he swung back out. "I'll go relieve your father. Take your time eating."

He went poof in that vampire way, leaving me with the feel of his mouth on my lips. And a big smile.

Fortunately for customer wait time, Glynn stayed the rest of the day. Unfortunately for me, the crowd, heavy and a little aggressive, kept us busy right up until I had to pack my instruments. Even if I was hoping for a little nooky—which I *wasn't*—I didn't get any.

We waited in the hallway for the limo. I might've hoped for a quick orgas...I mean kiss, but Glynn said, "Emerson's called a council of war tonight, directly after the show. I must attend."

"Oh." No nooky right away. "After that?"

"Junior." He took me by the upper arms and started speaking earnestly. I watched his gorgeous mouth, not really hearing him, standing breast-to-ripply-abs and ultra-aware of our size difference—and ultra-aroused by it, to the point that my body was screaming "damn the commitment, full speed ahead".

Until his words cut through my slobbering brain. "...better if we not indulge. Easier. So I won't be seeing you anymore."

"*What?*"

The limo's horn cut me off. Before I could screech *What do you mean you won't be seeing me anymore?* Glynn nudged me out the door and zipped with my sax to the limo. I dashed after, but by the time he stowed sax, shoveled me into the limo and slammed the door, he was the color of boiled lobster and his cryptic remark was the least of my concerns.

I laid a hand on his forehead, flinched at the unnatural heat. "Are you okay?"

"I...will be. In a moment." He was panting.

"Damn it, why didn't I notice this before?"

"Softer...day. And I...disguised it."

"Glynn can't shapeshift yet." Mishela flashed brightly inquisitive eyes between the two of us. "But he can morph small things like his face. I can't wait to do that. No more greasepaint for me. So what have you guys been up to all day? Alone. Together."

Which explained the brightly inquisitive. "We did retail, and not alone." Unfortunately. Except *he didn't want to see me anymore.* I shook my head. "Vampires can shapeshift?"

"After we reach a thousand."

"A thousand what?"

"Years." Mishela ignored my gaping. "Glynn doesn't have long to go."

Nearly a thousand years old. And I'd thought we might have a chance at a real relationship?

No wonder he didn't want to see me anymore. My heart ached. What could be worse?

Well, sure. Having only six people in the audience. Twyla, Nikos and Mayor Meier were joined by all three members of the Teapot Jihad, a radical sect of Meiers Corners teetotalers. (Really. They picketed the Alpine Retreat and Bar on Labor Day, bombed Nieman's on Independence Day with red white and blue smoke balls, and every St. Patrick's they took out an ad in the *Zietung* newspaper pushing green milk. If you think that's yuck, they also distributed pamphlets with full-color close-ups of drunks and toilets, too gruesome to describe.)

Onstage the cast put out SRO energy, singing and dancing their little hearts out. But without audience feedback, without applause or laughs or even a chuckle, it was hard to keep up. Like a balloon in the freezer, the performance slowly deflated.

Oh, there were moments. Toto tried the golden leg-lift on the captain of the Winkies. The captain, wearing tall black rubber boots, just smiled—until Toto started humping black rubber. The captain tried to shake the dog off, but Toto grabbed boot with all four legs and rode it out. It looked like the dog was actually enjoying it.

I snorted into my sax. Which, since the part was half-note stings, was fine.

Aside from that, the show was awful with occasional squalls of horrendous. Which fit my mood. *I won't be seeing you anymore.*

Now, too late, I wished I had processed, wished I'd confronted my feelings after our incredible night together, wished I'd confronted *him*. If we'd hammered out what was going on between us—a bout of sex, a short-term affair, or something more—then I wouldn't feel so confused. So lost.

So why not confront him now, hammer it out now?

Immediately my confusion vanished and my mood improved. The moment our disaster of a show was over, I ran to the dressing rooms, where he'd be hovering over Mishela.

Empty.

Oh, yeah. The actors did a meet and greet in the lobby after performances. I had time, so I packed up my instruments. Then I went to the lobby.

Empty.

Except for the mayor, who looked a little lost. No tourists, and he'd know what that meant. I wondered how much he knew about the added-value issue, the vampire turf wars. No, this was only temporary. The show would be successful. Eventually.

The mayor saw me and brightened. "*Ach*, Gunter Marie. How are you?"

I could have run, but why? No Glynn. This would be the first time he hadn't seen me home in...dammit, I wasn't wistful. "Hey, Mayor Meier."

"*Ach*, I didn't tell you this morning, all my attention on the GLBT mayors, but how you have grown! You, who I have known since wearing diapers—"

"Wow, Mayor, thanks!" Rude, but I had to interrupt. The mayor has this thing about diapers—and whips. Not together, thank goodness. Any other city, it'd have been a scandal. Here, it was one of those small-town secrets, which everyone knows and nobody talks about. Because, come on. Santa in lederhosen with a whip and diaper fetish? So wrong. "What did you think of the show, Mayor?"

"I am dejected, *liebchen*. The attendance is in the toilet, *nein*?" Then he brightened. "But tomorrow is Sunday. The matinee will be better attended, *ja*?"

Well, who was I to burst his tiny beer bubbles?

Then I realized the matinee started at three in the afternoon, well before Fangs To You opened. There'd be no competition for the timeslot.

Rainbows and leprechauns and St. Murphy the Good filled my head. If people but experienced the joy of our show, they'd want to tell their friends. All we had to do was put butts in seats. "You betcha, Mayor! And I'm going to make sure of it."

Hey, if Camille could market with flyers, why couldn't a cute and totally competent sausage retailer?

Julian's limo took me home. But before I made flyers, I had that little outstanding issue to deal with. *I won't be seeing you anymore.*

I rushed to my bedroom to call Glynn, not as simple as it sounds. Before I called, I had to close my bedroom window, shut my door tight and stuff a sock into the crack underneath. Not that I thought the parents listened to my personal conversations. I *knew* they did. Hey, even paranoid people have parents.

When I was as private as possible, I touched my UK map for luck and called his cell phone. The line clicked open.

"Hello, *babi*."

Glynn's deep voice vibrated out of the phone and down my spine, echoed inside. Not hearing that voice ever again... Confused feelings fled. "What the hell did you mean, you won't be seeing me?"

A breath of air came over the line, a sigh. "Junior. I think I love you."

I sucked my heart into my throat, where it stuck.

"Perhaps we could have...ah, but we'll never know. I'm aware of your duty to your parents, your dreams of New York. But when I'm near you, all I want is to make you mine. Even today, with the sun a check on my libido, I wanted you so badly I nearly tossed you on the counter to have you a dozen times, despite the crowd, despite your parents. So I must stay away."

"But Glynn, what if I wanted to be yours? I don't know what I'm feeling, but I do know you're special. That we've got something special. While you're here, couldn't we at least see each other?"

"*Babi.* If you don't know what you're feeling, sex will only confuse matters. Can you honestly say you'd give up New York? That you'd choose me over your dreams?"

I swallowed. "But...couldn't we..."

"No, love." His voice was soft and full of regret. "We can't." He hung up.

Today's a matinee and our prospects are good.

Sunday morning I repeated that mantra as I stapled, taped and thumb-tacked flyers from Eisenhower to Cedar, from East Thirteenth to West. It took all morning (I skipped church and caught hell from Mrs. Gelb—that is, a stern finger-shake), but I papered the whole city.

It also took ten dollars' worth of paper and forty dollars of ink, but saving the show would be worth it. Saving the show—and Meiers Corners, by keeping Mr. Woo-Hoo Ancient from unleashing his Ray o' Vampire Deathiness. The show, Meiers Corners, Chicago—and maybe the world! Yes, I was one awesome woman, one big fish in this small pond, thank you, thank you.

Taking mental bows, I crossed Jefferson onto my block, saw the shreds of the Cheese Dudes' worm, and grinned at the display of Glynn's caring. Remembered he cared too much *I think I love you* and got depressed.

Wait. I'd saved the show. Was there a problem in the universe I couldn't overcome? No! I was SuperSausageLady, able to leap tall buildings in a single bound, catch bullets with my teeth and command the weather with a wave of my hand. Maybe not the last, but relationship troubles were easy-peasy. After I saved the show and the city and world, I'd just convince Glynn to come to New York with me.

Should have known when I started thinking words like easy-peasy that I was tripping, Yellow Submarining toward chicken buh-awking insane.

Totally oblivious, I headed into our shaded walkway, butchering the lyrics to "Singin' In The Rain". Felt the pound of a very different music.

Vague horror frosted my spine. I turned. Across the street, the sun glared off blisteringly shiny black marble. I squinted—what I'd taken for shadows resolved into a long line of black-garbed people.

The line was moving. Fangs To You was open.

Dad waited at our door. "*Ach*, Junior. That racket has been going on since eleven. Even Good Shepherd had trouble filling its pews today."

Numb horror bloomed into actual ice. Good Shepherd, with its cosmic whip, had trouble getting people in the seats? What chance did my little paper and ink carrots have?

I found out that afternoon. Two people were in the audience, Mayor Meier and the PAC's janitor.

We ran the show, but it was worse than the first rehearsal. The mayor was dejected, the pit was dejected, the actors were dejected. Dumas wasn't even yakking about Method acting.

Toto was still humping everything in sight.

But we were losing money, losing audience, losing tourists. Losing to Camille and the Coterie. And unless Fangs To You's novelty wore off damned soon, there was nothing we could do about it. Nothing *I* could do about it.

My entire morning felt like a lie. I wasn't a big fish, I was a very small fish floating in my tiny pond—on my side.

Worse, when I looked for Glynn after the show (I know, I was weak), I only found Mishela, who told me with a pitying look that Emersons would give me a ride home.

At home I ran up to my attic hideaway and threw off my concert blacks. Stomped naked around my room until a *bam-bam* from below told me I'd stomped too hard. No growls came through the window (it was still light out but I'd been hoping), so I gave up and tugged on cutoff jeans and a baggy T-shirt over my naked skin and moped for a while. I tried visiting the places on my wall, first escaping to the Globe Theatre, then sticking my arms out like the Rio de Janeiro statue and shouting inanely, "I'm the king of the world!"

But running in my mental background were the facts, an acid eating away at my manufactured confidence. No audience meant no impressed Broadway backer, no fabulous job in New York. No asking Glynn to come to New York with me.

Phooey. I was catastrophizing. It had only been three days. Surely the good Corners folk would come to their senses soon. Surely by Thursday the novelty of free drinks until you puke would have worn off and we'd have an audience.

Surely they'd get tired of Camille's before it was too late.

I had to believe that. Because, besides playing the very best reed two of my life, there was *nothing* I could do about it.

Sheesh. No wonder theater people were superstitious.

Although if our audience didn't come to their senses... Even supposing we survived vampageddon, I'd never see Glynn again...oh, God. What was I going to do?

I crawled into my roof crenel, stared into the warm evening. Now would be a good time for that all-powerful Ancient One to show up with a plan, or the mayor to find a spare hundred thousand in the budget. Deus ex machina would be very handy right now.

Instead I got Dirkus ex Ruffles. He called to sheepishly let me know that, since the matinee was over, my flyers were classified as litter.

Some days are so shitty, they qualify as their own sewage district. And Murphy, the ass hat, was laughing.

Slamming out of our home, I walked the city, ripping down my useless flyers. Ruffles wouldn't have called on his own. But who put him up to it?

Sure. The Cheese Dudes.

Maybe not, but they were the most likely. So when I got home, I stalked next door to "discuss" it with them. I don't think the discussion would have involved tweaked noses, but I never found out because either they were gone or holed up. I beat my fists for five minutes against their door without an answer.

It left me worn out and deflated, with nothing to do—except see Glynn.

My mood immediately improved.

Bend me over and spank me with a Knackwurst—the single bright point in my life was a male I'd first met Monday? How pathetic was that?

I still had duty. I still had dreams. I was still confused about whether sex with Glynn was a really hot affair or something more. But it's hard to argue with the tug for companionship when you're so damned dejected you want to smack yourself in the foot with a meat cleaver because it'd at least be hurting about something real.

Except he might love me, and because of that didn't want to see me. I should respect that.

The thudding music across the street was a painful counterpoint to the throbbing in my head. This was worse than Buridan's ass. I wasn't midway between two good things, I was sinking in a Bermuda Triangle of three bad. Which reminded me of Glynn's triangle of tchotchkes, which started my feet south.

They took me to Walnut and turned west. Not really just my feet—I knew what I was doing, homing in on Glynn for comfort. I just didn't want to admit it.

I won't be seeing you anymore.

His going all noble on me only proved he was a male of worth, as in worth getting tangled up over. Worth derailing my future? Maybe not, but he might say yes to New York.

That finally convinced me—just as I got to the townhouses. My feet had kept going while I argued with myself. They knew which side would win.

They'd made one stop along the way, to buy condoms. Glynn had only had the one, and I wanted to come...er, arrive prepared.

Chapter Thirteen

I knocked on the first townhouse door. Mrs. Hinz answered.

The Hinzes were "the new folk", having moved to Meiers Corners last November. They'd still be the new folk twenty years from now. Ironically, that didn't stop anyone from considering the Hinzes ours, or for them to consider Meiers Corners home. Strange and distinctly schizophrenic, but that's the way things were in our small town.

"Hello, Junior," Mrs. Hinz said. "You're here for Glynn?"

I wasn't surprised she knew. Even if Nixie hadn't blabbed, TV-DBGN (the Dolly Barton Gossip Network) would have told her. Dolly's network was so efficient, Mrs. Hinz might even know I'd bought the Peppy Peenie brand latex (they came in XXL). "Is he in?"

"Yes. I'm glad you're here. Perhaps you can 'cheer' him up." She put a strange emphasis on the word.

"I'll do my best."

"After the matinee, all four of them dragged in like something left out in the sun too long." She winked to let me know she was in on the vampire thing. "But while Master Julian and his wife have ways they can 'cheer' themselves up and Mishela is too young, Glynn needs a good dose of 'cheering' right now." She winked again, to let me know—aw, heck.

Gossip, okay. Knowing my deepest, darkest secrets, fine. But I draw the line at city-wide mental sex cams. "Um, yeah. Thanks, Mrs. Hinz. If I can just borrow your stairs to the basement?"

"Certainly Junior. This way." She led me through a cozy living room to the stairs, and I trotted down.

At Glynn's shut door, I took a deep breath and raised my hand.

The door flew open, to a wild-eyed Glynn.

He was wearing nothing but silken sleep pants. Before I could ogle, he pulled me into his embrace. His naked arms were strong, his muscled torso warm and supple. For a moment I just rested in the haven of his strength.

Then he groaned, "I tried so hard to resist," and tugged me into his room. When the door swung shut, he kissed me.

Ah, that fresh taste of his, like crisp breezes and clear mountain streams. His skin was warm as a sun-dappled meadow. And pulsing against my belly was the thick branch of his big ol' redwood. Apparently a checked libido wasn't the same as a dead one.

This was why I'd come. No one made me feel like Glynn. Made me glow. Made me feel stronger, smarter. Better.

Made me feel loved.

The plain fact was I needed him. For a week or forever, it didn't matter. I needed him and I needed him now.

I stood on tiptoe to return his kiss. Nipping those luscious lips was like tasting campfires and s'mores, all the best of nature. "More." I threaded my fingers in his hair and pulled.

He slanted his mouth across mine and one big hand cupped my head, holding me for hard, hot ravishment.

I wanted to ravish him too. I grabbed his ears and launched myself up, wrapping my shorts-bared legs around his lean waist, snugging us skin to skin. My feet found purchase on his muscular behind, my crotch pressed to his washboard belly, my breasts crushed against the hard muscles of his chest.

My mouth landed directly on his.

I tasted and nipped, reveling in summer sky and green grass, biting harder until I bit too hard and he jerked.

I'd forgotten what went with the nature druid—the vampire prince. With a growl, he threw me on the bed. Before I even stopped bouncing, he misted naked, sailed on top of me and started tearing at my jean shorts. I'd released something dangerous—and incredibly hot.

While he ripped open my zipper, I tugged my shirt over my head. Oh, the look on his face when he realized I wasn't wearing any undies.

There's a moment of truth when it comes to sex and pants. If the woman wants it, she'll lift her hips, just enough. Without that subtle aid, it's harder for the man to remove her last physical barrier to penetration.

It's the last psychological barrier too. That hip-raise is a vital part of the sexual dance. It's a nonverbal cue that tells a man how ready the woman is. More important, how the man handles it shouts to a woman whether he's in tune with her and listening to her needs.

I wasn't ready for intercourse yet. Oh, I wanted Glynn bad. But there were things I wanted to do before we got to penetration. Kiss him more, bite him, tongue his magnificent torso. Compare the taste of his nipples to the intriguing dent of his navel.

Ah hell, I just wanted to put my face between his pecs and rub.

I looked up to tell him and was shocked.

His eyes were blood red, roving over my naked breasts and belly. When his hot gaze landed on the hint of pubic curls in the V of my open zipper, his eyes actually started glowing.

More than his eyes had gone pure vampire. Fangs split his lips, still lengthening. His breathing was barely controlled. His fingers were tipped by long, sharp claws.

He knelt by my thighs. Putting palms on the sides of my shorts, he tugged, hard. He wanted in now.

The shorts didn't move. I hadn't done the assist. Sex would be awesome, but not yet. I half-lay on my elbows and waited to see what he'd do. I had no doubt that if I said stop, he'd stop. But the hip-raise was subtle, and he was aroused enough to miss it and strong enough to yank off the shorts without help. Animal lust rolled off him in waves. I certainly wouldn't blame him if he went for it.

His fingers curled on my hips. A slight prick through the denim told me just how close to the sexual edge he was. How close he was to, not even pulling my shorts off, but simply ripping them to shreds.

His eyes clamped shut. His nostrils flared white with his effort to control himself. His fingers spasmed a few times, as if they would go on without him to strip me.

But slowly, his fingers loosened. He immediately clenched his hands so they couldn't return. I only realized he hadn't retracted his talons when blood slowly dripped from one fist.

I sat up and reached for it. "Glynn—"

He shook his head, that sharp single shake. "Pain...helps me focus."

"I don't want you in pain."

His eyes opened, softened to a violet-blue. "You want time to touch me. This is the only way I can give you that."

Oh, sweet heavens. He not only knew I wasn't ready—he knew *why*. And he was doing everything in his power to give me what I wanted.

He was putting my needs before his. Friends did that. And family. And true love.

My heart was too full. "A cold shower?"

He smiled, but it was pained. "Junior, we...my kind...we feel everything stronger. Longer. Pain and pleasure are both vivid and they feed each other. This agony...ah, it's almost sweet." Another deep breath. Eyes closing, then opening, dark blue. "Pain and pleasure in eternal circle. Our poetry calls it the ouroboros of ecstasy."

The ouroboros was the dragon that swallowed its own tail. "Um...sounds intense. Vampires have poetry?"

His expression eased to a real smile. His fangs retracted and he sat back on his heels. "We do. Mostly about sex, all very dark and deep. But it isn't, is it? Truly it's just sex."

"Well, sure." I was relieved to see him not looking so pained. "Unless it's love."

His eyes darkened to royal purple.

Me and my big mouth. Even an underwear slip would have been innocent-sounding compared to the "L" word. Although slipping my tongue under Glynn's wear...yeah, not quite so innocent. But certainly less dangerous.

So I leaned forward to caress the velvet of his skin. Leaned more to press my lips to firm muscle. It was like lipping hot silk.

"Junior. I'm trying to give you a little time. A little space. But..." He gasped when I licked his pectoral. "But I'm still a vampire by nature. A sexual beast."

He was warning me to back off. But I was doing exactly what I'd wanted to do, exploring his body, and he was holding still for it. I found the puckered nib of his nipple, licked it lightly and enjoyed his shudder.

He cleared his throat. "A beast," he repeated. "My control won't last forever."

"I don't want it to," I said and bit his nipple.

He grabbed my head and crushed me to him. I sucked and his nipple tightened even more against my tongue.

He seized my hand and pressed it to his erection, smooth, fat and throbbing. "Ah, *babi*, feel what you're doing to me." In my palm, he swelled even bigger.

Which gave me an idea.

195

"Unpin my hair."

"What?"

I squeezed his cock until he gave a sharp groan. "Unpin my hair."

Pins flew. My braid rolled down my back.

I curled my legs under me and swiveled up on my haunches, sitting knee to knee, mirroring Glynn. Naked but for my open jeans shorts. I combed my fingers through my hair until the braid was gone and kinked tresses rippled from my crown to my butt.

His breathing grew more and more ragged as I worked, his cock bobbing eagerly. A glistening drop appeared at the tip.

I parted my hair at the back of my neck and drew crinkly blue-black veils over my breasts. I leaned forward to kiss his chest again.

As I did, my hair feathered along his thighs, trailed over his erection. His cock jumped. Lusty little beast. Or big beast, actually.

I smiled up at him. Planting a stabilizing palm on his chest, I wrapped a tress around a finger of my free hand. Still smiling, I sucked the tail into my mouth.

Glynn watched me with hot focus, an almost glazed aspect to his stare now.

I released the tress to twist it into a rope, then wrapped it around his shaft, snug. He watched as if this were something he'd never seen before. With another smile, I drew the coiled strand up his erection like a silken noose.

He stiffened sharply and his eyes squeezed shut. Pain or pleasure, I couldn't tell. Maybe there was something to that vampire poetry.

I stopped just under the crown, drew the hair a little tighter. He grimaced, but his cock got fatter and his fangs slid out from between his lips. He reached for me.

I released my hair and launched myself back along the mattress by thrusting my legs straight, landing on my butt a few feet back. The coil of hair ratcheted around his cock like a motor starter.

He roared, choked it off. Dropping forward onto his fists, his head fell over my thighs, his shoulders heaving as he panted for control.

I pursed my lips, studying the back of his bowed head. Still all that control.

Fisting his hair, I pressed his face into the opening of my shorts.

He snarled wildly and seized the waistband with enormous talons. I laid back and lifted my hips, the only thing that saved the shorts from being shredded. He wrenched them to my knees, threw my bound legs over my head and opened his mouth on my exposed vulva.

I arched into the bed, my hair spilling all around me. His tongue slid into the seam of my sex, a hot lick that ignited me. I gasped, caught between wanting to clench my thighs tighter and burning to spread them wide.

The shorts banding my knees made it impossible to spread. I moaned, rolled my hips against his lapping tongue, my honey-dewed vulva sliding along his smooth fangs. He released me and yanked the shorts off altogether.

I grabbed his head and pulled him down onto my mound. He came obligingly. His mouth opened, his tongue slapped along my slit and his breath heated my entire pussy. His fangs unsheathed—

They sank into my mons. I went haywire with orgasm, full-body spasms that would have shaken bones loose if not for him holding me firmly. He plunged his fangs deeper and roughed up my clit with his tongue.

Heat rushed through me, bursting every cell. I came hard in a flush of fever, fire dilating veins and pores and my very self, transforming me into a phoenix rising brilliant and glowing from the heart of climax.

I lay in the stupor of its aftermath. Until with a flick of foil, Glynn mounted me.

He'd found the XXLs.

A ripple of belly buried him inside me. I felt every inch, every rigid, thick vein run into me, slick and electrifying. My eyes popped wide and I gave a little shriek as another small climax hit me.

Glynn, rising like a sea monster between my legs, smiled. Smug.

I growled, clenched my inner muscles hard. That wiped the smile off his face. Replaced it with a look of savage possession. In his hot eyes, I saw hard thrusts and bouncing bodies. Silky skin and panting breath. Plunging, over and over.

Glynn dropped fists next to my head, trapping my hair, and rode me so hard I thought I would shatter.

And then I did.

I arched into him as I climaxed again. He thrust so deep his balls slapped my butt, contracting hard as bellows. Scorching liquid heat filled me, even as he kept thwacking into me. It flooded me, wave on wave of molten pleasure, until the pieces I'd shattered into burst, an explosion of bright gold.

My muscles relaxed, my mind emptied. I was at peace. Glynn's fists still trapped my hair, his head bent as he brought his breathing under control. He softened inside me.

I gingerly started to sit up.

Glynn's cock jerked tight in me. Hardened. "Junior, don't—"

WTF? I elbowed myself sitting. It drew him from my body. His face seared with intense pleasure/pain as his glistening erection emerged.

Erection, as in fully engorged cock, even bigger than before.

I stared. His controlled breaths weren't to bring down his heart rate, but to bring down his erection. To meet my human expectations of a single male orgasm.

I touched his cock in wonder.

He groaned. "*Babi*, please don't—"

"Glynn, please *do*. If you can go again, so can I."

He gave me an incredulous look. I smiled and patted myself in invitation.

It was all he needed. He threw me under him, rolled my thighs up along my ribs, and with a lion's roar, drove into me. He started thrusting, pounding with almost animal ferocity.

I'd already come three times, so I simply smiled and relaxed. Lying under him, I had no end in mind, no goal, except to enjoy his beautiful body, his rippling muscles, his skin glistening with desire.

He kept thrusting. My enjoyment sharpened. Desire returned, wrenching a little mewl from my throat.

His eyes burned bright red at the sound—he'd been waiting for it. His thrusts slowed. His fangs lengthened and his mouth opened on my neck.

Hot breath steamed bright need onto my skin. Sharp points pricked, focusing desire. I throttled a moan...throbbing fangs sank in, releasing it.

Ultraslow, I burst. A full-body climax, lengthened and extended by slow rolls of his hips. I shuddered, wave after wave quaking from brain to toes and back again, crisscrossing until the crests were ecstasy and the troughs were peace, and I shimmered into a full, flowering being.

I was still shimmering when he wrapped me in his strong arms and rolled, brought me on top, cradled in his warmth.

Time snapped into place and I knew. Not just that I loved him. But that he could be the one. Mine, the male I'd spend the rest of my life with.

I lay panting atop his impressive chest. His erection nestled inside me, not wilted after that orgasm so much as waiting quietly. If I moved again, it would grow. It made me very aware of just how different vampires were, that the males could have multiple orgasms.

Which brought to mind the questions that should have been foremost in my head from the start.

I might want to spend the rest of my life with him, but would he want to spend the rest of his life with me? And even if he would—*could* he?

Serious considerations for postcoital bliss. But if he was The One, there were things I had better find out.

Breathing slightly less like a bellows, I managed to raise my head, look him in the face and ask my first question. "Are you married?"

"Of course not."

"With the deal you made about home...girlfriend? Significant other?"

"Junior, no. Not now or in the recent past. I wouldn't get involved with you even on a temporary basis if I belonged to someone else."

Not in the *recent* past. Vampires were both long-lived and highly sexual. In a hundred years Glynn might have had thousands of encounters. How many of those women were still alive? How many still pined for him?

Were there any he pined for?

That pushed me off his hard torso. I jumped off the bed and paced away. "How recent is recent?"

"Years. Decades." His eyes followed me. "Why?"

I opened my mouth to ask the kicker. *How old are you, anyway?* But something else caught my eye.

Something new sat on the little round table.

Just above the center tealight was a single bronzed shoe. Small, not much more than a bootie, with a pointy toe. Under the bronzing was evidence of ornamentation, bands of leather or cloth.

"What's this?" I moved to pick it up.

"Nothing." He was instantly there, a restraining hand on my arm. "Please don't."

199

"This shoe wasn't here the other day."

"I bring it out when I'm considering something."

"Like a concentration focus?" Despite the bronzing, or maybe preserved by it, I could see scuffing.

"Something like that. Junior, don't—"

I turned it over. The sole was worn. "It's been used." I set it back on the table. "It's not a doll's."

"It's not." The bald statement, his flat tone, screamed pain to me.

But I had to know. Not because of Nixie, or because I was curious. But because maybe I could help. "It's a child's shoe," I prompted. "Yours?"

I meant his child's, and he nodded, but to my surprise he added, "It's the first thing that I knew was mine."

I stifled my surprise. "Who owned everything else?"

"My abductor."

Ice rolled through my system. I just stood there as Glynn returned to the bed and sat with unnatural heaviness.

He clasped his hands between his knees. "You'll be curious about that too, I suppose."

For such a strong male to be so sad... That got me moving. I sat on the bed next to him and put an arm around his shoulders, or tried to. My arm wasn't quite long enough, so I snaked it around his ribs instead. "Kidnapping is traumatic. Something you should talk about."

He just sat there, staring at his clasped hands.

I rubbed his spine. "You'll feel better."

"Will I?" He laughed, not a happy sound at all. "Fine. A vampire took me from my home when I was too young to remember."

My hand kept moving on his back, patting reassuringly. But my chest froze.

"His name was Fychan." Glynn shook his head. "I don't think it was his real name. He didn't sound Welsh."

A vampire had kidnapped Glynn as a small child. I breathed past the shock. Kept my tone normal when I said, "Maybe he took a name from someone in the area, to fit in."

"Perhaps." He fell silent.

"So your earliest memories are of this vampire Fychan?" I prompted.

He drew a bushel of air, let it out slowly. "Fychan, and the road. Sleeping in hay lofts and open fields, moving at night. Staying a day or two but never very long. Always hungry...for food, but for simple human comfort too."

I wrapped my other arm around him, an awkward hug. "Why did he keep you?"

"I was his early warning system while he slept. Also a decoy to catch humans unaware. A watcher for witnesses while he drank. And sometimes, when he was particularly inept at the catching, his source of fresh blood."

I couldn't help it, I jerked. "That's...that's horrible."

"It was my life." Glynn's voice was hollow. "For eight years he dragged me across Wales and England and Scotland, barely one step ahead of the lynch mobs. One night he got drunk on whiskey piss without hunting first. He drank blood from me, too much. It killed me, and I woke like him."

We sat in silence. I rubbed my cheek against him, giving and seeking comfort. "You were turned as a boy? How did you survive?"

"I found others like me. Young, just turned. We watched out for each other. I grew to manhood with them...vampires become their ideal age, no matter how old they are when they die. My little gang...we did the best we could, but we weren't a family." He sighed. "Because of the vampire, I had no family, no home, and no childhood. Except..." He gazed at the table and his face softened. I thought he looked at the cookie press.

The love in his eyes was evident even after all these years. I wished with all my heart that I could inspire such a love. "Who was she?"

"A farm wife. A big woman with an even bigger heart. Her name was Nesta." His voice warmed from that hollow, distant tone. "We stayed in her barn one of the last summers I was human. Fychan pretended to be a farm hand. He did some work at night and I did the rest during the day.

"It was the best summer of my life. Not only did I get enough to eat, but we stayed in one place long enough for me to get to know people. Nesta made cookies for me. That was her stamp. She gave it to me."

"And the pipe?"

"Her husband John relaxed with a pipe of the evening. I found the

201

smell soothing." He swallowed several times. "One night, in the barn, John discovered Fychan drinking from his wife's neck. John stabbed the fool vampire with a pitchfork. While John went for the axe to sever Fychan's neck...well, one of my duties was to save the vampire from his own stupidity. I pulled out the pitchfork and we fled."

"Was Nesta okay?"

"For all his faults, Fychan wasn't a killer, or not intentionally. Both John and Nesta lived to a ripe old age. They had a small army of grandchildren and great-grandchildren. When I went back to Wales as a young vampire, I...watched over them from afar. Helped them as I could."

He'd watched over them. Despite never having a family, he knew how to care for one. "That was good of you."

"It felt...right. When the family died out, I bought the holding. I live there two months out of the year as my home."

He traveled to Wales every year. Called the only place he'd been happy his home.

I could see the yearning for a true home in every tense line of his body, every gesture and word. In the glistening of his eyes. He still felt like he was on the outside, looking in. Vulnerable. So strong, so caring...yet he had no center.

It made my heart ache. He was right—I was lucky to have a home, a center, a base of strength. A place, as a youngster, to push against, safe enough to define not only who I was, but who I wasn't.

Glynn had none of that. Like his tchotchke table, his center was only a mist of unknown. Although that would make him even more dangerous, because he had no stake in anything at all.

But it would take its toll.

I stared at the mementos on the table, the cookie press, pipe and dragon... "If you wandered all of Great Britain, how do you know you're Welsh?"

"I had a blanket, long since rags but fresh in my memory, embroidered with a coat of arms bearing three heads. I looked it up later. It's Ednyfed, who was Welsh. A few half-remembered baby words... I don't know absolutely that I'm Welsh, but it feels right."

"But what about the vampire? Couldn't he tell you your name or where you came from?"

"Fychan claimed he didn't know. In a drunken stupor he once

mentioned that I came from a large Welsh homestead, and that the Ednyfed blanket had come with me. But my family could have been anything from the landowner to a visitor to a peasant who worked the land."

"So the vampire named you."

"No." Glynn barked a laugh. "He called me 'boy'. I adopted my own names, for people I admired. Rhys for Lord Rhys ap Gruffydd of Deheubarth. Glynn for Prince Owain Glyndwr, though he came later. And Jenkins because..." He took a breath, slightly hitched. "That's what Nesta called me. It's...like Johnny, or little John. I guess I hoped one of those names was truly mine."

How terrible not to even know your own name. "Did you try hiring a detective? I know this happened a while ago, but kidnapping usually makes the papers. Maybe there are records—"

"Junior. I died in 1240."

I blinked at him. Mishela had alluded to such immense age, but what he was saying was bigger than my brain. "Twelve forty? As in before the Renaissance? As in your life playing out against huge historical events? Queen Elizabeth I, the Inquisition, World Wars I and II—"

"I was there for it all." Glynn's smile was tired. "But mostly I just tried to stay alive. Or undead, I guess."

Now I knew why home was so important to him. And Wales was his home.

Not New York.

I couldn't ask him to come to New York with me, not now. Not after hearing what Wales meant to him. How could I be so selfish as to ask him to give that up?

Although maybe he would ask me to come with him to Wales.

But no. How would I earn money to send to my parents?

God. Maybe some things were not meant to be. I swallowed my pain and wrapped him in my arms. We sat in silence until it was time for me to go home.

The more I knew him, the less important how he made me feel was, and the more I just wanted him to be happy.

Entr'acte

When Junior left, Glynn missed her so much that he was out his door and into the garage before he realized what he was doing, the urge to follow an actual physical tug on his heart.

He reminded himself it was better she'd gone. He had much to think about.

The strength of his feelings troubled him. He'd spent centuries looking for love. He could hardly believe he'd found it in the arms of a woman he'd just met.

But he'd never felt like this before. With all the women through all the centuries, he'd never had this connection. Junior's taste, her smell...the way she was genuinely interested in his tchotchkes...and he just plain liked her.

The kicker was when she'd listened about his childhood. She'd stiffened her spine and supported him. Caressed him. Held him. No woman had done that.

What he felt for Junior could be true love—the kind that lasted a lifetime.

He wanted a lifetime. She kept surprising him, with her courage, her inventiveness in sex, her diverse talents. His heart glowed at the thought of a future with her.

Centuries of restraint pulled him back. If he truly loved her, he had to consider, not just what made *him* happy, but what was best for her.

She put duty to her parents first. Even going to New York was based in the practical reality of supporting them. She couldn't do that if he took her with him.

Wales, the only place he felt something approaching peace, was home only two months out of the year. The rest of the time he traveled, troubleshooting for Elias. Junior could come with him, but bouncing around the country would kill any career. She'd have neither duty nor dreams.

He could go to New York with her, but how long would he last without Wales to center him?

Their lives were headed in different directions.

His Wales visit was scheduled right after the show closed. Up until this week, he'd been looking forward to it with hungry longing. Now he wouldn't even discover if his feelings for her were real before he was gone.

Maybe after he returned, they'd take up where they'd left off.

Unless she found someone else in the meantime. Two months were an eon in the life of a young human.

She should find another love. Glynn could only give her a secretive nature and no real past. She deserved more. A real life. A family. A home.

Loving Junior meant letting her go.

Good. One thing decided. Glynn turned from the garage and glided back to his room. Now to decide another.

Camille.

He and the female had a past. Nothing like his relationship with Junior, though Camille'd had delusions. But his past could have an impact on Junior if both stayed here.

Camille got jealous.

Worse, she took out her jealousy on, not the male in between, but the other female, though never directly. Junior wasn't in any physical danger—if she were, he'd have dealt with Camille as he dealt with any rogue. Decisively.

Not directly, but Camille was the queen of sin. She'd make Junior's life hell with temptation, suffering and crushing Junior's happiness any way she could.

All because Camille wanted Glynn for her own.

She couldn't have him. He'd told her that centuries ago, but said it in a way that didn't burn bridges. Long-lived vampires waved adieu, never goodbye.

But with Junior's happiness at stake, he had to be sure Camille had gotten the message clearly. Junior's safety was paramount. If he had to, he'd even completely burn the bridge. Best case, Camille would hate him instead of Junior. If that didn't work, he'd destroy Camille, her minions and the whole damned Coterie. Whatever it took to make sure Junior was safe. And happy.

In a life without him.

So for Junior, he needed to clarify things with Camille. But for Camille, he'd do it in person. For what she once was—or rather, what they'd all been to each other.

He waited until just before dawn, when Mishela was snuggled in for the day and Emersons were at it again—for the fifth time. Before Junior, Glynn would have raised an eyebrow at the waste of time. Now he was envious.

He strode out into the cool air, noting the bright moon and stars. No clouds to ease his return if he wasn't finished before sunrise. He'd just have to deal with it.

One try to talk Camille into leaving. Into abandoning whatever plan Nosferatu had here with the club. They'd been friends once. Hopefully that still counted for something.

The windows he passed were dark, the humans still abed, so Glynn kicked into the gliding run of his kind. Mist would have been faster, but the mental focus needed to hold the dispersed form made it viable only for short distances. The glide got him there quickly enough.

Glynn paused outside the black marble facade of Fangs To You. If anyone saw him here, it might be considered betrayal. Talking directly to the enemy? He wasn't sure he'd disagree.

He firmed his resolve and shouldered his way through the door.

This late—or early—the bouncers were inside. Again two, different from last night but in the ubiquitous black. Without a line to manage, they simply stood on either side of the door, the muscles bunched up by their aggressive, cross-armed stances prominently displayed in their sleeveless T-shirts. Glynn tested the air for vampire.

Hot scent crashed into his nose, a heavy wash of perspiring humans, cloying perfumes and smoke both legal and illegal. A stench like burning rubber snaked up from trays of little cheese curds scattered around the room. The stink all but masked any vampire signature.

But Glynn was trained to observe too. The larger bouncer's working jaw and clenching fists did not completely hide fangs and claws. Judging by build, the male was older, perhaps two hundred. Not a fledgling, but not Glynn's strength either. The other was either a small vampire or moderate-sized human. If it came to a fight, Glynn would win.

Suddenly cinnamon and anise bit into his nostrils like shards of sugared glass. His nose wrinkled.

Camille.

He could take the bouncers, but she was another story. She was his age, and not only knew all the tricks—she *liked* to fight dirty.

No. He had to believe he could still connect with her somehow.

"Glynn, darling. How good of you to come." Fingers curled over his shoulder, nails pricking. "I have a room waiting for you. All the pleasures."

He turned and beheld her. Glossy black hair, perfect skin, pouting lips and green eyes lined in thick black—just as beautiful, just as treacherous as he last remembered.

"This way." She glided through the crowd as serenely as any queen or goddess. He waited for the pang of unwanted desire to hit, never able to avoid it, only barely able to suppress it and then only using his considerable will.

But this time, nothing.

He followed, slightly off-balance. He felt—nothing. No distracting desire, no disturbing attraction. For the first time in eight hundred years—or actually seven hundred, as the first century she'd been sweet without the bite—he felt nothing for her. He shook himself, reached out for it—still felt nothing.

Except free.

Well. Elias was right again. When the right woman came along, all the others faded away. Too bad he and Junior had no future. It would almost be worth giving up his home for this bliss.

Pulsing heat and music assaulted him as he followed Camille to a glass elevator. The inside pulsed with psychotic red lights. When she reached past him to insert a key in the pad, she crowded him, deliberately pressing her large breasts against him, her pulse pounding with sexual invitation.

Glynn felt the start of a headache at all the pounding pulsing.

One floor up the doors opened to air both cooler and quieter. The headache receded.

An exposed walkway overlooked the seething mass of people. Glynn took note of the layout, automatically cataloging tactical advantages and disadvantages. He wasn't planning to fight his way out, but he'd lived this long by being prepared.

Several doors lined the walkway. Glynn let his senses extend, smell and hearing but also taste and touch. He'd saved a dozen humans once sensing a drop in air temperature just before a vampire attack.

The smell of drugs and sex, the coos and shouts of ecstasy were unexpected. Free beer, yes. Maybe even a bit of marijuana as a naughty curiosity. But he couldn't believe the good townsfolk of Meiers Corners would allow the kind of depredations he sensed here, much less indulge in them. Perhaps visitors to the second floor were all vampires from Chicago. "You're using prostitutes?"

"We call them sex workers, darling." Camille gave him a simpering smile over her shoulder.

Long ago, her smile would have been sweet and he'd have returned it. Later, he'd have felt the sexual tug of those glossy, plump lips. Now he felt—nothing. Amazing. He was truly free. "Vampires?"

"A few. Mostly humans though, especially for the marks too drunk or stoned to care. It's cheaper and easier. More cost effective. Your little plaything would appreciate that."

The barb jabbed home. Junior, a businesswoman, would appreciate cost-effective.

Then he rolled his eyes. Camille had become the goddess of trickery. One person's time might be paid more than another's, but one *person* was never more valuable than another. Junior would approve of cost-effective goods or work, never cost-effective *workers*.

And that was their difference. Junior saw the humanity behind the business. To Camille, these people were nothing but numbers.

But it meant his hope of calling on their old bonds of friendship was dimming.

She opened the last door and stood back, waiting. Wary, Glynn looked in.

Red-flocked walls, black lacquered furniture and iron candelabras dripping guttering candles gave the room a heavy, oppressive feel. Thick, yellowed mirrors skewed what illumination there was into a mockery of light.

The heart-shaped bed, covered in red silk, should have been a valentine. The mirrors and candles twisted it into a dungeon piece. The trio of shackles hanging from the ceiling didn't help.

The naked human women writhing in the shackles were certainly Camille's crowning touch.

"They're for you," Camille purred. "Just titties. I remember you don't like danglies as much, though I don't remember why."

"Are these locals?"

At her sly smile and coy nod, Glynn stifled his immediate reaction, which was to tear the chains from the ceiling and smash the funhouse mirrors. The young women weren't frightened—he'd have smelled it. Still, the drugs he could see in their blown pupils might have made a mockery of their will. Something stronger than marijuana and, he'd guess from the eyes, hallucinogenic. Which might explain why the shiny-new, as Nixie had called it, hadn't worn off and life hadn't returned to normal. How had Camille gotten local folk to try drugs, much less get hooked? "Let them go, Camille."

"But darling—"

"I said release them." He turned on her with a snarl. "Unless you want me to walk out right now."

"Pooh. You've become such a spoilsport." But she waved her hand.

A scrawny human male, naked but for a slave collar and black leather lederhosen—Glynn closed his eyes; only in Meiers Corners—applied key to shackles. When all the women were loose, they and the young man shambled out, stopping just outside the door.

Glynn stalked into the room, far enough that he couldn't see the waiting humans. He spun. "Why, Camille?"

The vampire woman sashayed past him to pick up a crystal decanter and gold-rimmed glass from a tall blackwood table. She didn't pretend to misunderstand him; perhaps her tribute to what they'd all been to each other, perhaps just caprice. "Why? To make money, of course. I'd certainly rather be at my downtown club. It's a hell of a lot more fun, but expansion is good for business. If you're not growing, you're dying."

He lost his temper. "And corrupting the humans? Is that for money?"

"It's because they're *humans*." She whirled. "We're *better*, Glynn. Nosferatu woke me up. These damned short-lived apes are already corrupted—by death." She slammed the decanter down on the blackwood, shattering it and slicing her hand.

Glynn's nostrils flared at the punch of blood-scent. His fangs descended, but not with desire.

209

She considered the slash on her palm. Her eyes rose to his. Slowly, she licked the trickle clean.

He scowled. "You're being a bit obvious, aren't you?"

She flushed and looked away. "Besides, these Meiers Corners humans are such babies. So easy to corrupt."

"So it's *their* fault you tempt them? Their fault you drug them?" His blood flamed. "We *ought* to be better, Camille. We live long enough. But we aren't better at all."

"Of course we are. Watch." She beckoned with one long, red fingernail. The lederhosen man came like a puppy. Smiling all teeth, she petted him like one. "Is this not proof?"

Treating the man like a dog. Glynn shuddered with the memory of Fychan, treating Glynn like an animal or worse. "Oh, indeed. It proves things quite well."

"Somehow, darling, I don't think we're talking about the same thing." She pushed the man away and he wandered out the door. Then she smiled at Glynn. "Perhaps this will help you see my point."

She released a tie at her nape. The drapes covering her breasts fell.

Glynn, watching her shoulders for an attack tell, couldn't avoid seeing her round globes bared.

As a new vampire, Camille had been pretty. Conical little breasts with dainty coral nipples. As she grew into the change, her breasts became large as musk melons yet high as a teenager's on her chest.

Glynn waited for the automatic surge of lust that being a vampire made impossible to avoid.

Nothing.

He swallowed. Free. He was truly free. He owed Junior more than she'd ever know. If he hadn't loved her already, that would have cemented it.

His anger cooled, and he remembered he'd come here to connect. "We were friends once, Camille. What happened?"

"Friends? We were lovers."

He snorted. "The way a pack of puppies are lovers. When there were just the five of us, you were different. Caring."

At first, she didn't get it. He could see it in her wide, confused eyes. She looked almost as he'd known her then, when they'd been fledglings with only each other for support, innocent and new and scared, but together.

Now she had only Nosferatu. The Coterie's head was not known for his understanding.

"Please, Camille. Tell Nosferatu this won't work. Tell him there's no profit in corrupting Meiers Corners." Glynn reached for her hand, in the spirit of what they'd once had.

She jerked away. Her eyes narrowed. "I brought you here to give *you* one last chance to see reason. Your side is outsmarted and outnumbered. Switch to the winners before you get hurt."

"Strange. I came to talk sense into you." He could afford to be gentle now; she had no more hold over him. "The Ancient One isn't too happy with you. He's rather fond of Meiers Corners."

"Even your precious Ancient won't save Meiers Corners this time." She snapped her fingers. The humans, doped-up thralls, dutifully came. She snapped again. The young man bent to one of her large, high breasts, and a woman to the other. She pressed their heads to the ruby centers. Her lids half-closed, her nostrils flared, her mouth dropped open in pleasure. "Remember this, Glynn. Remember the humans of Meiers Corners are *mine*. And remember you could have shared in it all."

Glynn shook his head, saddened. "Camille. A share of emptiness, no matter how large, is still just a pile of nothing. I won't let you harm Junior."

The vampire's eyes narrowed to slits. "Who says I care? Play around with your little human if you want. I got over you a long time ago, Glynn. I have bigger fish to fry."

"You'll leave her alone? Your word?"

"Yes." She smiled. "My word."

Glynn left. He'd gotten what he came for—Camille had agreed to leave Junior alone.

But his headache had returned, perhaps because he knew the value of the word of the queen of lies. As empty as that pile of nothing.

Chapter Fourteen

So there we were. The city had put all its financial eggs in one basket, tourism. But CIC Mutual was pressuring our business shells from the outside, while Camille sucked cash flow yolk from the inside. Crunching was inevitable.

Too many defaulted loans would kill the Sparkasse Bank, which would topple the whole town. Which would start a vampire war, top of the not-good food chain.

More personally, *Oz, Wonderful Oz*'s attendance was in the sewer and morale was even lower. If we were this pathetic closing night, we wouldn't get to Milwaukee, much less Broadway.

Could things get any worse?

Yeah, I apparently enjoy flushing my head down Murphy's toilet. Yay, swirlies.

"Get the hell out of my way! I saw this scarf first."

"I had my hand on it. You get the hell out of my way."

I sighed, gave up facing boxed sausage and shut the clanking cooler door to make my way to the combatants.

Were they big city nobs, no patience and less humanity?

I wish.

"All right Mrs. Gelb, Mrs. Gruen. Break it up." I pushed them apart. They glared at each other, jaws jutting. The contested scarf fell to the floor. "I thought you two were friends."

"I thought so too." Mrs. Gelb's jaw jutted so far I thought her nose would fall in. "I was wrong."

"You're no friend," Mrs. Gruen blasted back.

"I've got more scarves in back," I said. "You can both have one."

"I wouldn't touch it now." Mrs. Gelb turned away with a sniff. "Not if *she* wants it."

"Me either. Not if *she* does." Mrs. Gruen stomped off for the door.

Then, to my everlasting hope, she paused. Sneaked a glance over her shoulder.

Mrs. Gelb gave her a stiff back with a side of cold shoulder.

Mrs. Gruen huffed out.

"How dare she?" Mrs. Gelb glared at me like this was *my* fault. Then she too stomped out the door, leaving me to pick up the scarf.

I brushed the dirt and indignity from it (okay, there wasn't any real dirt, thanks to the Stieg broom fetish), and sighed as I folded it and returned it to the shelf. Meiers Corners matrons making scenes—worse, making *messes*. What in blazes was going on?

I didn't know what had gotten into *die Frauen*'s morning Schnitzel-O's, but whatever it was, I didn't want it to get worse. I called Pop to bring out more scarves.

Proactive Junior, making sure things didn't get worse. Yeah, next time I'll just take a mallet to my head. It'll be faster and less painful.

I was handing Hermy a jar of creamed Braunschweiger, the new Summer Spices collection, for Tiny to test when Twyla Tafel sailed through the door.

"It's Armageddon." Twyla slapped her hand on the counter. "I swear the whole city is going van Gogh, cut-my-ear-off insane. Did you hear what happened at Der Lebensmittelgeschaft?"

"The grocery store? No, what?" I got down a second test jar and opened it.

"Traffic accident. Mrs. Schwartzkeller cut off Mrs. Weiss with a wide right turn and a wider right gesture."

"Parking lot?"

"Produce aisle. Knocked an entire display of casabas to the floor with her shopping cart. "

I stuck a spoon in the jar and handed it to Hermy, then got Twyla's order together. "A few smashed melons isn't the end of the world."

"No, but then they started a *catfight*."

"I don't believe it. Pillars of Meiers Corners society don't spar in the produce aisle."

"Spar? Try screaming and scratching and hair pulling."

"That's bad." I watched Hermy offer a spoonful of creamed Braunschweiger (with chives) to Tiny as I bagged the city's order. "But still not Armageddon."

"It gets worse. The melons pulped into a muddy mess. Mrs. Weiss tore off Mrs. Schwartzkeller's blouse and Mrs. Schwartzkeller ripped Mrs. Weiss's skirt to her ass...and, well, both of them ended up with bruised tits and black eyes and tickets for disorderly conduct. The video's already on YouTube."

"Okay, that might qualify for a couple apocalyptic horsemen. Were they drunk?"

"Not alcohol, but Elena thinks they were jacked on some sort of psychedelic, though they swore they hadn't done any drugs. But that's not the worst of it."

"You're kidding." I rang her order up.

"Elena fielded an armed robbery at the Alpine and Ruffles had a case of domestic abuse—not bedroom games getting out of hand but broken jaw battery."

"Good heavens." I stopped ringing and stared at her. "What's going on with everybody?"

"Call the CDC. It's an epidemic of stupid."

I handed her the bag. "Strange that it started just when Fangs To You opened. Coincidence?"

"Maybe corruption is infectious."

"Thank you, Typhoid Camille."

The door bell tinkled, but before I could even hope for a shiver, Rocky ran in.

"Junior! I know you hate those things, but you'd never hurt my mother like this so please tell me it wasn't you."

Twyla grabbed Rocky's shoulders. "Breathe, kiddo."

She breathed, barely. "Someone shot my mom's pink flamingo and stole her gnome!"

The flamingo wasn't a crime, but stealing a gnome was just plain despicable. "It wasn't me, Rocky."

The bell rang again. Mrs. Blau stopped in the doorway, her expression outraged. "What are you doing?" She strode to the counter. "That is for *babies*."

We all just gaped as she struck the jar of baby food out of Hermy's hand.

Hermy blinked big eyes. "But Tiny is a baby. My baby."

"Now look here." Mrs. Blau grabbed Hermy by the snug sack

straps. "Tiny is a cat. C-A-T. He has claws and whiskers and licks his butt."

"He's my baby."

"Your baby died. And the sooner you realize that and get over it, the better!"

I reached out a hand. "Hermy—"

"He's my baby!"

I'll never forget the way Hermy's face crumpled as she ran out.

It was the last straw. I had no idea why Fangs To You's novelty hadn't worn off, why Meiers Corners not only wasn't returning to normal but getting worse. But one thing was clear.

Camille's hold on us had to be broken.

Of course the question was, if not the free drinks, what was Camille's hold? I needed more information.

I called Glynn that evening to get some background on her. They seemed to have some sort of history.

I told him about all the strange behavior and my belief that Camille was at the bottom of it. "I think she's gone beyond just stealing our business. I think she's stealing our souls."

"Camille does like to corrupt," he said reluctantly. "What if I said you were right?"

"Then I'd find some way to grass her ass."

"*Babi*, no. We have no idea how she is subverting people. You need to stay away from her until we know more."

"I can't do *nothing*. These are my people. Meiers Corners is my city."

"Your home," he said softly.

"My home, yes, okay." I blew a disgruntled breath. "I feel so helpless. We beat the kidnapping attempts only to find Camille had a plan to lure away the tourists. Even if we win back the tourists, I think she has another plan after that—to corrupt our people. Even if we save Meiers Corners, how do we know she doesn't have another plan after that? And another?"

"Junior, shh. It's okay." His voice deepened, gentled. "One plan at a time. We defeated the kidnapper. We'll win back the tourists."

I shook my head. "That's my job, not yours. You're supposed to guard Mishela. I'm supposed to win tourists. Well, me and the show."

"Your job is to stay safe. Mine is to keep you that way."

"Hard to do after you leave town." I gulped. "Sorry, that was uncalled for. If it makes you feel better, I'll stay away from her, safe in my bedroom. Um...you could come over here."

"My scent is on you, love. It needs to wear off. Something happened and I don't want to remind Camille that you and I...well, it's complicated."

"It always is. I just promised I wouldn't go anywhere for a while. Since I'm stuck here, you might as well explain."

He sighed. "Friday, she smelled me on you. That wasn't a problem because vampires have casual liaisons all the time. But if she smells me on you days from now, if that scent is actually stronger... Camille is not stupid. She'll know you and I have gone beyond a casual liaison. She's quick to exploit any vulnerability."

He was staying away to protect me.

When I hung up, it was with a lump in my throat. I wished hard for vampire senses so I could smell him on my skin too, and be a little less lonely.

Tuesday was worse. Friendly waves were gone. Eye contact was a thing of the past. My mother put on *I Pagliacci*—not only tragic opera but one about clowns. Yeah, we were really wallowing.

I knew Camille was responsible but not how. The obvious thing to do, the thing I *wanted* to do, was head straight across the street and scope out Fangs To You. But Glynn wanted me to stay out of her way and I'd honor that if I could.

So I called my resources. Twyla promised info on Camille's permits. Rocky said she'd check the connection between CIC insurance and Fangs To You. I tried to tease information out of the customers, but all they did was babble about free drinks and fizzy cheese curds.

Glynn called again that night but didn't come. Um, come over...visit. Whatever. I did my usual routine but it felt flat, like a dieter getting a taste of real food and then being forced back onto pap. I'd only known him a week, but that didn't stop me from a lifetime's worth of wanting. Contrarily, I resented his being unavailable. Yes, he was doing it to protect me. Yes, he was leaving at the end of the show's run. I was counting on it, needing it to get my feet and my rainbow dreams back under me.

But all I could think of was that Glynn and I only had a few more days together, and I wasn't even going to get that.

Wednesday I got a call from Elena with orders to come to breakfast at the Caffeine Café. As a cop with a very sharp knife, a very big gun, and an even bigger gun, nobody except hubby Bo argues with Elena. I went.

At the café, Tammy led me upstairs to a private room I didn't know existed, containing a single round table. Six women sat around the table, two-thirds of them pregnant and all involved in good-natured arguing.

Elena, Nixie and Twyla were on one side, brunette, blonde, brunette. On the other side were three blondes. Gretchen Johnson was Elena's sister, with the looks of a cheerleader and a sweet, mothering nature. Liese Schmetterling was a computer geek, wholesome as a dairy maid, recently married to cover-hunk-gorgeous Logan Steel. And finally there was Liese's mother, Hattie Stieg Schmetterling Gillette. (Also my aunt. As I mentioned, everybody's related in the Corners to some degree or another, even the people who've just moved here. The genes rub off.)

"That's all of us." Elena pointed me to the last empty chair. "I hereby call to order the first meeting of V-spouses of Meiers Corners and Nearby Surrounds."

"The door's shut," Twyla said. "We can use the word vampire."

Pulling out my chair, I stopped. "Vampire spouses? Why am I here?"

"Because of Glynn." Twyla said this, but everyone nodded.

"But...he's leaving at the end of the week."

"Su-ure he is," Elena said. "Ring or not, you're part of our world now. Sit."

As I mentioned, gun, knife, and way-bigger gun. I sat.

Nixie started things off. "Okay, the beef on the table is as follows. Camille's got her lacquered claws in our collective hides. Julian's working his ass off to get a legal crowbar under her. Meantime, Scary Ancient's got his undies in a bundle. Since he's badder than Blade, we're officially worried."

217

Liese cleared her throat. "We don't know that. The badder than Blade thing. None of us have ever met Elias in person."

The door opened and everybody shut up. Tammy slid in with a tray of food and drink, including my regular order. Since she was part of the Emerson household, discussion started again.

"Liese, you work for Elias, right?" Nixie unwrapped a muffin, her third, from the paper wads on her plate. "You've talked with him on the phone?"

"Yes."

"Okay. Superman or Blade?"

"Um, Blade."

"Blade or the Terminator?"

"The Terminator, I guess."

"The Terminator or Elias?"

"Elias...oh."

Having made her point, Nixie popped muffin in her mouth and moved on. "Nosy's the ruinator behind Camille, hacking at MC tourism to chapter seven the city. That happens, Scary Ancient'll start a war and our hubs'll be front line."

Aunt Hattie raised her hand. "Translation?"

"Nosferatu's ruining our tourism, Mom," Liese said. "To bankrupt us, make us ripe for takeover. The Ancient One won't allow that, but it might put Meiers Corners in the middle of a vampire war, with Julian and the rest out front."

"They'll need all the help they can get," Nixie said. "That's us."

Elena slammed her mug on the table. "We'd be more help if we were vamps."

"That would be nice," Liese said. "Not just for fighting. With us aging and them not, it'd give us happily ever after, emphasis on ever."

"You know we can't convert now." Nixie rubbed her belly. "We couldn't make rugrats as vampires."

Elena's sister Gretchen laughed. "That wouldn't be so bad. My second baby was born in March, and I'm already pregnant again."

That brought on a round of congratulations and frappe toasts. I leaned toward Nixie. "I thought vampires couldn't get humans pregnant." At least, that was what Glynn had said.

"Sure, if you and the vampire aren't mates. Then nothing takes.

But you are..." She pointed at her rounded belly. "Bang. Everything does."

That sat me back.

Elena was still arguing. "Even after our kid's born, Bo won't make me like him. He won't even *try*."

"It's really dangerous," Liese said. "The chances of a successful turning are very low."

"Steve turned," Elena said, referring not to Shiv but to Gretchen's husband. "Over a year ago."

"But it was horrible. He was murdered by a gang of vampires." Gretchen looked away. "He still has nightmares."

"And I sympathize." Elena rubbed her sister's shoulder. "The thing is, as a vampire I'd be able to kill rogues without arming up like a SWAT team. For me? Totally worth it."

"*If* turning were a sure thing." Liese pulled out her smartphone and a stylus. "But it isn't. I've been doing some research. It's incomplete and I had to extrapolate parts instead of interpolating, which is always dangerous and my statistical app isn't Steel Software's but—"

"Eyes glazing over here," Nixie said. "Bottom line?"

"Well...current turning rate assumes...hmm, a hundred forty-four million bites...seven *billion* humans..." Her stylus flew across the phone's screen. "You have a better chance of getting hit by lightning."

"That's crap." Elena bit her toast like she was the vampire.

"There's a way to better your odds."

Elena stopped mauling defenseless bread. "I'm listening."

"If you're eviscerated, that raises the chances to one in a thousand. Or if you have AIDS."

"Eviscerated?" Twyla's fork hand slowly dropped. "Like split belly, strewn guts? I don't feel so good now."

"You're probably pregnant," Gretchen chirped.

"What? I sure as hell better not be! Nikos would insist we get married, my sister would *never* let me hear the end of it—"

"Not to mention the mayor." Nixie smirked.

Twyla swore, tossed her fork to the plate with a clatter. "Look, what's the deal with turning and happy-ever-after? Why not just enjoy the now?"

"Hello," Elena said. "Super strength, super senses, super speed?"

"Super sex." Hattie grinned.

"*Mother...* I didn't bring her up like this," Liese said to no one in particular.

"What do other human-vampire couples do?" Gretchen asked. "Surely we're not the first women in this situation."

"Race said the Lestats use up their human lovers," Hattie said. "'Drink and screw until they're through'. At least our guys nurture us."

Liese covered her face.

"I don't care," Elena said. "After my kid is born, I'm making Bo turn me."

"Elena, you can't." Gretchen thumped the table every bit as hard as her sister. "You'd have to die, and there's no certainty you'd come through. We need more of a guarantee."

"We need more information." Liese uncovered her face. "Maybe Mr. Elias knows something."

"Yeah." Elena patted her hip. "Let's shoot that ancient fucker and get him to talk."

"I didn't mean—"

"Hello?" The door opened. Instant silence.

A tiny woman bustled in, all bust and hair. Behind her, Tammy hauled in a chair. "Thanks, sugar," the woman said. "Free bikini wax for you."

"Um, no thanks, Ms. Barton." Tammy handed her a mug that smelled like full-throttle chocolate before shutting the door.

Dolly Barton, queen of the MC grapevine, had arrived.

To say Dolly was the town gossip was like saying J. K. Rowling made a little money on those quaint wizard-boy books. Dolly knew *every*thing that went on, sometimes even before it happened. Some people said Dolly had WiFi in her head and that at night she spirit-walked as a webcrawler.

She was a seventy-year-old platinum-blonde dynamo, four foot eight, forty-two D, exactly like the country singer except older and shorter. She wore pink fifties diner-style uniforms and chewed a wad of gum as big as your head.

At her entrance, a tinkling bell rang in my head like her beauty shop. Pavlov instead of Freud. Or I'd backslid from the genital stage to the aural—ha ha.

"Hey Dolly." Nixie was the first to recover her cool, but she rarely lost it. "Sup?"

"I heard about the meeting and thought I'd take a break from haircuts and mani-pedis." Dolly twirled the chair to the table (she was small but strong) and sat, beaming at us. "What are we talking about?"

There was a lot of hemming and hawing because v-guys were secret and we needed to keep our mouths shut.

And Dolly was the Queen of Open Mouths.

Hey, oral-stage Freud was back.

"I was surprised you hadn't invited me." Dolly reached for the condiments basket, snapped up three packets of real sugar and tore them into her mug. I blinked. I was a whopping five-two and it only took a couple extra pounds to make me feel like a blimp. I wondered what Dolly did to work her calories off. Then I thought of the bedroom workout Glynn had given me...

Queen of Open Mouths. I decided I was better off not knowing.

"Gosh, sorry, Dolly," Elena said. "But we're just having a sort of—" she waved vaguely around the table. "Impromptu grade school reunion."

"Hattie was in your class?" Dolly raised eyebrows at Liese's mom.

"Uh..."

"Oh, pick up your jaws. You look like beached fish. I know about vampires."

Whatever mouths hadn't been open, dropped.

Elena went for her gun, stopped herself. "How... I mean where...or why...?"

"Always the detective." Dolly's eyes twinkled. "Stark, of course."

"Solomon Stark?" I frowned. Of Stark and Moss Funeral Home, Solomon Stark looked the part of undertaker, as tall, gaunt and striking as a Tim Burton character—or if you don't know Burton, think Spock from *Star Trek* in an Abe Lincoln hat. Or just think Abe.

"What about Stark...no." Comprehension hit Elena's face. "Oh no."

"Oh yes." Dolly calmly drank chocolate. "We've been lovers for fifty years."

"Fifty?" Liese worked her smartphone. "But that would make you—"

"One hundred and two. I've been with Sol since my fifty-second birthday." She smiled, a small, secret smile. "Don't look a day over seventy, do I?"

"But what...I mean how..." Elena covered her eyes with a hand. "Scratch that, I don't want to know."

"I do," Nixie said. "Julian waited over a thousand years for me. Doesn't seem fair he gets me only sixty, seventy tops."

Gee, what would happen if I stayed with Glynn for seventy years...no. I had New York and he had Wales, and while both were east of Chicago, there was this little matter of the long-distance swim.

"So gimme the 4-1-1," Nixie said. "You've found a way for humans to become immortal, like vampires?"

"Vampires aren't immortal," I muttered.

Everybody looked at me. I flushed. "What? Glynn says they're not. He made a big deal about it."

Dolly laughed. "Well, this won't make you immortal or even stop you aging completely. But it will keep you younger longer, and chase away the aches and pains when the old chassis does start rusting."

"Spew," Nixie said. "What's the secret? Does it involve drinking v-blood?"

"Not exactly. But your lover can help you to heal faster, better."

"How, exactly?" Liese's stylus was poised, her eyes a bright blue.

"It's a secret."

Several women exchanged glances. Elena finally said, "More secret than vampires?"

"Yes." Dolly leaned in, lowered her voice. "Even if your lover shows you, you must *never* speak of it. Not in euphemisms, not in code. Never, ever, not one word, not even among yourselves."

Coming from Dolly, this meant something.

"Why?" Elena demanded.

"If the wrong people *ever* learned of it—" Dolly shuddered. "They'd die."

"Who'd die?" Nixie frowned. "Us? The people who found out? Our vampires?"

"I can't say any more." Dolly rose. "If your lovers want to, they will show you." And on that cryptic note she swept out.

"Huh," Liese said. "Dolly Barton, keeping a secret. Who'da thunk it?"

"Looking like that at a hundred and two?" Gretchen sighed. "I'd like that."

"Not me," Elena said. "I still want to be a full-fledged vamp. Super strength and speed, *plus* a gun? That's a no-brainer."

"But no children," Gretchen said. "Vampire women can't have them."

"Did anyone say why?" Liese asked, paging through her phone. "If the males can make babies, why can't the females? I know the females have periods."

"You do?" All eyes blinked at her.

Stylus paused over phone, she blushed. "I did some research with Logan's female lieutenant. And, um, made a database." Her blush faded. "I'm surprised you didn't know that, Nixie. Since Julian has a female lieutenant too."

"Never came up." Nixie shrugged. "All I know is Julian says no female vamp's gotten pregnant, but they don't know why."

Elena snorted. "They never know why."

"Be fair," Liese said. "They've been hiding the fact that they're vampires for centuries. How would they do the research?"

"How do you do it?" Elena countered. "By asking questions, by looking at reality. By using your head. Know what? I bet they know. I bet it's another secret."

"You think Scary Ancient Fucker knows?" Nixie frowned.

"It's like this anti-aging thing, which we wouldn't have known about if not for Dolly." Elena slapped a hand on the table. "This is exactly why we vampire wives need to stick together." When Twyla cleared her throat, Elena amended, "Why we v-SOs have to stick together."

"He may not know," I put in. "I mean Elias."

"Come on. He knows everything. He's not telling us because he wants to fuck with our minds. Or because he's keeping it back for control."

I shook my head. "That doesn't ring true. Elias is a huge humanitarian, at the forefront of all sorts of charities. Why would he screw us behind our backs?" I was a newcomer to vampires, but in the business world, where a lot of people were out for themselves, Elias was one of the good guys.

Elena opened her mouth, then closed it. Then sat back. "I'm just saying."

"And we hear you, Elena," Liese said. "But Junior has a point. We already have philosophical differences with the Coterie. We don't need to divide our own ranks by imagining disparity when it's simple deviation."

Nixie blew a raspberry. "You sound like Julian. English, please?"

Liese blushed, slid her smartphone into her purse. "I mean we already have enemies. Let's not make more, just because they don't think exactly like us."

"Well, I'm asking Steve about this," Gretchen said. "I want to keep young with him. I can't believe Dolly's over a hundred."

"Me too," Liese's mom said. "Fifty is the new forty, but I'd love it to be thirty-nine."

Nixie snorted. "Hell, if Dolly's right, fifty will be the new twenty."

"Which still doesn't answer the dying thing," Elena pointed out.

"But it's a step closer." Gretchen smiled and began to eat.

Twyla stopped me before I left, gave me a quick update on Camille's permits, which were unfortunately all in order. I got back to the Haus just in time to open. Like the previous Wednesday, trade was brisk. I barely had time to practice and no time at all to think of another avenue for Twyla to try. I hoped I could let it slide a day.

Wednesday night we had a brush-up rehearsal. Normally brush-ups are incredibly fun, with the cast ad-libbing hilarious variations. But aside from Toto humping a potted scenery tree and getting splinters in his doo-dah, it was as dry as a chewing cardboard.

I talked with Rocky at intermission. She'd discovered that Camille was connected to some high mucky-muck at CIC but didn't have a name. I have to admit I was less interested in who the connection was than whether I could break it somehow. Rocky said she'd look into it.

After the rehearsal, I was surprised to see Glynn waiting outside the prop room, not looking very happy at all.

I cast around, but he was alone. "Where's Mishela?"

"Gone home with Emersons." He scowled. "They all took great delight in reminding me you live directly across from Camille's club. That walking home alone would be dangerous."

224

"Friends are such a pain," I agreed. "Happily married matchmaking friends are the worst. I promise not to put any moves on you."

"You're breathing," he noted flatly. "That's a move. Your heart beats. Another."

"Tough to be you." I tried not to smile as I headed out.

His eyes clamped shut. "Walking. Yet another, the worst of the lot." He followed, eyes still shut.

"Poor baby. Aren't you going to run into something?"

"I wish. Perhaps it would dull my senses if I smashed my face against the wall. But I'd still have the image of your graceful hips swaying. The memory of your luscious feminine scent."

"Nice, but the grimace on your face kinda takes the poetry out of it. Maybe you should open your eyes anyway. To watch out for bad guys."

His eyes snapped open. "I don't need to see them to kill them." The tips of his fangs flashed as he spoke.

"Aren't they already dead?" I pushed through the back door into the warm May night, enjoying our banter.

"Destroy is a more accurate term. But kill is so much more satisfying to say." He paused. "Junior."

He sounded so hesitant I stopped. We weren't playing anymore.

His eyes were off to the right somewhere. "I know I should take you straight home but...would you like to get some food at the Caffeine Café? I'll buy."

Wow, that was sweet. And if he really was having fantasies involving nothing but breathing and heartbeats, incredibly dangerous. "Love to, but I'm still burping up muffin from this morning. Elena called a powwow of all the v-SOs. I'm surprised you didn't hear about it."

Glynn stuck hands deep in his pockets and started walking. "Oh, I did. Mishela and Rebecca were cross that they weren't invited. I pointed out the sun was up and got my head taken off for my troubles."

"Not literally, I hope." I fell behind, just to watch him. Tongue-worthy ass, but his shoulders were hunched and his head down. Maybe from the grief Mishela and Rebecca of Sunnybrook Farm had given him, but maybe... Frowning, I caught up. "We can go somewhere else, if you want. Nieman's. Still buying?"

Glynn sliced me a glance. "Am I that obvious? I would like to spend time with you. It's dangerous, but...well, I can't be in the same city as you and completely ignore you."

I smiled ruefully. "We're a couple of goofs, aren't we? Don't want to be together, can't stay apart. If I didn't know better, I'd say we were in a teen angst flick."

"Teen angst?"

I flung my arm across my forehead. "Oh, I love him. But he is a vampire. Woe is me, we are from two worlds, destined for agony and never to be together. Star-crossed lovers like Romeo and Juliet, Tony and Maria, Richard and Kahlen—"

"Alien and Predator?"

I dropped my arm and laughed. "Yeah." Seeing the black marble facade of Fangs To You, I sobered. "But the danger is real."

"It is." Glynn took my elbow and escorted me across the street, dropping contact almost immediately. "From our enemies and our hearts. Junior, I don't know if this physical attraction we have is love. But I do know it's real."

"Yeah." My arm still burned where his fingers had pressed. "What are we going to do about it?"

"It's up to you. I only want what's best for you."

"And me for you." I turned to face him. "What's best for *us*?"

"Junior...there is no us. Not yet. That's what you have to decide."

Whoa. This load of sausage was heavy, and I couldn't even begin to calculate the costs. I needed to lighten up, pronto. "There's an *us* tonight, at least until you pay for my soda."

"There is indeed." His lips curved. "Why don't you stow your instruments? I'll wait outside."

"You got it." I slipped inside the house and raced up the stairs as silently as possible, dropped my cases in my room and raced back out. As I flew past my parents' landing, their door started to open.

"Junior—" Mom.

"GoingoutwithGlynnbebacklaterbye!" If it were important, it'd have been Dad. If it were really important, they'd call my cell.

Outside, I smiled to see Glynn waiting for me. "Hey. You didn't run off."

"I'd never do that. Besides, I owe you a drink."

Time slowed as we walked together through the warm, sweet-smelling night. Meiers Corners flowers marched in military-sharp garden rows, but it didn't stop them from perfuming the air.

We walked all the way to Nieman's without talking, silent yet saying all kinds of things to each other. He matched my shorter stride, saying *I care*. My hand sought his, saying *I need*. His warm return clasp said *me too*. Our smiles said...oh, God. Our smiles said *I love you*.

We got to Nieman's. The neon was dark and the door locked.

I stared. "This is impossible. They're never closed."

Glynn glanced north. "Camille's club has been bad for Meiers Corners in more ways than one. You know the city better than I. Where to now?"

I was still stuck on Nieman's being closed. That was just wrong. "Practically every block has a bar but none as good as Nieman's. Let me think. Von Bier's on Settler's Square has a nice selection of specialty lagers, raspberry beer and such."

"Isn't that near your Uncle Otto's?"

"Yeah, okay. Scratch that." While I thought, his fingers threaded mine, parting them like his cock parted my... I cleared my throat. "Well, there's the Alpine Bar and Retreat on the outskirts of town. But that's a couple miles away. It'd take nearly an hour to walk—hey!" Glynn had picked me up.

Actually, he swept me into his arms, full romantic-hero style. I was so flabbergasted I didn't protest when he kicked into motion.

He shot forward and buildings blurred and wind snapped and my braid fluttered behind us and I realized we were going *fast*. Faster than the five mph I jog, faster than the twenty-two a racer runs. Faster even than my bike.

After I got over the shock, it was exhilarating. "This is fun," I shouted into the wind. Glynn smiled down at me, a soft little smile that said he liked making me happy. It should have scared me, but the sense of freedom, of speed, of enjoyment shared and so doubled was far too precious. I clasped arms around his neck and urged him faster.

We reached the Alpine in a couple minutes. The lights were on and cars were in the lot, but instead of stopping, Glynn careened around the place and spun out again, a starship slung by gravity into

227

an even faster trajectory. He raced to the opposite end of the city and spun around Mr. Miyagi's *dojang*, then flew even faster northward toward the AllRighty-AllNighty.

He probably could have run all night and I would have enjoyed it, but I said, "Aren't you afraid someone will see you?"

"I should be." He slowed to a walk. "Most people don't understand how fast I'm going. But some do."

After the exhilaration of thirty or forty mph (which doesn't seem like a lot when driving, but try pacing a car on a bike and you'll see what I mean), walking was, well, pedestrian. Me and my big mouth. "Sorry. I was having fun."

"Me too." He smiled down at me, still snuggled in his arms. I snuggled closer.

The blue of his eyes darkened. "Junior, don't." He shifted me as if to put me down.

But I didn't want this closeness, this night to end. A fairytale, sure, and all fairytales have The End, but not yet. Not now.

I wrapped desperate arms around his neck and kissed him.

Wanting and waiting had taken their toll on me. My lips, tongue and teeth all got into the act, tripping over themselves in urgent touching, tasting, nipping.

He slammed me against the first open space, a broad tree trunk, and devoured me in return. Wanting and waiting had apparently taken an even greater toll on him.

Ever open a screen door in a storm and had the door torn from your hands? I was needy, but still only a-hundred-pounds-and-change of female.

He crushed me against the tree, drove his muscled thigh between my legs and impaled me with his tongue. He thrust so deep my jaw ached. His hands found my breasts, kneading, hefting, pinching, and the ache shifted to my belly. He pressed forward with his thickly muscled leg, grinding into my mons, and the ache exploded in my groin.

"Who's there?" a voice rasped.

Glynn lifted his head, panting. Behind him I saw a patch of perfectly clipped grass, one of Meiers Corners's many beautifully manicured (Nixie would have said ruthlessly manicured) lawns. A beam of light played across the green, flashing over a park bench. A

Meiers Corners public park.

We'd been kissing and pinching and leg-pumping in public. Not quite as bad as doing it on the front walk but certainly exposed.

Exposed, and, as the circle of light swept nearer, about to be more so.

Chapter Fifteen

Fortunately, Glynn was already moving. He hoisted me and skimmed around the tree. The flashlight beam cut to both sides but didn't catch us.

"Well, I thought I saw someone, but now I don't. Maybe I was imagining it." The rusty tenor was Detective Dirk's. "Guess I'd better call Detective Strongwell and report all's quiet. I wonder if she'll be breathing heavy like last time."

Off-key humming and the boop-boop of a cell phone receded. I sighed. There were times Dirk's social obtuseness was a blessing.

"That was close." Glynn set me down.

It put my face at pecs level. My mouth landed on the swell of one cotton-covered mound as if I couldn't help it. I could have, of course. The decision was still mine, each time, to risk forging a forever-type bond.

But I'd made the choice several times already and each time was getting easier. Maybe it wouldn't have if Glynn were an ass hat, but he was talented, caring, and, as I tugged his shirt out of his pants and fastened onto bare, pale gold skin, tasted really good.

"Junior," Glynn groaned. His chest lifted like he was grabbing something overhead. I slicked my tongue over a nipple. Wood cracked. His hands came down, a thick, leafy branch between them. He groaned again, this time in frustration. "We shouldn't."

"Yeah," I panted. "But I'd give half my poster collection for a bed right now."

"Give me a moment." He shucked his jacket and draped it over my shoulders, then ran off while pulling his T-shirt over his head.

I barely had time to process the shock of those sweeping lats flaring like a rising cobra when he returned to whisk me up—against his naked body.

I clung to truly awesome muscles. "What about Dirk?"

"He's gone. I found us someplace private." He stepped under a waterfall of willow tree branches and we were in nature's secluded bower.

He'd lined the springy ground with his soft T-shirt and worn jeans. Laying me on this impromptu bed, he covered me with skin warmer and smoother than any blanket.

I spread my hands on his back. My fingers rippled over acres of pure muscle. His mouth descended on mine, and his taste was as wild and darkly sensual as our outdoor cocoon.

With the world shut out, his urgency changed, taking his time, kissing me thoroughly with soft swipes of tongue and lips, light nips and tastes. I loved the feel of his skillful mouth—loved even more the occasional slips of control, those jags of impatience, quickly contained, that meant he wanted as much as me, but was making sure I had my fill of pleasure first.

I stabbed my tongue between his lips and demanded my own back.

His mouth opened and his dark taste intensified. I kissed until I was drunk on him, until my body throbbed and my blood pounded and I desperately wanted more. I tried to open my thighs, but my legs were pinned under his. I wriggled.

He lifted slightly, the male version of the panty hip-lift. Immediately, I spread my legs. He settled between them, heavy and hot. My jeans and panties were thin barriers to his pulsing erection and my blossoming need.

He wrapped both hands around my waist and swept up, raising my tee and bra over my breasts. He fell to suckling.

Sweet need filled me. I marveled at his dark head, nearly as big as my whole chest, and his shoulders broad as airplane's wings just beyond. Need intensified to ache. I cupped his silky head and pressed him closer.

Birds chirped around us, masking our quickening breaths and soft moans. At my urging, he suckled harder. My fingers clenched fistfuls of black hair. He made a small sound, pain laced with pleasure. I consciously eased my grip, but was too aroused to stop my hands from rubbing him with ever increasing desire.

He raised his head and I skimmed fingers over his face, his strong cheekbones, his lips...his fangs. Their smooth warmth drew me and I stroked them with my thumbs. They lengthened and throbbed under the pads of my fingers. I stroked again.

He groaned, a tight, throttled roar. Every muscle around his eyes clenched tight, his jaw clenched even tighter. His cock expanded up my belly like a balloon, dripping hot desire.

I blinked. Teeth as a G-spot? But the evidence was before me, so I plucked them between thumb and forefinger like nipples.

His reaction was immediate and extreme. He reared back, mouth open wide, and sank them into my breast.

Lava desire poured into me, seared me. Lust surged, flooded every nerve ending, every organ. My body filled, swelled almost painfully. The pressure built without an outlet, without release, until my hips jerked, drawing my jeans-sheathed sex over his hard erection. Friction burned hot, pumped my ballooning need. I whimpered.

With fangs still embedded, his lips clasped my nipple and pulled. He suckled me, hard. I swelled brighter, hotter, as if I were filling with the exploding universe. The erotic suction was so intense it bent me in an arch into the soft, clothes-lined loam.

I rubbed myself frantically against his thick cock, seeking release. My flexing hips scraped denim over his bare shaft, hard enough to scour him raw. He didn't seem to notice, suckling me with eyes closed, his expression pure bliss. "Ah, *babi*. You're so sweet. So lovely."

"Glynn...please, enough." I was terribly aroused and having trouble breathing, trying to keep my moans and pants under the natural noises around us.

He lifted his head. His fangs emerged from my breast, red with my blood.

It was a surreal moment. I might have been horrified, but the sheer joy of his bite filled me to bursting. Liquid heat welled near my nipple, trickled down the curve. Coppery-smelling.

Glynn's eyes closed, his nostrils flared. "Ah, Junior. My love." Lashes thick and black against his druid's cheeks, he touched a worshipful tongue to the hot thread. Began to lap, gently. His complete immersion in the act, engrossed to the point of communing, thrilled me. His tongue, his breath, his passionate celebration inflamed me to flashpoint.

As he licked, he thrust a hand into my waistband. His fingers found my clit, stroked. Like the blown side of a mountain, I orgasmed.

His low rumble started, a dark purring not even vaguely human. I barely noticed. With a final lick, he came to hands and knees over me, grabbed my jeans and pulled them off.

I lifted my hips with a languid roll but neither of us cared. Comfortably sated, my legs fell open. The scent of my satisfaction was so strong even I could smell it.

His gaze riveted on my sex, pupils flaming bright red. His fangs shot out like swords and his cock was so hard it stood straight up.

I slid my hands down my belly to my thighs, framing my vulva. "What are you waiting for?" My seductive whisper barely rose above the crickets' chirps.

The soft spring air caressed my body. Watching him, I ran a finger over the wet silk of my sex. Overhead, slivers of starry sky shone through the willow's leafy fall.

Nature at its seductive best. And the prince of nature's fertile magic knelt between my thighs, staring at me with red, red eyes.

"Come on." I wiggled in the snug nest of his clothes, trailed one finger along where I wanted that throbbing cock. He still didn't move a muscle, so I slid the tip of my forefinger in.

He growled, grabbed my thighs. Spread them roughly. Dropped his head and began to feast.

The instant his tongue branded my slit, I arched with intense pleasure. It jerked me against his hold, but he was so inhumanly strong, it was like jerking against the weight of the earth. His fingers bit into my thighs, his mouth opened wide...my vision went red as his fangs sank into my swollen labia.

I screamed a climax so big and shockingly fast it was a *whoosh* of wildfire. I gasped, panted, then keened when he started sucking on my pussy while it still flexed. Heaven help me, his mouth, all hot, wet suction, sent me even higher. I grabbed hunks of hair and felt the world buck beneath me. He sucked and tongued, impaled me on fangs until I was wound so tight and coming so hard it was pain. Not dull aching or rasping hunger but blistering, screaming, fuck-me-oh-*please,* open, ravenous wounds.

In the midst of my screaming, Glynn pulled away and fell to one fist over me, chest pumped. The other fist held his fat, sheathed erection. He guided it toward my spasming pussy and I thought *thank you,* but he only touched his fist to my vulva, thumb positioned over my clitoris.

I writhed under him, trying to impale myself on him, but his hand was in the way. His fist pressed to my open sex and he started feeding cock through it, slow as a glacier. I was an out-of-control wildfire, and he was feeding me heaven inch by screaming inch.

The head popped through first, stretching me. An inch of shaft. Two. I grabbed his shoulders, my clutching fingers barely denting ironwood muscles. I writhed to leverage my hips onto him, thrashing to jam heaven home. He froze me simply by pressing his thumb against my clitoral sheath, bearing down with heavy, dark pleasure. I sucked in a breath.

The thumb wiggled. Jagged bolts cut through me like branched lightning. He grunted and fed in another inch of thick shaft. At this rate, I'd burn to ashes long before he got all the way in.

He did a one-arm pushup. Biceps bulging, his head lowered to my throat, his thumb still assaulting my clit, up and down now, like thumbing a lighter. I cried out, not caring if the world heard me. His breath brushed hot against the sensitive skin of my neck. I wrenched my head back, exposing my throat. His teeth nipped flesh, his incisors sharp, the fangs lying smooth alongside.

Another inch of cock. Two.

I was beyond frantic. I grabbed his head, his hips, and shoved. Urged him to bite me, screw me. But he only nipped and nibbled and teased and oh-so-slowly drove me insane.

Another inch sank in, finally kissed cervix. He was completely filling me, eight or nine inches of shaft and glans—and he still hadn't removed his fist.

I was out of my head with need for him and *he hadn't removed his fist*. Like his kiss, he was restraining himself, hanging back, focused totally on my pleasure—and ignoring his.

Fuck that.

I grabbed his ears with both hands, tried to shake him. Like shaking a cliff. "Damn you, Glynn. Take me. Let go. Find your own pleasure, dammit."

He lifted his head. His face was flushed, his eyes heavy-lidded with desire, the red gleam under them the only sign of his preternatural hunger. "Your satisfaction comes first. Your pleasure triggers mine." His lids drifted shut, then open again, fully. "That's not right. Your pleasure...it completes mine."

I was wiggling like a worm on this hook of lust and didn't see the difference. "I'm satisfied, damn you. Twice. Three times. I don't know how many."

He smiled, lazily. "Not enough." And releasing his cock, he thrust me into the center of the earth.

Ever been pounded into the mattress? Powered into by a male so strong it's like being bedded by an oil rig, whacking its great thrusting piston into you?

Glynn's hips rolled and plunged until I was pulverized. Until I shattered in that sweet, dark night. And when I shuddered with release, he didn't stop. He kept driving straight through my climax, rode me until I lay limp and utterly spent under him.

Then, with a growl, he stabbed his fingers into the soil next to my head.

Energy crackled up his arms, spread through his chest like he was calling up magic. His face glowed, his eyes shone brilliant as the sun. All his muscles expanded, pumped so big and hard the earth itself must have filled them.

It raised the hairs on my arms. My blood pounded in my ears. The short wisps in my braid crackled like a thunderstorm.

All that power, all that weight, slammed into me. I clenched in reaction. Was slammed into again, deep, so deep I whimpered. Was slammed again.

Something inside me awoke. Something dense and heavy and deep, like molten iron at the earth's core.

Slam.

It shook me. Literally, my breasts and hips shuddering, but that was only the outer manifestation of a deeper, more electrifying jolt. I'd already climaxed several times and was now a yielding receptacle for his pleasure.

And he, by the simple fact that he put me first, was making me come again.

Growling, he pummeled me, riding me with the rhythm of the rising sea. His male magic commanded my body, my blood, my very soul. I rose with him. Dark as the night, powerful as the earth and vast and irresistible as water, he thrust into me. An ocean's wave of pleasure swept in with him, swelling bigger and bigger with no crest in sight—and rolling directly toward me.

His climax was coming. And if he continued to take me with him, mine.

I shrieked my denial. An orgasm that big would destroy me. I clung to his massive, pumped biceps, pleaded for him to finish before he demolished me.

He rode me harder. His balls slapped my buttocks and his teeth opened over my throat and I'd gotten what I'd wanted, him out of control, but I hadn't reckoned with the cost. I opened my mouth to scream—just as he sank fangs into my throat.

I imploded. Fractured all the way to my soul, shattering. Seismic waves stripped me of all my pretenses, anything civilized falling and breaking like so much crockery in an earthquake. My body gloried in a pleasure so complete it remade me in its own image. I howled, began pumping my own hips in reaction, flailing desperately and instinctively until I was riding atop the waves, pushing them longer, farther.

I seized him with my legs and beat up, my force that of a woman instead of the earth, but enough for him to roar in counterpoint and churn his pelvis so tight and fast we both burned to cinders. Then he bit me again and the cinders exploded.

Bits of ash floating in the dark were all that was left of me.

Time passed. Rumbles of lazy pleasure stirred the ash. Soft licks here and there recalled a body once real. Warm night brushed bedewed skin, rumpling it into goose bumps. Slits of vision opened to sapphire eyes soft and deep as the night.

Heels slid off muscular buttocks, thumped to spongy ground. Mine, I realized somewhat dazedly. "What...did we...?"

"No one heard. No one's near." He touched a finger to his nose.

"Some sniffer." I yawned. Stretched. I felt clean, new, like I'd gotten a great night's sleep.

Until reality crashed into my head. I'd had sex with Glynn, again. Not just sex, but sex so cataclysmic it qualified as more. As physical intimacy. As—gulp—lovemaking.

It's not the decision itself, I told myself frantically. *It's what I do after.*

Great words, and I knew they were true, but it was now way *after* and I had no idea what the hell I was going to do.

Glynn noticed my dismay and tried to persuade me to talk as we slowly dressed and made for home. His idea of persuasion was soft kisses and gentle bites, and I admit they would have worked if they hadn't led to more lustful pursuits, three times in quiet, dark corners of the city. The only talking we did then was with our hands and mouths and the occasional groaned name.

So we didn't talk about it. Just as well. I still had my duty and rainbow dreams, and Glynn still had to leave at the end of the show.

Nothing had changed, just because everything had.

I loved him. I'd thought that before, but this was the kind of love that would throw away duty, forget dreams, simply to stay with him a few moments longer.

Feelings that big should move mountains. It's absolutely incredible to me that they don't even ruffle the real world unless action is taken.

Since most emotions don't last and most actions do, it pays to be very careful to know for sure what's real. The saying "think before you act" is just good business sense, and I was nothing if not all business. Well, except for the music part.

But my emotions were so overwhelming, thinking was almost impossible. Right now my saying was more, "When in danger or in doubt, run in circles, scream and shout". Cap that with city businesses plunging toward financial ruin and Elias's Armageddon marching one day closer, and maybe panic was a sensible reaction.

I needed simple again. I needed to reduce my life to problems I could solve.

Okay, good. Glynn first. Leaving at the end of the show, traveling to the home he loved. I'd already decided to let him go. Loving him even more didn't change that.

Vampires? I might be able to make a difference there, as part of Nixie and Elena's group. I tucked that away for later.

CIC Mutual? Too big for me to knock down.

Camille and her club?

There, as another business owner, I could prove useful. I'd see things the others might miss: ways to get her out of Meiers Corners, means to pull her well-manicured claws out of our citizenry.

Once I could think again, that was.

Thursday morning I discovered the city's financial crisis was closer than anyone thought.

Before I even unlocked for the day, Rocky Hrbek was knocking frantically on the door. When I opened up, she ran in, breathing fast, locked the door behind her and drew me away from it as if we could be heard. In a low voice, she said, "They did it. I never thought they would. It's *personal*, Junior. Almost evil."

"Calm down. Another stolen garden gnome?"

She gaped at me from behind her huge glasses. "Are you serious? No, this is important. A friend at work called me. They posted yesterday. You'll get yours today."

"They're mailing out stolen garden gnomes?"

"No!" Rocky rarely lost her temper, but that did it. "CIC is demanding full premium payment."

"Your supervisor is demanding payment?"

"Would you listen?" She glared at me like I was the slowest tricycle on the planet. "The directive came from the president of the company himself. All premiums are due immediately."

That finally got through. "W...what? But they can't."

"They think they can, and they have some nasty, ruthless lawyers who agree." She lowered her voice even more. "I know Julian's good, but they've got a whole cadre of sharks ready to stab us with lawsuits. Even if we're in the right, we'd bleed out before we win. And dead is dead."

An imperious knock at the door spun her. "Crap, it's Mrs. Blau. You'd better let her in. She's gotten crabby lately."

"Everyone's gotten crabby lately," I muttered. Camille's doing. I went to the door, Rocky following.

"Maybe it's catching," she said as I unlocked the door. "That would explain why Mr. Nosferatu went all Snidely Whiplash on us."

"Nosferatu?" Unless there was more than one, that was the vampire who stood against the Iowa Alliance. "How do you know him?"

"He's president of CIC."

If she'd whapped me in the face with a bassoon, I couldn't have been more stunned. Yet it made obvious sense. Nosferatu, the vampire attacking Meiers Corners, was behind CIC, the insurance company attacking Meiers Corners. Nosferatu was the high mucky-muck at CIC Camille was involved with. Why hadn't I put it together before this?

I had a lot of time to think about it that day. We had customers, but they perused the sausage in stony silence. When they spoke, it was to criticize. Our receipts were way down, and I knew we weren't the only ones.

Worse, we got our dunning notice in that morning's mail. The letter carrier looked almost sick delivering it. It wasn't the first he'd seen either.

The envelope rattled in my shaking hand. This was intolerable. I had to do something. We needed money, but even business guru Kai Elias's cash was tied up helping the truly penniless. And besides, no self-respecting MC businessperson would accept a handout.

So what we really needed were tourists.

But Camille had grabbed those tourists somehow. She'd hooked them as surely as she'd grabbed our own people. And I had no idea how.

I opened the envelope. It was as Rocky said, twelve thousand dollars due by the end of the month. We could find other insurance, but it'd be hard to bind a new policy in time to stay open. Yet to pay this, we'd have to sacrifice the cooler fund, our savings and my instruments.

I felt cornered and out of options. Business Truth #7 said I should just wait, that the solution would become obvious. An obvious solution to citywide meltdown, and two ruthless vampires?

I didn't have a lot of hope.

The theater that night was nearly empty. A dozen people sat in the audience, mostly parents.

Takashi's beats were listless. Director Dumbass's sparkling swish was gone. Even Mishela's voice wavered as she wished upon that star.

What's more shattered than heartbroken?

We didn't bother playing the bows. I trudged back to the prop room, sluggishly disassembled and swabbed instruments.

Glynn appeared in the doorway. "Walk you home?"

"I'm not good company."

"I thought perhaps..." He stared at his feet. "Maybe you could come to my room. I have a real bed." He raised his eyes. Deepest blue, they were filled with such longing that it stole my breath.

"Bed?" The bower had been awesome, but the thought of Glynn's huge mattress...a door to muffle anything louder than gasps and moans... My hormones revved directly into desperation. I stuffed instruments in cases, grabbed his arm and hustled us out the door.

Our hands found each other's skin on the way, sliding under clothes and exploring so fast we were practically undressed by the time we hit Glynn's door. He turned the knob with a hand borrowed from my breast, immediately diving back under while he kicked open the door. He scooped me off my feet and twirled me across the threshold—and ground to a stop.

His nostrils were flared, his fangs full length and his eyes burned bright red and not in the good lusty way. I followed his stare to see—

The small table was bare.

Glynn rushed to it and frantically patted it like a blind man, like maybe his tchotchkes were still there, just invisible. He hadn't put me down, had simply baled me into one arm like a sack of groceries. I wasn't insulted at being treated like cat litter; I was amazed. He'd held on to me.

In the midst of a nightmare, he'd only clutched me tighter.

"Oh, *Duw*, where are they?" He whispered it like a prayer, as though he were actually asking God. He dropped to his knees, twitched aside the heavy brocade tablecloth, but I knew he wouldn't find his tchotchkes there. If they were anywhere in the room, his preternatural nose would have at least detected the pipe, the unglazed ceramic holding its cavendish essence.

He rose and circled the room in search anyway. Round and round, checking the same places two or three times. His directionless search screamed his loss.

"Glynn." I caressed his hair. "Glynn, stop. Sit down. We need to think."

It took five minutes of petting and gentle words before he finally collapsed on the foot of the bed.

"Why?" His voice broke. My heart broke with it. "Why would someone do this? Who would do it?"

He was incredibly vulnerable right now. Of course, his very vulnerability made him deadly dangerous. Not to me, but I didn't want to touch off that powder and have it explode on someone else. So I spoke slowly, carefully. "Who knew what those items meant?"

"Nobody. I never talk about them." He took a deep breath, making a visible attempt to calm himself. "You know. Elias knows, I suppose. Nobody else."

"Not what they symbolized. Who knows how important they are to you?"

His eyes focused, for the first time since seeing the empty table, on me. "I can't believe I didn't think of that. Many people. Emersons, Mishela, some of the Alliance vampires. And—" His eyes abruptly unfocused, like he'd been shot. "Oh, bollocks. I can't believe...it can't be."

"Can't be what?" Or rather, *who*?

The pain contorting his face confirmed a "who", someone close. Betrayal by a friend.

But there was anger in his face too. A friend, but not a heart's friend. I was incredibly relieved—until he said her name.

"Camille."

I shuddered.

He shook his head. "How could it be her? Wouldn't I smell her?"

Camille knew about the tchotchkes, knew how important they were to Glynn. She had, at one time, been close enough for him to feel hurt and betrayed now. Close enough that he remembered her scent.

Close, to guys, usually meant sex.

Damn.

Yes, Glynn wasn't mine. And yes, I knew he was eight hundred years on this earth and had to have had sex before me.

But it hurt. Not because Glynn had belonged to someone else first. But because he might *still belong to her*. The male I loved so much that he'd become a part of me, might still be part of someone else. Wouldn't he have forgotten her scent otherwise?

I wanted Glynn to belong to *me*.

Well, mostly I wanted him to be happy. And maybe he wouldn't get that belonging to me—but he sure wasn't going to get it with *her*.

Damn it, I just wanted him to be happy.

Oh God. I loved him. The real deal—not just first-blush euphoria or giddy sex, but the nitty-gritty, daily grind, your-happiness-matters love. I'd run away from it, then deluded myself that it was a business decision. I'd lost both those battles. Having never felt quite this way about anyone, I thought maybe I'd lost the war as well.

And there went my rainbow dreams.

I was singularly less impressed with losing them than I'd expected. Maybe shock. Maybe because Glynn was still here, at least for a few more days. Or the sense of inevitability. Mom had fallen, so would I. How many children actually ended up completely different from their parents? How many molecules escaped the liquid as gas? *All of them* whispered my brain, but I hadn't done that well in chemistry and couldn't trust the answer I wanted in the face of the answer I had.

"I'd smell her," Glynn said again, sounding lost.

I put my feelings to one side. I could deal with them later. Glynn was suffering now.

I stroked his hair. "You just need to do a more thorough search."

His eyes focused on me like I'd thrown him a lifeline.

"Start in this room. Go over every inch again, using all your senses. Search the entire basement, both townhouses, and the yard."

"Why?" He made a half-gesture at the table. His eyes dulled. "They're gone."

"You'll find traces. Clues to what happened." I took his beloved face in both hands. "Get Julian to help you, and Nikos and Rebecca. Even if you're distracted, they're good. They're sure to find something." I put more certainty in my voice than I felt. If the thief were human, I'd have had no doubt. But I had no idea what a vampire could hide.

He nodded and I could practically see his intellect come online. "I'll ask Mishela too. Both her acting and Elias have trained her to observe."

"Great." Now came the tricky part.

Glynn and I might have no future, but my love demanded I do at least this much for him. I needed to at least try to get Glynn's pieces of home back. But I knew what would happen if I told him I was going to visit Fangs To You. He'd try to stop me. I couldn't let that happen.

Safer for me if I asked him along. But he still remembered Camille's scent, was still lost and hurt at just the thought that she might be the thief. He was so vulnerable my heart broke.

Besides, I didn't think I'd be in any real danger. Hey, I wasn't intending to announce myself. A little luck and she'd never know I was there.

I released his face. "Look, since you're using vampire senses, I'll just slow you down. I'll head home." He frowned again, so I added, "If you come up with anything, give me a call."

"Well...you must be tired. You work too hard, Junior." He managed a small smile. "Thank you. You're good for me."

I covered my embarrassment by pressing a kiss to his gorgeous lips.

Enough of Glynn's protector self was left to insist on driving me home. I managed to not give myself away on the drive home, but his sad face made it hard. With a quick kiss I jumped out and ran inside. I ran to the front store window and watched the limo purr away. Then I wrote a note explaining where I'd gone and slipped it onto my dad's desk. I wasn't expecting trouble, but I was going into the lair of a she-bitch vampire.

For Glynn. For the pain she'd caused him.

I took a deep breath. *Showtime.*

I locked the door behind me. Because a vampire owned the club across the street from my parents, sure. But the Cheese Dudes lived right next door and they were tricky.

Stoking my courage with my love, I walked across the street.

I didn't have one of Camille's flyers, so I had to fork over twenty bucks cover (and show half a dozen forms of ID to prove I was underheight, not underage. Stupid long-lived vampires. I bet they thought two hundred was still jail bait).

Inside, the smoke and pulsing light made it hard to see. But when my vision cleared, I saw it wasn't just free drinks Camille was offering.

Barely clothed women and men strutted around, offering customers trays of rancid-looking cheese curds—and themselves. I sucked in a surprised breath. How had this gotten past the planning commission?

I nearly choked on that breath. The smoke was nauseatingly sweet. Marijuana sweet. I coughed. Hookers and drugs? How was our good, upstanding MC citizenry not only not up in arms over this decadence, but participating? Body snatchers?

I needed to focus. I'd come to find Glynn's pieces of home. I looked around to orient myself.

The long bar to the left was stocked with the standard taps and bottles, littered with bowls of peanuts. The only unusual things were the near-nudity of the bartenders and the plates of cheese being gobbled by everyone in sight.

I frowned.

Shouts from a nearby table turned my head. A pumpkin-headed man knocked cards and chips off the table with an angry sweep. A woman in skin-tight leather leaped to her feet, snapping out a whip.

No, not Camille's lackeys, or even tourists, but Police Captain Titus and the mayor's secretary, Heidi.

Tempers escalated. More shouts. I thought things would get messy (Heidi could do more damage with her whip than most people could with a Mauser), but she threw aside the quirt to shove Titus. Snarling, Titus shoved back.

The ensuing fight was not much more than grade school butting. I looked away, embarrassed for them.

And caught the action at another table, where a woman reached for a card tucked in her shoe. The card was a queen of clubs, and the hand was Anna Versnobt's, Miss Better-than-everyone in school.

Meiers Corners folk, brawling and cheating. Good grief. I needed to find Glynn's tchotchkes and get out of here before whatever it was affected me too.

Fangs To You was built like a hotel atrium, with an open main floor facing a two-story, motel-like front, upper walkway shading a lower. On the ground floor was an elevator and a door through which staff shuttled with their ever-freshened trays of cheese. The kitchen. There'd be restrooms and storage and maybe offices nearby. Good place to start. I wound my way through tables toward the gallery.

One of the waiters stopped me on the way. "GObubble?"

Actually he shoved his tray of curds in my face. Lucky I'd had all that martial arts training. My head recoiled just in time to save me an impromptu nose job. "No, thanks."

"Are you sure?" He teased the tray in front of me. "They're Go-go-goooood."

About to refuse more vigorously, I caught sight of his eyes. His pupils were blown like popped balloons. Drugged, and more than mere weed.

"Okay then." I snatched a couple cheese curds. They crackled in my fingers, like bubblewrap. GObubbles, huh. I grabbed a napkin from the tray, wrapped the curds, stuffed them in a pocket, and headed on.

I slowed as I crossed the main floor. The whole place was low-light, but I'd seen staff step down a few feet out of the kitchen. Searching with my toe, I discovered raised marble.

I stepped up, was dazzled by a thousand tiny lights.

The underside of the upper walkway was studded with them. The overhang had blocked them like a cloud covering the stars.

The elevator was right in front of me, doors wide like a hungry maw. I swallowed, sidled away from the bloody gullet. To my right were four doors labeled in red. *Fangs. Blood.* The hair on my nape went up. *The Dungeon.* My scalp prickled.

Storage.

Okay, that was soothingly prosaic.

Fangs and Blood were subtitled Men and Women. My hair settled. The Dungeon was the kitchen.

Storage was my first search target. Since I wasn't dressed in the official uniform of lederhosen and pasties, I backed up to the door and watched The Dungeon for a break in the tray traffic. The instant no one was looking I pulled open the Storage door and spun inside.

And jumped back, spine against the door, horrified. Ye gods, whoever did their shipping and receiving should be shot.

Haphazardly stacked boxes of expensive wines and cheap booze cluttered a hallway far too narrow for fire safety. (My father's cousin's wife's half brother Herbort was in the assessor's department. Why keep a family Bible for genealogy when you can use the phone book?)

Several boxes were stamped with stylized fangs and a red slashed circle over a man stick-figure. Vampire-only rotgut? I edged in until I could see the printing. In red letters was the slogan "Bomb your blood with Vamka!" Maybe a play on the word vodka, but the small print simply said mannitol hexanitrate. I made a mental note to look that up on the Internet.

They were plenty big enough to hide a few small knickknacks, but none of the boxes looked opened. I tested the seams on several with my fingers. They all seemed solid, factory-sealed. I moved on in my search.

Four more doors lined this narrow hallway, helpfully labeled Cool, Cold, Office Supplies and Props. I guessed Cool was storage for cheese and preserved meat, and Cold for uncooked foods. Office supplies seemed self-explanatory.

But Props?

I peeked. It was a moderate-size room with garage-style shelves loaded with boxes of studded leather, lederhosen and personal lubricant—strawberry. And, strangely, a whole rack of chainsaws on the back wall.

Oh boy. I didn't want to know. But for Glynn, I started for the first box.

The door slapped open behind me. A big goon filled the doorway, dressed in the black-on-black of security. "You. Come with me."

"I just got lost—"

"Now, Ms. Stieg. Or do you want me to carry you?"

I grinned and followed him. He led me, not to the exit, but to the open maw of the elevator. I gulped, stepped inside. It rose smoothly but when the door opened, the guy held it and gestured me out.

Camille was there.

She wasn't looking at me. She stood at the balcony railing, the overlord surveying the scurrying ants. Paying ants, by the avaricious twist of her lips. Hey, I'm in business. I value good service above profit, but I know the grin o' greed when I see it.

I looked over the rail, tried to see the floor action from her perspective. Slow, dull-sensed humans, their lifetime not much more than a pet's. To her we were merely animals, deserving no better treatment.

But that didn't explain what she'd done to Glynn.

"Camille." I growled her name.

She turned. "Well, well. Glynn's little human whore, come to save the day." Her carmine lips curved, more sneer than smile.

I saw then that even the most perfect features can be ugly.

I sneered back. "Says Glynn's discards." It was a shot in the dark, but by the thunderstorm in her eyes, it scored.

Another clue was that she seized my ear, nearly pulling it off my skull.

She tried to yank me in, but I'd studied hapkido with Mr. Miyagi. I grabbed her wrist to control our distance, then used my other hand to seize her little finger. With a firm grip established, I wrenched on it.

Vampires, I was pleased to prove, were actually more sensitive than humans. She let go with a squawk.

And the score was Junior two, Vampbitch zero.

"Why are you here, slut?" She stepped back with a glower.

Apparently we were getting right to the point. Fine with me. "Where are Glynn's tchotchkes, asswipe?"

"How should I know?" She rolled her eyes. "Glynn's missing little trinkets have nothing to do with me. Why would you think they do?"

"You like people vulnerable, Camille. Glynn rejected you, you wanted to get even, so you took them."

"Nonsense. I rejected him."

Her nonanswer was answer enough. "Give them back."

"Or else what?" She spat it. "You'll simper at me? Cast your human stink on me?"

"I'll figure something out. Just know I'll get them eventually."

She snarled. "You think to buy Glynn's affection with his little pieces of home, but he'll leave you anyway. You're a flash in the pan. I'm eternal, with centuries of experience pleasing a male. I'm built for sex."

"And I'm built for love," I snarled back. "Besides, you're not eternal, just long-lived. I'll get his tchotchkes back, Camille, if it's the last thing I do." I nearly smacked myself. I was talking like a bad vampire soap opera. So I offered her a combination of my father's and mother's best sign language instead, a stiff middle finger and a slapped arm. "Sit and twirl, Camille." Spinning on my heel, I hit the elevator and jabbed down.

The black-clad security goon caught me by the shoulders as I steamed out. Ham hands clasping me tight, he hustled me through the gambling, boozing and fighting. The bouncer at the door saw us coming and swung the door wide just in time for the goon to toss me through.

I stumbled out onto the pavement. Gathering myself, I brushed specks of indignity off my sleeves. Then I glared at the black marble facade. This was worse than I thought.

She had Glynn's tchotchkes; I was sure of it. But how would I find them now that she knew I was looking?

And what the hell had happened to the good folk of Meiers Corners? What I'd seen in there wasn't just free drinks gone wild nor temporary madness. That was the complete corruption of our small-town values.

And our good folk embracing that corruption.

I slapped dust from my pants. Maybe I was overreacting. Maybe this was just the inevitable backlash from all our straitjacket niceness. Taken to the extreme, Meiers Corners was inbred, narrow-minded, and valued cleanliness and efficiency *über alles, sieg heil.*

But if this backlash went on too long, well. Beyond killing tourism, it would kill the spirit of the town itself.

As I slapped more dust, I heard a crackle. Those damned GObubble cheese curds. I pulled them out of my pocket, unwrapped the napkin and sniffed. Stench burned like nasal buckshot. My head spun. Wheeling, I braced myself against marble, breathed anywhere but that napkin. Gradually my dizziness faded.

The memory of the stink, sharp as crystal, didn't. It beckoned, urging me to take another whiff. To bite into that juicy pungency. I lifted the napkin. Opened my mouth. Extended my tongue...

My cell rang. It snapped me out of it. I stared at the curds. What was in this stuff? I rewrapped the curds, rammed them deep into my pocket, smashing them. Pulled out my phone. It was Twyla.

"Junior. What the hell is going on?"

Stink rose from my hip. The aroma was so bad it was good. Tempting. I wanted a taste so much. I swallowed hard. "What do you mean?"

"Glynn looks like he was hit with a bus. What did you do to him?"

"Nothing. It was Camille." I touched my pocket. It crackled slightly. I needed to get these curds analyzed. And *not* by eating one. I fled across the street, dissipating the stink. "She stole his tchotchkes."

"Ouch. Sorry. Nikos smelled you and we jumped to conclusions."

"It's understandable. But maybe you can do me a favor." I hopped up onto the other curb and told her about the curds. Twyla would know what to do. She had connections with the whole world.

"Drugged, addictive bar nibbles?" Twyla tched. "That would explain why everyone's so crazy. My cousin Synnove is studying to be a doctor in Chicago. I'll get her to look at them."

"It has to be fast." What with vampire Armageddon coming and all. "Oh. And if we're right, we'll need an antidote."

"Believe me, I understand. I'll be there in five to collect the sample."

As I waited for Twyla, I replayed the confrontation at Fangs To You. I was angry that Camille had stolen the symbols of the only home Glynn had ever known. But then to pretend she hadn't? She was playing emotional head games with little pieces of Glynn's heart, and I was furious at that.

Camille was going down.

The purr of an engine caught my attention. Julian's limo pulled to the curb. The passenger window buzzed down, revealing Twyla, a couple large posters resting against her knees. Her sig-O Nikos was at the wheel.

I handed her the napkin of cheese curds.

"I'll get these to my cousin tonight, after Nikos and I hang these posters." She started to buzz the window back up.

"Wait," I said. "I want to help shut Camille down. What can I do?"

She nailed me with a stare. "*Don't* go back to Fangs To You."

"Sure," I said like she hadn't read my mind. Besides, it wouldn't do any good. The bouncers knew my face now. "But I have to do something."

"Julian and I are working on legal ways to get her out. In the meantime, there's not much you can do."

"I could hang those posters for you."

She grimaced. "I suppose. These go on the front and back of the PAC."

I understood the grimace only after she'd opened the door and slid the posters out. They read *Closed until further notice.* "What's going on?"

"CIC." Her expression was as angry as I've ever seen it.

"Demanding full payment by the end of the month? I know."

"No. Demanding the PAC's full payment *now.* Unless we fork over the money, the PAC's insurance policy is canceled effective midnight tonight. No coverage, no show."

"What about another insurance company?"

"Frankly, to get coverage bound by tomorrow night, we'd have to walk in to that company cash in hand. And cash is one thing the city is short of right now."

Cash in hand. Ideas started percolating. "What about the show itself? Is that insured?"

"Yes, but... Junior, what are you thinking?"

"Hold off on this." I shoved the posters back at her. "I've got a couple ideas."

"But you won't tell me what they are? They're insane, aren't they?"

"Of course not. Well, one isn't. Better hurry with that cheese."

She was shaking her head as Nikos drove off.

If Camille had been even one bit ashamed about addicting and corrupting Meiers Corners...if she'd been the least remorseful about stealing Glynn's keepsakes...but she wasn't. I was almost hoping my sane idea didn't work, because the crazy one would truly piss Her Bitchiness off.

The reasonable idea was simple. Get a personal loan to pay for insurance. The crazy one? All I'm saying is that it involved angry vampires and office supplies.

So, just in case, I needed to print up a large poster or two. I ran inside our store, into the office.

I'd just started printing when my mother swept in. She glared at the page coming out of the printer. "What is this, young lady?"

"A poster."

She squinted at it. "The show is changing venues? Why?"

I explained about the insurance problem, then made the mistake of adding, "But this is only my backup plan."

"Your backup plan?" She transferred her suspicion to me. "I thought the PAC was the mayor's responsibility. So if this is your backup plan, what is your primary plan?"

"Um, try to get a loan?" My lameness always seemed magnified in the face of her naked disbelief.

"With what as collateral? The only thing we possess that a bank would value is our building." She fell back a step, hand to breast, with a theatrical gasp. "You would mortgage the business your father gave his life to, the business we Stiegs have spent generations creating?"

I recognized the start of the death spiral argument too late. "Mom, it's not that I don't appreciate what you've done for me." Still, I tried again to make this conversation come out different. "But—"

"Why are you not grateful? You are not on the streets, starving. Or worse, doing drugs or...or a punky rocker like that Schmeling girl."

"Nixie's married now," I said tiredly. She'd already scripted the next line, what else could I do? "To a Boston lawyer. Even by your definition of success, she's made it."

"I gave up my career for you," she said. "A star mezzo with the Italian opera."

The same conversation that we'd had a week ago, a year ago, forever ago it seemed. I felt like I was Neo from *The Matrix*, stuck in an infinite loop of simulated reality. All I needed was the blue pill of "business comes first" and I'd be trapped in the Matrix all over again.

"Always remember, Junior. *Business comes first.*"

God, get me off this train. Whatever I said next would be the wrong thing. She'd slap me and tell me my dad didn't have to marry her. Defending him, even though he'd seduced her.

Wait.

I'd always assumed that he'd seduced her. That he'd ignited the lust in her, the temptation that had overwhelmed her. But what if they were like Glynn and me—both just that horny for each other?

I'd never asked her.

She waited, fire in her eyes. I wasn't going to ask now, at least not straight out. Even deciding on the red pill of *get me out of this*, I wanted to avoid the whole ripping needles out of my spine.

So I stepped back. "You never told me how you and Pop met."

She blinked. Her mouth, primed to harangue, closed slowly.

"I know it was in Germany," I prompted. "At a shop or something?"

"Bavaria," she said faintly.

"What?"

"We were touring." She cleared her throat. "My opera company. We were in Bavaria, with *Die Fledermaus*. Your father was on a buying trip. He came to hear the opera. Your father loves music, you know." She glared as if I would challenge that.

I sat on the desk and gave her my full attention. "I know. He loves to sing hymns at church."

"You noticed." Mom nodded, sank into a chair in front of the desk. "After the performance, your father came to the dressing rooms—to tell me my German stank. I didn't understand him." She laughed. "If I had, I would have scolded him. I certainly wouldn't have thought he had the most beautiful eyes in the world."

She smiled, the soft smile of memory. I saw her as my dad must have, young and loving life. "So why did Pop make you quit opera? Because of me?"

She blinked in surprise. "No. Your grandparents would have loved to care for you, happiest with a dozen children in the house. If we could have had more after you...ah well, that's not your question. I could have left you with the Stiegs in good conscience. Your father would have said okay because he loved me and wanted the best for me. I could have—and maybe should have—chosen my career."

She stared at her hands, strangely quiet on her lap. When she raised her eyes, I could see she had made her own tough decisions long ago, and not only lived with them, but shaped them into a life. "Junior, I had a good career, but after I met your father, I realized that for me, what I had was empty without someone to share it with. The triumphs meant more by his side, the fears and troubles less. Difficulties were easier to meet, but also they had less importance, *sí?* Sharing life with him has made me happy."

"And the store? That makes you happy?"

"Not as happy as singing. But singing doesn't make me as happy as your father." She paused and some of the Mom I knew leaked through. "None of this changes the fact that your father and I have broken our backs for you. The Stieg family business comes first."

I nodded soberly. But inside I was smiling. She'd married Dad, not for business or even because she'd gotten pregnant, but because she loved him.

Chapter Sixteen

Popping out of a lifetime rut was surprising enough. But then, Friday morning, Mom and Pop walked me to the Meiers Corners Sparkasse Bank (lobby open at seven) to support me. I was grateful.

Sitting in Mr. Sparkasse's office with my parents behind me, I pasted on a trembling smile and told Mr. Sparkasse, "I need a loan." I swallowed hard and named a figure that was ten times my entire net worth.

"I see. And for collateral?"

"I was hoping we could do a signature loan. But I have musical instruments."

"I'm sorry." Mr. Sparkasse's smile became strained. "I'd need something more substantial."

"The Wurstspeicher Haus," my father said. "We will expand our mortgage, *ja*?"

I whipped around. My dad stood with legs spread, arms folded, and the mule look on his face. "Pop, no."

"*Ja.*" Mom linked arms with him. "We support Junior."

I swallowed hard again, for a different, better reason.

"I'm so sorry," Mr. Sparkasse said. "But I can't. Your business is already mortgaged to the limit. And there's another issue." He placed fingertips together. "Ours. Unfortunately, our loan reserve was seriously depleted after the hike in insurance premiums."

"You too?" I said. "Damn CIC."

Mr. Sparkasse shook his head. "Wrong alphabet. I'm talking FDIC."

That made me sit up. "The Feds? Why?"

"Because of all the failed banks. Federal Deposit Insurance premiums were raised for the surviving financial institutions. Like a car accident raises your auto insurance. I'm so sorry."

I tried a few more tacks (including my best sausage-selling smile) but Mr. Sparkasse continued to be sorry until we left. Good thing I had a backup plan. Woot. Too bad it involved two mobs of angry vampires. I'd have to work not to get caught between.

As we walked home I could see my parents exchanging worried little looks. "Junior," my father said. "I'm sorry you are disappointed. Your mother and I want to cheer you. How about a bratwurst cookout for lunch?"

"But what about the store?"

"For an hour?" my mother said. "We will close the store."

I'm not sure you can understand how remarkable that was. The last time they closed the store was when I was born. Even then, Mom worked the register until her water broke and Pop opened up again as soon as the cord was cut.

"You shouldn't." I couldn't quite keep the hopefulness out of my voice.

"It's no problem," my father said. "We want to."

"We will invite Uncle Otto," my mother said. "Make it a party. Why don't you call him, Junior?"

"Well, if you're sure." My cell phone was already out, and seconds later I was explaining to Otto.

"What the heck?" Uncle said, in tourist mode so he pronounced it *vat der heck*. "I need to walk Toto anyway, *ja*? We will be there by noon."

Aunt Ottowina was elbows-deep in smorgasbord, but Aunt Hattie, who lived at the B&BS with Race, was eager to join the party.

At eleven fifty Pop fired up the grill. I hung up my apron and headed for the PAC to put up my posters announcing the change in tonight's venue. Not that I expected any audience to see them, not with the GObubbles probably being addictive. Dreams beyond the rainbow, I guess.

As I returned I saw Uncle Otto and Aunt Hattie coming the other way on the sidewalk. Auntie held Toto's leash and Uncle spun with his ever-present broom. I waved. Toto yipped and Auntie unsnapped his lead. Smiling, I crouched to gather up doggie kisses.

And heard the hiss of a spray can.

I sprang to my feet, took a few steps toward the sound. The Cheese Dudes were just inside the mouth of the narrow walkway that separated our stores.

Dude One had a can of bright silver spray paint. He was spritzing Sistine Chapel art on our wall—not Michelangelo, but naked. The naughty bits were rather heroically sized.

I was too flabbergasted (by both Dudes and naughty bits) to move. Uncle Otto shouted, "Stop that!"

"What?" Cheese Dude Two jumped. He saw Otto, spun, and ran for the cheese store. Screeched to a stop when he saw me. "Hey. It's business hours. What the heck are you doing outside? Darn it." He ducked into their store.

Cheese Dude One kept spraying. He sneered at me over his taped, Hubble-lensed glasses.

Otto pushed off with his broom and spun up to Dude One. "I said stop!"

"Make me." Dude One sprayed. Much more and he'd spray a tripod.

Otto swatted the Dude's bony hand with the broom. The can dropped with a clatter.

"Ow! You want to fight?" The Dude whipped something out of his shirt pocket.

"What is all this racket?" My father stuck his head out the side door.

The Dude made shoving motions at Uncle. I couldn't see what he was doing but there was a snort and a couple seconds later Uncle was falling backward. I wasn't totally surprised, Otto being top-shaped. Without the broom or his ever-present sweeping to balance him, he probably had just tipped over.

Cheese Dude One waved a couple finger-sized sticks that looked like string cheese. "Whoo-hoo! Snort Limburger jalapeño sticks, buddy."

Ooh, this was bad. Not just because Otto lay on the sidewalk twitching, tears running down his face, cheese like cotton wads up his nose. But because Toto had jumped Uncle and was trying to hump his face.

"War!" my father crowed and ran back into our store.

I dashed across the sidewalk to help Otto. Cheese Dude One saw me coming, screamed "Keep away from me!" I didn't listen, intent on Otto.

The Dude grabbed my arm. I swung like a gate, my mouth

opening in surprise, which was when the Dude shoved a dynamite stick of cheese mace past my epiglottis.

Pain, shock...my throat swelled and my face was a running mass. I stumbled to my knees. Nothing worked. Everything warped like a nightmare.

Aunt Hattie shouted, Toto barked. My father shot out the front door of the store, a Wurstspeicher Haus apron girding him like armor, brandishing five pounds of summer sausage. "Rosalinda! *Sales maneuver twenty!*"

Yeah, my folks really had numbered these things, both the Business Truths and Sales Maneuvers—though there were so many Maneuvers I could never keep them straight. You thought I made that up, didn't you? Sorry, no. They even had the Business Truths printed and laminated. Pop carried a pocket version in his wallet, alongside his Wurst Sellers membership card and a picture of me playing my first musical instrument, an Oscar Mayer Wiener Whistle.

Mom shot out behind Pop. They grabbed each other's wrists and started twirling, spinning like a pair of demented skaters. Each turn swept them closer to Cheese Dude One.

Dude One hopped out into the sunlight, brandishing his last stinker cheese stick like a limp knife. He feinted as Mom and Pop neared, jumping from foot to foot, his pocketful of Nintendo DSi and pens rattling, a geeky prize fighter seeking his opening.

At the last moment, Mom let go of Pop. He sailed into Cheese Dude One, knocking the Dude into the brick of our building.

The Dude shoved Pop off, just far enough to swing his deadly cheese into position.

Pop slung his *wurst* like a machete and whapped the Dude's cheese hand. Summer is a dense sausage—five pounds makes a hell of a whap.

The Dude dropped his jalapeño stick with a howl. Pop swung the *wurst* again, hit the Dude in the chest. The DSi popped out of his pocket and crashed to the sidewalk, but those things are built to withstand family vacations. It was fine.

"My system!" *It* was fine, but Dude One wasn't. His face boiled bright red—and he leveled Pop with a good right cross. Pop went down with a small sigh.

"Gunter!" Mom dashed to him, fell to her knees and cradled his head.

Aunt Hattie shouted, "How dare you!" She snatched up Uncle Otto's dropped broom and bashed the Dude in the head.

Dude One raised his skinny arms in a vain attempt to cover. "Cut that out!"

"*You* cut that out." Aunt Hattie's cackle was somewhat maniacal under the circumstances.

"You!"

"You!" Hattie started spinning the broomstick like a ninja, flutter-punching Dude One's stomach. I watched through my tears, awed. What had Großmutter Stieg taught her grasshoppers with their little Christmas-present brooms?

"No, you—hey, look out!"

In the past, Hattie's aim had never been very good. The broom had dropped to the Dude's groinal area. She pulled it barely in time.

But she pulled too hard. The stick hit sidewalk—and rebounded straight up between the Dude's legs.

Dude One clutched his cheese curds and went down, another victim of Hattie's poor aim.

She cackled again. Hmm. Maybe Hattie's aim was better than we knew.

"*Gut* job, Hattie." Pop creaked to his feet, Mom assisting. Toto yipped circles around them.

Cheese Dude Two's white face pressed against the window of his store. Pop brandished summer sausage. "Coward! Come get your own whipping!"

Dude Two disappeared.

Pop strutted, hand raised in the age-old sign for *owned*. Mom blew the Dudes a full ear-and-tongue raspberry. Toto barked. Aunt Hattie did a rather obscene victory dance.

I closed my eyes. It's important for the younger generation to move out of the house. Some things make it critical.

An electronic "Cheese, Marvelous Cheese" assaulted my ears. I opened my eyes to see Dude Two emerging from his store with a tray of... "Duck," I tried to scream, but my mouth was still swollen and burning from Limburger jalapeño and it came out "Cock!"

LLAMA cheese balls sailed at us, a whole barrage, Cheese Dude Two flinging pus and mayonnaise fast as a semiautomatic.

Yeah, Limburger jalapeño is a caustic substance, but LLAMA balls are classified as weapons of mass destruction.

Mom and Pop ducked (hey, they'd understood me when my vocabulary was goo-goo and ga-ga). I wasn't so lucky.

Balls hit sidewalk, spattering me with goop. Uncle Otto, wobbling to his feet, got smacked in the head and went down again. Aunt Hattie darted to his rescue, slipped on cheese slime like a grotesque Slip 'N Slide and landed on her butt.

Toto barked and darted, erratic as a mosquito. Cheese balls plopped all around him but didn't hit. He stopped to sniff a puke-green one covered in fur. Or that may have been oregano. With a leg-lift, Toto gave his opinion of that.

Mom peeked out from behind her pole. Dude Two's eye twitched toward her.

"*Mom,*" I croaked—just as Dude Two launched a ball at her head. She screamed.

"Rosalinda!" Pop leaped in front of her in true heroic form, almost as good as Glynn, and took a Limburger-pus-and-onion full in the face.

All motion stopped.

Pop's nostrils flared. Sharp odor wafted potent in the air. His face turned white and his mouth dropped open.

Limburger goop dribbled in.

Sputtering, Pop tried to spit and choked. He doubled over, gagging. His foot hit the edge of the curb and twisted. He fell like a badly thrown bowling ball—hard and into the gutter.

"Oh, Gunter! My brave Gunter, what has that horrible man done?" Dropping, my mother ran her hands over Pop in anxious waves—got a good whiff of what she was wiping, snagged her handkerchief and used that instead. Mom may have started out as a Giraldoni, but she'd lived with the Stiegs long enough that she was incredibly practical. I guess in the ways that counted, she really was a Stieg.

"Enough!" Aunt Hattie scrambled to her feet, snatched up Uncle Otto's broom and poked it threateningly at Cheese Dude Two's crotch. I lurched to my feet and backed her up with my best Crouching Tiger, Puking Dragon position.

Dude Two reached for cheese ammo, but his fingers met empty tray. He fell back.

Toto jumped the Dude's leg.

"Aw, that's so wrong." Lobster-red, Dude Two whapped at Toto with the tray. When the dog danced back, Dude Two grabbed pill-bug Dude One and hauled him into their store. The door slammed, and a moment later we heard the click of the lock.

The battle was over. We'd won.

But at what cost? I sluiced goo off my shirt. Aunt Hattie scooped cheese off her neck, tried to flip it into the gutter, but the stuff stuck like snot. She had to practically shake her hand off her wrist to get rid of it. My dad and Otto looked like ads for LLAMA facial masks or cheese zombies. Everybody was covered with cheese goo and bits of cheese turds, except Toto.

Toto, his coat pristine, trotted a zigzag to pee indiscriminately on cheese balls, the forgotten spray can and the broom.

Until he trotted up to Otto, still on the sidewalk. Toto tilted his little head at Otto and I could see the evil little light enter his doggy eye. He glanced at his own hindquarters, then glanced back at Otto's face.

Lifting his hind leg, he exposed his little doggy faucet.

Hattie, shaking cheese slop, flung a gob at Toto, catching him square in the nuts. He yowled.

Yep, Aunt Hattie's aim had definitely improved.

Twyla called soon after with the news that her cousin had identified the addictive drug in the GObubbles and was formulating an antidote. Twyla was with her now and would drive the stuff back when it was done.

Fortified with that good news and the bratwurst, I could almost face the doom that was Plan B. Without insurance the PAC couldn't open. Without the PAC we couldn't perform.

Or could we?

My insane plan was actually quite simple, and on some level beautifully poetic. The PAC wasn't insured, but the musical was. And so was Fangs To You.

It took a while to convince Director Dumas *et alia* (musical term for the rest of the gang) but what alternative was there? Finally I just forced the issue.

"Everyone grab something and follow me." I hit the pit for my stand and music. "We're taking this show on the road."

Nixie grinned. "Invading Camille's!"

"Blowing down her doors." And when Twyla brought the GObubble antidote, I'd back up Plan B with Plan 2-B, a soliloquy hopefully worthy of Shakespeare, designed to bring the good folk of Meiers Corners back to their senses.

I sure hoped Twyla got there pretty soon.

We headed out. Julian followed with two stands, cello, bass clarinet and alto sax. Besides being strong, vampires were apparently quite dexterous. "Camille won't like it," he cautioned.

"Yeah." I grinned back at him. "Icing on the cake, isn't it?"

The vampire guards at Fangs To You were bigger and tougher than normal, and weren't going to let us pass.

But Julian and his lieutenants, Elena's husband Bo and his lieutenants, and Glynn, stood in a line—and smiled.

Seven versus two. It didn't hurt that Team Emerson's fangs were *way* longer. Still, I thought we'd have trouble until Glynn went toe to toe with the biggest and grinned down at him. "*Please* tell me you're going to put up a fight."

The bouncers stepped aside.

"Too bad." Bo shouldered his way in, toting a tree costume. Since he was a big, blond Viking, shouldering the door meant it slapped open like a storm hit it. "I was hoping for some action."

"There'll be plenty, don't worry." Glynn set down my sax and nodded at the parting crowd.

Camille sauntered through.

A gold, sequined tube top stretched over big round breasts. Gold lamé skinny pants shimmered on her slim hips. The whole outfit was at least five hundred bucks of overpriced yellow—the color washed her out. She was more of a winter.

Her mouth moved. No words came out.

Or rather, words came out, but we couldn't hear them over the roaring. Not roaring of the crowd, though. She grimaced, made a cut motion across her throat. A guy juggling chainsaws on the raised marble walkway caught them, stopped them and slunk off through the door marked Storage.

She resumed her smile, strained, and her saunter, cocking a hip two inches from Glynn. "Darling. So good to see you again. You can stay." Then she hissed at the rest of us. "You will leave," and underlined her Ms. Nasty Buns status by kicking Toto. Yipping, the dog fled.

I detest mean people. I jammed my stand under my arm in lance position, blade out. Dropping my head, I pushed off and hit ramming speed.

She dodged. I bulled past her like I'd missed.

Headed for my real objective, the raised walkway under the second floor gallery. With its stars-in-the-ceiling lights and the steel, glass and marble walls throwing the sound out, it would make a dandy stage.

Camille dashed in front of me, blocking my way. "You're going nowhere, slut human."

I got the impression "human" was a more deadly insult than "slut". I glared into her red eyes. "Sorry, got a show to do. Move."

"Make me." She folded her arms and glared back.

"Sure. Just remember you asked for it." I reviewed my hapkido. Grab and throw? Pressure point attack? Hapkido's primarily defensive. If she'd grabbed me first, I'd have had a lot more options.

Glynn solved the problem for me by picking her up and tossing her across the room. When I goggled, he shrugged. "The show must go on."

That just made me one happy slut human.

But as much fun as one-upping Camille was, we wouldn't win anything unless Twyla got here with the antidote. I kept casting glances at the door, but a watched pot never boils. Well, unless you're an X-visored Cyclops.

Our actors and crew set up the stage while the vampire lieutenants organized the floor to make a rough audience. The pit set up to one side, Julian positioning his open cello case on its back like a big tip jar, a hopeful twenty tossed in for seed.

Camille screeched the whole time, alternating between threatening bloody war and flaming lawsuits. She had to be physically swatted down a couple times. The last time she retired to her upstairs domain, shoving rudely through a clump of Munchkins to get to the elevator. In retaliation, Toto peed on her leg as she passed.

Good thing she was wearing the gold. Didn't show the, er, dirt.

And then, without scenery or mood lighting or anything but ourselves and what we could carry, we put on the best damned show of our lives.

The mixed audience of MC natives and tourists was cold and unresponsive at first. Camille had infected them with a nasty sort of cynicism coupled with a jonesing for superficial highs.

But then Twyla banged in. She raced through the crowd, armed with several cans of aerosol. Giving me a brief thumbs-up, she sprayed the front row. Frowns turned puzzled. Cleared. Smiles broke out. Twyla covered the whole room.

Within moments feet were tapping to the Scarecrow's zombie ditty, "Brains Ain't Everything (Unless You Don't Got One)," and laughter followed Toto's antics. The aerosol must have been lighter than air because even Camille came down from on high to watch Dorothy skip off to Oz. She was almost smiling. By the end of the first half, the audience was detoxed and cheering. Good deal, because I had that 2-B pitch to make.

Before the applause died down at intermission, I stood. This would be the hardest sell of my life. I'd known some of these people since childhood, but thanks to Camille, they were as much strangers as the tourists. I could only hope their personality damage, without the addictive GObubbles, was reversible.

"Ladies and gentlemen. Let me introduce myself. I am Gunter Marie—"

"We know who you are, Junior," someone yelled rudely from the bar.

"Okay. So you know me." I blew my frustration out as a stream of air. "A lot of you know me, have known me all my life."

"Since diapers you were wearing!" someone else shouted from the back in crude imitation of the mayor.

"Diapers." I whirled toward the voice. "You not only know me, you know about Mayor Meier. You know everything about everyone in town, the good and the bad. Why is that?"

"Because this is Meiers Corners!" A dozen people raised beers high.

"Exactly." I hid a grin of triumph. They'd played right into my hands.

But now came the tricky part. I tried to read faces, but thanks to Fangs To You's goth lighting, they were only shadowy red clumps. "Could someone raise the floor lights, please?"

A moment passed, and then a moderate white light clicked on. Tables of folk blinked, shaded their eyes.

"We all know each other's secrets." I scanned the crowd, gauging them. "That's one of the bad things. Change is ice-age slow. You're remembered in your diapers, frozen forever in time. You can grow up and become a responsible adult and everyone still remembers you blowing up the toilet in ninth grade with a cherry bomb that wasn't even yours."

"Whose cherry bomb was it?" shouted Mrs. Gelb from the bar.

"Nix—never mind!" Sheesh. I got to the point. "There's no place like home!"

"So why would you want to live there?" yelled Anna Versnobt from the back. Several people snickered.

"Because there are good small-town things too. People aren't just nosy for titillation. They're nosy because they care."

"One good thing, whoop-di-doo," Versnobt said.

"There's more. We make eye contact driving at a four-way stop and wait for the other guy rather than just bulling through."

Someone shouted, "That's so important?"

"It is," I shouted back, letting my anger show. "In Meiers Corners, you're not a number in a crowd. You're an individual *worthy of simple courtesy.*"

The laughter died.

Still, Versnobt made one last attempt. "Everybody knows everything...including crap that should stay private."

"Meiers Corners's greatest strength of all. Despite knowing each other's weaknesses, *we're friends anyway.*" I looked around the room, meeting eyes. Some slid away in shame, but I kept going.

"We know the dirt, but we're still friends." I thought about the Cheese Dudes that morning. "Sometimes fighting friends."

My parents exchanged a glance.

"The point is, you're doing it wrong. There are good and bad things about a big city, and good and bad things about a small town. If you want big city, good and bad, live in a big city. You're just taking what's good about Meiers Corners and corrupting it. Killing it." I

263

paused for effect. "We care about each other. *We love each other.* Act like it."

Someone applauded. Anna Versnobt, of all people. Others joined her. More.

I smiled my relief. And capitalized on the moment by waving my hand toward the open cello case and its lone twenty...which was gone. Dammit, someone had stolen the seed money.

Anna Versnobt, face red, slunk up to the case and put the twenty back.

More applause broke out, harder.

Dumas, bless his performance timing, took that as his cue to start the second half of the show.

At the end, when Dorothy tapped her heels together and said, "There's no place like home" I heard a few sobs.

After that, the five thousand dollars collected in the cello case seemed almost anticlimactic.

Chapter Seventeen

We were playing the bows and almost home free when the doors slammed open and thugs flooded the club. In hoodies and *Matrixy* sweeping black leather, they were dozens of the meanest vampires I'd ever seen.

I'd known Camille would call for backup, but hoped the two-hour show would be too short for the Coterie to gather help. Or no, the thug branch was called something else.

"Lestats," Bo bellowed.

Oh yeah. The Lestats' vampire muscle attacked with mundane switchblades and guns, but their hard-shell faces, red eyes and pointy mouths were definitely not. Audience screamed and ran. Cast, crew and pit froze at the sight of so many armed and fanged attackers. Rocky turned sheet white. Another call to Iowa would be in order.

As if the good-guy vamps had trained for it (and maybe, considering General Ancient, they had), Mishela and Gretchen's husband Steve gathered the frozen humans and escorted them out while the remaining six Alliance vampires, in a rather compelling show of cool, clicked open switchblades and calmly met the charge.

Elena roared, "Kill the Lestats!" and threw something at Nixie before whipping out her even-way-bigger gun. Nixie caught the tube Elena threw her (was that a *bazooka*?) and, yodeling like Xena, waddled into the fray.

I knew I'd better get in there and fight because it was eight of us and thirty-plus of them with Camille and her goons. Several of the younger Lestats fell almost immediately, but the odds were still more than two to one. Besides, I needed to get my feet wet since vampire Armageddon would only be worse.

But how, without a weapon?

From what I knew, and the size of guns Elena and Nixie were wielding, vampires were hard to stop. The head-chopping Glynn had done on Shiv wasn't easy. Necks were thin, sure, but bone and meat weren't easy to manage on a cooked chicken, much less a raw, bloody...yeah, getting gross even for a sausage queen.

Anyway, I probably needed major equipage. Something big and scary that would cut— I snapped my fingers, remembering the extreme juggler.

I ran for the doors behind our impromptu stage. Fangs, Blood, The Dungeon and...I found the door marked Storage and flung it open.

The lights cut.

I froze. Emergency lighting clicked on, glowing softly behind me.

The storage corridor remained pitch black, except for the red exit light above me. Shoot me, I didn't remember which door was Props. I hunted with my hand, found and flicked the light switch just in case it cued the emergency light. Nothing. I wondered if the blackout was coincidental or a tactic by Camille to gain the upper hand. The vampires might not care much, but Elena and Nixie would definitely be at a disadvantage.

And me.

Still, I'd be helpless without a weapon. I inched in as far as I could without closing the outer door. Still couldn't see, so with a deep breath I let go. The door swung shut with a fatal-sounding clang.

In the dark, all sounds intensify. My rasping breath filled my ears. The whoosh of my speeding heart thundered. The adrenaline pumping through my system didn't make it any easier to think. Air circulation was nonexistent. Sweat popped on my scalp, trickled between my breasts. I tried to picture where the doors were through the rush of blood but couldn't.

I took a deep breath, pressing it out slowly to ease my heart rate. *Thumpity-thump* slowed from hummingbird to chicken.

Outside, the sound of fighting seemed closer, the defenders falling back. Not good. Ready or not, I had to move. I took a step.

And promptly went sprawling over sharp cardboard edges. Pain nicked my shins, my flailing palms. A thud, followed by a muffled crash-tinkle-tinkle and the sting of liquor biting my nostrils told me the bottles weren't packaged nearly as well as our sausage. Hopefully only the cheap stuff had spilled.

Very hopefully it wasn't the "Bomb your blood!" Vamka. I'd looked up mannitol hexanitrate. It was a vasodilator for heart conditions, which explained the blood part of the slogan. But the bomb part was quite literal too. Mannitol hexanitrate was an active ingredient in explosives.

I righted myself. Waving my hands in front of me, I advanced again, bumping another stack of boxes with a more expensive-sounding crash before finally hitting a door.

My hands slid down and found knob. I twisted it and cracked the door, was overjoyed to see dim emergency light, just enough to make out the cases marked Gorgon's Ola—I was nasally sucker-punched.

"Piquantly Pungent" my ass. This stink was Limburger eaten by a skunk and excreted into a vat of cow farts. In fact it smelled like—I mentally slapped forehead. GObubbles, G-O as in tiny chips off the old Gorgon's Ola block. My eyes were watering from the fumes. I breathed through my mouth and my tongue started to bleed. Not really, but in massive quantities the stuff wasn't enticing in the least, but toxic with a capital Ick. I couldn't imagine how it was the Cheese Dudes' big seller unless they used it as paint stripper.

I backed out and slammed the door. I needed to destroy that stuff. I mean, what if the military got hold of it? Or worse yet, LLAMA? Cow-fart cheese balls with a hallucinogenic side effect? Definitely Weapons of Mass Destruction.

The fighting was rattle-me loud. Okay, destroy killer cheese later, hunt weapon now. I felt along the wall for the next door, knocked into another stack and nearly puked at the *crash tinkle*. I hate the sound of product breaking. To a retailer, it's as bad as car metal crunching. So I was inordinately grateful when I located a knob, opened the door and saw The Chainsaw.

It was in back, resting on the top shelf of a rack full of juggling saws, just under the emergency light. Huge, gleaming, The Chainsaw was the kind of equipage that conjured up a full soundtrack of messily dying violins.

I ran in, wrestled over a ladder, clambered up it, grabbed that sucker and raised it high. Now I'd get me some vampires. Bone and meat was easy with this little—I lowered it and took a gander at its label. Well, talk about things going my way. With this little FRDe 5000.

Hugging Freddy, I started out, realized I'd be blind in the corridor again unless I could prop the door open and went back to deposit Freddy on his shelf. Back at the door, I popped it open with my hip and scanned the hallway for something to...hell.

The boxes I'd knocked into had been a tiny bit bigger and an eensy mite fuller than I'd thought.

Liquor streamed from broken bottles, pooling on the floor. Soaked bottom boxes sagged, stacks of product leaning like old drunks. Oily strings of vampire rotgut glistened malevolently on liquid and cardboard. Without fresh air, the alcoholic fumes topped by residue de stinkbomb was overwhelming. Feeling faint, I dropped my head to my knees.

Naturally that was when the battle broke through the outer door.

Clawing, yowling, stabbing vampires rolled in, red eyes flaming and talons slashing. The shrieking balls of destruction were headed straight for me.

I jerked up. Ran for Freddy. The door swung shut behind me.

It slammed opened. I spun.

Oh, God.

The dark form of a vampire filled the door, eyes glowing red, huge chest sawing like bellows.

I was too far from the chainsaw. I was going to die.

The vampire spoke. "What the *hell* are you still doing here?"

Blessedly, thankfully, stuff-my-heart-back-down-my-throat, it was *Glynn*. My first reaction was to leap for him and throttle him with a hug.

But the way he reached for me, he was going to grab me and skedaddle. *Not* going to happen. I was born to carve up vampires and this was my chance.

I swayed just out of reach. Faked right, then scrambled up the ladder. Or more staggered, since I was still under the effect of fumes so toxic my brain was slime, but I managed to snag Freddy and yank the starter rope just as Glynn shimmered to my side.

He scowled great thunderstorms at me. "What the fuck is that?"

I swung it up to show him—and shoved a couple hundred rotating steel teeth of death right in his face. He gave an infinitesimal flinch. Oops, but that flinch proved I could do some vampire hurt. I grinned. "It's a chainsaw."

"I can see that."

"I'm going to decapitate vampires."

"The hell you are." His tone was quite mild, but his teeth were clenched.

"No, really, I am. Elena has a huge gun and Nixie has a bazooka. I'm going to use Freddy here. Zip, zip." I demonstrated with a figure eight, nearly slicing off both his arms and my leg. He was nimble; I was just lucky.

"Junior." His mouth clamped so tight his fangs drilled holes in his lower lip. "Guns and bazookas kill from a distance. *You* would have to get close. As a human, that's not possible."

I considered that. "You could get me close though, right?"

Blood trickled from his lip. I could practically hear enamel cracking.

"Please?" I batted my eyelashes. When that ad campaign didn't work, I turned off Freddy. I needed better marketing.

One-handed, I lifted my top.

Glynn's jaw didn't so much ease as unhinge. Then he simply closed his eyes and nodded.

Note to self. Breasts make *great* sales tools.

I grabbed his hand and headed for the door. We swung out into the hallway just as the rolling mass of vampires knocked over the tallest tower of liquor boxes.

At the top was a case of Grand Marnier, the pricy special-edition stuff. It hit with the *thock* of thick glass shattering, tinkled with the nerves-edge flaying of almost ten dollars an ounce.

On the plus side, a pleasant orangey smell covered the stench of vampire rotgut and the lethal injection of Gorgon's Ola (leaking past the room's seal, another sign of shoddy construction. Cousin Herbort in the assessor's office would have to have a little sit-down with Camille).

That's when it hit me. I could actually see. Which meant... I looked up. The door at the far end of the hallway was open, held by Camille's red-tipped claws.

She stood like some heathen idol, golden hip cocked, liquid-gold-covered breasts heaving. "Kill them," she ordered in a ringing contralto. "Kill them *all*."

Glynn whipped into fighting stance.

Redoubling their efforts, the rogues rolled nearer. Snarling, Camille herself entered the fray. Before the door swung shut, I saw her jerkily slashing, like a monster in a sixties Hercules movie.

I pulled the start cord on Freddy and...

Nothing.

The door clanged shut. A flame flared in the darkness near me. One of the vampires, lighting a match. I wondered what kind of vampire couldn't see in the dark, decided it had to be a newbie, confirmed when the light flicked his claw of stylish gelled bangs into view before sputtering out.

In the darkness, I pulled on the cord again, harder. Nothing.

Maybe I'd flooded the engine. I set Freddy down on the wet floor to get purchase, put my foot on him and pulled that starter rope with everything I had.

Just as the vampire lit another match too close to his bangs. His hair caught like dry grass. He yelled and dropped the match to slap his fiery do—Freddy started up.

I'll never know if Freddy sparked, or if the dropped match did it. Glynn said it was the match and his vision was superior.

But a liquor-infused box caught fire.

Liquor doesn't normally burn very fast. Mixed with cardboard in that hot, enclosed space—well, even then we might have been okay. Even when the burning newbie Lestat panicked and tried to escape into the cool room, releasing noxious hydrogen cheesefarts, we might have been fine.

But mannitol hexanitrate is an explosive.

I heard a *whoosh* from the cool room, the rush of H2-charged air toward the flame-licked vampire rotgut. I released the FRDe 5000 with my suddenly nerveless hand.

Bo and Julian shouted. Seized their pregnant wives and ran for the exit.

The only exit. My exit—except a dozen Lestats clogged the way.

Glynn lifted me off my feet and set out at a dead run. I screamed at him. No matter how strong he was, he couldn't bowl through the sheer mass of vampires in our way.

He was running the wrong way. Away from the exit, toward the boxed canyon end of the hallway.

Yellow flame burst behind us. Lestats scrabbled like cockroaches, screamed as they caught fire. Nikos grabbed the three slowest and simply tossed them out of danger before shimmering away. Thor and Rebecca, inside the storage area, dissolved into mist and shot out the door.

Glynn couldn't mist and get away, not with me. I shouted something stupid like, "Leave me and save yourself."

He ignored me. Spun, curled protectively around me and hit the wall with his back. He blasted through, wallboard and wood rupturing like paper, brick shattering like sand. More shoddy construction. Cousin Herbort was going to have a field day.

Glynn hit the alley running.

Fangs To You exploded.

He cradled my spine and put on a burst, was out of the alley in milliseconds. When he finally slowed a couple blocks away, we were both breathing hard.

Black smoke plumed in the sky. Flames started showing above the surrounding buildings. Fangs To You's marble wouldn't burn, but anything frame was toast. Sirens shrieked.

"My folks!" I struggled to get down.

Glynn set me down and misted away. I ran after—straight into his chest. He'd returned in seconds. "Your parents are fine, Junior."

"But the explosion...the fire—"

"The explosion was in back of the club. Bo opened the fire hydrant in front almost immediately. The fire department's arriving now, getting the worst under control. There's some smoke damage to buildings next door, but the ones across the street weren't even touched. Everything's fine."

"Except Fangs To You."

He grinned, savagely. "Except that."

I took Glynn's hand and we walked to my place, stood on the street for a bit, watching the fire department work.

Camille stormed by, eyes red in her sooty face. I would have tackled her to see if she'd rescued Glynn's tchotchkes, but I could see from here she wasn't carrying anything, not even a purse, and her clothes were so tight they wouldn't have hidden a credit card. Catching sight of me, she shouted, "I'll sue. I'll sue Meiers Corners, I'll sue the Alliance. I'll sue every-fucking-body!"

Behind her trotted Toto. In all the fuss, I'd forgotten about him and was glad to see he'd made it out all right.

"I'll sue the makers of Gorgon's Ola," she shouted. "And I'll sue the pants off that show of yours."

Toto nipped her heels.

Camille shrieked, started running. "I'll sue you—and your little dog, too!"

Toto made a truly prodigious leap for such a small dog. Teeth bared, he caught her in her golden globe.

Heh. Our first award.

Whether it was my plan bringing Meiers Cornersitians back to their senses or the sudden lack of competition, Saturday's show (in the PAC with five thousand bucks of newly bound insurance) played to a sold-out crowd. We had money to make up, so we added a Sunday night show to the matinee. I was worried we wouldn't have enough people, but word of mouth advertising whooshed faster than even the fireball. Sunday's matinee was packed and the evening was SRO. Not only was it SRO, ticket scalpers were getting fifty bucks a head until Mayor Meier scolded them, guilting them into returning all the money.

Meiers Corners was back, baby, and it was good.

During the runoff music, as the house lights started coming up, I caught sight of the backer himself. Big bushy eyebrows and the kind of smile you find only on a Texan. Gene Roddenberry looked a lot like the *Star Trek* producer Gene, but of course couldn't be.

Director Dumas, watching from the wings, saw him too. Dashed out onto the stage, waving at the Roddenberry clone. "What's the good word, Gene?"

Mr. Backer made no indication that he heard Dumas. As the house lights rose, Gene shimmered, his body twinkling in the half light as if he were caught in an alien beam or a transporter effect or was a vampire misting—and disappeared.

What kind of life did I lead, that of aliens, future technology and vampires, the last was the most believable?

Just before Mr. Backer disappeared, he raised two thumbs up.

We were going to New York.

Camille made good on her threats to sue everyone and anyone, but Julian managed to hold off any proceedings for several months.

A glowing review of the show in the *Tribune* brought in advance money for the next PAC production. Someone leaked the story of Camille's club and her addictive cheese curds to the alternative press, bringing in tourists on the weird-places circuit. We never found out who told, but the headline was "Explosion Has *Der* Vampire Drug Club Ge-Leveled", in the mayor's best Eng-Glitch. A video of the fire had gone viral on YouTube. Curiosity seekers came from as far away as Japan and left laden with all things Quainte and Costlye. Money poured into the coffers and Elias called off his war. The only bad thing was I didn't have time to recover Glynn's tchotchkes. I hoped they weren't destroyed in the explosion.

Glynn didn't mention them, but he was busy in the aftermath of Friday. It took him and the older MC vamps the whole weekend to convince Friday's traumatized audience that they'd only seen bad dentistry.

We were both busy, so we didn't talk much, especially not about us. But we were intimate several more times, the kind that's more love than sex.

So as I packed instruments that Sunday evening, I was cautiously optimistic. I had another plan.

This one wasn't cunning, but rather straightforward and sweet. After taking my stuff home, I'd go to Emersons' townhouse. I'd talk to Glynn and convince him to come to New York. Not to stay, and definitely not to give up Wales, but to visit me. I figured all we needed was some time to come to an understanding.

Of course, if he balked at straight and sweet, I had a backup sales plan. No bra. And I'd written "New York" on my breasts.

If that didn't work, well, I wasn't flying out until Thursday. Four days, with that big bed at Emersons, would be plenty of time to convince him.

As I walked to meet my vampire, I wondered if he could smell me coming. If he'd meet me at the door. When I arrived, the door banged open. I raced the last steps to throw myself into the arms of—Nixie. Running into a pregnant one hundred thirty pounds was like hitting a sandbag. That wasn't the only shock to my system.

"You should've been here earlier." She hugged me. "The Iowa group's already gone."

"*What?*" Glynn's sweetness loving me, his frequent glances and secret smiles...were all my imagination? Beneath trees and in alleys and in his bed...had it been only sex after all, no love required?

I nearly slapped my face. Of course it had. *I* was the one to insist on it. No commitments. No claim, no foul.

"Isn't this kind of sudden?" My voice was disturbingly pitiful.

"Mishela had to get back to Iowa before dawn." Nixie led me into a small den, pulled a beer out of a refrigerator and handed it to me. "Apparently, she's got this stupidly strict curfew. Douchebag Ancient. Glynn went straight to O'Hare."

"But...he didn't...*they* didn't say goodbye."

She knew what I meant. "Glynn apologized for dipping out. He's off to Wales for his two months." She handed me a folded note. "He did arrange floodlights for your walkway before lamming. Said he knew you were jonesing for New York or he would've asked you along to Wales." She paused, considered me. "You okay?"

"Dammit, Nixie, before Glynn, everything was black and white." I rubbed the cold can against my forehead. "Duty was first, my dreams on hold. Now I have a chance to fulfill the dreams...but I can't stop thinking about him."

"That's why you're here? Good-bye sex?"

"I *was* going to ask him to go to New York with me."

"Instead he's gone home." She watched me closely, her blue eyes shrewd. "Dorothy said it. There's no place like home."

"But what makes a home?" I popped the can, had a long, cool drink. Went on, a little calmer. "I was thinking about that during the show. To Dorothy, home is Aunt Em as much as the farm. Uncle Henry and the farmhands, people as much as place. Home is safe people who love you even if you're you. Somehow, in the last couple weeks, Glynn's become my safe place."

I set down the beer and opened the folded note. It said simply, "Junior, Be happy in New York. I love you. Glynn" I drew a tearful breath. "I wanted a chance to become his safe place too. I was hoping...I wanted to be the place his heart called home."

"Awww. Embroider that on a pillow. Call him, you moron."

I managed a smile. "That'll work." I slid the note inside my shirt next to my heart, then pulled out my cell and punched up Glynn's number.

It went straight to voice mail.

That wasn't good. I left a terse, "Glynn. Call me," clapped my phone shut and stuffed it into my pants. "His phone's off. Why do you think his phone's off? Do you think he got in an accident? You think he's okay?"

"Settle, girl. He probably powered down for flying." Nixie paused before adding, "But he may not turn it back on during vacation. Two months until you'll hear from him." She whistled. "*Two* months."

If she did it for effect, it worked. "I've got to reach him. Does he have a land line in Wales?"

"Dunno. I can ask. Julian!" She bellowed the last, loud enough to make my ears hurt. She's small, but as a punk singer, can drown out a whole barroom. Give her a mic and she's been known to rupture eardrums.

Her husband shimmered into the room, solidified from a stream of mist. Even in the midst of my frustration I thought, *Wow. Way cool.*

"Ice cream?" he asked her immediately. "Chocolate? Or pickled artichokes this time?" His eyes closed. "Not the yogurt and smoked Thüringer hash again."

"Junior was asking if Glynn has a land line in Wales."

His eyes opened, blue lasers targeting me. "Probably. Do you want me to find out?"

"Please."

He whipped out a phone, punched a speed dial. After a few terse words, he slid it away. "He does, but he's going first to Vienna to make a delivery. I'm texting you his number in Wales. You'll probably be able to call him within the week."

"But I'm leaving for New York Thursday." And after that I'd be neck-deep in my new life.

They exchanged a glance. Nixie said, "He might call before then."

I'd be able to speak to Glynn in a week. He might even call me before then.

But the way he'd torn out of here didn't give me a lot of hope. Didn't suggest he'd leave the only home he knew for a potential new home in me, or even a visit.

Thursday marched closer and closer, and still no word from Glynn. In the vacuum, I chafed. Fretted. Dreamed up all sorts of possible scenarios, from Glynn declaring his undying (heh) love to him snubbing me with a terse "I never cared" to his simply not calling me at all.

Wednesday night I barely slept. When Thursday came, I was awake to see it. Still no phone call. My suitcase and instruments were all packed. Before dawn, I sat on my bed and stared at my posters. India, Japan, New York.

Part of me wanted to stay in Meiers Corners just because that was where Glynn knew to find me.

But my dreams were in New York.

Glynn had gone on with his life. It was time for me to go on with mine.

I stared at my ticket. Maybe I should stay for my parents' sake. They were strong, but even with the money I sent home they'd never be able to hire help as good as me.

Then Mom and Pop came up to say good-bye, and even that excuse disappeared when I found out they weren't as helpless as I thought.

"I love you." I hugged Mom. "Don't worry. With the show, I'll have plenty of money to send you guys."

"Don't worry about that," Mom said. "Just enjoy New York."

"It is good you have a shot at your dreams," Pop said. "Play well."

"What?" I looked from one to the other. "You've said for years that I couldn't leave. That everything I needed was here. Now you're encouraging me to go?"

"These 'dreams' you had before were nothing but pipes." Mom waved a dismissive hand at my posters. "You were not listening to your heart. "

"I had ambition," I countered.

"*Nein*," my father said. "Ambition is hard work, making things happen. *You* were running away."

"Now you are finally listening to your heart," my mother said.

"But Mom. You, most of all, hated that I wanted to leave. You did everything you could to stop me."

She smiled, the added soft touch of hand making it a little sad. "I didn't want you to make my mistakes. Sometimes you *want* career or dreams. Sometimes you run for *want* so fast that you miss what you really *need*. Follow your heart, Junior. It will tell you what you need."

"Junior." Pop took my other hand, squeezed it briefly. "Be the best person you can be. And be happy."

I sat slowly on my suitcase, staring at them. At these people I'd known all my life—or thought I knew. All these years I'd thought my parents needed me in their small pond, keeping me from becoming the big fish I knew I could be.

They were just waiting for me to figure out what being a big fish meant.

It was a bit freaky to realize they'd understood me all along, maybe better than I did.

"Of course we expect you to come home to visit," my mother added briskly.

"And we know you'll send a little money home," my father said. Then he hugged me and added, "But most important, be safe and happy."

"Now you must go." Mom made shooing motions. "Or you will be late."

I had to go. Glynn, if he came back, wouldn't find me here.

Follow my heart... If I truly followed my heart, it would take me on the swim of my life. Maybe I could use a kayak.

Instead I picked up my suitcase and instruments, and reluctantly headed for the airport.

Entr'acte

Glynn pushed his way through the masses at O'Hare, thought about turning on his phone but decided against it yet again. Why? It wasn't like Junior would have called.

He'd been packed in airborne sardine cans for most of the last three-plus days, racing through his mission to get to Wales, only to turn around almost immediately for Chicago. Even with his preternatural vampire resiliency, his butt was dragging.

Awareness struck him like Elias's size twenty boot in the face. His taste buds sang and his nose quivered. He snapped straight, all fatigue gone.

Junior was here.

He breathed deep. Luxuriated in the awareness, until its significance struck him. No one knew he was returning. What was Junior doing here at the airport?

For a moment he dreamed she was flying to Wales, yearning for him as much as he was for her. But no, she was probably just headed to New York.

She had New York and she had Meiers Corners. She'd never consider Glynn her duty or her dream.

It was why he'd finally given in and come back. He'd fought his attraction because he didn't want to give up his home for anybody. Fought until he was so miserable he'd been forced to admit he'd give up anything for her.

At Heathrow, waiting in a private vampire lounge, he'd realized that wasn't quite right. He wasn't giving up his dreams of a home, not for her or anyone.

But how to tell her so that she'd understand? He'd tried to find the right words the whole trip. Nothing had come. Now he was back and she was here and his time had run out.

He closed his eyes and located her in his mind. With the ease of centuries, he used the blood-memory to single her essence out of a thousand beating hearts, her smell/taste his burning beacon of joy. He opened his eyes and ran.

He saw her moments later, winding her way through the crowds. He couldn't help himself. He shouted her name.

She looked up. Their eyes met and it was like a fist to his gut. Elias's, as oversized and iron-hard as his boots.

They stood frozen in time. And then she was running toward him and he toward her—

A flash of scarlet intervened. A hand planted on his chest and pushed with inhuman strength. He stopped more out of surprise than anything.

"Hello, Glynn." An exotically beautiful face smiled up at him, green eyes glittering.

"Camille." He stepped back with a growl vibrating up from his belly, ripe with his disgust and anger.

"Now, now, darling. Is that any way to greet your old flame?" She touched a red nail playfully to his chest. He remembered how quickly her touch could turn from play to pain.

His eyes flicked behind her as he tried to calculate how much danger Junior might be in. She was still a few feet away but closing fast.

Camille growled. "Don't pay attention to your whore, Glynn. It will only make things worse for her. And you."

His eyes snapped back to Camille's exotic face. How could he have thought it beautiful? "Lay one finger on Junior and I'll destroy you."

Camille's red nail dug deep. "You're not in any position to make threats, Gly—"

Junior slapped Camille on the back. "Hiya, v-bitch. How's it goin'?"

Camille's finger slipped and her nail broke. "Why, you..." She spun, nails sharpening into claws.

Junior danced out of range with a grin. "I mean, how's it goin' considering your club's nothing but rubble and the mayor won't give you another building permit and Julian's tied your lawyers up for months?" Her normally sweet face was lit with a smug expression that Glynn could only think of as *owned*.

Camille's eyes flashed back to Glynn. Her smile turned distinctly predatory. "How interesting you brought that up, human. That's why

I'm here."

Glynn heaved a mental sigh. He'd rather not have Junior involved in whatever shit Camille was about to dish out. But telling his Junior to back off wasn't smart. It would only make her more determined to stay.

So he snagged Junior by the neck, tugged her into his side and sheltered her under his arm before challenging the other vampire. "That's right, Camille. Why don't you tell us your oh-so-nefarious scheme?"

He hated the little smile on the vampire's plump, glistening lips. Hated even more the triumphant twinkle in her eyes. "It's simple, darling. I have your tchotchkes."

Junior sucked in a breath. He soothed her shoulder. "They survived the explosion? So?"

"So if you go back to Wales and stay there—and I'll know if you don't—I'll send them to you after an appropriate interval. If not—" She ground her palms together then made a *poof.*

Under his arm Junior started struggling. "You bitch!"

Though he knew Junior had martial arts training, he rather thought from the way she squirmed that if he let her go, she might have tried to scratch Camille's eyes out.

Camille's smile thinned. "Careful, human cunt."

Glynn growled, short and savage.

"Excuse me, human female. Remember, you're in Lestat territory now. We have minions everywhere."

Junior snorted. "Ask me if I care."

Glynn glanced down. She stood with her chest puffed out, her eyes blazing gold. He was so proud of her. He couldn't let her take Camille's wrath. "Let me get this straight. You want me to move to Wales, permanently. I get a home, something I've always wanted, *and* my mementos returned."

"That's it." Camille's full-lipped smile returned. "A win-win."

"Except Elias loses one of his best trackers and bodyguards. The Alliance loses a knight."

"A rook, darling." Camille's lips plumped fuller as her smile turned coquettish. "You're a more valuable piece than a knight."

"Elias doesn't consider us chessmen, Camille. How did you find me anyway? Today, here at the airport?"

"Why, darling. The blood scent/taste, of course." She flashed eyes at Junior. "You remember our bedroom romps got a little...strenuous."

"We were never *that* intimate, Camille. Nosferatu has an eye on O'Hare traffic, doesn't he?"

"Pooh." She moued. "Well, it doesn't matter how I found you. I have your little knickknacks. I hold the cards. Either you make your home permanently elsewhere, or I take the things you care about most..." Her eyes wandered again to Junior. "...and destroy them."

Glynn's gums flared hot, his fangs fighting to descend. "If you even touch Junior—"

"Darling, no." Camille fell a step back. "Your tchotchkes only. I wouldn't dream of threatening your little whore." Yet her gaze was predatory, resting on Junior.

"Whore?" Glynn's vision went red, his talons throbbed to extend. "For the last time, that is not an acceptable term."

Camille took another step back. "Fine. Your little *friend*. I won't touch her." Her chin kicked up. "But make no mistake, I'll happily destroy your pipe and dragon, your cookie cutter and the child's sweetly bronzed shoe."

Glynn smiled. "Go ahead. Destroy them."

Under his arm, Junior started struggling. "Glynn, you can't. They mean everything to you."

He took in her pained expression, wanted to kiss the frown off her face, kiss her forehead, her eyes, her lips and never stop.

But this first. "You think you're offering me the world, don't you, Camille? Everything I want—not only my symbols of home, but a permanent home. But I was just in Wales, the only place I've ever known peace, and you know what? I enjoyed it for all of two minutes. Then I thought about showing Wales to Junior. Of taking her the places I'd been, of us seeing all the places I haven't been yet. And then I was thinking only about *her*. I even have a tchotchke for her, see?" He took the clarinet reed from his pocket.

Camille frowned.

"But this isn't a replacement for Junior." He stared deeply into Camille's eyes, trying to make her truly understand, trying to reach even a ghost of the fledgling she'd been. "None of those things, the pipe, the dragon and the shoe—not even the cookie press—is a replacement for what I lost. My childhood was stolen from me. I'll never replace it. I can only face the fact and go on."

Camille sneered. "You're a fool."

He shook his head. Camille's exotic beauty had intrigued him at one time, even captivated him, ensnaring his imagination and his cock. It was nothing compared to Junior, who'd invaded him heart and soul. "All my life I've wanted a home, a place to feel safe and secure. I wasn't going to give up dreams of a home, not for Junior or anyone.

"But I don't have to, you see. Home is where I can be safe, and if that doesn't describe Junior, I don't know what does. She's my home." He crushed the reed in his hand. "You can keep the rest."

It was a brave speech. His mementos had grounded him for a long, long time. He'd miss them.

But they were only symbols, not a real life, one of the things he'd realized in Wales.

So with his heart and soul, his *real* life, still secure under his arm, he turned from Camille and from his past, and walked away.

Chapter Eighteen

"I can't believe you came back from Wales just for me." I snuggled into Glynn on our way to an on-site hotel room to wait out the daylight hours. I'd missed my plane to New York, but it didn't matter. Glynn rebooked me for a flight tomorrow morning—with him in the seat next to me.

In the meantime, we were desperate for each other.

Oh, there were still issues to talk out. The usual things like do you want kids, do you hog the blankets. And some unusual things, like did vampires even sleep in beds? He also wanted to talk to my folks for some reason, but he said that could wait.

So for now, we were back in the same time zone. We stumbled into the room, kissing each other like maniacs, clawing off clothes (in his case, literally) and generally *not* talking.

Sometimes sex is slow and sweet, with a lot of foreplay. And sometimes the instant you're naked, you push your partner flat on his back, climb on and yell whoo-hah like a cowgirl.

Glynn fell obligingly onto the bed when I shoved and even helped me into the saddle. But when I rolled my hips in long, delicious undulations, he grabbed me with both hands and started thrusting straight up, so hard and deep I took off like a rocket.

Planting both hands on his pecs, I slammed down with equal force. The slap of our hips was underlined by panting breaths and deep moans. Delicious buildup flushed both our chests, dampened our skin. Fangs erupting, he arched into me. I grabbed him with my thighs as his hot pleasure took me sailing over the edge. My climax was hard and quick.

He switched his grip on my hips, started rubbing against me, purring. The rumble rose from his chest, where my hands still dug into his pectorals.

His fangs gleamed white against his flushed lips. I leaned over to kiss him. A particularly forceful stroke of his hips sent me cascading open-mouthed into his face, and I ended up Frenching him savagely.

He released my hips to grab my face with both hands and kiss me back. His erection pulsed heavily inside me, a *basso continuo* to the counterpoint of caressing lips and quick, brilliant leaps of tongue. A crescendo of sensation overwhelmed me. I stopped thinking and doing and became a symphony of feeling.

My arms collapsed, pressing my body flush to a hot, hard male torso. His panting breath rubbed silky skin and ribbons of body hair against me, a dance of heat, texture, taste. Sheathed within me, stretching me in the fullness of throbbing pleasure, was his patiently waiting cock.

All that swelling feeling finally burst into action. I thrust my tongue into his mouth again. My fingers dug into his rock-hard muscles. My hips beat a savage rhythm. My whole body tightened with need. Where I sheathed him clenched tightest of all.

He shouted my name. Thick arms wrapped around me, shoulders to hips. He yanked me tight and spun us both. My back hit bed with my feet high in the air.

He pounded wildly, pummeling my mons, firing shockwaves with every stroke. His shaft grew thicker and longer, finally jarring into my cervix. I sucked in a cry.

He swept my legs onto his chest. With my feet framing his chin, my body doubled between us, he would go *deeper.* I opened my mouth to howl.

He sank fangs into the thick of my calf.

Climax, lightning-sharp, streaked through me. Pleasure lifted my cervix, and when my howl emerged, it was filled with satisfaction. He wasn't too big now but just right. He rode my orgasm out, stroking into my contracting muscles until I lay limp and sweating beneath him.

He shifted our heads to the edge of the bed—and over.

I bent backward, my limp torso coating the side of the bed like melted wax. He tossed a couple pillows onto the floor, cushioning the crown of my head. Bracing a hand on the floor next to the pillows, he cupped my nape with the other. Belly to belly, his hips pinned mine to the mattress.

In this position, he pummeled me raw.

His chest, swelled to boulders, heaved over me. Or under me. It's a strange position to be in, upside down and being screwed senseless.

Blood rushed up...down...until my cranium was heavy and throbbing, like my sex. He thrust deep and hard, over and over. Lust built, sweet and powerful, the pressure increasing both in crown and pussy until it was unbearable.

Until it was no longer lust, but more.

His head bent, his rasping breath hot on my throat. I turned my head to give him greater access. Fangs pressed gently against my neck, all the more poignant for the wild thrusting of his hips. Tears sprang into my eyes, not of pain or fear or even need, but of intense happiness. Joy. Love.

He bit me. Climax raged through my body, igniting from neck to toe. Burned hot and fast, razing everything in its path.

His strokes slowed and shortened, the small after-strokes of lengthened fulfillment. His tongue touched my neck, swirling over the trickles of blood. I luxuriated again in sensation, suspended in a bright spot behind my closed eyelids that would settle into afterglow.

His tongue lapped once, twice, then paused.

"Growing up without a home, I learned to be self-sufficient. To take care of myself first, even with sex. Especially with sex."

"Mmm." I thought he'd taken care of me pretty well.

"I have care for my partner's satisfaction," he said as if he heard my thoughts. "But my own was always a concern. Until you. With you, I don't worry about my pleasure. I thought it was because my satisfaction is wrapped up in yours. But there's more. You take care of me too."

My pussy flexed.

"You confronted Camille. You tried to get my tchotchkes back...sometimes I think you don't even realize how you take care of me. You care about me. And I love you for it. I love you, Junior."

I opened my eyes, saw his face through dark, spangled vision because I was still on my head. "I love you too, Glynn."

He groaned and drove his cock into me to the hilt. And bit me again.

My blood-rushed brain detonated. Pleasure burst, a heavy liquid torrent. I screamed. He shuddered over me, quaking violently. I clawed at his back, seeking purchase in the raging consummation thrashing me. My hands met acres of skin, miles of muscle, vast shoulders.

Another massive wave rose up, crested. Collapsed, sweet oceans of pleasure drowning me. His thighs and butt clenched, driving another wave. It ebbed and I started to breathe—he rolled a few short strokes and sank his fangs just a little deeper. Yet another surge struck me. And another.

It went on and on. Even after he'd stopped moving, little aftershocks sparked. Even after he'd rolled us back up on the bed and his licks settled into nuzzling, even after he tucked me, with a few purrs, spoon-fashion into the crook of his body, small pulses glimmered. Even as we sank into sleep.

Much more than lust. It had been almost three weeks, not long but in some ways an eternity. And there were still many, many things to resolve.

But the basics were in place. I loved him. He loved me. We'd work it out from there.

Until, after we woke, I asked him why we he wanted to talk to my folks.

He said, "I must ask your father for permission."

"What permission?"

"To marry you."

"Junior. I *will* speak to your father."

It was two weeks later, on my one night off from rehearsing the show in New York. Arms crossed and grimaces firmly in place, we sat on opposite sides of the taxi, headed from the airport for Meiers Corners and my folks' home. Our first fight. Speaking of working things out. If I hadn't been so mad, it would have been sweet.

"This isn't the dark ages, Glynn. I make my own decisions. If you want to marry me, you ask me, not Pop. And I've already said no."

"Your father will not say no. He needs money; I have money. He needs help with the business. I can help."

"At what cost? You'll never see Wales again. The very idea of you selling your Welsh homestead in some misguided notion of helping my folks—"

"I love you, not pieces of land and crumbling castles."

"A hell of a lot of land that you spent all your life getting, peopled with folks you care for, friends. It must mean something, yeah? I don't want you giving all that up."

His gorgeous face set. "I'm going to talk to your father. End of conversation."

It wasn't, of course. We argued until the taxi pulled up outside the Wurstspeicher Haus, at nearly ten that night.

"You are not selling—hey." I alighted from the cab, a neon orange TENFFOEG landing on my shirt. "The lights are on."

"Your store has evening hours." Glynn pulled out our overnight bag. "That's why you had to hire help to play the musical."

"Yeah, but even when I was home we closed by nine. And now my parents are the only ones running the place. They said they'd shut at five."

His black brows pressed together. He took a step closer. His nostrils flared and he hissed. "*Vampire*."

I ran straight for the door. "My folks—" I folded in two around his barring arm. Rubbing my middle, I backed off with a glare. "*Vampire* means they may be in trouble."

"Exactly why you'll stay here."

I rolled eyes. "Because there are no vampires outside in the dark."

"Bollocks. All right." He reached into his ever-present black jacket, snicked out a long, silvery blade, and advanced. "Stay behind me."

A bell tinkled as he opened the door...and an electronic tune squealed with guitar distortion. The tune sounded damned familiar.

"Welcome to *Wurst Und Käse*. How may I help you?"

The voice sounded familiar too. I peeked around Glynn's black leather.

Cheese Dude Two stood behind the register. Cheese Dude One, beside him, was busily stuffing away fifty dollars' worth of blood sausage into a green cloth sack.

The latest outrage. "They're stealing our product! Attack!"

Glynn and I both charged at superhuman speed, Glynn because he was a vampire and me because I was fed up with this crap.

Cheese Dude One threw his hands up. I braced myself for a jalapeño stick hit but kept going at ramming speed—

I smashed into a wall of chest and bounced sprawling onto the floor.

Not Glynn this time, because he sprawled next to me. Standing over us, arms folded, was Julian Emerson.

"What the hell?" Glynn leaped to his feet, fanged and ready.

Julian waved him down. "Relax. I'm making an emergency food run for Nixie. Liver sausage and cream cheese, yum-yum. And some *blutwurst* for me. I appreciate only having to make one stop now. I didn't want you to screw that up."

I shoved to my feet, dusted off my butt. "What do you mean? We've sold blood sausage alongside our regular *wurst* for months."

"But not the cream cheese. Or the Limburger." He turned to the register. "Better add half a pound of that and some garlic summer. She's on a stinky food kick too."

"You got it, Mr. Emerson." Cheese Dude One trotted over to the cooler...which was suspiciously clean and shiny, and hummed without a clank.

I whipped around. *All* the coolers were new. And inside them— rounds of cheese marched alongside sticks of sausage. On the shelves, silver cow charms were displayed pinned to sausage scarves. Yellow foam wedge-cheese hats even sat on the top shelf.

Mom and Pop would never countenance wasting precious retail space on someone else's merchandise. I whipped back. "Where are my parents?"

"Dead to the world," Cheese Dude Two said.

Horror catapulted me over the counter. I'd snap his fat neck with my bare hands.

Dude Two sprang aside with amazing agility, eyes wide. "Wait, no! The parents are just fine." He flapped his meaty hands. "Better than fine. They're asleep. Good thing, after all the work they've been doing, installing the new coolers, moving product."

"That's a lie!" I said. "They barely had enough money for one cooler."

"We footed the bill." Dude One trotted behind the counter, hands full of cheese and sausage. "Our goodwill offering to our new partners."

"*What?*"

"Junior? What are you doing back?" A cookie elf came shuffling out of the back. Pop blinked, caught sight of Glynn. "Ah, *gut.* Welcome home, son."

I whirled. "Pop, what's going on? Why are the Cheese Dudes here? You hate them."

"Ah, Junior, your mother and I...we heard you speak at the

musical, and...it was mature. Sensible. And we were tired of the conflict. So when you left that morning, we went over to the Dudes' place and hammered out a partnership."

"But Pop, so fast?"

"The Cheese Dudes are making big profits." Pop smiled. "And now we are too. Don't worry. We'll still leave the family store to you and Glynn and the little *liebchens* coming."

While my mouth was hanging open, he shuffled back to bed.

"I heard about your speech," Dude One said. "You really did a number on the collective city guilt gland. Coolers installed in less than a week, and we've got a contractor starting tomorrow to connect the two stores."

Dude Two chimed in. "But until that's done, we're consolidating the best-selling product here. Mom and Pop Stieg run the place during the day and we run it at night. That way we can keep the store open 24/7 and get more customers."

Julian nodded. "It's nice being able to shop whenever Nixie's cravings hit."

"How can you side with them?" I glared. Julian was supposed to be my friend. I was annoyed with him, even more annoyed that the enemy Dudes were calling my parents Mom and Pop like they were sons too. "And you Cheese Dudes...you hate us. You have since you moved in."

"Don't blame us." Dude One rolled his eyes. "The smell was driving us *nuts*."

"Says the guy with the stinky cheese," I muttered.

"The blood sausage." Dude Two licked his lips. As his tongue darted out, I caught a flash—of two tiny fangs.

"But now we've hammered out a deal," Dude One said. "All the *blutwurst* we can suck. In return we run the online *Wurst Und Käse* store and man the registers after sunset."

I'd always said we needed an online presence. But... "You're a vampire?"

Dude One hugged Dude Two. "Both Ralphie and me. My name's Vaughan, by the way."

Glynn took me by the arms. "Do you realize what this means?"

"Yes," I groaned. "The little *liebchens* really do get everything."

"Not just that." He started purring.

"The apocalypse has come?"

"Your parents are set. Even after the musical closes, we can live in New York or wherever we want. Even Wales." He yanked me in for a hug, my chin crushed between his pectorals. "As long as it's together."

"Yeah," I said, kinda muffled by muscle. "And as long as we come home for Thanksgiving."

Bows and Playoff

Glynn and I walked hand in hand through the rolling green meadow, the soft scent of nearby farms not Iowa corn but tidy hedgerowed Welsh crofts. We were on our honeymoon, coinciding with a two-week break in the sell-out crowds for *Oz, Wonderful Oz*.

"Mishela looked great on Craig Ferguson last night," I said.

"She did," Glynn said. "She does a fantastic interview."

"It'll be great for her career. You know, I always suspected Ferguson was a vampire."

"He's not. But a number of his viewers are."

I smiled at him. We were together at last, but only because of Nixie, Julian, Rocky, Mishela, the Cheese Dudes, Mom and Pop and a dozen more people. I used to think it wasn't the choice itself, but what I did after. I was wrong. It wasn't just *my* choice. It was my interacting with dozens of other people interacting with thousands more.

Long run? Theater people were right, in a way. Life was chaotic; life was magic. I could only control my own actions, not my own fate.

Still, without my actions, without trying to corral small children that first night which got me rescued by Glynn's big warm hands, without falling in love with Glynn...without love, I might have stayed in Meiers Corners or gone to New York, but I'd still be searching for my rainbow. "You know, Dorothy was right."

He smiled down at me. "About what?"

"About home. I'm glad to have grown up in Meiers Corners. It taught me what home is, what it can be. Duty, but more. Being the best you can, both for yourself and for the people you love."

"Dreaming in a safe place." He traced my cheek. "Launching from that safe place to realize your dreams."

"Yes. I took all that with me. And now I'll use it to build a strong home with you."

"I'll do everything I can to make you happy, Junior." Glynn shifted his grip, held my hand more tightly. "I meant what I said, *babi*. You're my home now."

"I'll be your home—for as long as I'm alive. Which, from what I understand from Dolly, could be longer than the eighty or ninety years I was first figuring on?"

"Ah, yes. The secret." He bent, whispered in my ear.

I felt my eyes bug out. "You're kidding, right?"

"I'm not."

I swore. "You guys would be hunted like whales if anyone knew—"

"Shh." His finger covered my lips. "That's why it is a secret."

"But you'd do that for me? Just to extend my life a little?"

"In a heartbeat."

I squeezed his hand. If I hadn't already known he loved me, I did now.

We walked in silence. When we passed a crumbling folly, I said, "You mentioned a Lord Rhys when you told me about your name. I looked him up. He and his daughter, a Lady Gwenllian, were alive around your time. Did you know them?"

Glynn laughed. "Everyone did. Lady Gwen was quite the social force. From entertaining kings to nursing sick children, she did it all. She was married to Ednyfed Fychan."

"I read that too. And that Ednyfed and Gwenllian had six sons."

"At *least* six. The vampire who kidnapped me was always hanging around there. It seemed there were dozens of children in the yard. The vampire talked about capturing another boy..." He stopped. Cold.

"*Another* boy." I grabbed both his hands. "The vampire named himself Fychan, like Ednyfed Fychan. And you had a blanket with three heads—just like the Ednyfed coat of arms. Glynn, what if you're one of Ednyfed's sons? His grandson was Tudur Hen. You'd be a *Tudor*."

"I'd be...good heavens. After all this time, a possible family." His eyes misted, the bright sapphire silvered by the moon. "Will you research it with me?"

"I'd love to."

Then he bent his head and kissed me. "But it doesn't matter as much any more, because I have another family now." He stroked my belly.

"Despite your telling me I couldn't get pregnant." I smiled into his eyes.

"When I told you that, I didn't know you were mine." He smiled back. "My mate, my heart."

We walked our land hand-in-hand. The moon shone down upon us, bright as a followspot. Behind us, long shadows trailed the green grass.

Love had put us here. Our love, but more. Love of friends, of family. Love of a whole damned annoying city.

There truly is no place like home.

About the Author

Mary Hughes is a computer consultant, professional musician and writer. At various points in her life she has taught tae kwon do, worked in the insurance industry, and studied religion. She is intensely interested in the origins of the universe. She has a wonderful husband (though happily-ever-after takes a lot of hard work) and two great kids. But she thinks that with all the advances in modern medicine, childbirth should be a lot less messy.

Visit Mary at http://www.maryhughesbooks.com, Facebook (http://www.facebook.com/MaryHughesAuthor) and Twitter (http://www.twitter.com/MaryHughesBooks), or write Mary at mary@maryhughesbooks.com.

He's a candy box of sex appeal wrapped in a golden bow.
She's on a diet.

Biting Me Softly
© 2010 Mary Hughes
Biting Love, Book 4

Blood, sex, violence. Blood, okay, but computer geek Liese Schmetterling had enough S&V when her cheating ex fired her. Now security expert—and lip-smacking gorgeous—Logan Steel saunters into her Blood Center, setting fire to her libido. And threatening her job.

Visions of pink slips dancing in her head, Liese tries to push Logan away without touching his jutting pecs...or ridged abs. Or petting the Vesuvius in his jeans. He's hiding something, but it doesn't seem to matter when his smiles stun her, his kisses crank her to broiling and his bites rocket her to heaven. Fangy bites which, if she weren't grounded in science, would make her think ampire-Vay.

Centuries old and tragedy-scarred, Logan's mission is to fortify the Blood Center's electronic defenses against his nemesis, the leader of a rogue vampire gang. He's ready for battle but not for Liese, who slips under his skin, laughs at his awful puns, charges beside him into dark, scary places—and tastes like his true love.

No matter how often Logan declares his love, Liese can't bring herself to trust him. But when his archenemy comes after her, not trusting him may cost her life...

Warning this book contains explicit vampire sex involving absurdly large male equipment (hey, they're monsters), unbelievable stamina (just how long can he stay underwater in a hot tub?), hide-your-eyes violence and horrendously bad puns. And, just when you think it can't get any worse, a computer geekette trying to play Mata Hari.

Available now in ebook and print from Samhain Publishing.

It's all about the story...

Romance

HORROR

www.samhainpublishing.com

CPSIA information can be obtained at www.ICGtesting.com
Printed in the USA
LVOW081323110613

338038LV00003B/75/P